FUDOKI

Tor Books by Kij Johnson

The Fox Woman
Fudoki

FUDOKI

Kij Johnson

TOR®

A TOM DOHERTY ASSOCIATES BOOK

NEW YORK

This is a work of fiction. All the characters and events portrayed in this novel are either fictitious or are used fictitiously.

FUDOKI

This book is printed on acid-free paper.

A Tor Book
Published by Tom Doherty Associates, LLC
175 Fifth Avenue
New York, NY 10010

www.tor.com

Tor® is a registered trademark of Tom Doherty Associates, LLC.

Library of Congress Cataloging-in-Publication Data

Johnson, Kij.
    Fudoki / Kij Johnson.—1st ed.
        p. cm.
    "A Tom Doherty Associates book."
    ISBN 0-765-30390-6 (acid-free paper)
        1. Women soldiers—Fiction. 2. Metamorphosis—Fiction. 3. Japan—Fiction. 4. Cats—Fiction. I. Title.

PS3560.O379716F83 2003
813'.54—dc21

                                                                            2003053345

Printed in the United States of America

0 9 8 7 6 5 4 3 2

For Chris and for my parents: a tale told under your eaves

These times have passed, and there was one who drifted uncertainly through them, scarcely knowing where she was. . . . Yet, as the days went by in monotonous succession, she had occasion to look at the old romances, and found them masses of the rankest fabrication. Perhaps, she said to herself, even the story of her own dreary life, set down in a journal, might be of interest; and it might also answer a question: had that life been one befitting a well-born lady? But they must all be recounted, events of long ago, events of but yesterday. She was by no means certain that she could bring them to order.

—*Kagerō nikki (The Gossamer Years)*
translated by Edward Seidensticker

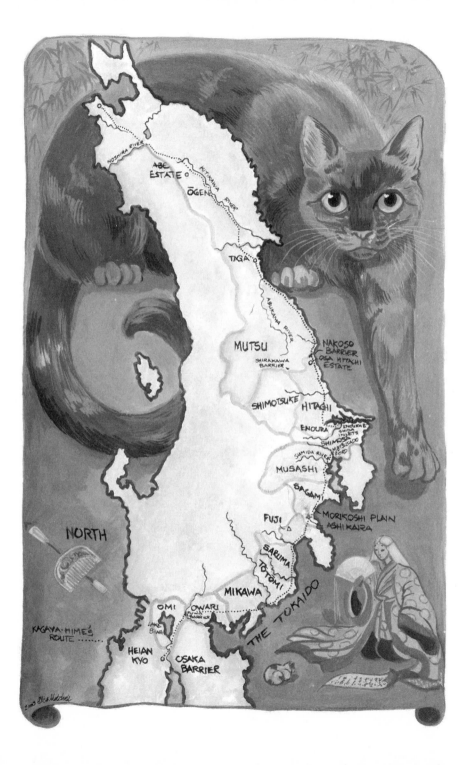

NORTH

NOSHIRA RIVER

ABE
ESTATE

ŌGEN

KITAKAMA RIVER

TAGA

ABUKUMA RIVER

MUTSU

NAKOSO
BARRIER
OSA HITACHI
ESTATE

SHIRAKAWA
BARRIER

SHIMOTSUKE

HITACHI

ENOURA

ENOURA &
SHIDA
INLETS
SHIMOSA
MATSUCADO
FORD

SUMIDA RIVER

MUSASHI

SAGAMI

FUJI

MORIKOSHI PLAIN
ASHI KAGA

SARUMA

TOTOMI

MIKAWA

THE TOKAIDO

OMI

OWARI

LAKE
BIWA

KAGAYA-HIME'S
ROUTE

HEIAN
KYO

OSAKA
BARRIER

2003 Elisa Mitchell

CHARACTERS IN THE PRINCESS HARUEME'S TALE

Fumiya no **Shigeko,** Harueme's primary attendant

The emperor **Shirakawa,** now dead: formerly the prince Sadahito; Harueme's half-brother

The emperor **Horikawa,** now dead: formerly the prince Taruhito; Shirakawa's son; Harueme's nephew

The emperor **Sutoku:** formerly the prince Atsuhito; Shirakawa's great-grandson; Harueme's great-grandnephew

Fujiwara sammi no **Kenshi:** Shirakawa's consort; mother of Horikawa

Fujiwara no Yorimichi: Harueme's maternal grandfather; her **foster father**

Fujiwara no Morozane: Harueme's **uncle**

Mononobe no **Dōmei,** a guardsman from Mutsu province

Shisutāko: Harueme's first cat

Myōbū: Harueme's current cat

The cat **Kagaya-hime**

Osa Hitachi no **Nakara:** a road-met companion to Kagaya-hime

Osa Hitachi no **Kitsune:** Nakara's adopted brother

Junshi: Nakara's primary attendant

Seiwa Minamoto no **Takase:** commander of the war band

Suwa: Takase's attendant

Onobe no **Kesuko:** priestess with the war band

Abe no **Noritō:** head of the Noritō clan

Uona and **Otoko:** Kagaya-hime's female and male human attendants

FUDOKI

1. THE CLOUD-PAPER NOTEBOOK

I am the princess Harueme, daughter of Fujiwara no Enyu and the emperor we now call Go-Sanjō. More to the point, I am old and I am dying.

My life (what remains of it) does not look so different from the outside than it has anytime in the past fifty years, since I first came to court. I kneel on a straw mat laid on my oh, so familiar boxwood floors, though the padding is thicker than it was when I was young, and despite it my knees hurt rather more. I wear silk as I have since I was a child today; my robes are the *susuki* grass color combination, a private favorite of mine. My screens and curtains of state and eye-blinds are elegant but worn—but so they have been through all these years. I cannot recall ever having completely new hangings.

And there is a cat watching me as I write, a tabby female with green eyes whom we call Myōbū for her grand-lady manners. Before her there were others, but she fills the same place in my life that they did. The individuals may change, but there are always cats, there are always robes, there are always mats. These do not change.

I am old, but it is not age that kills me. There is a pressure deep in my chest, as if my liver and lungs are pushed aside by new and unknown organs. To breathe, my lungs steal back territory from these encroaching organs, and then they must do it again for the next breath. Each time they reclaim less and retreat sooner, so

that I see a day when they find the price of this war too high, and
we will die, my lungs and I. I can only hope that these usurping
organs will be required in the Pure Land, and my body is simply
premature in generating them. Even in hoping this, I grasp for a
reason, like a falling monkey catching at vines. My half-brother
who was the emperor died some months ago; I follow him rather
sooner than either of us expected.

I know I am dying, though my great-grandnephew the emperor
and a thousand medical men—herbalists, diviners, eccentrics of
every stamp—do not seem to believe me when I tell them. Or perhaps they do not choose to believe. Believing in a thing can make
it so; how could they risk such a thing? If it is possible, what else
might be, as well?

I cannot die here in the palace, of course—to do so would stain
the purity of the sacred enclosure, and therefore it would be bad
for my great-grandnephew the emperor—so I have already made
my plans. Soon a priest will administer certain vows, give to me a
new name and cut my long hair, and I will be a nun. It is as simple as that.

Not quite so simple: in my lifetime I have acquired and filled
what seem to be a thousand trunks, and these must be emptied
and removed. Their contents comprise an odd sort of midden
heap: close-writ diaries; broken antiques from China or beyond,
their value only in their provenance; a half-finished translation of
The Thousand-Character Classic; torn robes in no-longer-fashion-
able color combinations; love letters twisted into the clever little
knots that girls think can conceal secrets. And there are notebooks I have never gotten around to filling, their pages full of
promise, or emptiness.

Pick up a *biwa*-lute, and you can't help but strike a note or two.
Watch a cat sleep and you long to touch it (often to the cat's
annoyance). A new brush begs you to grind ink. A cup makes
you thirsty; dice in your hand demand to be thrown. The mind
follows what the hand touches.

A blank notebook demands words. Which words? I wonder.

✿   ✿   ✿

At a time now past, a cat was born. The emperor Ichijō brought the first cats from Korea—my great-grandfather, though this was long before I was born. This was not so long after that, when cats were still rare, and all in the inner provinces near the capital.

This cat was a female, the smallest of her litter of four, and her fur was at first a blurred darkness. As she grew it changed to black flecked with gold and cinnamon and ivory, like the tortoiseshell of a hair ornament. Her eyes when they opened were gold, like a fox's. She was small but fierce: in no way but size a runt, for she lacked the gentle resignation of the weak.

She lived on the grounds of a *shinden* residence on Nijō avenue, in the capital's west side. It filled a city block, and it had once been very fine, though that had been before even the emperor Ichijō's time. The owners abandoned it to build a house closer to the heart of things (and that heart had moved east, to where the retired emperors lived); there were fires and droughts and earthquakes; there was the slow erosion of apathy. The main house with its three wings still stood, but the roofs leaked and had fallen in places; the walls were furred with mosses. Some outbuildings were no more than piles of wood and cedar shakes. The grounds were overrun with ivy and weeds, and the three little lakes and the stream that joined them were green with neglect.

Three people lived here. They called themselves servants to justify their presence, but they were no more than cuckoos squatting in a nest that did not belong to them. They lived in the north wing, what had once been the primary wife's rooms, and cooked on the pavement of what had once been the bamboo courtyard. Their trash they tossed into a heap beside the covered walkway to the west wing. A goat also lived here, too wily to catch and be eaten.

Cats have their estates, as well: their gathering places and private wings. A handful of females, fellow-wives and sisters, shared the residence's grounds, which had not inconsiderable resources viewed from the perspective of a cat's tastes. The ruined garden and the kitchen yard seethed with mice and small edible things, and the brook and the lakes contained slow, fat frogs that attracted what seemed consistently stupid birds.

Each adult claimed her slice of the grounds, where she hunted and mated and bore kittens in solitude. These private spaces met at the center, like the petals of a dogwood bloom, and on pleasant days when the sun was warm the cats gathered at the midden heap and the space around it, matrons dozing as the kittens chased one another.

Most kittens were sired by one of two toms, each of whom claimed half the grounds (and sometimes more) and visited when their responsibilities permitted. Sometimes a strange male infiltrated, like a guardsman secretly visiting a nobleman's wife, and there would be a kitten with unusual markings or strangely colored eyes. Apart from these occasional visits, toms had no part of the cats' lives: were irrelevant, in fact.

The cats (the female cats) of the residence's grounds shared another thing, their *fudoki*, which is self and soul and home and shrine, all in one to a cat. The *fudoki* is the chronicle of the females who have claimed a place, a river of cats that starts with the first to come to that place, and ends with oneself—when one grows experienced enough to have a tale to tell. It is also the place itself, and the cat whose story it is, and the immaterial shrine in which the household is honored. A cat may lose her tale by leaving her family and place, but then she is not the same cat. Mothers taught their daughters the *fudoki*; if the mother died too soon, the cousins and aunts and fellow-wives did so. Some (though not all) of the kittens would live; the tale would go on, an unbroken stream.

Though she was fairly young, the tortoiseshell cat had survived kittenhood and not run away. She had not yet earned a place in her tale, though her aunts and cousins had taken to calling her The Small Cat. This would change when she had earned a true name and a longer story. The tortoiseshell's *fudoki* was many cats long, and she knew them all—The Cat with a Litter of Ten, The Cat Born the Year the Star Fell, The Fire-Tailed Cat.

❊   ❊   ❊

The Fire-Tailed Cat. I wrote those characters as my woman Shigeko came to me, to warn me of the impending visit from the latest healer my great-grandnephew has sent—a yin-yang diviner this time, with the good looks and arrogance that mean he will go far in his profession. He wasted half a day of my none-too-long life, but as I waited for his rather silly rituals to be completed I at least had ample time to ask myself why I am writing in this note-book. For the pleasure of watching the characters shape them-selves under my hand? Do I distract myself from pain or boredom or fears for the future (for of course I am afraid. I am not so enlightened as all that)? I know the ending of my own story: do I long for a tale with an end I do not yet see?

I have written much before this but always notes about things I have observed. Never a tale (which is, after all, a lie, without proof or relevance). And why a cat? —Which is the easiest of all these to answer, for Myōbū sat beside me, sunlight in her green eyes as she stared into air, or nothing. What does she see? And when I look at her, what do I see? Cats. Who can tell?

There was a day, beautiful and very hot: summer, though autumn would begin soon enough. The first gingko leaf had turned, a sur-prising brilliant gold fan against dusty, dry green. Ducks slept on a pond as still as enamel, out of reach of ambitious cats. Pollen choked the air with a haze like smoke. The afternoon sky had leached to the color of tin in the heat.

The cats were gathered at the midden, five adults and a hand-ful of half-grown kittens. There were not many, because it was not a good summer for cats: the cat distemper had killed some, and a stray dog others including the oldest female, The Cat Who Found the Jewel. Most of her kittens—too young to have earned places in the *fudoki*—died, but one survived, the small golden-eyed tortoiseshell. She sat on a wall, looking down at the court-yard, blinking as the sun moved into her eyes.

Adults dozed tight-muscled in the dappled shadows cast by the garden's trees, or stretched out on the gravel under the sun,

looking dead. The kittens played idly with fishes' tails retrieved
from the midden, pausing to rest in the shade of the raised walkway and buildings that formed three sides of the space. One cat
licked clean the ears of her half-grown daughter. The *fudoki* rip-
pled over them all, slow and warm as a summer brook. A wind
started.

The ducks panicked suddenly: awoke and whirled up from the
lake in a ragged spiral like a dust devil. The cats did not move
from their places, but in a blink slipped from sleep to hunters'
wakefulness. They watched the wheeling ducks, all thrashing
wings and strange cries. The air had changed; or something.

A duck broke from the spiral and arrowed toward the cats.
The others followed her; and when the first duck slammed into
the side of a storehouse they followed her there, too, and died
with her. The last broken-necked duck had not hit the ground
when the earthquake struck.

It was not a large quake, nor a long one. Across the capital,
screens and cooking braziers rattled or fell. Humans and animals
screamed in their various ways. Tree branches tossed; leaves rustled as if in a gale. Temple and shrine bells jangled in their frames
without rhythm.

The ground shuddered and gave a deep sound the cats felt
through their paws. Some had experienced earthquakes and hun-
kered down, ears flat and eyes wide. Some bolted for safe places,
under buildings or up trees.

The tortoiseshell did not know earthquakes; her *fudoki* (and
there were quakes in the *fudoki*) could not prepare her for the
ground moving. She jumped to her feet, teetered, and lost her
balance, falling to the wall's base in an awkward heap. Plaster fell
around her in heavy flakes. She staggered to the courtyard's center, braced her legs against the bucking ground, and hissed.

The residence's main house collapsed slowly, almost painstakingly. Old timbers groaned and broke like river ice. With odd
musical noises, cracked roof tiles shook free, slid, and shattered
on the dirt. More fell; they sloughed in sheets like snakeskin as

supporting pillars flexed. A dislodged beam crashed down. Another splintered with a noise like fireworks, or thunder. Slowly, the roof crumpled in on itself, vanished into the building with a wave of white dust and a sound so loud that the tortoise-shell fell, stunned with the weight of it.

She could not tell when the shaking stopped being the earth and became instead the falling building. She streaked up the ragged bark of a *hinoki* cedar, to an abandoned squirrel's nest she knew. She heard noises outside the grounds: shouts, cries; on the street to the west, frightened horses that had kicked down their stable doors; the frightened (or irritated) bleating of the estate's goat, fading as it bolted away. The last cat she saw was an aunt vanishing beneath the west walkway.

The bells chimed randomly for a long time after the earth-quake ended.

Despite the earthquake's damage, it was the fire that destroyed the *shinden* residence and its grounds. The eighth month is a dangerous month: the gardens are dry, and wood-and-paper houses catch fire as quickly as brazier coals. In the capital's southeast quarter, a tipped lantern set fire to a floor mat. A length of summer gauze hanging from a curtain stand flared up and lit an old reed eye-blind, and that was the first house to burn. In the afternoon's rising breeze, flames spread to the north and west, a bright fan across the city.

Crouched in her tree, the tortoiseshell smelled the fire before she saw or heard anything. The air grew sharp and stung her eyes, made her wrinkle her nose and sneeze: a greasy, complicated smell. She shook her head to dislodge the tang.

There were more shouts outside the grounds, more hoofbeats, wagon wheels screaming under weight. Bells rang again, their discord rhythmic, in earnest this time. Behind all was a steady roar, like a festival crowd cheering.

The heart of a *hinoki* cedar is not a good vantage point, and the tortoiseshell crept along a limb until she could see out through the needles, over the broken outer walls. Through the dirty air she saw that everywhere to the south and east was smoke. Where buildings burned, thick dark plumes seethed upward; where there was grass or gardens, pale shreds crawled toward her. And there were flames.

She knew fire, convenient little blazes that the residence's people used for their mysterious purposes, but this was not the well-mannered glow of charcoal or lamplight. This was chaotic, full of angry colors: the source of the roar she had heard, the shouting crowd. A sudden gust of hot wind slammed into her. She retreated along her branch.

When she was small, she fit into the squirrel's nest, had hidden here as the dog killed her mother. But she was larger now, and it was no longer a refuge. She climbed as high as she safely could, and pressed herself into a little hollow where a branch joined the trunk. And then she waited, panting, for the fire.

We—humans I mean, peasants and nobles alike—know about the fires. I had not lived more than a few summers before I had learned of them. They always start with something small, but if the weather is dry or the wind is strong, they can destroy everything—or nearly everything; fire is as whimsical as the gods. Flames settle into one place, burning for days with choking black smoke and leaving the ground too hot to touch, mysteriously poisoned for years afterward. Across the street, they cross another residence with no more damage than black-scorched tips to the banquet field's grass. The flames disregard entirely the gardens of a third residence, happily beyond the range of the winds' vagaries. Within a few streets one may see all of these, and more besides: a thatched stable with a roof like a pillar of flame, its walls hidden in the smoke that pours downward; a storehouse half-burned, half-untouched; a garden pond filled with boiled, once-ornamental fish. One shop is abandoned, screens and grilles gaping as the owners flee with the best of their stock in a wagon pulled by their strong-legged sons. A shop next door remains open, and a woman buys gourds in a net from an old man. Except for the cloths over their mouths, they seem oblivious to the burning city.

If the wind blew safely away from where I lived, the fire became exciting, like riots in another quarter of the capital. "What is the news?" we all called to passersby. The rules were forgotten, and noblewomen (even princesses, if no one was attending closely) ran barefaced and barefooted into the street to catch at the sleeves of the guardsmen hurrying past: how many houses are gone, what streets, what lives? We ate our rice cold on the verandas where we could watch the smoke. We prayed desperately to the kami, to the Buddhas, to all the gods and demons, begging for an easy fire, begging that the wind stay kind.

We know about the fires, but the tortoiseshell did not. There were stories in the *fudoki*, of course, but a story does not choke you with fumes; the grass in a tale doesn't hiss like a kitten as it burns. She crouched in her tree and watched through eyes slitted against the smoke.

At sunset the wind eased, and the flames slowed. The fire seemed brighter with dusk, its movements clearer. The smoke glimmered red and amber. She heard individual noises within the roar now: a whistle like an overblown *shō*-pipe, low wooden sighs, an angry metallic squeal.

To the east was a *shinden* residence like this one, old and forgotten and dry. The main house and its wings were half-hidden from the tortoiseshell, but for a time what she could see remained recognizable and was even made beautiful by the fire. Flames defined everything, tracing the shapes of screens and supports, railings and walkways. Smoke gushed like water along the roofs, but she could not tell whether it moved up or down.

The flames hesitated at Sai avenue. Lanky weeds and half-grown trees muddled its neglected surface, but it was broad, and the border-ditches still carried water, if not much. Cinders showered up from the burning buildings and started small fires in the weeds. The neighbors' gatehouse collapsed outward, and coals caught in a young *katsura* tree in the avenue. Smoke oozed from the tree's crown until the fire became visible and destroyed it.

The tortoiseshell's grounds caught in a hundred places. Flying sparks settled on roofs and in dead pines and cryptomeria. Fire slipped into the ditch, leapt across the reeds that bridged the slimy trickle, crept up to the outside wall, and swarmed over it.

The residence burned for most of the night. Thatch and shingles went immediately. Woodwork took a little longer, the perfect grid of a screen or a carved phoenix over a doorway outlined for a time in light. The buildings' heavy-beamed skeletons settled in like *Urabon* festival bonfires as the timbers turned black and then white and cherry red. The smoke thinned somewhat, for the wood here was well aged.

The air was very hot, not quite unbearably so. When a coil of smoke curled around the tortoiseshell, she pressed her face between her paws and breathed through the fur of her inner leg, leaving tears and smears of the dirty mucus that trailed from her nose. Her claws had been out since sunset. Her muscles trembled with exhaustion.

Through the gaps left open by her second eyelids, she watched the flames flicker, quick as birds or lizards. Sometimes cats looked up through the hot, wavering air with shining eyes and glistening mouths that said things she could not hear. They might have been the cats of her *fudoki*, her cousins and aunts. They might have been ghosts, or flames, or illusions. She could not tell.

A live cinder settled on her shoulder: a tiny smell of burning fur. It was a moment before she recognized the pain. She screamed and scraped herself convulsively against the bark, but there was nowhere to run, nothing to fight.

Fire is not constant. Trees near her burned, but the *hinoki* cedar did not. Needles on the lower branches sizzled as they flared, and then smoldered like incense sticks. She smelled the changed air, and pressed herself harder against the trunk. The squirrel's nest below her remained intact, though the smoke would have been fatal. Her retreat was high enough that fresh air found its way to her, and so she lived.

We understand what fires are like, in the same way we understand about riots and wars. We hear tales, rumors, reports from the front. They interest us, but they do not threaten us. Long before we are truly endangered our careful attendants hustle us off to some safer place: the summer house at Biwa lake, a relative's home in a quieter quarter, a temple in the mountains.

There are some who know fire (or riots, or war) intimately, who see it as the tortoiseshell did. I am not one of those (my so-careful attendants have prevented this), but I have watched bonfires and braziers and walked in a garden after a fire once. I guess what she might have seen or felt, the acid touch of scorching air in her lungs. I imagine; I dream, even when (especially when) it frightens me.

"What are you writing?" Shigeko asks me. It is afternoon, and I write out on my veranda, enjoying the sun's warmth and the low voices of my women as they put together a robe for me to wear when next I am summoned to visit my great-grandnephew the emperor.

Shigeko is my primary attendant, as old and weathered as I, and so she dares ask such a question, when other, younger, lesser women might instead remain silent. The perfect attendant (and I have had many of them in my life) asks no questions. She brings what is requested; she cleans up what is spilled; she laughs and cries appropriately, as required by her mistress's mood. Shigeko has never been the perfect attendant, despite her inarguable skills: managing the other women, overseeing my wardrobe, and intercepting unwanted visitors and letters. —Though she certainly has been the most interesting of them.

My brush was moving when she asked this, and so I have written her words and now my thoughts, quite as though they were part of this tale. Now her politeness is at an end, for she has said, her voice sharper: "My lady?" I think I must put down my brush and answer her—

"Nothing," I told her.

She frowned: she knows I lie. I am not skilled at lies, and she is expert at detecting them. Why did I not tell her, "A *monogatari* tale"? I have written a thousand things and shared them with her: my notes on the number of legs and the wing-colors of whatever vermin I was observing, my letters, even my diaries. Why am I unwilling to show her this?

I have shared everything in my life with others. Not much has belonged to me alone.

The cat did not sleep so much as fall unconscious, and she was not aware of doing either until she startled awake, her claws still sunk deep in the bark, her burning eyes sticky with clotted tears and mucus. She was hungry and very thirsty. Dirt and ash caked her fur and clotted at the roots of her whiskers and sensing hairs. The air smelled strange, of char and ash, every scent changed beyond recognition.

The sky was pale and smoke-pillared in the southeast, smeared indigo and black to the west. Several buildings retained their shapes but were hollowed out and seared. Others were only heaps of charred timber, unrecognizable piles of smoking gray and black, red light peeking through cracks in certain logs. The fire still burned in the northern wing where the "servants" had lived, but with the idle half-interest of a well-fed cat teasing a mouse. The great trees of the garden stood, though their lower branches were charred or gone altogether. Everything else was scorched or destroyed, leaving the garden a tangle of black shapes that might have been shrubs or branches, and might not.

The tortoiseshell *niyaan*ed softly, and then loudly. There was no response, no sound of any sort: no morning songbirds, no people swearing and spitting and clattering pottery in the north wing. No cats. The only living creature she saw was a soaked rat climbing from the stream, which was chalky with ash. Setting foot on a patch of still-smoking ground, it made an anguished noise and leapt back into the water, then swam off to vanish beneath a collapsed bridge.

She was alone. She knew this, though she could not have explained how, or even what, she knew. We, who are more familiar with the gods of our land than she, might have said that the garden's and the residence's kami were gone—dead or angry or distracted, or something else that men cannot understand. But her people were new to the Eight Islands, and neither knew nor cared about our gods. She knew only that the heart of her home was gone.

She climbed down, carefully feeling her way along the soot-slick branches. She paused on the lowest and then dropped the final distance. The earth was hot enough that she shifted from paw to paw trying to find a comfortable place to set her feet. Around the base of the *hinoki* cedar was a scattering of dead birds fallen in the night, but her thirst was stronger than her hunger. Startling with every step, she walked down to the little stream. She found a place where she could crouch without burning her paws and lapped at the water. A taste like sulfur caught at the back of her throat, but she drank.

She returned to the dead birds. She pushed the closest one with a paw but it was already rigid despite the heat. She wrinkled her nose and turned away. The next bird had been badly burned, its eyes melted away, its clawed feet curled against its breast. It was unpleasantly crunchy, and she turned away from this one as well. The third was a late-season nestling, scarcely a mouthful.

The fourth she ate. The meat was smeared with ashes that ground against her teeth, but she was too hungry to care. The blood in its veins was stagnant but warm and helped ease the sulfur taste at the back of her throat. Feathers were always bitter, and she clawed them from the bird when she could; otherwise spat them out as she ate. She tried to groom the blood and feathers and ash from her fur, but her mouth was dry. After cleaning her forepaws and face, she gave up and explored her world's remains.

The continuing silence frightened her. She had always lived in a cloud of noises large and small. Leaves rustled, birds sang, water chattered over rocks in the stream; the people in the north wing had yelled and whispered and snored through their days. Now she heard noises outside the grounds, but the silence within seemed absolute. She listened to her own rasping breath and a steady fast thump like a small drum: her heart beating. She *niyaan*ed again. The sound did not carry, muffled by ashes.

One of her aunts had slipped beneath the walkway, so the little cat searched there. She found no one, only a smoking shape that might once have been a cat, pressed into a depression in the ground. She sniffed carefully and caught the memory of a scent, the black-and-white cat, The Cat Who Talked to Moths. "Aunt?" she asked. When the tortoiseshell tapped with a paw, the shape that might have been a cat crumbled.

She searched throughout the grounds and the destroyed structures, but she found no other cats.

Beside the north wing, she found a dead woman caught beneath a beam that had fallen in such a way that half the wood was untouched and the other end burned away to a blunt point. The woman had been pinned and died there, of the smoke or injuries. A ghost knelt over the corpse, patting it as one might try to wake a child and sobbing, "Get up, get up!" Though there was no wind, its hair and clothes moved like water weeds in a storm.

Cats see ghosts, of course, and speak with them, too, when they have not yet passed on to wherever they must go. Can you doubt it? "Where are the other cats?" the tortoiseshell asked.

The ghost looked up with red-rimmed eyes. "Help me wake up."

The tortoiseshell said, "You're dead. I don't think you'll wake up from that."

"I have to," the ghost said. "Where will I go? I was a bad Buddhist, but I don't want to go to Hell. I won't have to, if I can just wake up." It shook its corpse, and ash flew from its clothes.

A flake fell on the tortoiseshell's nose, and she shook her head to dislodge it. "Where are the cats, my cousins and aunts?"

The ghost stopped shaking. The tears that fell from its eyes were blood. "They are all gone. Cats and mice, people and kami. I am all that's left."

"No," the tortoiseshell said. "*I* am left. *You're* a ghost. If my kin are dead, where are their ghosts, then?"

"Why would I know?" the ghost said bitterly. "I am no cat. If cats go to Hell perhaps I will meet them there. Unless I can wake up."

The tortoiseshell returned to the midden heap to think.

Individual cats are not important. Even if the other females were gone, she lived, and the *fudoki* continued. Grass and bushes would grow again, and mice would crawl from their holes or move from other, less damaged residences. Humans might or might not return, but they were of only minor usefulness. Perhaps other females would find the grounds and become part of the tortoiseshell's *fudoki*. Eventually, the males would visit again. If they did not, new males would take their place. She would have kittens, perhaps many litters, and some would be daughters. The tale would continue, and she would take her place in it: The Surviving Cat. She was frightened and alone, but the tale remained, and this comforted her.

There were sounds within the grounds: men's voices, heavy footsteps. The fire left a thousand new hiding spots, but they were unfamiliar and frightening, so she leapt for the top of a wall. *Up* had always been safe; had been safe through the night's fire.

She landed with her full weight on her front paws, driving them down onto the still-smoking top edge. She screamed and twisted sideways in the air, fell full length onto a raised stone walkway, still scorchingly hot. The pain closed down her mind, and she ran.

All through the night, when her life depended on it, the tortoiseshell had not panicked. With morning, the enemy was no longer immediate and all-threatening. It could be avoided, and so there was no longer a reason to panic. But she was weary to staggering, and queasy with the poisons of the night's unused fear. When she burned herself, the pain overwhelmed what strength she still had.

Cats do not like to run far at a time—their strength is in their patience, not their legs—but she could not stop herself. She was past the wall in a flash, and streaked south, in the shadow of the weeds along Sai avenue's western ditch. Everything was strange. The noises that had whispered at the fringes of the frightening silence were all around her now, and they were all made by *things*, blundering objects that moved unpredictably, any one of which might be a threat. There were horses and oxen, dogs and carts and people. Smoke still choked the streets, and she smelled fire, old and new, everywhere around her, and she could not tell what was dead and what still lived. With each step, new pain seared her feet. She jumped forward, away from the pain, but it stabbed at her with the next step. Whenever she managed to overcome the reaction caused by the pain, a noise or blundering *thing* would startle her, and she would run again.

In the end, the exhaustion that began her flight also ended it. She missed a step and sprawled. Because she fell on her unin-jured side, for a moment there was no sharp shock of pain. In that moment, the goddess Kannon was merciful, and the tortoiseshell fainted. Small and injured as she was, she had crossed more than a mile of the capital.

It was not, perhaps, the ideal place to fall: in the center of the dog-walk, the walkway that ran alongside Rokujō avenue, which is always busy with the doings of the common people who live in the south of the capital. But she was both fortunate and unfortunate in the day: unfortunate, for had there been no earthquake, there would have been no fire and no deaths, no burned paws and terror to drive her from her home and *fudoki*; fortunate in that her own troubles were mirrored in those of others, and no one paid atten-tion to the corpse of a small filthy cat in the middle of the path. People saw her and stepped aside. There are a thousand ownerless dogs in this city, but they were all busy elsewhere. It is true that a dun-and-black dog examined her, leaving a moist nose-print on her shoulder; but he was called away by his owner, who had lost much in the fire and feared to lose this last thing, his dog.

It seems I have fallen asleep over my notebook. I do not recall the shift from awake to asleep. I was thinking of this small cat and all her losses, and then I was standing naked beside a cold river, in a place so far to the north that it has no name, watching blue-green fish tremble under the water's surface. I did not seem to realize that I am old and cannot swim and have never been farther north than a visit to Funaoka hill, and that this must therefore have been a dream.

When I nodded off I trailed one of my sleeves in the ink, leaving dust on the dried ink stone and a feathery stain across my writing desk and this page. Worse, I dropped my favorite writing brush to the floor, where the wolf's fur bent into an awkward curve and then dried. I am forced to switch to this brush, stiff-bristled and narrow-tipped, though I do not like the flightiness of its line. I loved that wolf brush, which gave my calligraphy a soft elegance that it doesn't really deserve.

Shigeko woke me, entering my rooms to force the latest batch of herbs into me. Mercifully she was sidetracked into getting the ink cleaned up and replacing my outer robe with a clean and (I observe) darker one. She is no younger than I am, has been with me since I first came to court fifty? sixty? years ago; and she forgets things as much as I do. "I came to ask you"— she hovers before me, trying to think of why she came in; then guesses, incorrectly to my relief—"whether you wish to be read to?— though I see you are occupied."

"I am," I tell her, and hold up my brush, this irritating scratchy new brush. I have had to make new ink, which (since I am a princess and do not always have to suffer the effects of my actions) I am doing on a new ink stone, in preference to cleaning the old one. "Kneel. Keep me company."

Shigeko eases herself down to her knees. I hear their cracking, like twigs in a fire. "I am so sorry, I should not have awakened you."

I gesture with the brush to the floor beside me, still shining with water from the cleaning. "It's better you did. Sleeping with ink is, well, dangerous. For my surroundings, anyway."

"You shouldn't have been writing at all, my lady: the healers

Kij Johnson

say it is bad for your hands, and you need your sleep. More than writing, anyway."

"No," I say, and then smile at her, the old joke: "I can sleep when I'm dead."

After all these years, she still does not find this amusing. Worse, she remembers the herbs and so I must now drink this vile tea.

—I see that I have ruined all the pages after this one in this notebook. No matter: I have others as empty as this one once was.

2. THE PLUM-COLORED NOTEBOOK

The tortoiseshell woke in the sheep's hour, when the afternoon sun threaded through the trees beside the walkway and warmed her fur. For a moment everything was all right; she was basking by the midden heap with her cousins and aunts around her, though she couldn't understand why she hurt everywhere. There had been a terrible nightmare, with flames and fear, but it made no sense for her to ache from running in a dream. She heard the breeze in a tree overhead, and she snapped awake. This was not the right tree, not *any* of the right trees, the trees of her garden.

She rolled upright and crouched there, gathering her bearings. There was packed earth under her sore feet, a ditch beside her. She smelled the air, and then opened her mouth to taste it: smoke; horses and oxen; cooking rice and radishes; stagnant water and rotting wood; a squirrel's musk and the tiny fresh scent of a chewed twig. She also smelled the dog who had touched her and stood nervously, salivating involuntarily at the renewed pain. She saw no dogs, but beyond the ditch was Rokujō avenue. Broad as it was, it seemed (to her) filled with people and animals and wheeled conveyances. In fact, it was not a busy day: the fire had not affected this corner of the capital, except as people from the north and east came here from their own, more damaged quarters. The *iroha* maple above her was untouched by flame.

She limped to a safe place under the raised floor of an ancient small building away from the road, where she inspected her front paws. The pads were sticky from blisters that had broken during her flight, and caked with ashes, dirt, shards of broken pottery, and splintered wood. The pads' leather seemed torn away, leaving only raw flesh. She licked herself clean, biting at the clots of blood and pus that kept her claws from retracting. The pain made her queasy, and sometimes she had to stop and wait for the dizziness to ease, but after a long time her tongue found skin under the filth, and blood began to flow cleanly from the cuts and blisters, a soft comforting taste in her mouth.

Her flank was less damaged, only a broad sore area that made her flinch when she nosed there. The exhaustion was worse: every muscle and joint and bone ached, and grooming was a slow and painful process. Once finished, she looked about her.

A human is a reasoning creature, or so we would like to think. After disaster, we assess our situation and make plans: make sure the stored rice is untainted, rebuild the main house's roof, borrow quilted robes from our sister until we can replace our ruined ones. The tortoiseshell's idea was simpler: find home. She returned to the avenue, and looked about her, but everything was new, unfamiliar. She took a tentative step first one way, then the other. Nothing smelled or looked right; no way led home, to her *fudoki* and her cousins and aunts. She could not help the cry of sorrow that escaped her.

She was lost, in every sense. There was only her. She recited the *fudoki* to herself, compulsively, one cat after another in their proper order: The Cat Who Ate Silk, The Thousand-Spotted Cat, The Cat Who Hid Things. But without a place and her cousins and aunts and fellow-wives to anchor it, the *fudoki* had no meaning, and the tortoiseshell was no one and nothing. She had been like a brazier balanced on three legs: tales, clan, and the ground they claimed. Each was necessary. Each was useless without the other two. Lose one, and she fell.

She was young and not very experienced and did not understand that one cannot simply tack on a new leg. In her thinking, if she had lost one home, perhaps she could find another. If she lost her clan, surely there were other clans. If she taught them her tales, they would somehow become part of the *fudoki*, which would settle easily over new ground, and she would be whole again.

Her burnt paws hurt, and she felt and smelled the beginnings of infection. She needed to find a safe range. The lot where she had cleaned her paw seemed unclaimed by any cat (or dog or human, either), but it was poorly drained, a reeking swamp even in drought. There would be food—frogs, insects; ducklings, come spring—but she would never be dry, and the heavy smells would dull her senses. The building's support posts were spongy with moisture, riddled with beetles. Worse, there was no one here to learn the tale.

She limped east and south.

I cuddle pain to myself tonight. My woman Shigeko watches me in lamplight, her eyes dark with concern; but I say nothing to her, only smile and continue to write. I could tell her of the pain; but what would that accomplish? She would fuss and flutter, and despite all she would not ease it. And in some strange way I do not wish to share it with her, any more than I share these words I write. I had a nurse who used to say that a princess possessed only two things she did not need to share, her death and what she dreamt at night. There is little enough that is mine alone.

There is a day I remember, as precious as the Three Treasures to me. My half-brother the emperor (Shirakawa they call him now that he is dead—how can you be dead, my friend?) retreated to the Toba residence—scarcely an hour's ride, but outside the city's walls, and that meant it felt like an adventure. This must have been fifty years ago, when we were both young and grief had not stained us so deeply.

It was the third month, and we all complained about the cold damp everywhere, the moldy smell every trunk released when it was opened. Not even braziers seemed to help. I remember

my toes were never once warm in the month we were there. The
garden was ruined; day after day of heavy rain drowned the new
growth and left slick-looking gray sludge where lawns and courtyards had been.

That day no one was out on the verandas, save the two of us,
emperor and princess. My half-brother sat under the rain, his
silks dark with water, his *eboshi* cap flattened. I had thrown an
extra set of robes over my head and stayed huddled back from
the eaves' edge, but even so I was wet through and shivering.

And then I joined him under the sky, tipped back my face and
drank rain with him, and laughed. I recall the taste of the rain,
sweet and toothachingly cold; the tiny blows of drops striking my
eyelids; my half-brother's laughter rippling in my ears.

I do not know what exactly had happened that day. Did he
send everyone away? Did he slip from their endless attentions?
Why did he share this moment with me, with me alone? Why did
I join him? What I remember is a moment of perfect joy, the taste
of rain, and my half-brother's presence beside me.

My half-brother is dead now. I suppose that makes this memory mine alone now. I would trade every secret I have ever
hugged close for the sound of his laughter again.

I do not wish to think of my life just now. Oh, these dark
nights.

"Who are you?" a voice hissed. "You do not belong here."
Another cat, a female. When the tortoiseshell turned her head
slightly, she saw the strange cat crouched just overhead on a
fence, a gray tabby with cold green eyes. The tabby poured off
the fence to land a few steps away, and began to groom her tail.

"I am nothing and no one," the tortoiseshell replied. She sat,
turned her face away, and waited.

Cats have a sort of game they play when they meet. A player
alternates between watching the strange cat and ignoring her,
grooming or examining everything around herself—a dead leaf, a
cloud—with complete absorption. It is almost accidental how the

two cats approach, a sidelong step and then the sitting again. This often ends in a flurry of spitting and slashing claws, too fast to see clearly, and then one or the other (or both) of the cats leap out of range. The game can have one exchange or many—and is not so different from the first meetings of women.

The tortoiseshell and the tabby played this game, the tortoiseshell with deadly earnest, the tabby with unknowable motives. The tortoiseshell played well, for when they were done the tabby ignored her existence, and she was allowed to stay.

The tabby was part of a clan, a dozen females whose ground overlapped in the back garden of a dirty and poorly run inn. There was room and food enough; they had lost three females to the cat distemper of the summer, and the tortoiseshell threatened no one. She slipped into the space between the ranges claimed by the tabby and one of her sisters, a gray-and-white female.

She explored her new range, which was smaller than she was used to. The inn's storehouse had a crack in its floorboards, and the mice had found this and prospered, so food was plentiful, and she did not need much ground to survive. There were moles as well, and birds, and sometimes people threw out spoiled meat or bones. The moon had turned and it was early in the ninth month, so that there was more color in the early-changing trees around her: the gold of gingko, the red of *urushi*-lacquer. Her favorite retreat was a fallen tree trunk, where she slept curled warm and tight against the tang of autumn in the air, and the rain that fell all one day and into the next.

The tortoiseshell pushed at the undrawn lines between her territory and her neighbors'. Whenever she saw one of the other cats, they played the meeting-game again. They hissed and complained, but she was desperate and they were not. After a few days they started ignoring her in earnest, and the game and the fighting were no longer necessary.

She spent a lot of time keeping her paws clean. The scabs became thick and healthy, and she walked easily, if still with pain. She slept a lot, but not well. Her dreams were uneasy, full of burning cats that stretched their mouths to speak, though she heard nothing but the crackle of flames, and the deep scream of a shrine bell breaking in the fire's heat.

One afternoon she sat high in a larch, where she looked into the inn's back garden and saw the cats there, touching noses as they greeted one another, dozing in untidy heaps, telling their tale. *Soon,* she thought. Soon they would accept her. They would become her clan, and she would approach the garden and teach them her *fudoki.* The world would become stable again.

The tabby spoke with the tortoiseshell sometimes now, when their wanderings brought them close together, sharing the things cats find interesting: a hanging pheasant in the storehouse (regrettably inaccessible, but one could hope), the male's visit after many days away, someone staying at the inn who had tried (and failed) to catch her gray-and-white sister. She said little about the fire, which had been only a strange bitterness to the air here, for they'd been out of the wind's reach.

The tortoiseshell approached the cats' gathering place slowly, over days. There were some flattened ears and sparring, and she responded with humility or ferocity, as required. But each time the females gathered she came closer.

There was a day when the oldest cat was teaching her daughter their *fudoki,* and the tortoiseshell crept forward to listen.

As she listened she shivered, and her fur lifted from her back. The tale was told in the correct way; the chronicles of one cat followed another in neat progression: The Cat Inside the *Biwa*-Lute, The Cat Born with One Eye, The Cat Who Ate a Poem. But these were the wrong cats, the wrong tales. They grated against her ears, and she felt parts of herself scraped away. Her stomach heaved, pushing gagging noises past her rigid throat. She could not move, her muscles locked in a tension that hurt like a cramp. This was *wrong,* as wrong as if it had been a dog's tale, if such an abomination could be.

She suddenly realized: her *fudoki* would never belong here. They had their own, and it was a thousand, a million cats long.

There was no room for her tale and all its cats. They would never learn it, for it was irrelevant to their lives. And if she stayed, and was accepted and became part of their world, she would no longer be *her*, but another cat in her shape, The Cat After the Fire or The Burned-Paw Cat—a cat in a different *fudoki*.

Where was *her* tale? Gone, the cats dead, the ground lost. She arched and backed away, tail shivering, teeth bared; and when she was far enough from the terrible stories, she turned and bolted. Howling as she ran, she streaked across Suzaku avenue, midway between the great gates that began and ended the avenue. Suzaku avenue is very broad; grief began her crossing, and her fear of an approaching bullock completed it. She slipped over a wall and into the east half of the city, and ran on.

She stopped in the east market. It was a large place, perhaps a hundred acres, and even this did not serve all the people of the capital: the west market, marshy as it was, had its share of workshops and storehouses, and there were other manufactories and shops throughout the capital, on the Street of Cloth and elsewhere.

It had been seven days since the fire had ruined the parts of the east market. Many of the storehouses and merchants' residences had collapsed, no longer identifiable save for a wall here, a fallen outbuilding there. The more temporary structures—tents, fences to hold in cattle or horses—had vanished altogether, though new ones sprang up to take their place, like mushrooms in rain. The air smelled of ash and wet flax and new dung and cooked (and now rotting) vegetables, where a vendor had lost his entire stock of early *taro* roots. New construction was everywhere, but the tortoiseshell found a quiet corner, crouched in the shadow of a blackened stone.

Life does not stop because of tragedy. People must eat. They must wear clothes to warm them or protect them from the sun; they must earn enough to pay their taxes; they must purchase and take medicines; they must continue with their lives. The time for people to mourn and tear at their clothes was past, and except for a few ancient grandmothers who yet bemoaned their lot, the people of the market were full of direction and mission. Some were dead or their wares ruined, but most had saved some stock, or brought new from storehouses elsewhere, outside the capital, away from the all-too-common fires.

Life does not stop because of tragedy—but it can be gutted, left light and hollow as a winter gourd. The tortoiseshell's tale was dead: she knew that now. She had told the tabby that she was nothing and no one, but she had not believed it. The pain that immobilized her had no material remedy, no torn flesh to clean, but her body didn't seem to realize this. Her second eyelids half-closed, as they did when she was wounded, and her chest ached as if she had strained her heart running. She *niyaan*ed, the weak frightened noise of an injured newborn. She longed for her life to end, for the pain to stop. At least then she might find the ghosts of her kin. Perhaps the *fudoki* would go on in Hell, wherever and whatever that was.

She didn't hear the dogs approach. Unsettled by the activity around them, a pack of feral dogs that had claimed the market milled from site to site, looking for scraps and mischief. Instead they found her, absorbed in her misery. They weren't hungry, and cats are not much food for a dog, let alone a pack of them; but cats generally stayed out of reach, and one sitting absent-minded on the ground proved irresistible. They barked at her— "Cat! Cat! Cat!"—and lunged.

She did not make a decision to live; her body made it for her. All claws and teeth, she scratched the first dog across the nose, and when he fell backward, she tore away, the pack yapping at her heels. Her instincts might have led her up high, but she still limped from the wounds left by the last time she had tried this. The market was full of hiding places, but it was also full of people and motion; there was no place safe. She found herself running faster than she ever had before. The scabs on her paws cracked. She might have been caught, but a gap between two foundation stones appeared, too obvious for her to miss. She streaked into the crack, which was deep enough to keep her from their mouths.

After barking insults at her for a time, the dogs wandered off (dogs are easily distracted from what appear to be fruitless situations). She slipped from her safe place, and continued south at a walking pace, leaving bloody paw prints where she stepped. When she came to the great Rajō gate, she climbed it and rested.

The Rajō gate is collapsing from age and neglect, and has been broken for many years now, but when she was there it towered a hundred feet or more, taller than most trees in the capital, and broad as a temple, with an impressive tiled roof. Back then, it must have been safe to climb. If one were inclined to do so, one would have ascended a ladder within the gate's structure, into a series of rooms above the passageways.

I do not know all this about the Rajō gate, precisely; but when I was young and first-come to the court, I ran away to explore the Red Sparrow gate. There were several narrow rooms with tall ceilings, and passages that went from one to the other. Some had guards in them and I avoided these. Another was empty except for an enormous cracked porcelain bowl gathering rainwater from a leak in the ceiling and, more mysteriously, a bale of silk fabric, riddled with (what I assumed were) mouse holes. The gate was full of mystery, like sneaking into storehouses when I was a girl, but so much more exciting because it was truly forbidden. Nothing happened; I was found by my old nurse and one of the menservants, and returned to my rooms before anyone realized I was not just in seclusion.

The tortoiseshell climbed a forgotten *sawara* cypress notch-ladder, and then climbed through the rooms of the Rajō gate until she found herself at its highest unfallen part, the hand-wide platform created by the roof's peak, which had been flattened in the Chinese style.

From here she could look down at the capital. Ours is not the biggest city in the world—great Chang-an is that, which tales say

is a hundred miles around its boundaries—but we are the heart
of our empire, and we spread for miles in each direction. Softened by late-afternoon light the warm pink of peonies, the city
glowed before her, tucked in its valley. The path the fire had cut
was clear, a blackened fan broken by the paler gridwork of
streets and avenues. Far to the north, beyond the Red Sparrow
gate, were the soaring roofs of the great palace buildings and,
beyond that, Funaoka hill, which shelters the emperor (and us
all) from ill.

She had climbed high in trees before this, but she had never
seen the city in its entirety, cradled between the Kamo and Katsura rivers, cuddled in this hollow of the mountains. She had
small imagination, and little ability to understand the significance
of what she saw. She only knew that the city was far larger than
she had realized. She would never have found her way back
home; the loss of hope had been an appropriate response.

She turned her head and looked south, away from the city.
There were buildings everywhere, and paths and roads threading
through fields and copses in a thousand directions. To the south,
the Kamo and the Katsura joined beside the abandoned capital
Nagaoka. The city's tidy grid of roads was still visible after centuries, a subtle brocade of lighter and darker grasses.

One road was greater than the others, broad enough for ox-
carts to pass. It marched off east to merge with another that
marched north beside the city and then lost itself in the hills. *We*
recognize this road immediately, even if we have never seen it
before, even if we have never left our dark rooms in the court and
the residences of our fathers and husbands, because we are raised
with the romantic tales of the savage east ringing in our ears. She
was a cat, and her stories are different from ours; she could not
know that this was the Tōkaidō, the great road that begins at Rajō
gate and skirts the sea for what seems a million miles before ending
in distant Mutsu province. She only recognized that the Tōkaidō
had a direction, a meaning, and that this made it unlike her.

❈   ❈   ❈

We ascribe meanings because it is our nature to do so. The Tōkaidō means mystery and wonders and adventure. We can no more see a thing without searching for a meaning than we can see a snag in a robe without pulling on the loose thread. When does this begin? With adulthood? Perhaps, for I remember when I was seven—the year before my mother's death—when the great comet came.

I do not remember much from when I was so small. I remember I had many nightmares and liked to play in dirt. I remember touching a snake once. It felt warm and muscular, and the gardener told me, "It's not the snake that is warm; it is the sunlight," though I had no idea what this meant. A story my nurse told me, something about monkeys and Kannon; but because I had once seen a picture of the goddess riding a carp, I thought Kannon was the fish, and so I did not understand the tale at all. A blue robe that my nurse wore always, as far as I can recall, that reminded me of the ocean, though I had never seen anything bigger than the garden's three ponds and the tame little brook that ran through them. That is all, really. And then the comet.

I heard of the comet before ever I saw it. The adults fretted among themselves—was it an omen? a kami falling? was it related to the drought we'd been having?—but since I had no idea what a comet might be, these statements made as little sense as all the other incomprehensible things adults said.

(*Was* the comet an omen? Had it a direction, a meaning? I did not think so then, but when I grew older I started to wonder, for we had been suffering from a great drought, and it was the year after this that my mother died. Still later, I decided that comets, like roads, have only the intentions we ascribe to them. And now I have no idea. If a comet is without meaning, it seems possible that a woman is likewise so; and I do not wish to think this of myself.)

There was one night when a terrible nightmare awakened me, and for once there was no nurse to coax me out of my tears—no one at all, and I was not used to being alone. Sniffling to myself,

I pulled my robes close and padded out to the veranda to find someone who would pet me and cuddle me (and, I know now, spoil me).

It was wintertime, and very dark; either the moon had not yet risen or had already set, or perhaps it was the new moon, the beginning of the month. The garden was silver and black, all color gone. There was ice everywhere.

I saw gathered in the garden a handful of tall shadows: adults, men and women standing, talking together. (Now I realize how strange, how improper, this was: no screens, no curtain-stands.) I suddenly felt shy, for I knew that the nights belonged to adults, that here was an entire world that I was not meant to see. Still, a visitor straying by chance into the private quarters of a monastery does not immediately leave; she looks about for a moment before she returns to the public areas. Before I returned to my rooms and sleep (my rightful domain), I would see what was so special about the adults' world.

The sky overhead was thick, furred black, spangled with a thousand stars, and dominated by the comet, which hung overhead, a blurred streak of silver as long as my hand. I thought I could see it shimmer as if it were fire, or water flowing over silk (I must have seen such a thing before, to think this); I imagined that I heard a tingling noise: the comet moving through the sky.

At least I think I remember this.

I do remember that night, the adults in the darkness; and all the talk about the comet. But the story my nurse told me of that night is quite different: she and the others had gone out into the garden to watch the comet, and heard a child's voice singing, and found me utterly absorbed in cracking the shell of ice from a twig. When she had held me up to see the comet, I looked with polite disinterest, then returned to cracking ice from the twig in my hand. "As if you'd never seen ice before," she said years later, "when you'd spent all afternoon cracking ice!"

A child (or a cat) is not awed by the same wonders that an

adult is, because everything is equally new and therefore won-drous. My nurse (and the adult I became) sees or imagines a comet and is struck dumb by the beauty of it. A child has not seen so much that she knows that ice on the trees is common, and a comet rare and therefore precious. It is only age that tells us what is precious, what is new.

Now that I am old, I think I have perhaps come back to this perception. I cannot afford to wait for another comet, and so I watch the tiny things of each day and am amazed by them. —Or I try to do this, anyway: there are a lot of days when I watch nothing at all except my breaths, and wonder how many more I will have.

The tortoiseshell cat dreamt of voices that night, tucked in a crotch between two beams high in the Rajō gate, under the quar-ter-moon of the ninth month. Dreams had always been silent for her: she chased prey or slapped fruitlessly at swimming fish in a world of scent, but without noise. Sounds were too important for dreams. Awake, they warned her of things she could not see, and even in sleep her ears were pricked, listening for threats or opportunities that should not be ignored.

But this night she dreamt with sounds, a thousand chaotic noises that flooded her, threatening to overwhelm her and send her into nightmares. She fought down the fear—nothing in dreams could be as terrifying as her waking hours had been since the earth shook—and noticed that there was sense to them, that the chaos she heard was actually myriad voices, speaking at every pitch and pace. Words flickered out of the background, like sparrows launching from a wind-tossed tree: *wave's crest, memory, heart, Tosa, rice, Why should I?*

She understood little, but I see much more than she. The kami do not speak to me, but they nevertheless speak, to others and to one another, and (if they are lonely, or have secrets) to them-selves. They are everywhere, of course, in everything from

my family's shrine to a dying cycad-palm on a beach in distant
Satsuma province; and their voices are everywhere, all chattering
or twittering or intoning at once.

Though they speak with the dead, cats hear neither kami nor
Buddhas. Cats are too fierce for gods; they came godless from
Korea many tens of years ago, and they worship no one. This is
good, for they are free in ways men are not; but this is bad,
because they are utterly alone in the world. Indeed, they seem
reluctant to see any god but the living emperor, and even him
they do not respect as they should. The cats at court (and there
are always a few, besides the kitchen cats) seemed to disregard
his presence altogether; when he was emperor, my half-brother
used to laugh and tell me that the cats were his only attendants
who did not bow and scrape and lie all the time. I said nothing in
response, of course: the emperor may laugh at himself, but no one
else is permitted to.

I cannot tell you why the tortoiseshell heard the kami—all the
kami—or why she heard them now, and not yesterday, or in the
fifth month, when she still lived warm against her mother's nipples in an abandoned fox den. Perhaps her ears had been attuned
by her grief, or by the echoing chambers of the Rajō gate. Or perhaps it was this: that one kami chose to speak to her, and by
opening her ears to its voice, it opened her ears to all.

"What are you?" something asked suddenly, close and very
loud in her mind.

The tortoiseshell knew she was dreaming, for she stood, not on
a perilous ledge in moonlight, but on a broad path as clear and
bright as crystal that curved off into gold-gray fog in both directions. "Nothing," she said. "No one."

"Unlikely," the voice said. "You clearly exist. You must be
something. And someone."

"I am a cat," she said. "That's all that's left to me."

"A cat," the kami repeated. "I am unfamiliar with your people.
But now that I think on it, I recall that I have perhaps seen some
of you before this, from the corner of my eye, as it were."

"What are you?" she said hotly. "I see no one here."

The road beneath her shook slightly, as if laughing. "And yet *I* also exist. I am this road, and those who walk it, and the trees and inns that line it. And I am the god who watches it all. And other things."

She tapped at the road with a paw, and ripples formed at her touch, perfect circles growing until they slipped off the road's edges and into the fog. "How can you be all those things?"

"How can you be a single thing, a *cat* and nothing else? You do not seem to be very creative, if that is all you've managed to become."

"I have no choice," she said bitterly. "I hadn't yet found a place in my tale, but at least I was part of my family and my ground. My *fudoki.* And that's all gone."

"Your *tale,*" the kami said. "A tale contains a thousand things. I think you are more than you believe."

"Not now," she said. "Not anymore."

"You would do better if you had gods," the kami said. "Then you would have something, at least."

"Well then, what is a god, and where do I find one?" she asked.

"I think you have already found one." The road's tone was perhaps a touch smug.

"I don't see how I can carry you with me." She tapped the road again, harder this time, her claws just bared. The road shook like a horse's withers, and she went flying.

"I just told you," it said, "though perhaps you did not listen very carefully. I am this road, and —"

"Never mind," she said. "I don't see what the point of a god is."

The kami said, "I do not see what the point of a cat is," and the tortoiseshell awoke.

When I was a girl, I longed for the voice of the gods — any kami, any Buddha or bodhisattva or saint. I prayed to a statue of Kannon my mother ordered erected in her room before she died. I thought I prayed for her health, but in truth I did not know her well —

losing my nurse would have been much sadder—and what I really wanted was a sign that gods—any god—existed. I wanted to see the robes we had draped over the statue move as she reached out with one of her thousand hands to touch my mother. This did not happen. My mother died.

After that I made up a kami. I have never said so to anyone, but I wanted a god of my own and so I picked a little pink-and-black-and-white rock in the garden, no larger than a cat, and I honored it. I made a little hut over it, and smuggled it a bit of rice each day. I gave it flowers I stole from elsewhere in the garden, and I wrote prayers on slips of fabric in my childish writing: *Let me be pretty when I am grown. May my nurse let me keep my collection of moth's wings. Let my half-brother the heir like me.*

When my nurse found out, she rapped my hands with a piece of bamboo and insisted that I never visit that rock again; but I did, and I found that others had begun to leave flowers and scraps of fabric there; and the hut had been remade, and better. I *knew* I made up the kami of that stone, and yet others worshiped it, as well. After thinking on this for some years, I decided that I was wrong: is not everything filled with kami, every stick and rock and leaf? Perhaps I had been the first to recognize and worship this kami, but that did not mean it had not been there, lonely and hungry for attention, like a bored little girl.

Now, so many decades later that I do not choose to count them up, I think there may be another truth to this—that the rock was worthy of worship because it had been worshiped—that every shrine in the world began as mine did, with someone's longing for something greater than herself. I wonder if the shrine to the little rock is still there, and I wonder if, a thousand years hence, it will be as honored and hoary as the shrine at Ise.

The tortoiseshell hears kami because I cannot, and even though I created her (as perhaps I created the kami of that little rock), I envy her. For her they may be strange, but they are as close and immediate as dirt.

3. THE GRASS-CHARACTER NOTEBOOK

How many notebooks have I filled in my life? I have trunks filled with them—and the other odds and ends of my life: old letters and calligraphy samples; fans and robes; hundred-pace incense, long dead but still haunted by scent; a man's sash forgotten before a dawn forty years ago; scrolls and fan-folded notebooks of the poetry collections I gathered when I was first at court, before I gave up even the appearance of interest in poetry; a set of shallow lacquered boxes filled with moths' wings; a sutra that I began to copy when I was twenty and never finished.

I discard these once-precious things more easily than I could have dreamt. I empty the shallow boxes, and moths' wings flutter to the ground, a momentary illusion of life. Even the notebooks are taken apart and dropped like autumn leaves into my brazier; without sadness I watch them flare and then vanish into smoke. The sutra has more merit than the rest; to die working to finish it would indicate virtuous intention, at least.

And yet I fill one notebook and start another. I am dying, but there are still many things to say—to myself, if no one else.

The tortoiseshell woke in the ox's hour, after the moon had set. She clawed her way down the Rajō gate's south face, and dropped to her feet on its wood steps. There were several guardsmen there, and one called softly to her, "Sneaking out to meet a lover, little one?" Another guard chuckled, and the first crouched down and made meaningless noises to her, tickling the dirt under his fingers. She crouched there watching him, unsure. She was unused to kindness from humans (the servants at the residence of her *fudoki* had a tendency to throw things, and caught up in their own problems, everyone else had ignored her as she fled across the city), but his voice sounded a little like the warm sounds that a mother cat makes when she is grooming, and his hand's movements were strangely intriguing.

"She's not going to come to you," the other guard said. "She's wild, can't you see that?"

"But she's tempted, isn't she?" The guard inched forward, and she stood up and tensed to run.

"Oh, leave her alone. Some girls just aren't susceptible to your charm."

"I suppose." The guard straightened and dusted his fingers off on his thigh. "Good luck, little one. When you return come find me. I'm here every night. Maybe I can show you around, hmm?"

She trotted into the shadows of a low shrub and watched him for a long time, but he did nothing else incomprehensible. The stars were fading when she crossed the bridge over the moat and moved on.

One generally travels with a goal. Even noblewomen travel to a purpose, however minor the journey ends up being: be at the banquet-pine grove by midday to view the cherry blossoms; be at the lady Chūnagon's rooms by dusk to watch the moonrise. This generates a sense of mission and of urgency, however spurious. The tortoiseshell had no goal. She traveled because with no *fudoki* one place was just like another, and there are small edible animals everywhere. It was easier to move than to stay still, for movement eases pain—or distracts one, anyway. She had not yet lived through a winter, so she did not know the comfort of a familiar warm sleeping-place; winter was months away, at any event—as incomprehensible to her as gods.

She followed the Tōkaidō's first miles more by accident than anything, and her pace was so slow that it was a fortnight and more before she came to the great Buddha just beyond the Osaka barrier, and that is only a handful of miles from the capital. The road was very busy in the daylight hours and into the evenings, and so she hid in trees and underbrush, and slept and watched passersby, and sometimes the little boats on Biwa lake.

She stayed with the Tōkaidō because its sense of direction and meaning were attractive to a cat with neither—even though the food was not quite so good as it might have been farther afield, where there were seed eaters in the fields. She caught a lot of squirrels. It was the time of year when squirrels seem to lose all the little sense they had, to run stupidly into the centers of kitchen yards and under the hooves of horses, and into the waiting claws and teeth of cats. She found them so easy to catch that she was not often hungry. Sometimes she caught them just to taste them, to learn what she could of the country she passed through, and she caught hints of *taro* root and horseradish.

A dog that loses a leg learns to cope, and after a time no longer seems to remember its loss. But on cold nights, when it is brought inside to doze beside the hearth pit, it licks the stump where its leg once was, and when it dreams, its remaining legs gallop in the pattern of a four-legged dog, instead of the three-legged gait that fills its waking hours. The tortoiseshell learned to cope with the loss of herself, and even found occasional joy—when she actually caught a fluttering *oban*-coot, or when she found a freshly dead fawn, miraculously unclaimed. But in quiet times, when she dozed or sat, the empty place filled her with despair.

She did not move far in any day: dogs and horses are designed to lope for endless miles, but cats are as brief-moving as an arrow. She would have lost interest quickly in any sort of disciplined movement, which in any event did not occur to her. It was just that the squirrels she decided to stalk were usually east of her, and when she was thirsty the water to her east always smelled better than the other possibilities. And there were times, at dusk or dawn, or during a lull in the middle of a beautiful afternoon, when she followed the road with nothing else on her mind but the even flow of yards into miles.

The voices of the eight million kami still chittered and chanted in her mind—*despair, hut, flowering fortunes, she was dead, monkey*—but they offered no guidance; did not seem to know of her existence. Perhaps the road's kami led her, though if so she was unaware of this.

The Tōkaidō is a great road, of course; it connects us with our most distant lands to the east, and binds our empire together. But it is not a *large* road, not in comparison to the broad streets of our capital. It begins impressively, just beyond the capital; but it thins and becomes hard-packed earth, wide enough for carts to pass; and farther east, past the Fuwa barrier and the ferry at Nogami, it becomes still narrower. I have never known anyone who has been to the end of the Tōkaidō. Perhaps it runs straight through Mutsu province and off our island, into the sea and along its bottom never to appear in the lands of the living again. Perhaps it does not end but tapers off: a road, then a path, then a deer's trail, and then a rabbit's, and then it is no more than a traveler's imagination.

Once, at the beginning of the tenth month, she said aloud, "Road?" and hoped it would not answer. She wasn't aware that it was the no-gods month, when they all come to Ise and transact whatever business it is that kami consider important. In any case, we often hear what we expect. When she received no response, she decided that the road-spirit that had spoken with her was a nightmare, like the cats of fire that still haunted her sleep. The voices of the eight million kami made her uncomfortable; mostly she chose to ignore them.

At first, totally cat-like, she stayed in the brush on either side of the road and hid when people passed. Over time, she started to do as the people did. Walking on the roadway really was easier than pressing through the shrubs and fields that fringed it, and no one tried to eat her; and so she did it. People stopped and drank when they passed an occasional well, and it made sense for her to do the same, lapping water from the puddles at its base rather than feeling her way on injured feet to the bottom of the many streams they crossed. Inns and houses looked so much warmer and more pleasant than sleeping under bracken, so she learned to slip into farmhouses and inns, and curled up in dimly lit corners.

There was more rain, and the days and nights grew colder. The cold did not bother her much, for her fur grew denser, and her foot-pads were thick. The rain was more irksome; she had never liked wet feet and fur. Worse, it drove the squirrels and other small things under cover where she could not reach them. Except for flies and fleas (which are always with us), most insects vanished altogether. She developed a taste for cooked fish, which could be stolen from bowls, if one was clever.

Cooked fish: I see now why I chose that rather than "cooked rice" or "buckwheat noodles" or "duck meat." I have been writing on the veranda again, for the weather is scorchingly hot, which is to say just barely warm enough for my old bones, and Shigeko and several other women are bringing a little table and series of trays. I suppose I smelled the fish cooking (it is *hake*), though I was absorbed in what I wrote.

This is hardly a profound reason to prefer "cooked fish" to all the other options. I have always assumed that the lady Murasaki weighed every word in her *monogatari* tale of Genji with the focus I might have applied to the making of a water-clock, where a badly shaped element may destroy all. But perhaps it is not like this: perhaps Murasaki selected Genji's robe combinations and the foods and trees for just such minor and immediate reasons, because she looked up from her brush and saw someone in cherry-shaded robes, and thought, *That's lovely. I'll use that.*

I wish my half-brother (Shirakawa, I must remember that this is his name now!) were still alive, so that I could share this thought with him. I think he would have been amused. No, I will not think of him just now—it hurts too much, and there is already enough pain for one day, in my chest and bones.

Cooked fish are not lovely, not even this cooked fish, with its elegant garnish of gromwell, now drooping dispiritedly. But they are necessary. "More necessary than words," says Shigeko, who tells me that the fish is growing cold.

There was an inn, not so far from the Omi-Owari border shrine. The tortoiseshell came to it one afternoon, when the sky was the color of old lead and had been weeping continuously since the night before, with an icy relentlessness that hinted at snow. She'd slept in an outbuilding at a little farm until an officious dog had rousted her, howling curses as she loped into the dusk. After catching an adolescent rabbit, she'd buried herself as deep as she could crawl into a mound of rice straw heaped around the base of an ancient and revered pine. But by midmorning, the dragon's hour, a drip found her and she heaved herself from the straw and moved on. She was soaked to the skin, and splashed to her belly with sandy dirt when she came to the inn, which squatted between rice fields filled with wet stubble and the mulberry trees that crept up the hill to the north.

It was an ordinary inn: which is to say, a farmhouse with rather more room divisions than is usual. The dirt-floored area was smaller than it would have been, and the raised section larger. Mats for sleeping were rolled up in a corner, beside an empty curtain-stand much too beautiful to be of local manufacture. This inn also grew silk when it was time, so boards had been laid on the horizontal beams overhead, giving an unsettling low flatness to the rooms.

It was special in one thing, that it had a cat. Remember, this is not so many years since the first cats came to the Eight Islands. Most remained in the capital, whence they spread slowly across the home provinces, like spilled syrup in cold weather. Some cats had come farther than that, though generally not voluntarily. Someone from the country saw a cat stalking vermin while he was visiting the city, or elsewhere. Inflamed with a sense of the possibilities (no mice ever again!), the hick purchased the cat from an enterprising child, or captured one behind an inn somewhere, then stuffed his prize into a closed basket and carried it home to a backwater in the provinces. Sometimes the cat died immediately, but often she lived a long time and became the pride of her farmhouse. Sometimes the hick was lucky enough to acquire a pregnant cat, or even a female and a young male. The innkeeper had been one of the lucky ones, and his cats had been thriving for a decade and more, their population expanding to fill the countryside around.

The tortoiseshell did not know this. There were no scents in the cold rain, and the cats themselves were hidden away, sleeping off their night's hunt. She checked for dogs when she approached the inn, but she didn't notice the smell of a cat until she'd found a corner behind an earthen oven in the dirt-floored kitchen area. She groomed herself dry, taking comfort in the warmth of realigned fur. She was mildly hungry but willing to wait: there was a spill of some sort on the dirt floor, and she would examine it whenever the people went to sleep.

"Leave," a voice growled. There was a cat a short leap away, a well-fed and much larger black female with yellow eyes so pale that they looked white. Her ears were flat and angry. "This is *my* place."

The tortoiseshell responded warily, her claws half-out. "I won't stay long. I'm just tired."

The black cat danced sideways at her. "My *fuδoki* is a dozen cats long and there will be a thousand more. And you are no part of it. Go *now*."

"I have no tale," the tortoiseshell said. "My place is dead. Let me sleep here, just for tonight."

"Why should I?" the black cat said. "I am The Cat Who Killed a Hawk."

Cats fight as they run, in short spurts. The black cat and the tortoiseshell fought in quick snatches of great ferocity; in the pauses they groomed themselves with a cold rage. Ordinarily, the tortoiseshell would have left immediately, but the rain-turning-to-snow depressed her, and she was cold and sick at heart, and tired of having no place to call her own. For one day at least, she wanted to sleep safe and warm.

And so she tried something she'd seen men do, when they drank wine and started pushing one another around. During one of the grooming times, she attacked without waiting for the other female to finish, and surprised her. The tortoiseshell slashed the black cat's neck and jumped back, out of range.

Despite this, weight and experience mattered in the end. The black cat pinned the tortoiseshell, and raked her again and again: "Storyless cat!" she snarled.

She would have killed the tortoiseshell, for cats are like people: they are uncomfortable in the presence of those who have suffered disasters that might happen to them. But the cats had drawn the attention of the servants in the kitchen house, who threw water over them to stop the fighting. Soaked and bleeding, the tortoiseshell fled into the gathering dusk.

She might have hidden in another building in the inn's compound — the stable or an unused room, perhaps — but she was thoroughly unsettled, and smelled cats everywhere now. Ears folded back and eyes half-closed against the rain, she trotted east along the Tōkaidō, through wet flakes of snow as large as her paws.

She came to a small wayside shrine: a hidden inner room and an open-fronted antechamber, in imitation of the great shrine at Ise. The shrine was small, perhaps waist-high to me, though built on a mound of stones that brought the structure to eye height. (When I was a very small girl and not yet properly respectful of the gods, I would have looked at this tiny shrine and longed to place dolls in it.) She stepped under the antechamber's peaked roof and looked around her. Wooden tablets painted with prayers hung everywhere from the roof. When she brushed past them, they clattered softly together. Bowls and packets lay scattered on the antechamber's floor, most empty, but a few still containing grains of rice or fraying scraps of fabric. She was hungry, but everything had been fouled with birds' droppings, and the floor was spangled black and white with them.

She pushed into the inner shrine. There was nothing she might make sense of here, only mysteries and shadows; but it was dry, and just large enough for a small cat who needed shelter. She licked clean her scratches and bites, then curled up to sleep.

She found herself on a path as clear and bright as crystal. The cacophony of voices had been with her since the night in the Rajō gate, a gabble in her mind, but she had not heard the single one, the road-kami's. Until now.

But she was a cat, and thus stubborn. The kami had not answered when she called for it. She had wondered about this at the time, simultaneously hurt and relieved. Now, nursing her miseries, she was bitterly, proudly, alone. The kami might have shattered her loneliness, and so: "Go away," she said, and refused to listen.

The kami's voice faded, leaving only the gods' chittering— *under robes, violet, Kuji district, the lit candle.* For the rest of the night, she dreamt that she walked along the road looking for a way off, and found none.

Kami are in certain small ways like people: some seek company and the admiration of friends and strangers, while others seem to be content to exist without worship, in silent corners of the world. (Perhaps the kami of my pink-and-black-and-white rock was one such, and I disturbed its rest. Perhaps this explains certain sorrows in my life.) Though she slept in its shrine, the tortoiseshell ignored the road-kami's voice; and it is possible that she wounded it, or made it angry. There is no telling whether turning the tortoiseshell into a person was meant to be a punishment, or a lesson, or even a gift of some sort. —If the kami in fact did this thing, and not some other, unknown force. Who can tell, with kami?

When she woke, she was no longer in the inner room; and she had become a woman. She lay stretched on the ground before the shrine, a small, fine-boned woman with thick black hair to her shoulders and gold eyes under straight brows. She was wrapped in a moss-colored traveling cloak, with grass stuffed into a spare robe and rolled tightly to make a pillow. She sat upright and tipped her head first to one side, then to the other, listening to the crackling of her stiff neck. A beam of dawn's light made the fog of her breath gleam cherry-red. She stood stiffly and brushed the thin layer of wet snow from her cloak. Her bare feet were very cold, and her hands and her nose.

She must have still been half-asleep, or thought she was dreaming, for it wasn't until now that the change sank in. She dropped to her knees, staring at her hands—clearly hands, and clearly *her* hands, for they were scarred across their palms with healing burns. Her neck and sides burned from the inflamed scratches left by the black cat. She touched her face and felt eyebrows, cheekbones, soft lips. There was something snagged in her hair, and she pulled it free to see a comb carved of tortoiseshell, plain except for the character for cat, *neko*, carved into it. She clenched her hand around it and made a sound, a human sob.

It was just after dawn. The clouds that brought the rain and then snow were gone, vanished like a dream; the sky was the brilliant blue of turquoise. Grass stems and small rocks poked wet and shiny from the snow, which was barely a finger's-width deep. The first travelers were already on the road. She heard someone whistling as he walked toward her, west on the Tōkaidō. She crouched, ready to run, ready to jump up and fight. She no longer had hackles, but her shoulders and the nape of her neck tingled. She fought the temptation to hiss, afraid of what she would sound like.

It was a peasant man, dressed in sturdy hemp cloth, with a garland of teals strung by their legs around his neck. He stopped. "My lady." He bowed slightly, the ducks squawking at the motion. "Have you lost something in the snow? Can I help you?"

"No. Go away, please." Surprised, she heard words coming from her lips. She scrambled to her feet and bowed back.

He smiled and then bowed to the shrine, clapped his hands, and bowed again. This made the birds squawk more loudly; he laughed at them, said, "Yell all you like; kami don't listen to ducks," and passed on. She watched until he was out of sight.

She looked at her hands again, and her bare feet. She was still human. "Road?" she said suspiciously, not knowing who else to ask; but there was no answer. And that was all there was to it: cat to woman.

Even for people, changes can be this arbitrary and extreme. Yesterday I was a girl, living in my foster father's house, sneaking away from my attendants, and kilting my robes high enough to wade after frogs when he ordered the servant-boys to stop catching them for me. The sun sets, the sun rises; a palm-walled carriage comes for me, and today I put on robes in tawny yellow and violet and dark red to take my place at court, serving my half-brother the emperor. My poetry (which has always been clunky, at best) is now elegant, "modern"; my music (I play the *biwa*-lute adequately, the six-string *koto* with an almost total lack of skill) is politely praised. In a single night, I become unrecognizable, even to myself, even though I have been raised for this my entire life.

And another change: I passed through a thousand thousand days, and each was made up of hours and moments; but they might as well have been a single day, for they are all past. Yesterday I was that girl chasing frogs (unsuccessfully, I add, and just as well: frogs are better left an unattained goal). And today I am very old. And tomorrow I will die. Is this any less strange, any less arbitrary and extreme, than that a cat becomes a woman?

Still, in our minds, there are changes we expect, and those which we do not. To us, this is a miraculous thing, this change, cat to woman. But to the tortoiseshell, this was only the latest part of something that began with the earthquake, back in the capital. It was neither more nor less surprising than that the ground should move and the city burn.

She made no choice to be human, performed no magic. I do not guess whether cats will ever be tricky like foxes and *tanuki*-badgers, which change their shapes to do us mischief. It seems possible—they have the same intense desire to have things their own way. Perhaps they used to do such things when they lived in Korea, or whatever distant end of the world they originated. Here they do not; not yet.

She was not beautiful, for her hair was far too short, and her
eyebrows unplucked; far from being a perfect moon, her face
came to a point at her small determined chin. Still, she was lovely;
to change any of these things for a more conventional attractiveness would have been to ruin all.

The cat-now-woman shook the grass from the robe that had
been her pillow and pulled the garment on over the robes she'd
slept in. The under robes were well made, of a high-quality
padded silk in dark blue and ivory; the over robe was woven so
that multicolored dyed threads made patterns like fallen leaves or
a cat's fur: black and cinnamon and russet and ivory. The cloak
was simpler, dark green oiled cotton, a rice-straw knot protecting
the center seam of the back. In her sash, which was the bright
orange of *take* bamboo berries, was a knife with a blade the color
of claws.

She stepped into the wooden clogs beside her feet and started
walking east. She noticed the change most as it affected her ability to do things. Fingers and thumbs were good, as was being
able to eat things other than meat. She found these both out at
midday, when the sun's warmth finally seeped through the heavy
cold air. She stopped to remove the cape (and tied it into a tidy
bundle she could wear over her shoulder, as easily as if she had
made knots all her life), and sat for a time on a low stone divider,
the perfect height for walking along, if one were a cat. An *amagaki*
persimmon bush hung over the wall's side. It had been picked
over, but there were a few little orange fruits that she could pluck
and did. They were smooth-surfaced and chilly, but when she bit
down they popped, and juice poured onto her tongue. She'd
never eaten plant matter before, except the half-digested chyme
from preys' bellies, and grass when she needed to vomit. Nothing
prepared her for this odd little burst of tart sweetness, so different from the texture and warmth of animals' blood. But she was
not entirely changed: she saw a cricket on the ledge, logy from
the cold, and she ate that as well.

Smell was different, she found. Things that had seemed obvious before—warm scents, like dung and the musk of other animals—were muted in her nostrils, while others—pine and cypress, distant hearth smoke—were sharper than she remembered. For a time as she walked she tried to imagine what people might gain by smelling such things so strongly; but she gave up at last, not seeing the point of smelling anything she could not eat.

Standing upright was not such an advantage. She saw much farther, but not as far as she could have in a tree. As the day passed her back ached, even though her muscles as a woman seemed better adapted to a long day's travel than her cat's body ever had. She had seen people pass her bearing sticks they leaned on. When she found a fallen branch, she used her knife (again, she knew just how to do this, as if she had been born with fingers) to lop off the unnecessary bits, and carried it as she had seen them do. It did not seem to help, but she liked swinging it at overhanging tree limbs to shake down pine cones and acorns.

People were pleasant to her, and this was also new. This was far from the capital, so most passersby were peasants and countryfolk, with none of the fixed stare and polite inattention of the city-dweller. And, for the first time, she noticed the strange things they carried everywhere, and knew what they were, which had not been the case when she was still simply a cat. When she was near the ocean (and as the days passed, the Tōkaidō spent much time within sight of the ocean, generally a sullen eleventh-month gray), she saw men carrying over their shoulders fishing nets caught up on long poles that snagged in branches overhead if they were not careful, or strings of dried cod, or flat baskets filled with mackerel strips. Once she saw a man who led a black ox with wheat straw loaded across its shoulders in a pile so tall that it dwarfed the ox. A dog slept on top of the straw, and did not notice her.

There was a night, when she was in Owari province. The moon was new, and the nights were very dark. She was tired of sleeping wet, and eating cold food she couldn't see properly, and so when the light dimmed with dusk, she looked for a place to stay. A path left the Tōkaidō, and trailed north toward a hulking blackness capped with a dim luminous triangle, high up: firelight and smoke through an eave opening. Frosted grasses closed over the path, and she had to feel her way through, listening to them slide against her skirts. Another disadvantage: she missed her fur sometimes.

A dog barked. She stopped until it came up to her, yelling, "Hey! Hey! Hey!" and then it, too, froze.

They eyed one another in the near-dark, the woman who was a cat and the little dust-colored bitch. "Why," the tortoiseshell woman said, "you're no taller than my knee."

"You're—what are you?" the dog asked.

"Bigger than you," she said, and threw her stick at it. The dog tumbled backward into the grasses and vanished, and she did not see it again that night.

She continued to the farm. She looked around: there were a number of buildings, and she could tell what some were simply by their smells: a barn, a food-storage house, a granary. Everywhere were spaces into which she might have crawled had she still been a cat, all too small and unwelcoming for a woman. She stood indecisively in the farmyard's center.

"Hey," a voice called. The tortoiseshell woman spun and dropped into a fighting crouch: ready.

"Easy, easy, now," the voice said, comfort and laughter in its tone. She saw its owner: a man, barely more than an outline under the farmhouse's eaves. "I mean no harm, miss. This is my farm, is all. My wife here, she'll want to invite you in. Yukio?" he called into the farmhouse. "Come on out here."

A wood door slid open, and a woman stepped out, outlined in the dim light from inside the building. "Where—" she said, looking around. "Oh, there you are, husband. And miss. Come in, stay the night. We don't have much to eat, but you're welcome to it, such as it is. You shouldn't be out at this time of night. Wolves; other things."

The tortoiseshell woman took a step forward, then another. It is not an easy thing for a cat to trust people. They keep their own counsel even in the best of circumstances, when they are cherished pets (indeed, Myōbū, who pats at my damp ink stick as I write, has clawed two women I asked to take her away, and refuses even my touch); how much harder it must be for one who had never felt a gentle person's hand. She might not have come in at all, but the wife gestured. "Come on up here, where I can see you."

The tortoiseshell woman stepped through the sliding door onto the dirt packed hard as stone that floored half the house. She slipped off her clogs (another thing she knew without knowing) and stepped up onto the boxwood floor of the raised section, following the couple to the square hearth pit. Mats were clustered here, and trays crammed with little metal bowls.

Here she learned one of her first lessons about people: "not much to eat" is a matter of opinion. As a cat, she had lived on whatever animals and insects (and, to be plain, garbage) were most easily captured or found, which had necessarily limited her options; as a woman her options had not broadened much. But the farmer and his family were not constrained. They grew many things and traded for others. It was autumn, so there was much to eat, and she tried it all: cooked rice with sweet vinegar and beans, and fresh and salted fish, a soup made of sweet potatoes and gromwell, little pickled quails' eggs, dried slices from a pungent orange melon, and preserved plums so sour-salty that her eyes watered after the first tiny bite.

The three of them ate together on the polished floor that surrounded the hearth pit. On the other side of a wall that lost itself in the shadows of the immense eaves were laughs and conversation from the two servants.

We—people—may not always recognize the feeling, but we can tell when a thing is not right. We walk into a room and know immediately that something has changed, though it may be days before we realize that it is the eye-blinds have been replaced. The farmer and his wife knew that the tortoiseshell woman was not what she seemed, even though they could not have told you precisely what she seemed to be. She was no peasant. She might have been a noblewoman—the weave of her robes was very fine—but her hair was chopped short as a nun's or a servant's. She might have been a nun, but she did not wear the drab grays that would be correct, and she neither begged nor offered prayers; if she were a wealthy nun, she had no servants. If she were running away from home, she would be attended by the lover who had talked her into eloping. That left only two possible explanations for her presence.

"Are you on pilgrimage?" the farmer asked.

"No," she said. "I don't think so."

"Then you must be selling something," he said with total assurance. "What is it?"

"Sharpness," she said, listening to herself with surprise. "Claws and teeth."

"Needles?" his wife asked, as if she'd heard different words. "I need one. Mine is bent."

"I don't—"

"They'd be in your pack, yes?" the wife said. "May I get it for you?" She stood and crossed to the sliding door, and gathered up something that had been there. It was a footed wicker box with straps so that one could carry it over the shoulder, like the packs the monks carry.

The tortoiseshell woman frowned. "This is not mine."

"Of course it is," the wife said. "We saw you bring it here. You put it right there when you came in, along with your cloak and other things."

The tortoiseshell woman opened the basket. Inside were bundles of various sizes. She unwrapped the first: a handful of needles pinned to a scrap of the indigo cloth that peasants use for everything, rolled tight to protect them. She handed this to the wife, who *ooh*ed over their sharpness, the lack of rust. There was a larger lumpy bundle of oiled cotton, as well. She unrolled it on the floor, and found wrapped in rabbit-patterned silk nineteen knives.

"Those are nice," the farmer said. "What do you want for them?"

The knives were each precisely as long as her palm, each identical to the one in her belt. "I—cannot trade these," she said, looking at them.

The farmer shrugged. "Someone else wants them, eh? It's a pity, they look good and sharp." But despite the fact that she had nothing to give him, he gave her a cloth filled with goose meat and rice balls.

They slept soon after that, and she was nearly asleep when she heard the farmer's wife whisper: "My lady? Men, they see little, but you are more than a seller of needles, or even a flighty girl running away from home. Who and what are you?"

"I don't know," she answered, honestly but warily, remembering the last time she'd answered this question, for the black cat who had attacked her. "No one."

"No one is no one," the farmer's wife said. But nothing else happened, and when she went her way at dawn the next morning, the farmer's wife said nothing of this.

I try to write of the common people, but, really, what do I know? I have never met any. I have never slept in their homes, eaten their food. Even my servants are of good family, elegant and civilized women all. I imagine what their lives must be like, yet my imaginings are necessarily naïve. But what else do I have? Is it better to write and think only of what I have myself experienced? Most *monogatari* tales are about what their authors already know: life as a court noblewoman, the mannered round of exchanged poems and misunderstood intentions. I am intimately familiar with this world: I was born for it, and have lived at court for fifty years. And here, where I tell the tale of the cat who became a woman, I confess frankly that much of my life bored me senseless.

I have watched the full moon many times, crossing the same arch of sky between the same mountains to east and west, lighting gardens that were nearly interchangeable: here the three lakes, there the stand of reeds and iris, the pagoda from China, the perfect little bridge. Yes, it is always beautiful, each month's moon unique. But all my life I longed to see a place where the eye was drawn, not by delicate nuances in oh, so familiar sights but by utter newness, by a blow to the mind. Perhaps this is why I write a tale now, something so foreign to my experience — because in doing so I am for a minute or a month freed from my life.

I have traveled as much as was allowed. I have gone as far north as Funaoka hill, and been on pilgrimage as far away as Ise, Hase, Yoshino mountain, two days' travel and more from the capital. I even saw the moon rise over the ocean once. But every night the tortoiseshell woman sleeps under a new sky and a new moon. She has lost everything, and still I envy her from the bottom of my heart.

In the morning it was raining. The wicker pack was still there, and so she shrugged into its straps. There was also a basket-hat, deep enough to conceal her face, with a trailing veil of ivory gauze. She had not had this the day before; but she took it without comment, along with the walking-stick beside them.

She crossed the border to Mikawa province, and stopped to eat her goose meat and rice. Her hands were cold and clumsy (a mixed advantage: fingers were better than paws had been, but then paws had never felt cold, even in the rainiest weather. Still, she was young and had not lived through her first winter; she did not know the numbness that snow brings to even the most leathery of pads) and she dropped several of the rice balls. She was not a lover of rice, so she left them where they lay, hoping some edible animal would find them and grow fat and slow, ready for her should she ever return this way.

There were few people on the Tōkaidō that day. No one traveled for pleasure, and even men who *must* travel—for pilgrimage or with news from the provinces for the capital—find there are days when they cannot quite bring themselves to hustle about. Such a day as this—cold, wet, and monotonous—encouraged a certain lack of discipline, and everyone who could stayed inside. But the tortoiseshell woman did not travel for pleasure or because she was required to, by gods or man. She traveled because there was no reason not to, because her misery was independent of weather, and so she moved on.

That evening it was still raining, steadily and everywhere, so she stopped in an abandoned roadside temple. (She slept much at shrines and temples: they were near the road, and they did not require her to talk with people, which became fatiguing sometimes, with their interminable chat about families.) There were no priests or monks, and not even a statue to show to which of the ten thousand Buddhas and saints the temple had been holy. All that was left was a bell the color of verdigris, its silver tassels tarnished and frayed; fading vermilion paint on the beams; and empty stone pedestals: the ghosts of Buddhas. The little stones once heaped before the statues were still here, scattered to the temple's corners. With each step the tortoiseshell woman kicked aside now-purposeless pebbles. The roof was more cracks than shingles. Water fell through everywhere.

Using wood she broke from a ruined screen, she started a fire on the largest pedestal. Her wicker pack held many things, it seemed, though she only found them when she needed them; one was an oiled deerskin bag with a flint, and a bundle of dust-dry grass. The fire was small but bright, for the wood had been resinous. It spat colored sparks, and hissed when rain fell into it. Smoke seeped upward and let itself out at the cracks in the roof. She shook her cloak dry, and was soon warm again.

I cannot say quite how it was, but she was still a cat in some ways. Her robes never got as wet as they would have on a person, as if they were fur and she could shake and then groom herself dry whenever she wished. She did not know that this was not normal for people, and so she never thought of it. But I do. I have taken everything else from her: home, family, story. I know some of where she goes, into winter and conflict and more loss. And I find that I cannot make her physically miserable, as well: not tonight as she huddles in an unfamiliar body, anyway. We—the gods who create things, even we small gods who write *monogatari* tales—find that there are limits to our cruelty.

She ate the last of her food from the farmer, and curled up in her cloak to sleep.

She was dozing when something bit her hand. She killed it without waking up fully, and only after it was dead did she look at the little creature. It was small enough to fit in the palm of her hand, fat, and the dead-white of rice or ghosts. When she turned it over, she saw that it had either no legs or myriad tiny legs, though she couldn't tell which in the dim light of the dying fire. She felt another bite, on her ankle, and slapped at it, killing another of the little things. She was ready for the third one, and caught it between her hands when it sank its teeth into her calf. "Stop that!" she said.

The thing squirmed. "Let me go!"

She felt it trying to bite her fingers, so she shook it and then cracked a little opening to look inside. It was like the others, small and white; when she looked around, she saw several more, just out of the firelight. "Stay back, or I'll squash this one." She flattened her hands a little, and the others squirmed back into the darkness.

She returned her attention to her catch, which lay rigidly still in her hands. "What are you? Killing animal, prey, something else?"

"I am a rice ball," it said with a certain pride.

It did look a bit like one, though. — "Rice balls don't talk, or move. Or bite me," she added as it tried to do so, and she closed her hands and shook it again.

"I'm not just *a* rice ball," it said when it could talk again. "I am one of *your* rice balls. You dropped us. Remember?"

"You weren't alive then."

"You *abandoned* us," it said, full of a sense of ill-usage. "Bad enough that you eat my brethren; bad enough that my *destiny* is to be eaten, but then you don't even do that! You drop me on the ground, where mice or foxes will find me. Wasted!"

"Hey," she said, and shook the rice ball again. "I said something: you weren't alive when I dropped you. What happened?"

"How do I know?" the rice ball snapped. "How do *you* know, for that matter? Maybe we *were* alive, and you were just too much of a clod to notice."

She considered the rice ball. This was the first time that something she might eat had ever spoken to her. Prey animals didn't have souls and could not speak—her mother had taught her this, and it must be true.

"You have a soul?" she asked dubiously.

The rice ball said, "Why do *you* care?"

"If you do, then perhaps mice and rats and all the other prey animals have souls as well. I'm curious."

"Would that stop you eating them?"

"No," she said honestly. "Not if I can catch them." (Cats are like that.) "But it might make things a little more difficult."

"Why?" said the rice ball. "Life is all about eating and being eaten."

"I suppose," she said. "What do rice balls eat, then?"

It was an unanswerable question, and so it tried to bite her again. She popped it in her mouth and bit down. There was a single squeak, and her mouth was filled with cold sticky rice. The other creatures rolled to her feet, their life gone: no more than rice balls now. After eating two more (for she was hungry), she pushed the rest into the fire. I cannot say whether this was a touching attempt to offer them a Buddhist cremation, or whether she was making sure they would not come back to life and harass her in her sleep. Perhaps she meant both these things. It is seldom that our motives are uncomplicated.

"Perhaps now you are willing to listen," the road said.

She stood on a road as clear as crystal, fading into fog at either end. Ten thousand voices chittered, growled, chanted in the back of her mind: *turn; cedar; emulate; I hear it now; rain-wet sleeves.* "Go away," she said as she had before, but added: "Did you make the rice-ball creatures?"

"The farmer made them," the kami said. "His wife and the little pregnant servant-girl, actually. You take cooked rice and a bit of vinegar and—"

"No, I mean did you make them live?"

The road shrugged, causing the tortoiseshell to stagger. "I am the road."

She gave up. "Did they all die?"

"Why do you care?" the kami said, echoing the rice ball.

"Because—" She sat down. "If they didn't all die, they might breed. Perhaps someday they might tell tales to one another. I wondered what a rice ball's story might be like." (As do I, though I cannot tell their stories myself. I must pick carefully what tales I tell in the time I have left.)

The road was warm, with a pulse like a heartbeat against her legs, she curled down until her face and side were against it. She found herself purring at the warmth. She had not felt warm all the way through since winter had started, and that had been at the border of Owari province, miles and days back.

"So why are you here?" she asked at last. "I told you to go away, the last time I saw you."

The kami's voice in her head sounded a bit like a snort. "You made an offering. And I came."

"I did not!" She straightened. "And this is a temple, not a shrine. It wouldn't be an offering to *you*, anyway. Even if it were one." It was another thing she knew without knowing, the difference between the Buddhas' temples and the shrines of the kami.

"The Buddhas were done with it," the kami said, "so I took it back. And there was an offering. Water in a fallen leaf. And rice. Though it would have been nice for you to offer something else, as well."

"The rice balls? They bit me, and then they turned back to rice and I threw them on the fire."

"Quite. Was there anything else you wanted to give me?"

The tortoiseshell woman sighed. "I suppose you could have the cloth they came in. It's in my wicker pack. As if you cannot tell."

"An excellent gift"—as it was. The cloth was linen (if a little sticky and greasy), and flax is always appropriate for a kami.

There was silence for a moment—or an age; there is no telling about time when it is dark and there are no watchmen to sound the hours—and then the tortoiseshell woman spoke. "What are these voices?"

"The gods," the kami said. "The eight million gods, speaking all at once."

"Are they all roads?"

"That would be a lot of roads. No. They are peace. War. Rice, barley. A thousand forges, ten thousand gates. This lake, that pond, the other river. The houses of Fujiwara, Minamoto, a dozen others. A tree, all trees, a forest, all forests. I am not here to discuss theology."

"How can there be so many of you, and I have never met a god before this?"

"How would you know if you met one? You cats live in a cat-shaped world. There do not appear to be any cat-shaped gods."

"And now I am not even a cat," she said bitterly.

"You are no more and no less than you ever were," the kami said. "You lost nothing that was yours in the first place."

"I am nothing and no one. Is that all I ever was?" She tipped her face toward the darkness, and felt hot tears on her cheeks. "I did not ask for this shape."

"Do you hate it?"

"Yes! No. Sometimes. Parts are good. But," she added, "I'm sure there are good things to being a mouse, and yet I have no desire to become one. I want to be a cat again. Change me back."

"Who says *I* did this?" the kami asks. "Eight million gods and all the Buddhas and all the demons and all the dead; foxes and *tanuki*-badgers, snakes and spiders. Monkeys. Magicians. Any of these might have done this, or encouraged it to happen, or convinced you to do this to yourself."

"I wouldn't do this. I think you're a nightmare," she said. "I don't think you're really here at all—you or any of the others. At least rice balls are real. But what are *you*? No one can eat you."

"I exist," the kami said. "But never mind."

"Wait—" she began, but it was gone. She had no more dreams that night.

When she awoke, she saw tiny pawprints in the dust on the floor and the cold ashes of the fire. Mice had crept past her as she slept and had eaten the rice balls.

A journey can be defined by miles or by days. Hers was defined by both, for each day meant more miles under her clogs. The Tōkaidō is a comparatively easy road, though in winter it can be blocked by drifts of snow taller than a man's height, or muddy wallows tens of feet across and knee-deep in the center, which stay liquid in all but the coldest weather. As on even the best of roads, there are ruts that can break a cart's axle, but constant usage keeps much of the path free of tangling weeds. Even the Hakone pass is not high. Roads and trails trail off to both sides. Some have signs painted or carved into wood stakes stabbed into the ground at the fork; others say nothing, keeping their mysteries to themselves.

Her wicker pack contained more things that surprised her. The knives were there. There was also a doeskin pouch filled with ancient coins: copper *wadō kaihō*, gold *kaiki shōhō*. They were not very useful as money, of course, but the countryfolk wanted them as good-luck amulets, and she found them handy to barter for rice and a roof, when she did not find her own. Inns and villages string along the Tōkaidō's length like beads on a cord, though they grow farther apart (and more barbarous) the farther east one goes.

Winter threatened, and the traffic along the Tōkaidō thinned, so that entire days would pass when she saw few people except in the villages that followed the road for a while, like idle dogs seeing one off their ground. The remaining traffic varied so much that there was no predicting what she would meet: a wagon pulled by horses, bells jangling on their necks; ox-carts with two wheels, with four; flocks of oxen tied neck to neck, being led to new pastures. Messengers and their guards cantered along the Tōkaidō on sturdy, wet, irritable horses. Begging priests walked barefoot through icy mud, their *fudō* scarves tight over their heads against rain.

Many people called greetings as they passed (for she did not walk fast, as she retained a cat's lack of enthusiasm for long marches), and when she stopped at the side of the Tōkaidō, to eat or rest or inspect her blisters (a disadvantage: her feet were always cold, and the clogs rubbed her toes raw; feet were not as durable as pads had been), others rested near her, and sometimes offered a bit of fish or *taro* root. She did not trust them, but no one threw anything at her, and after a time, she accepted that people generally meant no harm to this new shape. From them she learned to use the immense leaves of bog rhubarb to shelter her head, and even how to make the cheap rice-straw foot-covers that all peasants can make for themselves and their horses and oxen, and which they throw away whenever they please.

There were robbers from time to time, for they are common as lice on the Tōkaidō. Some she avoided, others she fought or negotiated with or simply gave something to: different solutions for different situations.

Somehow, no one asked her for papers or tolls. The guards at the barriers and the posting stations bowed deeply and let her pass, as if it were an everyday thing to see a woman in silks walking alone in winter. The ferryfolk did not charge her for their services, though they found themselves carrying her at times that they did not intend to cross this river or that bay, with the water icy-cold and foaming white as rice powder. The bridge-men and ferryfolk and guards never seemed to realize how irregular their actions were.

She still recited her *fudoki* to herself. She, the cat of that *fudoki*, was dead, and the tale with her. But sometimes, when the nights were cold and wet, and she was alone (and lonely, though she would not have recognized the concept), she would recite the familiar chain of cats to herself and take comfort in them. In this she was becoming human, that meaningless words can ease loneliness. We have all received enough empty poems from lovers to have learned this.

The dreams of fire-cats ended, as well. She knew—and had known, even when she spoke with the ghost of the servant, two and more months ago—that her people were dead. For cats there was no afterlife except one's place in the *fudoki*. Our Hell, filled with fire and demons and arcane punishments for breaking the precepts, did not frighten her, for she had no god or Buddha to send her there for disobedience or neglect. She'd left the cats of the Eight Islands far behind. Now she walked through country that had never seen a cat, and never heard a cat's story.

Nor did it now, for she was no cat, though there were things about her that remained very cat-like. She did not feel squeamish at the taking of life, as any good Buddhist would; little as she understood of the kami, she understood still less of the Buddhas, which were as pointless to a cat's sensibilities as poetry would be. I pray for her enlightenment, as I pray for the enlightenment of us all; but I must confess (honesty is a good thing so close to death) that I think she was perhaps better off for not believing in the Buddhas.

She enjoyed the hunt, though it was different than it had been when she was a cat, since her prey was bigger and had different habits. Her favorite prey was the little serow deer, as tall as her thighs, for their abrupt movements and bright black eyes reminded her a bit of mice. She stalked them when the craggier bits of the forest came close to the Tōkaidō. They were wary, but she knew in her bones how to wait, and she caught them almost as often as she failed.

She reveled in the feel of her knife sliding along bone and through meat, the pulse of hot blood across her hand. She loved the slowing of their heartbeats, the shallow breaths, the silence. She did not thank the kami for the meat as some hunters do, but she understood the importance of their deaths. She caught enough that she traded meat sometimes. She usually remembered to cook what she ate.

She had always watched ducks and wondered what they might taste like, but as a cat they had been too clever for her. Now she learned to wade into marshy waters and wait for them to come close enough to kill by throwing one of her knives. They tasted better than she even had hoped, warm and grainy: an advantage to being human. At other times, she caught grouse, deer, monkeys, turtles, a crane once.

When nights came, she found she missed her night vision (though her eyes were still sharper than yours or mine might have been), and the messages her whiskers and sensing hairs had given her; so she slept wherever she found herself at dusk. She was fortunate, for it was a surprisingly easy eleventh month. Frost came some nights, snow others, but it did not accumulate. She watched the moon grow and rise, earlier each night, until the full moon of the eleventh month was bright through dead reeds or pine needles, or shredded clouds, or the tears that sometimes flooded her eyes.

But there were also times when she forgot her sorrow and her state and enjoyed something, the taste of pheasant, the warmth of the sun, a rain so soft it was scarcely a hissing on her face. She was learning something about grief, that it begins with a great blow, but heals with a thousand tiny strokes.

To me her life is perfect. The cold is of no account; we are all cold in the winter. She owes nothing to anyone, and does not fret over the shape of her eyebrows or her robes' color combinations. She catches what she eats with her own hands, and sleeps where she likes. Every day she sees new sights, *real* things—an ancient pine struck by lightning, a shining green field frosted with melting snow and grazed by ink-black oxen—and not merely yet another well-painted screen.

And yet I have invented her, and her perfect life. These sights are not mine, but are secondhand. I have heard them from lovers, or read them in tales; in truth, I have more firsthand experience with well-painted screens than with anything in her world.

I must not forget that her life is her own. Her miseries, her longings, are not mine. For her, even this perfect month was filled with tears. Life is like that.

She was fortunate, for she traveled for some time before a man tried to rape her, an apparent woman traveling alone. It was in

Suruma province where she was attacked. As so many other nights, there were no stopping places close to hand, and so she ended her traveling for the day in the shelter of a great pine tree with branches that swept the ground around it, close to a slow stream. She started a fire and cooked her food in a thin-hammered black metal bowl she found sometimes (though not always) in her pack. It was nearly dark, only the dimmest glow to the west, when another traveler, a man alone, joined her.

He dismounted and led his horse into the firelight. "May I share your fire?" he asked. His horse was a small stocky bay, and his garb was such that any reader of *monogatari* tales could have instantly told that he was, in fact, a bandit, for he had leggings of *tanuki*-badger skin with the fur still on.

The tortoiseshell woman did not read stories, and so she only shrugged. "If you wish. You might as well get some use out of the fire, as well."

He laughed. "An interesting perspective, my lady." He unsaddled his horse, and crouched across the fire from her, a tall man with a missing tooth in the front of his smile. "If I put something in the pot, may I share your dinner?"

"If you wish," she said again.

He handed her strips of salted deer meat and dried eggplant. "What do you have in there?"

"Rice, boar meat," she said.

"Boar? Where's a pretty woman like you getting boar meat?" he asked.

And so it began. He wanted to know her name ("Call me 'Crow,'" he said, though she did not ask). She was obviously a lady, perhaps even a noblewoman ("Above my touch," he said, and leered), so where were her attendants? Close? Within earshot? Her robes were very fine; where had she gotten them, from a husband, a lover, someone with power? Had she a brother, a father, waiting for her? He had a little barrel of plum wine, and he rolled it close to the fire, dragging it out every so often to drink from it. He offered her some, but she had discovered she had no taste for wine, and thus refused. She answered none of his questions, for they seemed pointless.

Every woman is born aware that a man can force his attentions on her. All our romantic *monogatari* tales are filled with circumstances where a nobleman slips behind the curtains of a woman who has repeatedly expressed a lack of interest, and has sex with her. Paralyzed with fear at what people might think, she says nothing, not a single squeak to awaken one of her women; and when it is done, she vows eternal love to her (to put it bluntly) assailant.

I was never like this. Courtiers (and others) crept behind my curtains from time to time, for, however inadequate my skills as a musician or poet, I was very beautiful when I was young—and I was a princess, and thus attractive to ambitious men. But I squeaked—emphatically—if I did not want them as lovers.

The tortoiseshell woman was not without defenses, though she did not recognize the exact nature of the threat. The man, Crow, stood and crossed to her side of the fire. She stood as he approached, and when he reached out for her, she slapped his hand away. "I do not choose to be touched," she said as he nursed his stinging hand, anger darkening his eyes.

He grabbed at her again, and she attacked. She did not consciously pull her knife, but it was in her right hand, and she buried it to the hilt, straight down into his shoulder. It grated on bone and jammed there. Holding him with the knife and her left hand on his arm, she slammed her knee into his groin, lifting him with the force of the blow. She pulled him down in stages, knee to belly, then to breastbone, then to throat and face. He fell from her hands to the ground, blood pouring from his nose and mouth and neck. She kicked him in the ribs twice, though it was not as satisfying as it would have been had she still been a cat, for she had no hind claws to sink deep in his belly. When the blood stopped flowing, and his terrible wet breathing stopped, she pulled her knife free and wiped it clean on his clothes.

When she left in the morning, she took his horse with her, but she did not ride or keep it, for (whatever its reasons) it had loved

its master, and it feared and hated her. The blood on her robes
(and there had been much) had vanished in the night, and there
was nothing left of the bandit and his intentions.

—I do not know that it would have been like this. My experiences, as I said, were not violent; but there were nights when I
shared robes with a man I had invited and then realized I had no
interest in; and yet I could not send him away without the mating
he craved. So I lay beneath him and made the correct noises, and
imagined how I might stop these movements had I not been a
princess and unwilling to expose myself to the questions that
would arise. Perhaps this is a sort of assault, that I did not feel I
could say no; though I had not thought so.

From time to time, other men tried to attack the tortoiseshell
woman, but these attempts were never successful. She usually
killed them silently, but there were times, when the black empty
place that had once held her *fudoki* seemed overwhelming, that
she laughed. When she had been a cat, killing meant food, survival. It came also to mean peace.

When she crossed into Sagami province, and stopped for a
time at the border shrine, she found a lovely sorrel stallion tied
outside its walls, a bridle and rosewood and inlaid-shell saddle
wrapped in oiled hemp-cloth at the sorrel's feet. Perhaps by the
sheerest coincidence they were abandoned here by some noble
who had staggered into the woods to die (for the horse and the
tack were very fine; no one would willingly leave such a treasure). Perhaps they were created by the magic that placed flint
and knives in her basket—which had also, somehow, changed, to
waxed saddlebags of leather patterned with tiny dark blue flowers on an ivory background. Perhaps the horse and its gear were
an apology or a lesson or something completely different, from
the road-kami or another.

We try desperately to make sense of the world, to see the *why*s
behind how things happen. We make up things that might help:
sukuse, the law of cause and effect; perhaps even the gods. Perhaps
even Buddha. But sometimes there is no *why*. The tortoiseshell

woman didn't wonder why the sorrel was there—or the *why*s of any of it: the earthquake, the fire, the journey, her unfamiliar body. In this she was purely a cat. She approached the horse cautiously (always wise, when meeting a strange horse), and ran her hands along its legs and belly and back. She understood horses, she found. She also understood this horse, its temperament and the strength in its bones and its great-lunged chest. She pressed her face against the sorrel's long nose, hands on its cheeks. They stood there for a time, woman-who-was-cat and horse. And then she saddled and bridled it, mounted easily, and moved on.

Miles: days. Or a journey can be measured by sights, the smooth exchange of vista and intimate detail, shrine and temple. She saw the great mountain Fuji when she was as far away as Yoshida, back in Mikawa province, though it was many days before she saw it a second time, for the air hid it in clouds or mist. She crossed under the sullen black forests of Ashigara mountain, and overheard the elegant savage songs of the countrywomen there. She led the sorrel across the plains of Morikoshi, where she saw no flowers (and did not know enough to look for them, having no experience with the poetry we have all read a thousand times). She passed through reeds so tall that even standing on the sorrel's back she could not see over them. Mountains, rapids, marshes that stretch for days, dunes dusted with snow as white as the sand. Skies that stretch a million miles east across the endless ocean. A lake so clear that she could watch a sleeping fish as long as her arm, suspended as if in crystal.

I have not seen these sights, but I have heard of them, and longed to hear more. When I was young, I foolishly imagined myself in love with a guardsman who had been sent from Mutsu province. He was handsome, though his eyes were unsettling, for they were not properly black but instead liquid gold.

He could not write poetry, but I didn't care. Poetry did not laugh the way he did, and it did not come warm to my bed on certain brilliant moonlit nights. Poetry did not tell me about the great mountain Fuji at dawn, when it is the color of roses and pearls and peaches. Fuji captured a cloud sometimes, he told me, round and flat as a mirror. "You cannot imagine how big it is," he said to me, and I reached under the bed robes and grasped him. "Not that!" He laughed, and told me more, about the plains of the Kantō, which run to the very foot of Fuji, so that it seems but a handful of miles away, instead of the seventy and more that it is. There are many herds of half-wild horses there, each a hundred or more together, all more beautiful than anything you've ever seen.

He told me about all these places, and others besides. I did not write them all down back then. I regret this now, even though I would be burning those notebooks tomorrow in any case.

"You love it there, don't you?" I said to him: a little wistfully, for his eyes never shone when he looked at me, not as they did when he spoke of *azumi*, the east. "You will leave someday, and return there."

He said, "I serve my emperor as directed by my father; but come dawn of the first day my duty is done, I'll be gone."

And so he was. I cried a bit, for he had been very handsome, and was a kind lover. But mostly I cried from envy for his freedom, and because there was a place he loved like this.

Strange, how I have not let myself think of him until now.

One night, when she was still in Sagami province, she slept outside, for there were no houses or inns close—though there had once been a salt-making place close by; the silvered wood ruins looked and felt like ancient bones. The sky was clear and brilliant with stars, for the three-quarters' moon of the eleventh month was not yet up. She was very near the sea here, on Morikoshi plain. She could hear the surf, and feel it in the darkness, a great restless weight to her right.

She unsaddled her horse and hobbled him, and he began to pull up grass, and to strip the needles from a small tree stunted by the wind.

She built a fire of driftwood and watched the flames leap up taller than her own height. She had flinched the first few times she'd made fire, but that was many nights and miles (and sights) ago. She no longer saw the fire-cats who had tried to speak to her with their distended mouths. There were no cats, fire or flesh, in these lands she passed through. She was the first, which only increased her sense of loneliness and loss. The words of her *fudoki* were rather pain than comfort, though she could not help but recite them some nights, as a child cannot help sucking her thumb.

Her ears were still sharp. Even through the crackling of the fire, she heard a tiny rustling in one of her unstrapped saddle-bags, and so she flipped it upright, and began to remove things carefully until she saw her intruder. It was a straw-brown mouse, small as her thumb. Its black eyes stared up at her. "Mouse?" she said, and got no answer. "Do you speak? Do you feel? Have you a soul? Do you have gods?"

It only stared at her, vibrating with fear, and so she tipped the saddlebag onto its side and let the mouse go. Mice were less than a mouthful these days, anyway, and she would have gotten little satisfaction from eating this one.

She came to Musashi province at the end of the eleventh month, and forded Sumida river a few days into the twelfth month. The air was crisp, and heavy forest crowded the Tōkaidō on either side, so she buried her hands in her cloak, and let the sorrel pick its own path. Through a thinning in the trees she saw a wood yard, and a great tree propped up to be sawed into planks. A wiry little man in a loincloth stood atop the tree, pulling through the wood a saw as tall as he was. Sawdust drifted down in the heavy still air. Two other men watched him and said something—but she could not hear it, for by that time, she and the sorrel were past, and she had been craning back in her saddle to watch.

There was little traffic. She watched her breath puff in front of her and thought of mice. Ahead, a large party had pulled off the road near a roadside shrine to Inari. A well-dressed provincial woman and her women laid a packet of silk and a little barrel before the moss-green statues of Inari's foxes, bowed and clapped. The tortoiseshell woman picked up her reins, and helped her horse choose a path through the cloud of servants and guards and horses and oxen that clogged the road. The noblewoman lifted a hand and hailed her, and the tortoiseshell woman stopped.

"We are about to eat," the noblewoman said. "Would you be so kind as to join us?"

The tortoiseshell woman looked down from her saddle for a moment. The noblewoman was of middle age but still lovely, with a clever expressive face and merry eyes. She had kilted her padded robes to her knees, but this had not prevented their hems from being splashed with mud. The noblewoman looked down at herself and said, "I must look a perfect demoness to you; but I promise I'm hardly that. I don't exaggerate when I say it would be a kindness for you to join us. We've been on pilgrimage for half a month now, and we are sick of each other's faces." She laughed and her attendants laughed with her. Provincials have a very different sense of the proper relationships between a master and the various sorts of servants. "Please."

The tortoiseshell woman trusted no one, and yet she found herself sliding from her saddle. One of the noblewoman's menservants reached for the sorrel's bridle. "My horse doesn't like—" she began, but the sorrel finished the statement by lashing out at the man, teeth slamming together with an audible sound a hairsbreadth from his arm.

He laughed and grabbed its bridle. "Settle down, biter." He caught the tortoiseshell woman's eye and said, "I like 'em feisty. Horse like a dragon, here."

"He'll make sure your horse gets some food and water," the noblewoman said. "Please, come." She bowed and took the tortoiseshell woman's hand. If she felt the burn scars she said nothing, only led her to a rush-walled ox-carriage and helped her up into it.

It was warm in the carriage, and when the noblewoman followed her inside, it was crowded. There were five of them, all women, kneeling on thick cushions. They passed around little

boxes filled with food of various sorts, and each helped herself
with smooth little sticks to pickled cabbage, cold fried rice cakes,
salted eggplant, and sea slugs. The tortoiseshell woman had
never used sticks to eat, but she found a pair tucked into her
sash—a thing she understood without learning, like horses and
knives and knot-making. When the women were done, they
handed the boxes out of the cart, and the men filled them with
hot tea. She sniffed it warily (cats do not like hot things to drink),
and carefully sipped. The warmth soaked right through her,
along with a sweet, bright grassy flavor. She remembered with
bitter clarity that summer afternoon, crouched on the wall at her
grounds, the last moment she had still belonged. Her eyes filled
with tears and she turned her face from the women.

There was little talking until the tea.

"I realized I have said nothing of who we are," the noblewoman said suddenly. "I am the oldest daughter of my family.
I've been to the temple at Takeshiba to pray for my youngest
brother's success in an endeavor. These are my women." She
named each, but the tortoiseshell woman frowned. She didn't
understand names: unlike a cat's place in the *fudoki,* they said
nothing useful about a person. The noblewoman laughed at her
expression. "Never mind, you can ask again later, when there
aren't so many of them. Now: who are you and where are you
from?—because this is the middle of nowhere, you know. Hitachi
province is not the end of the world—that would be Mutsu
province"—the women laughed—"but we can certainly see it
from here, on a clear day anyway."

"I am nothing and no one," the tortoiseshell woman said. "I
have no ground."

The noblewoman looked at her from the corner of her eyes.
"Ah. The Buddha says that this is the way to wisdom, to understand that family and property are nothing. How enlightened of
you."

"This Buddha is wrong, if it says that," the tortoiseshell woman
said, her voice hot, anguished. "Family and tale are *everything.*"

The noblewoman smiled, but her eyes were suddenly sad. "And you have lost both, I surmise. I am so sorry. Such loss I can understand."

Somehow, though she never later understood how, when the tortoiseshell woman climbed out of the ox-carriage and returned to her sorrel, it was understood that she would travel with them. And that was how she met Osa Hitachi no Nakara.

I had friends when I was a small girl, before I came to my half-brother's court. Most were boys, and were inevitably of lower rank, but I loved them dearly. Their toys were so much more interesting than my own—mulberry bows and mugwort arrows, stilts, riding whips made of vine, hoops, and mock swords—and they could do so much more. They played between the horses in the stable and chased mayflies across the garden. They ran the streets around my home in the eastern quarter of town, all equally ragged and breathless, and told me stories of their achievements, when I could sneak away to see them.

I could not join them, but I had my own interests. I used to watch vermin, green caterpillars eating lacework holes into leaves; ants running about or walking in formal trains, bearing gifts to shrines hidden deep underground. When my attendants restricted this ("Squatting like a peasant? My lady!"), I bribed the household boys with rice candy to bring me things—moths' wings and beetle shells and birds' eggs—whatever my interest of the moment was.

I eventually discovered mice, when a boy caught one in the gardens and brought it to me, a tiny black-eyed brown thing crouching in a tall lacquered box. Its whiskers were finer than silk thread drawn taut. Carrying it in my hands, I asked a gardener who knew of such things to tell me of mice. As I watched and listened, tiny pellets appeared from the creature's hindquarters, black with a small earthy smell. The gardener told me such creatures slept in cracks and crevices and ate seeds and grasses. "A small life, and a short one," he said. "Everything eats them—dogs, hawks, owls, foxes."

I frowned and shifted the mouse to my other hand, shaking the soiled one clean. "Then what's the point of being a mouse? They're not going to learn anything, so they'll just have to come back as a mouse again next time. What's the good of that?"

The gardener laughed a little. "Maybe that *is* the point of being a mouse, little one—being eaten. Maybe the lesson they learn is grace in the face of unavoidable tragedy."

This made sense to me: *monogatari* tales are full of women (and sometimes men) dying gracefully. But—"What's graceful about mice? They don't write little poems before they die, or throw themselves into Uji river because their lover forgets to visit"—for my nurse had been reading to me from Genji's tale.

He laughed louder. "You think most people face tragedy with poems? No—we are a lot like mice. Some of us squirm under the cat's paw. Some fight, some freeze. I suppose a few have dignity."

"*I* will behave with dignity," I said. "With grace. But no poems." I wrinkled my nose and peered down at the mouse, a tiny quivering hot spot in my hand.

The gardener leaned closer to me, or perhaps the mouse. "Little one, the truest grace comes *after* the squirming and the fighting and the panic. To accept tragedy without despair. Can you do that?" I could not tell to whom he spoke.

I did not know the answer then. But I thought about it when my father died; and when my golden-eyed lover returned to the east, betraying us all; and when Shirakawa died; and now, as I feel my lungs fight this losing war to breathe. At last, perhaps I find an answer.

To show grace in tragedy? All those irritatingly stupid women in *monogatari* tales exhibit this, with their elegant little death-poems, their lovely corpses floating on willow-clogged waters. And they *are* stupid. What man, what lost love or deceased kins-man is worth death? The space in my life that my half-brother once filled is now an aching icy pain, like the hole left after a tooth is pulled, and I am dying in weeks or months—and yet I still fight for life, as every mouse does, until the final beak-blow. The grace in tragedy is not to succumb, but to fight on.

I knew none of this back then, of course: certain lessons come late. I was eight when I received my first mouse. What did I know? I made a cage of silk gauze and wood, but it ran away, as did the next and the next. For a time, I made up little stories about the mice, as dramatic and full of event as any tale from Ise. As I learned to keep them for more than a day or two (pottery stopped them, as did wire mesh), I told fewer stories involving thrilling adventures. The more I learned of them, the less convincing the stories were, even to me. I've found that's often the way with stories. Perhaps the only reason I tell the tale of the tortoiseshell cat is that, even after decades of living with cats, I still understand them not at all.

After a time I didn't keep the mice caged, but still they stayed. Mostly it was food that kept them, though I liked to imagine it was love. They slept in my sleeves, so that I learned physical grace because I did not want to crush them. They hid in my hair and startled my tutors and nurses, if I didn't have time to return them to their box. They allowed me to touch them, to feel their ribs fine as grass stems, the shapes of their delicate skulls. Their hearts beat fast in the palm of my hand.

I no longer kept mice when I came to court, nor did I engage in any of my less-acceptable hobbies. I wrote my notebooks strictly for my own satisfaction, though my woman Shigeko was forever asking to read them. I read the Chinese classics, because, while irregular, it was not unheard of for a woman to do so. I built water-clocks only when my monthly courses or illness kept me away from court and I returned to the cinnamon-tree courtyard at my uncle's house.

When I came to court, I studied the first cat I met there with the same interest I had reserved for mice and other vermin. Our cat was small and gray, with blue-gray eyes. We tied bright-colored cords around her neck, choosing colors that were appropriate to the seasons, but she tore them off and played with them, tiny gaudy snakes. After a time we took to calling her Shisutāko, the little nun, because of her dislike of finery and her soft gray color.

Shisutāko was not exceptional in any way. She did not grow up to be arrogant, as so many cats do, and she did not grow loving, as so many of us hoped she would. She remained a creature of teeth and claws, and the only way we could show affection in an acceptable fashion was to fold paper into shapes and thread them onto string for her to chase. She slept near us, but she spent the rest of her time elsewhere. Sometimes, we heard her screaming in the garden; several months later she would vanish, and return with kittens.

We offered her bits from our food, but she was as picky as a pregnant empress. She was uninterested in sweet rice candies, but she liked fish and the hot-tasting pickled vegetables. She also begged from the kitchen house, but mostly she found her own meals, sometimes bringing them to us. I was less squeamish than the others, so it often fell to me to remove the mice and voles. I examined one once, its tiny broken bones like twigs, and blood and saliva at the back of its neck. It was panting, eyes bright and fixed on me. I killed it.

"What have you done?" one of my women gasped.

"I stopped its pain," I said, and handed the mouse back to the cat to eat. Typically, she was no longer interested, absorbed instead in cleaning her paws, eyes half-closed as she lay in a patch of sun on the veranda. This was my first experience of a cat's nature.

And now: Myōbū has been sleeping on the sleeve of my maple-colored robes since this morning. I was wearing those robes but had not the heart to disturb her, so I slipped my arm free, and eventually discarded them altogether to change into another set, leaving her in undisputed possession. If I were to ask her what the point was of being a cat, what would she answer?

And what is the point of being a woman?

✽   ✽   ✽

I cannot say why the tortoiseshell woman and Osa Hitachi no Nakara became close. The cat-woman expressed no affection and had little in common with Nakara, and yet they were friends. Nakara had her own concerns, so perhaps she saw the tortoiseshell woman's grief and her strangeness, and pitied them, and her. And Nakara had certain experience with the creatures who could take human form, and it is possible that she saw a cat's nature in her companion, and so understood not to expect what she might from a woman.

It is also true that Nakara was tired of her people, for there were only nine of them for a month's travel; and she was used to the hundreds of people always to be found at the Osa Hitachi estate. Because she was on pilgrimage she observed the ten prohibitions, and perhaps she was bored. There had been little company on the road, and even the monks and priests at the shrines and temples had been surly, as they settled in for what was becoming a cold and wet winter.

People of the provinces are not like people in the capital, and Nakara was not like a court woman. For one thing, she spoke to all her people, men and women, even the lowliest boy brought along to tend the oxen for the trip. For another, she saw no necessity to hide her face behind fans or sleeves; she had no die-away airs. If she wanted something, she simply asked for it. If she didn't want something, she said so—very unlike the women of court, who on occasion find themselves married because they are unwilling to say no. She could use a Chinese abacus, but was hopeless at the poem-matching game.

She was capable of skinning out a deer or commanding her estate's defense from bandits, in the unlikely event that her brothers (and all their useful, strong, martial men) were far away. When she had been younger, barely a girl, she had served as nurse at an estate in Hida province. There had been a terrible disaster, and she had escaped with the clothes on her back and a ten-year-old boy, the only survivor. Together they walked two hundred fifty miles through the mountains in the dead of winter, to her family home in Hitachi. She avoided bears, wolves, and robbers, managing so well that on arriving she and the boy were well fed, clad in fur, and bearing weapons.

We would have considered her at best uncouth and at worst a barbarian, and she was both these things—but there is nothing to stop me from speaking the truth, however improper it is. She was brave and full of laughter and wisdom, and I would have liked to have called Osa Hitachi no Nakara a friend.

The tortoiseshell knew no one. Her clan were all dead. In her traveling, she met people on the road for no more than the shared instant of passing. Her meetings with the kami on the crystal-clear road were short and without satisfaction. She had no skill at conversation, polite or otherwise. She was moved with quick powerful grace, and there were moments of contentment or even happiness that softened her eyes; but the black grief at her heart made her less-than-light company. And though no one would have guessed she was a cat, there was something people did not recognize about her, something strange. We avoid those who grieve; we avoid those who are not like us; and so she was doubly distanced from her fellow travelers.

Friendships are strange. I meet one woman and I like her instantly. Another I dislike and distrust as quickly. They are both of good family and have beautiful manners and taste; they both laugh when I say something I consider clever. My woman Shigeko resembles a thousand of the women who have served me, her independence of thought her only difference—and even in that, there have been others. And yet she is one ear, and I the other.

Osa Hitachi no Nakara was another twenty days on the road returning home. Many things can happen in such a time. A woman can have a baby, or fall in love, or lose a loved one to death or indifference (though that can happen in an instant). The tortoiseshell learned about people. Nakara gained a friend.

The weather was mostly cold, for the twelfth month is solidly winter. Snow fell and lingered from one day to the next, until the

oxen pulling the cart could not get through in places, and they had
to stop until things became easier. When the sky was clear, the tortoiseshell woman rode beside the ox-cart, or ranged far ahead of
the Hitachi party, tasting air so cold that it burned her lungs. For
reasons she did not understand, she returned each evening to
Nakara's people, to sleep wherever they did. Often she brought
back animals she had killed, rabbits or *sika* deer draped across her
horse's shoulder. The sorrel did not seem to mind the smell of blood
or the twitches of dying prey; in this he was his mistress's match.

Though they considered their pace quick (particularly for winter), the party traveled far more slowly than she would have alone.
An ox-carriage is not exactly noted for its swiftness. These oxen had
been selected more for sturdiness than for fleetness of foot (if a fleet
ox can even be imagined), and they lumbered through cold mud
and hock-deep snow. The useful portion of the day was very short,
so that there were days it seemed that they had barely begun to
travel when the sun set abruptly over the mountains to the west—if
they saw it at all; the sky was often overcast, or even snowing.

Snow like this would have stopped dead the soft people of the
capital. We have snow, but it is not generally deep or long-last-
ing; and it is up to the servants and the guardsmen and the peasants to make their ways through it. We women merely watch
from our sheltered verandas, and admire it as if it were painted
on a scroll. It would never occur to us to take a winter pilgrimage
of a hundred miles or more.

The farther one travels on the Tōkaidō, the more real snow
becomes. No longer just pretty spangles on a robe, it grows deeper
and lasts longer. People can die in it, and not just because they
passed out in a ditch and drowned, overcome by too much *sake*.
They can die from this eastern snow due to even the tiniest care-
lessness, or karma, or simply bad luck. Storms come up where the
flakes fall so thick that a stranded traveler cannot see the eave-light
of a farmhouse a hundred—a dozen!—paces away. Someone lost
can scream until she is hoarse, yet her voice is swallowed as if she
shouted into a quilted robe. And these storms can last for days.

There are clear days, when the sky is a particular frozen blue, and the sun on one's face leaves no warmth. These days are bright, but oh, so cold. One's breath attaches itself as ice to one's clothing, and even tucked into sleeves, one's hands ache until they grow numb. Lakes and rivers freeze over and become solid for months instead of days; ferries become irrelevant. A cart can feel its way across the ice without falling through. (I have just realized: I do not think I will see snow again. How strange.)

Winter becomes harsher in the east, but the people somehow disregard it as we of the capital never can. They live and carry on their business even through snow and cold and darkness. There is no farming, of course, but the horses and cattle and other animals must be tended. Messengers still bring urgent business from outlying estates or along the roads. There is hunting and even fishing. My golden-eyed lover used to tell me about watching the fisherfolk of his district push their boats onto the sea on days when great snowflakes dissolved into its black water. *They like it,* he said; *snow keeps the waves down.*

Nakara and her people had adapted. They walked easily in high wooden clogs that no one in the city could manage with any facility. Their feet were often wet and always cold; but they shrugged this off as no more than an inconvenience. They did not panic if snow caught them unexpectedly; they sheltered themselves and made fire, and waited.

So travel was not fast. Beyond the limitations forced by the weather, the party stopped often for its own reasons. Nakara stopped at every temple and every shrine along the road, staying the night at the larger places, if they had guest quarters.

"Why do you stop so often?" the tortoiseshell woman asked once, when they pulled up for the third time in a day, before an unprepossessing little roadside Buddha cloaked in snow.

Nakara finished her prayer and laid her offering before the statue: food and a sheaf of votive papers, each printed with a hundred tiny Buddhas. She turned, her face sober.

"I had three brothers. Now I have one killed and one, my

adopted brother, gone to the capital. How can I not pray for them every chance I get?" She stepped onto a plank that had been laid over the ridges and whorls of frozen mud between the Buddha and the road.

The tortoiseshell followed her an arm's length behind, frowning. "You pray for males? They have no place in *fudoki*—clan, you would say."

"Don't they?" Nakara said. "And yet, I miss my dead brother every minute." She sighed. "I pray that the gods leave me the brothers I still have."

"Gods do not listen," Kagaya-hime said. "They just talk, talk, talk, and none of it makes any sense."

Nakara turned. "They speak to you?"

"Not to *me*," the tortoiseshell woman said. "Not anymore."

"Perhaps at least they listen," Nakara said, and turned away.

Tabu slowed them, as well. Nakara traveled with three women (and the tortoiseshell woman), and so there were days when they could not travel due to this or that one's monthly courses. There were directional tabus, which would not allow them to start a day's travel in certain directions; often Nakara ordered the party to head in an acceptable direction for a quarter mile (though this might lead through fields, or down a country road that led nowhere). The party then returned to the road, having addressed at least technically the gods' wishes. Delays were inevitable. There was a night when everyone was forced to stay up to protect their souls against demons, and they were too tired to travel far the next day. The tortoiseshell woman remained a cat in that she had no courses, and wondered at the delays of this and the other tabus.

"We have no choice," Nakara explained that night. "Well, not much. There are times when I have had to ignore the strictures, but I prefer not to."

The tortoiseshell woman snorted. "Do you think the gods notice?"

"Well, *I* notice," Nakara said.

And then there were the ten thousand things they stopped to see only because it pleased Nakara to do so. The east is strange and beautiful, and doubly so in winter. Nakara did not travel as much as she would wish, generally busy administering the estate, and she looked about avidly.

A waterfall splashed over black rocks, on either side forming great intricate sculptures of ice, and Nakara and her women pretended they were mandalas, and searched them for tiny Buddhas and bodhisattvas. The tortoiseshell woman looked with them, but saw nothing, even when one of the women (Junshi was her name) broke a bit off and pointed out the half-formed face and draped robes. And yet the tortoiseshell's eyes were clear enough that she saw an *ayu*-trout sleeping just below the waterfall, and threw her knife and startled it.

Later, just after they crossed Matsusado ford (now a stretch of slippery, dangerous ice that groaned under the cart's weight), they passed a wild black sow, the biggest any of them had ever seen, scrounging for stubble under the snow of a sunken rice field. The black against the white of snow and brown of earth was stunning, but Nakara stopped at the next farm to warn them that the pig was stealing their straw. The farmer explained that he allowed this because he knew where the old sow farrowed, and collected her piglets each year to sell. Nakara left a gift, charmed by the man's enterprise.

They came to a place beside a temple where a river had not frozen. Even though it was winter, a hundred ducks of every variety remained here, tempted by the open water and the grains the monks threw to them. A monkey moved among the ducks, squabbling with them as though he had been born from an egg. Nakara laughed until she cried, and stayed for nearly a day, using up all the fried rice cakes feeding this odd flock. The tortoiseshell woman did not laugh; perhaps did not know how to laugh.

Halfway through Shimosa province, there was a cinnamon tree as large as a *hinoki* cedar, alone in a field as flat as if it had been in the Kantō. Nakara and the women left the ox-carriage and felt their way across the field, which turned out to be less level than it looked, small stones hidden under moss and weeds and snow. The air was perfectly still, and they fell silent as they approached the tree. There was no shrine, nothing to indicate a kami was here (though of course they are everywhere), but Nakara saluted the tree as if it were a god, and removed her outermost robe and laid it at the roots. The tortoiseshell woman came close enough to see claw marks in the bark, as if a giant cat had scratched there. She pressed her face to them, but they smelled faintly of bear and not cat. She had known they could not be a proof of kin, for they were too large and too far away from the capital. Nevertheless, her sorrow nearly drove her to her knees.

They turned back, and when they got a certain distance from the tree, Nakara said, "I will tell my nieces and nephews of this."

The tortoiseshell woman frowned, abrupt in her unhappiness. "Why? What will you tell them? 'I saw a tree'? I have seen a million."

Nakara stopped and turned, surprised. "That tree is—you did not sense it? It is sacred."

"To whom? The gods? Which gods? Do we stop at all these places so that you may find sacred things?"

Nakara turned back and walked slowly. "Not really. I stop because I must, I suppose."

"Why?" the tortoiseshell woman asked, black grief forcing her to speak more harshly than she might have. "I understood the ducks and the monkey and the black pig, a little. But you can't eat a tree. One is just like another. Where is the use in that?"

"It warms my eyes and my heart," Nakara said, "and the world is cold enough. *That* is the use of that."

Their conversations were often strange, for the tortoiseshell woman did not always make predictable (or even socially acceptable) statements. Nakara was not shocked. There had been a time when she was young, when she had lived under an enchantment, attendant to a fox in distant Hida province. Her life had been filled with wonders and strangeness. A woman who was also a cat did not surprise her.

Nakara treated the stranger as a peer and a friend, and gave her a sobriquet: "Princesses may say what they like; the rest of us must be more circumspect," Nakara said to her at the end of one of their conversations.

"But then what is the good of speaking?" the tortoiseshell woman asked. "You might as well be silent."

"We are not all princesses," Nakara said. "And yet we have things to say." That was how the tortoiseshell woman came to be called *Hime*, princess. The sorrel they called Biter, for obvious reasons.

It is very late; the only light in my room is the brazier's dim red gleam and a faint sift of starlight that has somehow managed to ease its way past the screens and walls and curtains that otherwise protect me from the elements. My writing grows large and sloppy; I am sure that in the morning it will look to me as irregular as a child's.

Shigeko kneels across from me in silence, though I have written many pages since she first entered my rooms. She is pulling at a flaw, a loose thread in a sleeve. I can only trust that the thread is there; I see the tension in her hands and the soft puckering of the fabric, but the thread itself is invisible in this light. The night conceals her age; with her sleeping robes all askew around her shoulders, and her hair tied with paper tapes into a single hank to keep it from snarling, she looks like a small girl awakened by a bad dream.

"Shigeko, stop doing that, you'll ruin the fabric." She looks at her hands as if surprised they are hers, and places them in her lap abruptly. "Are you hungry? Would you like something warm to drink?" There is another attendant with me (there is *always* an attendant with me), a younger woman who silently bows and leaves, to try and find hot broth at this absurdly late hour. I no longer remember the younger ones' names; it seems pointless, like naming maple seeds.

Shigeko has stopped pulling threads; now she pulls the tapes from her hair and drops them into the brazier. Each bursts into tiny flames before vanishing utterly, a gold flare that illuminates her face's lines, touches the white in her hair.

I ask, "What's wrong, Shigeko?"

She does not answer immediately. Despite the tapes, there are tangles: she begins to comb out the knots using her fingers.

Except for visits to her family or the shrine at Ise, and her monthly retreats for her courses, we have been together nearly every moment of every day of fifty years. She seems to have no great dreams, no restless desire to be anything but what she is. For fifty years, she has been content to select robe combinations, sew even seams, exclaim about the weather, and exchange gossip with my other women—and to do it all again the next day, and the next. All these decades of shared minutiae have mounded up around us, concealing the fact that she is her own person, with yearnings and tastes of her own. I know her better than anyone, in the same way I know the texture of my own skin, or the shapes of my fingernails. There is a disadvantage to this: I do not always see what I am looking at.

The young attendant returns with bowls of hot *taro* soup and slivers of boar meat on a lacquered tray. I am not hungry: the growing thing that kills my body makes it difficult to eat, but I watch Shigeko drink her soup with tidy little sips, just as she has drunk every bowl of soup for fifty years. It is just as well that her manners are good, or she would have driven me mad, and I would have had to send her away. And this would have been like losing an arm.

The Tōkaidō takes to the great sea for a short while, on a long boat ride that just skims the Noumi peninsula, entering a vast inlet, landing the traveler at last in the Shida district of Hitachi province. This is (usually) safe in the summer months, but less so in winter, when snow can blind the pilot, and winds and strange tides may pull a boat far from shore before it can duck into the shelter of Shida inlet. The Osa Hitachi party waited for days before the weather and tides were such that the ferryfolk would take them. The only place they could stay at this time of year was a small and bitterly cold inn, mostly closed down for the season. Whatever their ranks, everyone gathered in the raised room beside the kitchen area of the main building, where the ovens kept things a bit warmer. The men went out often, for they had the animals to tend and various preparations to make, but the women stayed inside, and Hime often waited with them. They read aloud sometimes from a palm-leaf sutra they carried in a deerskin case; or from a handful of notebooks containing *monogatari* tales. Hime ignored the sutras (alas; she might have learned much from thinking of the Buddhas), but the tales intrigued her. "Though they are not very interesting," she said aloud.

Junshi put down the notebook from which she had been reading. "No? When Genji is exchanging such heartfelt poems with Aoi?"

"There is no fighting," Hime said. "No wonders, no strangeness. Not like the *fudoki* of my people."

"Tell it then," Nakara said.

"Tell you my *fudoki*?" Hime said, taken aback. She remembered all the cats' stories as vividly as if they were her own paws, but to tell them to one not of the group—this stymied her.

Nakara laughed at her expression. "I'm sick of *our* stories; I've heard them a thousand times. I say I'm praying for my brother's success, but I have to admit that a big part of my prayers is the hope that he brings me something new to read from the capital."

The Five-Colored Cat, The Cat with Three Legs, The Straw-Cloak Cat. She could tell the tales, and they would be heard, they would be witnessed. The *fudoki* would continue. But it would be wrong. The tale would be like the woman's ghost back in the capital, begging her charred body to awaken. "No," she said. Her eyes burned. "I have no tale to tell. Not anymore."

The other women begged a little, but Nakara said nothing, only poured tea for them all and led the conversation down safer paths. Hime left shortly afterward, to "see to the horse," and did not return for many hours.

She did see to Biter, and then stayed with the sorrel. Nakara might have been hurt had she realized this, that Biter was the closest thing Hime had to a friend. Hime did not speak to him, except the little nothings we say to our pets and our horses. He never spoke back. He did not behave in any human way; he was totally and unequivocally a horse, which is to say stubborn, occasionally stupid, frequently lazy, and occasionally savage. —Which is quite human, if I think on it.

Biter was an animal, and Hime, suspended between cat and woman, longed to be one. Perhaps Nakara would have understood this better than any of us might expect.

Nights were too dark to read anything, and so they talked, and Hime learned more of the party's mission. "It's complicated," Nakara warned.

Hime—thinking of the intricate interrelations between cats and people, dogs, horses—shrugged. "I will try to keep track," she said.

It *was* complicated, the sort of tricky political situation that usually ends with disaster of some sort. The *bandō*, the east, has always been a troublesome part of the empire. The original inhabitants were absolute savages (they wore furs and drank blood and carried arrows in their hair!), but they were controlled many centuries ago, when families from the central provinces and the southwest were sent by the empire to pacify them. Over time, some of these people became little better than those they defeated—though at least they did not drink blood. The eastern families are many months' travel from the capital, and generally well armed and well mounted (indeed, Osa Hitachi no Nakara's family is not atypical). The families develop independent ambitions and become fractious, and then the emperor (any of a dozen emperors over the past four hundred years) must send or assign troops to remind them of his absolute authority.

Or so it was explained to me so many years ago, on the one hand by my half-brother; on the other by my golden-eyed lover, Mononobe no Dōmei. My lover came from Mutsu province, as far north and east as one may go, and his perception of the situation was quite different from my brother's, naturally. I tried to find a medium between their varying reports, but I must believe my half-brother was right. Was he not emperor?

Nakara explained to Hime: there was a problem. The Osa Hitachi clan controlled a neglected estate somewhere in Mutsu province. (I cannot say in which of the districts, for they're all barbarous places; there's no point to keeping track. The only district I know in Mutsu province is Iwate, which was Dōmei's home.) The second Osa Hitachi brother managed the estate, which he did well, opening new land for rice fields and producing small amounts of gold from a mine on the site.

But after some years, the second brother offended a local family, an ambitious branch of the ubiquitous Abe clan. The initial cause might have been anything—disputed land; a stolen (or eloping) wife; a killing, accidental or intended; theft; an impolite letter; simple willfulness or pride or temper or greed. The Abe were very powerful, with allies and contacts as far south as Kurobe river, and they were used to managing things in their own way. They killed the brother, his family, and his followers, then burned the estate.

The governor of Mutsu province did not care about this—he had relatives among the Abe—but there were others who did. It is not a wise thing to kill the brothers of powerful men, and the oldest Osa Hitachi brother was vice-governor (and actual leader, for the governor would have been a cousin of mine from the capital, leader in name only) of Hitachi province, just to the south. The central government is uninterested in mere bickering so far from the capital—and a few tens of deaths a million miles away was hardly more than that—and so I think that perhaps the vice-governor lied in the letter he sent, claiming that the Abe family were not paying their taxes or had too large a household military force or were concealing weapons; and asking for a warrant to destroy them. He sent his adopted brother, Osa Hitachi no Kitsune, to the capital for a *tsuitoshi* warrant authorizing an attack on the Abe.

"So your oldest brother has asked your youngest brother to

lead an attack—" Hime said, setting things clear in her mind.

"Yes."

"—for someone who left their *fudoki* to found a new one—"

"I don't quite understand '*fudoki*,'" Nakara said.

"—home, then—because someone killed him to take his ground—home—when they had a perfectly good home of their own?"

"Yes," Nakara said.

"But he's dead, the one who left. Why do this?"

"He was my brother," Nakara said. "They killed him."

Hime frowned. "He was a male, and he was far away. He was not part of the *fudoki*."

"What the Abe did was wrong, against the codes."

"This isn't about codes, though," Hime said.

Nakara laughed suddenly, a humorless bark. "No. It's about revenge."

The day came when the ferryfolk were at last willing to travel, the sky overcast but calm. They left early, at the tiger's hour, to catch a tide that would drift them up Shida inlet. The air was so heavy and wet that everyone (except the oxen) shivered and fretted. The horses hated the trip, as did Hime, who hung her head and vomited for the duration. Nakara pointed out sights to her at first, hoping to distract her: the home of the great kami Kashima, the Aze passage, the Island of Nine Shrines. Later, when it became clear that Hime had no attention for such things, she left her alone. By the time they landed on Enoura inlet in the purple light of dusk on snow, Hime was too weak to walk, and had to be carried ashore, still retching helplessly. She was barely conscious when Nakara's women wrapped her in clean, dry robes and tucked her into a little curtained enclosure at the center of a room.

Hime awoke in the rat's hour, in warmth and darkness. For a moment everything was all right; she had been sick, but now she lay close to her mother's nipples, a sister cuddled next to her, other kittens pressing her down. She nestled closer, and Nakara sighed in her ear.

She was not home; she was not that kitten. The smells were wrong; the warm weight was robes heaped over her. Hime had been alone since her mother died. Her cousins and aunts had not cared deeply about her—cats came, cats went; only the *fudoki* remained—but even they were gone. A guardsman had scratched the ground before her, coaxing. She became a woman: a peasant with a necklace of ducks offered help; a farmer's wife took her hand and asked who she was. A provincial woman asked for her company. That was all the contact she had had.

If she had remained a cat, I do not think she would have seen just how alone she was. But she was not a cat, not entirely anyway. She made a single sob, and bit her lip to silence it.

"It's all right," Nakara said softly: awake. "We're on land now. Go back to sleep. You'll feel better in the morning."

"No," Hime said, "I won't," and she cried and could not stop.

When her eyes wept blood and her sleeves were soaked through, she at last calmed and spoke a little, of her mother's death, and her home burning down, and her time alone on the Tōkaidō since then. She never explained that she was a cat, for it didn't occur to her that it would matter. Nakara listened and held her until the sobs were finished, and she lay limp in Nakara's arms.

At last Nakara said, "What are you?"

Hime said, "Nothing and no one."

"I understand a little, what it is to be so alone," Nakara said.

"How can you? *None* of this is right." Hime shook her head, and tears flew.

Nakara leaned back. "I will tell you a tale, and you can decide whether I might know. It's about a girl who woke up one day and found herself nursemaid to a family in Hida prefecture. She remembered nothing before that morning. No: she woke up and there she was. There was a father and a mother and their son and servants and gardens, and everything was just the way you'd expect." She paused for a moment, and pressed her cheek to the top of Hime's head.

"But it wasn't normal, not really, because in the corner of her eyes, the girl caught glimpses of something different—foxes and bare dirt and rainwater in a fallen leaf. She feared that she was just part of the illusion, and she cried herself to sleep every night over this. You think you are the first one to look around her and realize that she has nothing, no one?" Nakara's laugh was brief. "You are at least real.

"After a time, she made up little stories about the life she wished were hers. She would be from a long way away, Hitachi province, maybe; and she would have parents who loved her, and brothers even; and she would have a hundred interests and a thousand friends, and they would all be real.

"And then there was a crisis, and all that was left was herself and the boy. She brought him to Hitachi province, and found it all just the way she dreamt: parents and brothers and home and horses. But she will never know whether she somehow *made* these things, or whether she was remembering what had always been there."

No more was said. Woman and cat-woman watched the brazier coals fade. Sleep came eventually.

We all cry all the time at court, and anything may set us off: a particularly delicate sunset, a *sika* deer calling to his wife, the purity of the lady Izumi's calligraphy. The disadvantage to this is that at times of great sorrow, we have no deeper expressions of grief than those we have already used for a thousand more trivial matters. I think this is why the women in all those tales died at the end. If the cherry blossoms move me to tears, then there was nothing intense enough to express my sorrow at losing my golden-eyed lover. Except for death.

I did not die, of course. I am a princess, descendant of gods, granddaughter and daughter and half-sister and aunt and great-aunt to emperors. We do not die for pretty young men who leave for their homes with only a scrawled note, with not even an attempt at elegant writing or a thoughtful poem. (*I will miss you,* it said. *You would have loved my home. I wish* . . . and no more.) I still wept at all the appropriate sights (moons and cherry blossoms), and never mentioned him to anyone. But there were nights when my woman Shigeko held me, and stifled my sobs against her robes until the tears, the true tears, the ones that taste like poison and leave one sick and light-headed, were past.

I have reached an age where I have known many people, but by now more of them are dead than alive. I look for them in the young people at court — hoping to catch a certain expression, or the movement of a head turning, that reminds me of someone I knew long ago. Sometimes it is there, but often as not this is because the young woman I see is the daughter (or granddaughter) of the woman I once knew.

Every cat is an echo of the first cat I knew, the little nun, Shisutāko. She remained as independent-minded as a scholar, but as she grew older, she began to spend more of her time with me and my women, curled up as close to the braziers as we allowed; for we could not believe that she would not inadvertently set herself afire, despite all the years of proof to the contrary. She caught less of her own food, relying instead on the bits of fish and fowl that we set aside for her in a little pewter bowl that eventually came to be used for no other purpose. She still had her wild moments, when she bolted from end to end of a room or across the garden. Her tail took ten thousand positions, each like a rapid brush stroke — the fluid calligraphy of a cat's life.

Certain cold nights she slipped between my curtains and coiled herself into a tight little knot on my bed robes. She did not like to be stroked much, but in these quiet hours, she permitted my touch and even purred under my hand. She was always gone by morning, but I cherished this shared secret we had.

There came a time when she moved only reluctantly, remaining always in my rooms, straying only as far as my verandas to raise her face to the sun's warmth. She stopped eating and developed a growth on her shoulder. "A tumor," said one of my women, whose family had cats and understood these things. "They get them, just as people do."

I kneaded the lump, a strange solid contrast to her dry fur and the skin thin as bird's skin that hung from her stick-like bones. "Then she will die."

"Oh, yes, my lady. I am so sorry."

And it was twilight one day in the ninth month, and the world was shades of dim purple, like my subtlest robes. The little nun stepped slowly off the veranda to a stone, and then to the round gravel of my courtyard, her fur taking on the same lilac tones as the air. She made her unsteady way toward the mossy shadows beneath a copse of red and white pine in the gardens. "Wait—" I said to her, but she was well beyond the sound of my voice, and had never attended me in any case. She paused for a moment at the copse's edge to carefully sniff some small bush; and then she stepped tidily into the darkness, and did not return.

Strange that it has been fifty years since she died, and she was a mere cat—and hardly affectionate—and yet her death moves me as even my half-brother Shirakawa's does not. Perhaps this is because I was young then and death was a strange land to me, a place farther than India even. Now that I am old, I know so many more people who are dead, and am myself so close to death that it no longer shocks me.

(I lie. Shirakawa does not affect me because I dare not let it. I still need my strength.)

Do not misinterpret. I am still terrified of death—terrified. If I thought anything could postpone it, even for a day, I would do that thing. I would give a thousand mirrors to the shrine at Izumo; I would write with my own hand a thousand sutras. But, unlike Kagaya-hime, the gods do not speak to me. Is there a Pure Land, hells, demons and Buddhas and bodhisattvas? Will my soul return reincarnated, perhaps with Dōmei, lovers for a thousand lives?

6. THE *GENJI*-POEM SCROLL

I can't imagine what I was thinking, keeping this paper for so many years—though I can see why I have not used it before this. I was never a lover of spring colors, and the scroll is busy with silver leaves and pale gray poems, an intimidating background to any words I might choose to record. Why would I write on something that is so obviously full of its own importance? But my eyesight is not what it was; the poems are mere patterns to me now, no more meaningful than the paw-marks of a restless cat on a rainy day.

I take a private joy in admitting this here, on paper; for my conversations have been all about poetry, lately. I have a former attendant visiting, a woman I have not seen in some years. She married a Kaya, and has been for some time off in the backwoods somewhere—Hida province? Shinano? Evidently her marriage is a trial, and she has left her husband and returned here. I invited her for a visit, grateful for her company, since Shigeko has a *kaze*-cold and is staying with a nephew somewhere on Nijō avenue until she has recovered. My guest's faith in the proprieties is touching: she is careful with her robe combinations and poetic allusions, as if such things mattered in the long run. This would be irritating if her critical eyes ever turned outward, but she judges no one save herself.

I say whatever comes to mind in my conversations with her, but there are times she thinks I speak in poems. I stifle a smile, for this seems to be all the difference between a poem and a statement, or a poem and a background pattern on scroll's paper: intention. And she can scarcely be thirty, too young to have learned that the intention is what matters.

It was a beautiful day when the Osa Hitachi party came at last to Hitachi province. Hime woke to bright daylight filtering down from the eave openings. The other women were awake and gone, but she heard shouts and laughing screams from outside. She stretched, and waited through the moment of grief she felt every morning, when she realized that she was still a woman, still with no ground and no *fudoki*, still alone. When her eyes stopped burning, she went outside.

Enoura was a posting station, and a fishing and farming village. Enoura inlet bordered them to the south, its open water nearly hidden by a tissue of mist, the only proof that there was any warmth in the thin sunlight. The houses of the village were large, with room under their roofs for cattle and sheep, though most animals (and people) were out, tramping through the stripped rice fields just up the hill from the inlet, hoping to find some overlooked treasure. A small fenced enclosure contained the border shrine, though the gate was open.

Nakara and her women stood at the covered well before the shrine's entrance. They dipped water from a bucket and threatened one another with it as if they were still children. As Hime approached, they settled down at last, and each washed her mouth and hands and clapped and bowed to the east.

"The god Kashima," Nakara explained when Hime was close enough. Recognizing the wariness that protected Hime's heart, she said nothing of the night's tears. "Agh, that's cold. I think my teeth will crack. Do you want to—?"

"No," Hime said.

"That's fine. We don't need to; it's really just a courtesy to Kashima. Let's register at the post, and then there will be hot food when we're finished." Her party straggled off, some back to

the inn; Nakara, Hime, and two of her men to the guards' post, a
large farmhouse at one end of the village.

"Do you know what this place is?" Nakara asked.

"Hitachi province," Hime said. "Yes?"

"We are in Hitachi, yes, and that means we are home. Or
nearly so. But it's more than that, too. You have followed the
Tōkaidō for a thousand miles. Or something. And now we are at
the end of the road."

"The Tōkaidō ends?" Hime said, taken aback.

"Of course it does," Nakara said. "Every road has a start and
an end somewhere. It ended at the ferry dock."

"But there is the road." Hime pointed past the posting station.
The road was clearly present, a band of dirt and frozen slush that
curved off to the north.

"That's Hitachi road. It's different."

Hime looked at her with startled eyes for a moment, and then
bolted back the way they'd come. Nakara called after her, but did
not follow.

Hime ran to the ferry dock, clogs clattering on the wood.
"Road?" she said. "Are you still here?"

The road said nothing, though the people by the dock looked
at her strangely. She knelt on the cold wood and closed her eyes,
tried to remember the path of her dreams: the crystal beneath her
feet; the golden fog from which it came, into which it vanished
(though she could not have told which way was which). "Road?"
she said again. "Please don't be gone." Silence. "At least change
me back. I don't want to stay like this." Water lapped the dock.

"Well, anyway," she said, "I didn't like you much, and I don't
understand you at all, but I am sorry you're gone."

One tear is lonely: she cried again, for the second time in half a
day. When she was done, she scrubbed her face pink with clean
snow and returned to Nakara.

They were in Hitachi province, but the Osa Hitachi estate is at its
northernmost edge, and that is some eighty or more miles from

Enoura village. Nakara stopped less for pleasure ("I have had sur-
feit of pretty things," she told Hime when asked; "now nothing will
be prettier than my own rooms"), but a storm forced them to halt
for several days. And then one of the women began her monthly
courses and they had to stop; and one of the oxen hurt itself on a
rocky incline and had to be rested until its foot healed. Hime did
what cats generally do when things are cold and not very pleasant;
she slept nearly all the time, even sometimes in her saddle.

It was the full moon of the twelfth month. The day before the cart
had fallen into a half-buried ditch some ten feet deep that crossed the
pathway, tumbling the women out onto the rocks and ice at its bottom. Junshi hurt her ankle, and the others were shaken. It took most
of the day to lift the ox-cart back to the road. They had seen no farmhouse or other place to stay, so they had bundled everyone possible
into the cart. No one slept well. Some slept not at all. At first Hime
enjoyed the warmth of so many bodies close together, but after a
time she grew restless and left the cart, to climb onto Biter's back
and sleep there, under a robe that covered them both.

Everyone was tired the next day, and this is why no one, not
even Hime, saw the ambush. Bandits are as much a problem in
the east as monks are here—they gather in groups and steal
whatever they please (though bandits are more likely to kill than
monks; that is one advantage to the capital, at least). Like everyone else in the east, the robbers do not stop working merely
because the weather is bad. They need food and clothing and animals, and these can be gathered in any weather. They have been
known to steal even the loincloths from parties they attack, leaving their victims to die, barefoot and naked in the snow.

I am told that there is a place where the Hitachi road is some
fifteen feet wide, a rutted dirt track that a thousand years of travelers have worn down until the land on either side is waist-high,
held back in places by stone retaining walls. Two well-treed hills
rise on either side. This is good, because the walls and the trees
cut the wind for a time; it is bad, because a robber gang can easily ambush careless travelers here.

The Osa Hitachi party was ten people: Nakara and three women in the ox-cart; the ox-boy leading his animals; four guards on horseback, two on point and two behind; and Hime, riding beside the cart. The robber gang—who can say how many there were? There might have been a thousand. Certainly, there were enough that their cries shook the trees, and their arrows struck two of the guards immediately, unhorsing them.

The narrow road broke into chaos. The horses of the fallen men panicked and bolted. The guards had all carried their strung bows across their horses' withers; the two guards still on horseback tried to control their plunging mounts with their knees as they pulled arrows from the basket-quivers on their backs. But there were no targets: the bandits were protected by the heavy trees; and the horses were too unsettled for easy shooting. There was no winning this fight, so the two guards on horseback lowered their bows to the ground and showed their empty hands.

Cats are used to watching a threat and ignoring it if it passes by; in this they are very like women—as I was, at any rate. I sat on my verandas and listened to distant shouts or carefully phrased reports: riots in the streets when droughts threatened to starve the common folk (and us, as well: we were not immune to the gods' vagaries); the monks in open warfare in the capital; the men and women who died of famine or plague or cold or despair. I listened; but I looked at my beautiful screens, and when I could no longer bear it, I thought of anything else, water-clocks' mechanicals or the change of caterpillars to moths—because even the human griefs were too much to bear, and there was so much more: dogs and horses that died of beatings, foxes frozen in a snowstorm, a nest of infant mice crushed by the sudden shifting of a trunk. What else could I have done? To understand the sorrows of the world requires the strength of a bodhisattva; to accept them requires a Buddha. I am not so enlightened.

Hime did not immediately react to the threat. The men killed were not her, nor her offspring, nor of her *fudoki*. She was mobile and (thus far) unattacked. She had her knife and knew that she was quicker than most people. Her horse was both fast and sturdy. A direct attack on her person would not succeed. She was wary, but there was no need to engage.

One of the women in the cart was married to one of the party's guards (it was not Junshi, but I cannot say precisely what her name was). She screamed her husband's name, and ripped the cart's door open. The other women caught at her and dragged her back inside, muffled her sobs. Nakara saw Hime, knife in hand, waiting to see what came next. "Get in here," she whispered.

Biter sidled under Hime. She calmed him, eyeing the hills, the stone retaining wall, the ox-boy crouched under his charges' feet; the two uninjured guards, empty-handed and dismounting now. "Why?" she said.

"They'll take everything, but there's no reason to let them—" Nakara slid the door open a little more to show that she held a long knife.

"They will hurt you?" Hime asked, watching. The robbers were emerging from cover, their bows still drawn: five to the right side of the road, more to the left—that she could see; there might have been another obstructed by the cart's slab side, and possibly others remained behind trees. Three of the men on the right stepped forward, the leader (he must have been the leader: he was the tallest of them, with a beard that trailed onto his chest and a hat made of wolf fur: very strange and alien) and two guards. Still perhaps sixty feet away.

"They will rape us if we are not careful," Nakara said, "though I will fight. Get in here, and I'll fight for us all."

"I don't think so," said Hime, and flipped her little knife in her hand to throw it at the closest bandit. He was a full thirty feet away, standing on the wall, but she hit him solidly in the hollow of the throat. He fell screaming, tearing at the knife. In the moment of shock that paralyzed the bandits, she caught up the bow across her saddle (though it had not been there even an hour ago). It fit in her hand, light and easy. She pulled a crow-fletched arrow from the basket-quiver at her back (and that was new, as well), nocked it over

her head and pulled the bowstring and arrow apart as she brought
the bow down, aimed, and shot, in a single movement, quick as a
cat's pounce. The second arrow's lozenge-shaped head buried itself
in a second bandit's belly before the first man hit the ground.

A cat is a highly experienced killer, and this seemed to transfer
to her woman-shape. She hit three men before anyone understood what was happening. By the time she sank an arrow into
the bandit-leader's shoulder, the two Osa Hitachi guards had
retrieved their bows and began firing. The robbers retreated, carrying some of their companions. Two remained behind, fallen
where they had been struck.

Hime had dismounted at some point to jump onto the wall.
She shot a last arrow after them. It hissed as it flew. When she
knew they were gone, Hime went to the first man she had
injured, to retrieve the knife in his throat. He still gasped a bit,
and the red bubbles on his throat grew and vibrated and burst,
tiny fireworks. She pulled the knife free. Blood steamed in the
sharp air, and drilled twin holes into the dirty snow, where it
dripped from his neck.

Hime made a noise, half snarl and half hiss, and she did not
realize that it was laughter. The blood and the bandits' flight
filled the black place inside her with a killing joy, sweet and hot
as desire, the only true joy she had felt since the fire, so long ago.
She touched the cooling blood, already gelling on his skin, and
laid the wet finger against her lips. His blood tasted like copper
and heartbeats and squirrel and dog and deer; and of something
else that might have been his soul.

His ghost looked up at her for a moment, surprised. "But you
are *not* a woman," it said, as if continuing a conversation they had
begun before he had died. "I thought—"

"Hime! Hurry—" Nakara's voice summoned her, and she
turned her back to the ghost.

Nakara and the surviving guards were bundling the casualties
(one dead; one injured and unconscious, bleeding from the nose
and mouth) into the carriage with the women. Hime helped, and

when the ox-boy whipped the oxen into a lumbering gallop, she stepped up onto Biter's stirrup as he passed, and caught the reins of the last horse, whose guard was dead. The ghost followed for a short while, crying tears of pus and blood, but it forgot its name soon enough and left her.

I have not been hungry of late, but for some reason I have just awakened feeling starved. I sent one of the women off to bring me food; but it is clearly very late. She'll have to find someone to wake a cook, which may take time, and so I write, content to watch words shape themselves under my brush.

I spent my life believing life is a series of nows, trying to discipline myself into accepting this, and enjoying (or suffering) the moments as they pass, instead of retreating into either memory or hope.

But I think that this is wrong. There is no now, or if there is, it is drawn with too fine a brush to see. There is what was, and there is what might (or what ought to) be. The line between them, which is now, is too small to see, and even as you reach it, it is past. *Now* is the edge of a page in a notebook.

Is this true? My old nurse would laugh sometimes. I would read or write a love-poem in a tale, and it would be about how "I" would love "you" for all the thousand years of the pine, how I want no one else. This is nonsense, of course—lies, in fact. I said this once to my nurse, and she laughed. "Lovers all lie, girl," she said. It is their nature—they lie to themselves, to their lovers, to the world. This is because what they claim to have is not real, what they seek is not real. But they must pretend it is, and since they already dissemble, it is simple enough to dissemble more.

When we were lovers, I believed that Dōmei did not lie to me. But in the end I realized he had lied twice: once, that he would never leave (the commonest lie of all among lovers), and once, that his loyalty to his emperor was steadfast. And then he left for Mutsu province, and six months later the great families of Mutsu rose up. He would have been among them, I am sure of it.

Wait. Tonight I have no reason not to see clearly, the hurt feelings over his abandonment so many decades old that they might as well be dead. Did he say he would never leave? Or did I want to hear it so much that I failed to listen to what *was* said? Perhaps it is not our lovers who lie, but our memories and hopes.

Still, he was in Mutsu province, and Mutsu rose against my half-brother. How can I have loved a traitor?

My broth is here, and just as well. I get no pleasure from my brush tonight.

The Osa Hitachi party paused at a covered travelers' well a mile or more beyond the fight in the sunken road. It was safer terrain. To their west was a gentle plain (soybeans in the summertime; now, in the twelfth month, snow). To the west were leafless trees and hills and then mountains. Any cover was far enough from the well that they would receive ample warning if anyone attacked. A short way ahead, a large farmhouse leaked smoke from its eaves. The tortoiseshell woman smelled tea and broth.

One guard was dead. The man whose wife had screamed for him was alive, the frightening blood pouring from his face a sign merely of his broken nose, damaged when the shock from a bandit's arrow shoved him from his horse. Hime's mouth watered from the hot coppery smell of his blood in her nostrils. The ox-boy trotted off to the farmhouse to acquire a cart to carry the dead man, since no one was willing to ride farther with it. Hime walked into the fields a bit, where the smell was not so sweet and strong.

Nakara came with her, shivering and pale from mingled horror and exhilaration, the aftermath of killing. "Brr," she said, and then, after a moment of silence, "Thank you."

Hime shrugged.

"There is blood on your mouth," Nakara said. "Like a court woman's lip paint."

Hime wiped and looked at the smear on her finger. There was more blood on her hand, darker than it had been when it poured from the bandit. She licked it clean. "Better?"

Nakara gave an unsteady laugh. "I suppose. You—shoot very well."

Hime's bow was in one hand still, and she looked at it, a great curve of tawny wood and black horn bound with ivory sinew. It was what warriors call a three-man bow (which is to say that it requires the strength of three men to string it, though in her case it was always strung when she needed it, like the tension of a cat's muscles sheathing and unsheathing its claws) and it was taller than she by a foot. She reached behind her back, felt the complex little basket that served as a quiver, a cluster of arrow-shafts springing like bamboo from a pot. She picked one at random, a humming-bulb head on a slim shaft nearly as long as her arm, fletched black and ivory with crow and goose feathers.

"Sharpness," Hime said to herself.

"Why did you not attack sooner?" Nakara asked.

"They were not threatening me." Hime lifted bow in right hand and arrow in left, high over her head. She caught the bowstring between her fingers, and brought her hands down and apart to the ready position, the arrow aligning itself to rest on her bow hand. All this was a single fluid gesture, formal as a girl in the Gosechi dances. She turned and released. The arrow howled as it flew, and slashed into the ground near the well. The two guards snapped around at the humming, saw Hime and Nakara—and no foes—and relaxed.

"But you could have escaped, I imagine," Nakara said. "You're certainly quick enough."

"I did not want you to be injured."

"Was that it?" Nakara said. "You were laughing. You killed them and you laughed. I come from a bow-and-arrow family, but none of us would laugh, I don't think." She shivered. "It is so cold. I wish we were home."

Hime said, "This"—her gesture took in the bow, the arrows at her back, the knife in her sash—"is the only thing the gods left me. If they exist." Her mouth twisted with the word *gods*.

Nakara touched her hand, fingers cold as ghosts. "The gods mean no harm," Nakara said. "We just—get caught up in their things, sometimes. They have their own problems, even Buddhas."

This battle was why Nakara started calling the tortoiseshell woman Kagaya-hime: Princess Glory.

The night after the robber gang's attack, Kagaya-hime had dreams. She slept in a monastery's guest house, tucked warm and alone under sleeping robes, for Nakara and her women tended the injured guard. In her dream, Kagaya-hime stood as a woman in gold-gray mist that somehow managed to seem both bright and dim. When she knelt to see if she stood on the crystal-bright road, there was nothing but mist under her feet, no matter how closely she looked. The voices of a million kami flooded through her (many sons, loyalty, stag's tail), but none were her road, though she called for it and searched the mist.

She did not find the road; but she met a mottled darkness that stared silently at her with a thousand green eyes, and said nothing, no matter how she spoke to it. With dreams'-reason, she thought it was a cat, a male whose territory she had strayed into. She averted her face. "I do not mean to stay—" and she meant here, in mist, without roads or sense. Though her own were closed, she saw the green eyes stare unblinking and heard voices say I/we/you, intentions, without significance/crucial. She could not tell whether this was the green eyes speaking, or the endless nattering of the million kami.

When I was young, and still fighting the new framework that shaped me, frog-watching girl to imperial princess, I met that darkness often in my dreams. I had no right to be angry that the world sought to form me to a shape I did not choose—none of us, peasant or emperor, have much choice, whatever plans we make. We do not choose to have one leg shorter than the other, eyes that do not focus well, weak lungs; but at least we have no illusion of control over these things. Yet even the things we pretend we control—our house's prosperity, our skills with a brush, a marriage's success—are beyond us.

I have always been told that the difference between intention and reality is karma, the unknown factor that makes one silkworm change to a moth and its neighbor rot in its cocoon. I conformed, because life demanded it, because it was my karma to do so. But I had such dreams, full of blood and anger. Some nights I had a knife in my hand, and I stabbed the darkness full of eyes, though the blade met nothing.

Another memory: my golden-eyed lover, Dōmei, and I stand outside. It is very dark, for it would be improper for him to visit me during the day; but we have placed a single torch in my courtyard, and inspect a target at its opposite end. Learning of my interest in small things, last night he told me of rabbits, the shapes of their small hearts. He used to hunt them with bows and needle-slim arrows. We talked of hunting, and he has brought me a mulberry-wood child's bow and a handful of arrows scarcely larger than my hand.

This is outrageous, of course—Shigeko (much younger, as were we all, forty years ago) is horrified, though it is she who has ensured our (more-or-less) privacy, here in the cinnamon-tree courtyard—but I revel in it. "Hold it thus," he tells me, "the arrow resting on your finger." Shigeko watches silently from the veranda, her expression strange to me, but I do not care. I am with Dōmei and I am focused on his breath in my ear as he places my hands. I drop the dove-fletched arrow a thousand times, and snap my fingers a hundred; at last I send it off on a single wobbly flight. It lands twenty feet before me, with all the power of a dropped fan. We try again, and finally I manage to get an arrow to stick for a moment into a support post (though that was not what I aimed at).

I laugh, and he laughs with me, and I think he believes I am merely pleased at this scrap of skill I have learned. It is not this. It is that, for the first time (and, as it turns out, the last), I have felt a killing action run through my fingers. I have been dangerous to someone besides myself.

I wonder if we all long to kill. I did not think it at the time, but perhaps Shigeko recognized this and hungered for it—her expression might have been envy. Dōmei had killed: animals, mostly, but bandits, as well. I envied him.

The party arrived at the Osa Hitachi estate at the three-quarters' moon of the twelfth month. After the attack, they had pushed on as fast as they could, with no halts for sightseeing or monthly courses or directional tabus. "I am sorry if the kami are offended," said Nakara, "but I won't be able to apologize if we are dead." Their arrival was well after the middle of the night, and Hime's first impression of the place was a chaos of buildings, walls, and trees, touched red-gold by torches, pale lilac by the nearly full moon.

The big country estates are as different from the capital as a mountain might be. Each is a town, really: many buildings serving myriad purposes, gathered within bowshot of one another. There is a stockade of tree trunks gathered from land cleared for rice and soya and hemp, but (in this case, at least) it has been a long time since there has been a serious threat, and many of the logs are tipped or fallen, or even taken away to serve other, more immediately useful purposes. Goats and chickens wander through the breaks in the wall, scrounging for food under the shallow snow. The children of the estate (and there are a lot, for there are more than a hundred regular residents here, to say nothing of the visitors and followers and mendicants) climb on them, playing Bandits.

The Osa Hitachi estate is all of this. To the east and the north, forest-covered mountains march all the way to the ocean; on cold nights, you hear wolves plotting to steal calves. A river runs beside the estate, fast and unruly, full of clear water so cold that my teeth ache even thinking of it, like biting into ice brought from the storehouses in the seventh month. Below the main buildings, something everyone calls the spider-leg stream crosses to join the river.

The Hitachi road threads through a series of steep-sided hills not so far away. Everywhere are trees, and because this is winter, they are bare mostly. The air is very cold.

Nakara was glad to be home. She slept for a night and a day, and then left lengths of cloth and paper and silk flowers at the altars of the kami and the Buddha. By the second evening, she had returned to managing the estate for her oldest brother, the vice-governor of Hitachi province.

The cat Kagaya-hime was more ambivalent. For months she had traveled alone, without clan or ground. The *fudoki* was gone, but the road had offered a substitute, and she had accepted it. Joining Nakara's party had not changed things so much. Kagaya-hime still slept on the ground, still killed her own food, still drifted north and east. And Nakara was far from her natural place, as well. A cat-woman on horseback and a provincial woman on pilgrimage are both unrooted from their worlds. But now they had come to the Osa Hitachi estate. Nakara belonged here, as did her attendants and guards and all the other scores of people. It was only Kagaya-hime who did not belong.

She did many things that were unconventional at best. Sometimes she wore women's robes, when she was with Nakara and her women. More often, she wore a man's hunting garb, knife at her waist and bow over her shoulder. The people of the estate did not seem to mind, or even notice her strangeness. People tend not to notice things that don't fit into their expectations, and it might have been this; or something else, of course.

Kagaya-hime's few expectations of people—that they tended to kick stray cats and were careless with food scraps—did not apply to her time as a woman at the Osa Hitachi estate, and so she noticed many things. Nakara had a lover, for instance, a bear-hunter who came down from the mountains one moonless night, and stayed until just before dawn. Kagaya-hime saw them say their farewells, as she returned from hunting with a serow deer across her shoulders. He passed her on the path without a look; only later did she realize how strange this was, that he appeared not to observe her.

She noticed the unpredictability most. People stayed up some nights, slept others; they ate, whether they were hungry or not. They changed clothes when there was no reason for it, and played games that taught them no useful skills, such as pouncing would be. People may think that it is cats that are the unpredictable ones, but this is only because we do not understand their thoughts. Within a cat's mind the sequences—sleep to hunt to groom to doze—all make sense.

The patterns of movement and interaction on the estate were bewilderingly complex, especially in comparison with her only other experience of a shared ground, her *fuдoki* with its ranked handful of cousins and aunts and fellow-wives, its careful separation of range from range. Even the *fuдoki's* overlaps were sharply differentiated; *thiи* cat used the wisteria courtyard in daylight only, *that* cat only at dusk. Perhaps such structure is a comfort to cats. Their lives are filled with a thousand sorts of danger; it may feel good to know precisely where one stands. Men and women also do this, but the dangers that threaten us are not quite so easy to identify as a hungry dog or distemper, and our attempts to give the world a pattern confuse even us.

The constant talking didn't bother her, for cats use their voices to say, "Here I am; where are you?"—and this seemed to be the primary intention of most human conversation, the words mere ornaments over the underlying purpose. The fact that humans seem never to be alone when they can help it bothered her more, and she found the constant companionship, as steady and irksome as dogs', annoying. She spent many hours in the stable with Biter, until one of the grooms saw in her a fellow spirit, and came more and more often to share stories of horses he had loved, brown, bay, and blue—the comparative merits of each—mares' tricks hiding their foals—the cleverness of certain stallions—a red stallion who had kicked off any saddle, however well placed—the comparative advantages of pearwood or cedar for saddle frames—the best workmanship available only from the capital, of course, preferably from the Yana family workshops.

After this, she spent time well out of range of the people, killing quail or whatever fell within reach of her arrows and knives.

She rediscovered another thing, as well, the charm of hunting for mice. When she was a cat, this had been as automatic to her as breathing, but a mouse was scarcely a mouthful to a woman, and she had fallen out of the habit. Once she began to see them again, she saw that mice, like smoke, were everywhere. There were nights when she walked down to the grain storehouses and crouched there, killing mouse after mouse with quick stabs of her knife.

One night, Nakara, walking down to an outhouse, saw Kagaya-hime turning something over in her hands. It was a dead mouse, or rather the scrap of fur and flesh that was left when a finger-wide blade pins a mouse to the frozen ground.

"Vermin!" she exclaimed, and then, crouching beside Kagaya-hime, said, "What are you doing, anyway?"

"Trying to see if mice have ghosts." Kagaya-hime gestured at a heap of mice by her foot. "So far none of them do," she added.

"Why do you care?" Nakara asked. Kagaya-hime said nothing, so she added: "Why are you killing mice at all? That's dogs' work."

"Your dogs are not very effective, then. It is good practice." Kagaya-hime scooped up her mice and stood. The broken mice barely filled her hand.

"Good practice for what?" Nakara asked, but Kagaya-hime was gone already, walking toward the stables where Biter stayed. When they met later, in Nakara's rooms, she did not ask her guest what she did with the mice.

I am cold, and so I write of the cold. It is winter in Hitachi province, and Nakara's world, like mine, is centered on braziers.

Nakara had many braziers. In the hinterlands, the proprieties are not adhered to quite so stringently as they would be here at court. At the Osa Hitachi estate, everyone who was acceptably clean—male, female, warrior, and ox-boy (if clean enough)— stayed near Nakara. The curtains designed to protect her from the eyes of men and lesser souls instead embraced them all, cuddling the braziers' warmth close. "What is the good of having all these charcoal makers on one's property," she said once to Kagaya-hime, though the cat-woman had made no comment, "if you get no good from it? It's like raising silkworms and wearing hemp."

In any case, Nakara's responsibilities as practical manager of the estate precluded her hiding behind curtains; but even when it might have been appropriate—entertaining functionaries or messengers from the capital—she did not often hide herself. When she did, it usually had less to do with propriety, and more to do with concealing her sometimes obvious signs of boredom.

Kagaya-hime stayed nights with Nakara and her women. Like any cat, she craved warmth, and the braziers and fires compensated for the occasionally irritating unending patter of conversation. And there was much conversation.

There was even a *fudoki* of sorts for the people, an unconscious mix of shared jokes and experiences with histories of the residents: The Man with the Two-Foot Penis, Great-Grandfather Falls Through the Broken Screen, The Three Clever Sisters. Some were funny, but others were less so: The Woman Who Gave Birth to a Demon, The Leg That Rotted Off. The stories—or even a slanting reference to one, for everyone seemed to know them all—wove these people together as much as the rooms they shared and their confusing relationships.

Kagaya-hime had no stories, or thought she had none, and their tales filled her with longing. The events of her life grew as great as a *fudoki* a hundred cats long, but she could not see that this mattered. Not yet.

I am come to the end of this notebook, and find I must begin another.

7. THE MICHINOKA-PAPER NOTEBOOK

I love the feel of this paper, soft and strong at the same time. I can see the patterns of the mulberry bark in it. Strange that this paper comes all the way from distant Mutsu province, just as the cat-warrior Kagaya-hime approaches its borders.

Strange that I write this at all. I am dying, I remind myself sharply. I have no intention of showing this to anyone. Why do I fill page after page with a *monogatari* tale that no one (but I) will ever see?

It is late, and my women are asleep, even my former attendant from the provinces Shikujo, who does not sleep well these nights; even my dear Shigeko, who tries to keep me company but cannot, not tonight and not through this final battle. There is a brazier lit because I am cold all the time, even though it is the eighth month and swelteringly hot. I refuse to wear padded winter robes, for it is not the season yet (I am still that vain, at least), but I admit to looking forward to the tenth month when I can switch from these thin robes without disgrace—if I yet live.

The light from charcoal is unimpressive, a dim bloodred, but the three-quarters moon is bright enough that reflected light creeps in from the peony courtyard. This afternoon my women and I opened one of the trunks from my storehouse, and I found a mirror there, a pretty handheld disk of silver and bronze, from when first I came to court. Now, in the solitude of my sleeping women, I inspect myself in the mirror. My hair and face are only hinted at by faint silver curves, here a cheek, there my brow. There are no wrinkles or white hairs in such darkness. But behind my eyes is dull red fire, which might be Hell or might be a hearth in the Pure Land. I cannot tell, though this will become clear to me soon enough.

Perhaps this is why I write—so that things will be clear to me. Now that I am old and dying, I think I write because I always meant to tell this story, and yet I never did, unsure of the ending. But I find I cannot rest, cannot cut this heavy hair and leave this world for the monastery, until I do this thing. I don't think it will be seen by anyone; but I will have done it and it will no longer tie me to this world.

There was a blustery day, at the end of the twelfth month. Nakara was writing accounts on a scroll in the stilted half-language of official reports; her women quilted silk batting into a sleeping robe for a newly born son on the estate. Kagaya-hime slept, curled up so close to one of the braziers that the tips of her shoulder-length hair sizzled when she shifted position. From outside came shouts, whinnies, hooves, heavy thudding sounds, as several men tried to break a recalcitrant stallion for riding.

"Mistress!" a man shouted from outside. Clogs clattered onto the stepping stone to the veranda; bare feet raced along a gallery. "Mistress," he said again, panting as he entered the room. Kagaya-hime blinked her eyes open, looked up at him from cat's-eye height. He towered over her as he bowed to Nakara. "Riders, my lady. From the west. There are banners."

"Whose?" Nakara laid her brush down and blew on her fingers.

"The wind blows them the wrong way. But one might be ours."

"My brother?" Nakara stood. Her women exploded upward like ducks rising at a sudden noise. Quacking with excitement, they trailed the man out to the veranda. Kagaya-hime paused to pull on another robe before following them.

The scene in the courtyard was so chaotic that she could not separate the new arrivals from the residents. There were men everywhere, leading horses away and pulling packs from behind saddles. Some of the women, barefaced and (occasionally) bare-footed, stood or danced in the frozen slush around certain of the men; others stayed on the veranda, in the gloom under the eaves. Nakara was one of the women behaving like an unruly child in the slush, her arms thrown around a newcomer.

After watching for a few moments, Kagaya-hime sorted through the sights and understood several things. The new arrivals were clearly the expected party from the capital, but they were far too few, no more than twenty; and they seemed disheartened, for all their happiness at being there. Since the youngest of the Osa Hitachi brothers had left with ten attendants of his own, that meant that the request for assistance had failed. Kagaya-hime had listened to Nakara talk often enough to understand that there should have been fifty or a hundred, or even more. There were a few strangers, but they had no part in the chaos of greet-ings, laughter, tears. Instead they attended to their horses and gear, all carefully not looking at the women, who in any case shouldn't have been scampering like puppies out in the open. And of these, there was one, an old man, heavyset, with eyes sharp and angry as hawks', astride a tall black horse, its own nose rather grizzled. He was their leader; he must be.

Kagaya-hime knew that the man Nakara embraced must be her youngest brother: the uncomplicated love on her face made this clear. And she also knew that he was not human.

Nakara had told her story to Kagaya-hime, but cats are literal-minded creatures, and I do not know whether Kagaya-hime understood it all. The family in Hida province had been a fox family, a wife and her human husband. Through magic I cannot explain, Nakara had been the child's nurse, but things had gone wrong, and she had fled here with him. There had been angry Buddhas and saddened Kannons, a jealous former wife—it is a long story, one I imagined when I was a girl myself, and pining for adventures that had nothing to do with Fujiwaras and Minamotos and boy emperors.

I made up many stories—I think every girl must; they are our best opportunity to become something unexpected. In some I was the heroine: a bandit-queen in the east, the empress Jingū conquering Silla. In others I was the victim, the princess who had been stolen away by a man of low rank in that tale from Ise. There were others, little tales I made up about people I saw and was fascinated by. I also made up stories about cats—*fudoki*, I suppose—for the little gray-furred cat Shisutāko and subsequent pets; and there were the stories about mice. Only now, as I prepare to die by emptying my trunks and, apparently, my mind, do I realize these tales are all connected.

Kagaya-hime knew foxes. There had been foxes on the neighboring residence's grounds, dirty little scavengers who occasionally strayed into her *fudoki*. They all smelled strong, even the smallest ones, who should have been scentless as kittens were, for protection's sake; and they were easy to avoid. She had seen them on the Tōkaidō, for she and they shared dawn and dusk as hunting times, and preferred the same prey, mice and small things. After she became a woman, she only saw them at a distance, a russet blur in twilight vanishing through a gap in weeds.

This man—Nakara called him Little Brother—did not look like a fox (or half-fox), except that his eyes were slanted, and flecked with gold. He moved quickly, but no more so than many men. Though he was some distance away, Kagaya-hime could smell him, for the wind blew from him to her. His smell was sweet and thick and slightly wild, too delicate, too human, to be a fox's musk. But animal knows animal: Kagaya-hime recognized him as readily as if he walked on white-tipped paws.

Foxes and cats do not like one another. It is not the guarded warfare of the cat and the dog, the fights and truces that so resemble court families vying for primacy with their emperor. No: foxes and cats do not like one another because they are so similar, though one is wild and the other (occasionally) tame. They are both clever and self-absorbed. They eat many of the same foods, and since mice are sometimes scarce (though this is hard to believe living at court as I do, where the mice seem to be like the gods, numberless), one cannot always afford to share. Adult foxes and cats will not fight one another because, though foxes are slightly larger, cats have more sharpnesses; but each will kill and eat the young of the other, and then complain that the kit (or kitten) is gamy and unpleasant tasting.

Kagaya-hime watched Nakara and her brother embrace. Cats do not like foxes; but she was the first to be jealous of one.

(Am I a fool? I think of Shigeko watching my lover and me play with bow and arrow. I am sure it was envy, but now I must ask: Of what? And of whom?)

There was a day when I first saw the guardsman Mononobe no Dōmei.

I had been at court for several years, serving my half-brother the emperor. My proximity and relationship to him covered all my imperfections with gauze, and emphasized the few skills I had that were appropriate to court. I was praised for my wit, mostly because I had read so much more than my peers. Observations culled from reading something other than the *monogatari* tales and the poetry collections, to which the other women were addicted, were hailed as witty or wise.

In six years, a woman can have many lovers. Whatever my skills as a musician or poet, I was justly considered an extraordinary beauty—though much of this was owing to the never-ending labors of my woman Shigeko, who ensured that I was never seen in unattractive robe combinations or with tangled hair.

I was also a princess and thus valuable as a lover or wife for ambitious men—even if I could not bear children (and this seems quite likely, when one considers how many lovers I had, and never a baby). My foster father retired and then died, and was replaced in everything—job, house, authority—by his nephew: my uncle. My uncle selected husbands for me, men who could help his branch of the Fujiwara family to maintain or even expand its power, usually men I had seen only once or twice at court, if so much. I was willing to marry whoever was chosen for me, though it meant leaving my brother and the court; but circumstance (or karma, circumstance's older sister) intervened again and again. The first husband died during an epidemic of smallpox when I was sixteen and he fifteen, months before our wedding. The second disgraced himself before the union could be formalized, and was sent to Satsuma province (which might as well be Korea, so far away it is), where he was killed by a disease or pirates or something. The third was nearly twenty years younger than I, six to my twenty-three, and my uncle was waiting a year or two before marrying us. I had met the boy and found him very ordinary, prone to runny noses and setting things on fire, but the alliance would be good for the Fujiwaras, and thus for the empire. As I waited for my husband to grow up, I stayed at court in desultory attendance on my brother and took lovers, always from the fourth rank or above, always amiable, talented men who cried at sunsets and fallen maple leaves.

It was autumn of the last year of the Eihō era. There had been drought all summer, and the dust made the sunsets unusually beautiful. The moon was the red-orange of *amagaki* persimmons when it rose each night, surprisingly large. I was not attending my brother, for he was at Ise visiting one of his other sisters, who served as priestess there (and presumably guarding his brushes; the people of Ise are perfectly capable of robbing their own parents). Several of his attendants, including Shigeko and I, rested on a veranda. The others were there to write poems, I remember; I was watching for bats, and hoping I might hear their wings beat, and the tiny nearly inaudible cries that sometimes scratch at one's ears.

Guardsmen at court are often importunate; their duties give them permission to wander about at all hours. Several happened by and, seeing us there, stayed to flirt. I was hidden behind one of the screens we providentially had placed around ourselves—but the screen was of wide-woven gauze, and I saw them all clearly,

four young men in identical hunting garb, with identical hair and
caps and expressions. As they talked, I corrected myself. One of
the men was a few years older than the others, though younger
than I, perhaps twenty. The folds in his soft black *eboshi* cap were
slightly different than those of his peers, but I could not decide
whether this was a daring aesthetic statement or mere sloppiness
on his part. And when he turned to respond to something Shigeko
said, I saw that his eyes were gold, even in the moon's cool light.

Young men and women together in the moonlight breed
poetry as oak trees breed mushrooms. I don't remember anyone's
poems—I was only half attending and they would be largely
interchangeable anyway, all about the coming dawn and longing
hearts, typical fare—until one of the guardsmen said, "But there
are four of you, and we have heard only three poems."

Shigeko and I exchanged glances. "My mistress does not share
her poems with every wandering rake," she said, "and she is not
the only one who holds silent. There are five of *you,* and only *four*
poems"—for the fifth guardsman, the golden-eyed man, had
recited no poem.

"Why should I?" the golden-eyed man, Mononobe no Dōmei,
said. "You have all said everything so much more eloquently than
I can." I hid a smile. So he had not been listening, either.

"You must forgive him, my ladies," said one of the guardsmen.
"He's from the hinterlands, practically a savage." Dōmei snorted,
and then we all laughed, for his amusement was infectious.

The moon eventually slid behind the clouds that rose during
the rat's hour, and the women and guardsmen wandered off; but
I fell to talking with Dōmei, and before dawn, he was behind my
curtains.

I knew Dōmei was no sort of lover for the daughter and granddaughter of emperors. He was of lower fifth rank, and unlikely to
rise higher. Worse, he was from the provinces, thought playing the
game *kemari* was a waste of time, and wrote pedestrian poetry when
he could be brought to write it at all. Certain of my friends at court
saw the appeal ("Those shoulders!" one sighed. "Those eyes! Such

a pity he's practically a peasant"), but the general opinion was that Mononobe no Dōmei was ultimately meaningless to court, just another in the endless stream of semi-civilized hicks the provinces seem to churn out and deliver for guard duty each year.

Everyone who knew was horrified — and of course everyone did know; a secret at court is like a hawk in a cage, it screams to be let out. But there are certain advantages to high rank, and one is that very few people have the effrontery — or courage, depending on one's perspective — to criticize their superiors directly. Shigeko shrugged at this affair of mine, only begging me to be more circumspect. From others there were sly comments, but I had no responsibility to respond to them in any way, and chose not to. I saw no reason to: I was blissfully, foolishly, in love.

He visited when his and my responsibilities permitted, a handful of nights each month; and we exchanged many letters, though we almost never wrote poetry to one another — a great comfort to me, as I was sick of producing *tanka* on demand, like a peasant making straw sandals to trade by the roadside. We made the usual promises that our love would last forever, even as we both spoke freely about our differing futures, his in the east, mine here in the capital. I cannot say exactly when I started disregarding the future, and believing the promises.

And then Dōmei left court and returned to his family. It was a year later that Minamoto no Yoshiee's war began in Mutsu province, and Dōmei fought against my half-brother's troops: a traitor.

We were in the middle of the Former Nine Years' War by the time I was old enough to be aware of anything beyond my nurse and my home. This was yet another war in Mutsu province, a million miles away, where they were apparently as common as the snowstorms there. "War" meant nothing to me, no more than did "sex": catalogued in my mind (and one of the notebooks I kept even then, childish calligraphy in large uneven lines down the pages; I found it this evening when we opened a chest I have not looked into for twenty years) as something important to adults but not as interesting as, say, spiders' eggs.

As far as I could tell, wars started when people rushed about killing one another with arrows someplace a long way from the capital. Some of the boys I knew had little bamboo bows and arrows made of mugwort twigs. I did not see how anyone could die in a war, for the arrows were so fragile that they tended to snap if they hit anything—which did not happen often.

I knew war must be like any child's game. You could play without interference if the adults were busy elsewhere and you were not too noisy about it. But if for some reason the adults noticed you, they would stop you. In war, this meant the government sent troops and generals into the hinterlands, and expected a certain number of severed heads sent back to show progress. (At the age of six, severed heads fascinated me.)

Even as an adult, I have not been able to discern why *this* conflict is considered worthy of the council's attention and the empire's resources, and *that* one is treated like the bickering of children in another room: only worth sending someone to see what is the matter if the tears and shouts become serious. The few people I discussed such things with (my lover Dōmei; my half-brother Shirakawa; the old Sugara man with whom I pretended to flirt as a cover for the time he spent leading me through certain of the Chinese classics) could not always explain the differences. "It is because you're a woman," they said in their various ways: "too complicated, really." Water-clocks were also complicated, and yet I had little trouble understanding them, so I knew this was a convenient lie to cover the fact that none of them—not even the emperor—really understood the differences. Still, war is a thousand years old, here since the gods made these islands— well, fights, anyway—perhaps it is as inevitable as death.

The year I was fifteen and came to court, the war in Mutsu province had been going on so long that I think everyone was surprised when it ended.

Dōmei had actually fought. He said little about it, but what he did say made it clear that war was quite different from the little boys of my childhood scrambling around with their feeble bows: different, even, from the court guards who could shoot through a poem slip on a board a hundred paces away. Dōmei had actually fought. He had fired arrows—three feet long and tipped with steel—directly at men.

"Did you hope to kill them?" I asked one night, shocked but thrilled.

"That's why I aimed for them," he said and then laughed, though it was not an amused sound. "Truthfully, what I hoped for was to get through alive and without letting my father down."

And that is all he would say then.

Shortly after he left, yet another war began in Mutsu province: Yoshiee's war. I grieved for the loss of Dōmei, (though I did not realize at the time that this is why I took lovers, why I cried without reason some nights, why my temper was grown so short), and this manifested in a fascination with war. It certainly had to be more interesting than my activities at court, which left me feeling trapped and desperate: a mouse gnawing hopelessly, endlessly, at the lacquered walls of my box.

I have strayed far from my tale, I find. The *monogatari* tales (for I have read them, despite my professed disdain), and the folktales the blind storytellers recite, and the parables of the priests all stay close to their topics, such as they are. Event follows event in tidy progression, poem and response, question and answer.

I have often thought that we humans sort our lives and their experiences very strangely. We see everything as a tale, event following event, birth to death. These are the years I could have borne a child, that is the year I wore mourning for my father; this was the month that I fell in love, that the day I ran away.

But time is very flexible, I think. I remember things from many years ago with crystal clarity—the brilliance of the red silk the Chinese traders brought to the capital when I was nineteen, the tiled skin of a snake I touched when I was six, the grass-bright smell of

Dōmei's breath—and they are clearer to me than the robes I wore yesterday. Today does not follow yesterday; *now* follows other *now*s.

There is another way to sort things, just as I can sort moths' wings by size, or by color, or by when and where acquired. Every line of this notebook—and all my other notebooks, and every letter and sutra and poem I have ever scrawled in a long and word-ridden life—has required that I make ink. On occasion the ink is gold or vermilion or the color of lapis; but it is most generally glossy black, and thick as paint.

The manner in which I make ink—the precise gestures of grinding the ink stick, adding water drop by drop, gathering and blending the two on a soft thick brush rolled against the ink stone—is always the same, whether I do it today or ten years ago or sixty, and it never fails to fill me with satisfaction—though this may be dispelled immediately afterward, when I drop the brush or find a long hair in the ink, or have absentmindedly made it too runny and must fiddle to correct it. Still, there is that perfect instant of brush and water and ink.

The instant that I make ink is closer to all the times I have made ink than to any other instant, even the moments surrounding it. I make ink, and a visitor is announced, someone I cannot simply send away. He approaches my screens bare heartbeats later, but his voice, the polite bow I see beyond the blinds, is almost infinitely far from the moment of the ink stone.

I have not lived seventy years. I have lived instead these things: the entwining of my days with a few men and women I have loved; a longing to walk on unpaved roads; the collecting of vermin, and other unacceptable studies; quite a number of unpleasant or tedious duties performed; the making of ink; eating and elimination and hair-washing and tooth-dying. My seventy years are only the frame on which they hang.

Very well, then:

Eventually the chaos in the yard settled down. The horses were settled, and the men were shown to quarters and fed, and given warm dry clothing. As bitter-cold twilight settled into moonless night, Nakara's brother Kitsune and the older man and several of their retainers were given places beside Nakara's omnipresent braziers. For once, Nakara banished much of the household, though Nakara's woman Junshi stayed, and Kagaya-hime: eight in total. The curtains that would more properly have been used to separate the men and the women, or the old man (who was the noble Seiwa Minamoto no Takase) from the lower ranks, were clustered around them all, the reflected light of lanterns and braziers making a warm little space that smelled of hot coals and men who have spent much time on horseback lately. The eaves were many tens of feet over their heads, blackened and shiny with soot and moisture, and the light lost itself in a tangle of beams that refuted the sense of coziness. No one but Kagaya-hime looked up. Everyone there knew that safety is an illusion; everyone except Kagaya-hime felt that sometimes the illusion is preferable.

Kagaya-hime's instinct had been right: Kitsune and his party had failed. There would be no official warrant to allow them to pursue and strike the Abe. The vice-governor of Hitachi province was not seen as the correct person to bring this to the central government's attention; however, if these allegations were true, they would surely be addressed by the next governor of Mutsu province, who would be named at the New Year's appointments.

"But that is many days from now, and then it will be months before he gets here," Nakara said, her eyes glittering with tears. "Months more before he acts—if he is not like the last one, allied with the Abe. My brother is dead and the Abe tramp over the land he kept and we have done nothing for half a year already." Her tears spilled over.

"*I* came," Takase said, as if that changed everything.

In many ways, it did so. There were the usual New Year's celebrations—the new men, Takase's attendants, made for more than usual humor among the unattached women of the estate; and children will celebrate in the midst of an earthquake, if need be—but they were muted, overwhelmed by the activities of a household preparing for war. Most winters the fields doze, and so do many of those who work them. But this year, gathering allies and supplies kept everyone as busy as silkworm season, when no one (not even the dogs) sleeps much.

Takase wished to head north with his troops as soon as possible, perhaps even in the second month, if the weather permitted. This urgency surprised everyone, even Kitsune and Nakara, eager as they were. Wars in the north can (and do) last years, even decades. Minamoto no Yoshiee's war, for which my Dōmei betrayed his empire, lasted four years; before that the Former Nine Years' War lasted twelve years. There is no need to rush into wars in the north; they will wait for you to begin.

Despite the untrustworthy weather (icy rain one day, bitter windless cold the next), messengers with letters flew like leaves in a gale. Some men chose to follow Takase because they owed it to his family, or they chose to support Kitsune's, or they hated the Abe for reasons of their own; or because, in the north, men are bred to war as horses are bred to run, and they pine if left too long without it. (Dōmei was one such man—restless without battle.) Warriors and their attendants arrived, three or ten or twenty at a time, bringing horses.

Takase pressed so hard because he was dying. The pain I feel, the bitter never-ending ache, the sense that my body is tired of its work—these are what he felt. And there was an old wound, where a barbed arrow had entered his side some years ago. It had never healed properly, but remained angry and wept pus from time to time. Takase had grown used to the red throb—had years to grow used to it—but now it grew worse again, the granulated flesh too sore to touch. He was dying, and he knew it (just as I know that I am dying), even if no one else could see it. Kagaya-hime also knew, for she smelled the wound and sensed the pain beyond it, the slow decay of his organs: a water-clock with a leak, nearly drained and useless.

In the flurry, Kagaya-hime was treated more as a member of

the household than as a guest—which means she was alternately left to her own resources and asked to help. Nakara asked for her assistance in preparing clothing, but Kagaya-hime had no interest in sewing. She had a single needle, so sharp and slender that the women all exclaimed with awe at it, and she was very good at sewing, the tiny pounces of needle into fabric coming as naturally as knife-thrusts to her, but sewing brought down no prey, did not fill the darkness inside. Instead, she caught birds for the arrow-makers to strip for fletching.

The noise and her hunting had discouraged most of the useful birds close to the estate, so she and Biter roved far, traveling into the mountains to the west looking for eagles. There were times they stayed out for a night or even two, and Kagaya-hime slept pressed against Biter's side, watching the ice-brilliant stars wheel overhead, threading their way through treeless branches.

She was gone for New Year's, sleeping in a thrown-together shelter of driftwood near the beach, where she had gone to look for geese. The air roared here with surf and wind, and perhaps this is why her New Year's dream was filled with the chittering voices of the kamis—*reed, despair, wives,* six wordless tones in sequence, *Wear red when you worship me*—when she had walked the crystal-bright road through golden mist. She searched for the road, or even the great mottled darkness full of blood and a thousand green eyes, but searching is futile when there are no landmarks, no way to keep track of one's movements. In the end, she gave up and sat as if on a riverbank, with her feet hanging into the mist. "Tell the road that I miss it," she said, and she awoke.

When at the Osa Hitachi estate, she watched the preparations with a certain curiosity. Cats understand combat—toms fighting for a female, females fighting to protect ground or kittens—but they carry their claws and teeth with them and they catch their own supplies as they go. War and its logistics—food and wine and weapons and tools to be carried to somewhere that is not one's *fudoki,* to fight a mass of others for no good reason—were incomprehensible to her.

It was obvious that, whoever had initiated this war, Takase was at its heart, and so she watched him most.

Two days after her New Year's dream, Kagaya-hime returned with two eagles, three osprey, and a crow across Biter's haunches. She left them with the fletcher (who would pluck their long feathers and pass them to the kitchen), and led Biter to the stables to clean and brush him before releasing him into the field with some of the Osa Hitachi horses. When Takase entered leading his own grizzled black, Kagaya-hime and Biter were pressed face-to-face, eyes closed, communing as horse and rider ever have. The black huffed and jangled its bridle. Kagaya-hime spun, knife in hand. "Ease up, girl," he said. "Inkstick and I are no threat."

"No." Kagaya-hime replaced her knife in her sash and looked up at the old man, her cheek against Biter's neck. "You are both old."

He laughed, a surprised snort. "Not too old to bite. Someday you'll be old; you'll see. I heard your story. You're the one who fought off the robbers."

Kagaya-hime knew this already. She said nothing.

He continued. "Is your sword any good?"

Hime's hand went to her waist and for the first time there was a longsword at her side, hung with amber-colored silk cords in the *jindachi-zukuri* manner. She slid it from its sheath: a short blade of the old design, straight-bladed with a ring pommel. She touched the steel, folded countless times so that blue and purple and indigo patterns chased one another across the metal, fine as slow-growing pine wood. "It's beautiful."

"It's not a necklace, girl. Give it to me." She handed it to him, and he examined the metal, his horse throwing up its head, restless. "Settle down, Inkstick. I don't recognize the maker's mark. Does your blade have a name?"

"No," she said. He handed it back, and she sheathed it, as easily as if it had been for the thousandth time. Teeth didn't have names.

Takase was silent for a moment, absently rubbing his horse's long grayed nose. "Your horse. Good sturdy one."

Kagaya-hime did not know Takase, but she said something that surprised her, and knew it was the truth even as she said it. "He is the only thing I love."

"I understand," Takase said. "I had a horse I felt like that about, a long time ago. Not Inkstick, here. He's a good horse, but I can't afford to care anymore."

Cats do not ask questions about one another, for there is no reason to do so. The *fudoki* tells all, or everything important anyway; if the information sought is important, it is in the tale. She cared for Nakara, but this did not extend to asking questions; the others of the estate (even Junshi, who was often kind to her) mattered too little for her to wonder about them. But she wondered about Takase, and began, for the first time, to ask questions of the men who traveled with him.

One of the followers, a nephew serving as bodyguard, thought Kagaya-hime beautiful, and he said much about Takase, mostly to keep her close to him. Takase's *fudoki* crossed sixty and more years, forty of them spent fighting bandit-gangs, pirates, refractory landholders. Takase had been a great general, and a governor somewhere in the south (Kagaya-hime did not bother to remember the place). Since his favorite consort had died, he had lived quietly, bowstring loosened, all thought of war gone. And he was ill—for even people could see this, though they could not smell or see that he was dying.

Kagaya-hime did not wonder about the half-fox Kitsune, but she watched him avidly when they were both at the estate, as a cat eyes a new dog. She did not choose to speak with him (what cat talks to dogs?), but she was often close, if safely out of reach. He would not have seemed beautiful to most of my friends at court (though there were a discriminating few). His face was thin, with straight eyebrows that flew up at the ends; and he had those sloped gold-flecked eyes, bright as a puddle reflecting autumn maples. He moved gracefully, with a fox's quick efficiency—not a tall man, as Takase was, but long-limbed and slender. Despite his fox-eyes and name, he often seemed no more an animal than

Nakara, and no one else seemed to think of him as anything but human. It was only sometimes, when his attendants were busy elsewhere and he was alone, that Kagaya-hime saw something in his expression that she understood.

By the end of the first month, the first horses foaled in their pastures, and wolves came down from the mountains to try their luck—successfully, for two foals were dead within days. A man in charge of the pastures alerted Nakara (for she oversaw this as she oversaw everything else: "The Osa Hitachi men are busy being men," she said to Kagaya-hime, "someone must make sure that the foals are counted and the taxes paid"). Because the men of the estate were busy, Nakara chose to attend to this herself, though in the end she did not go alone. "I am tired of being nice to people," Takase said when informed of her wolves: "I need to kill something." No one asked why Kagaya-hime joined them.

Three men and three women left on a bright clear day. Down at the main estate, thin dirty snow covered everything; as the horses climbed into the foothills, it deepened and grew cleaner, a jeweled dust, until the horses slowed, each step crunching through a white crust into hock-deep snow, with drifts to their knees. They rode for much of a day before they found the herd, in a windblown clearing nearly free of snow. This was one of the Osa Hitachi's far pastures, the only good place for foals right now. The smell of mares made the growing groups of bickering war-mounts fight among themselves. More importantly to anyone for whom the raising of horses is a livelihood and the waging of war a mere momentary madness, the stallions made the mares nervous and their herd's leader overprotective and militant. Even the six horses the hunting party rode upset the herd. Nakara directed them away, to a hut of sorts half a mile east, and settled there.

Six people and any gear they wanted kept dry (saddles: weapons) packed the little structure tight as herrings in a barrel: particularly busy herrings, for there was a fire to be set and a meal to be cooked and the herder to consult; and Nakara's only attendant fluttered around, trying to shield her mistress from the snow puffing in through the cracks in the hut's wall. Kagaya-hime slipped unnoticed under the cracked horsehide that covered the open doorway, and out past the hobbled horses nosing under the snow for anything edible.

It was very dark, for the moon was nearly new, but her eyes were better than mine have ever been. She walked easily in the black spaces under the trees and came into the open at the bottom of the horses' clearing. The pasture was a great sweeping fold between two wooded slopes that lifted to the mountains beyond, dark jagged outlines against starlight and an almost invisible green light that hung in the air to the north. The mares and foals milled anxiously at the pasture's center. The herd's stallion trotted some distance away, his head high, his ears and attention focused into the hills above the herd.

Kagaya-hime was more interested in a rabbit half-hidden under a low shrub near the trees. It had not seen her. The air was perfectly still and too cold to carry her smell. She dropped into a crouch before she realized she'd made the decision to catch it.

She moved carefully, but in any case the rabbit was distracted, its attention elsewhere. She was scarcely an arm's length away when it saw her. In the instant before it gathered its minimal wits to run, she leapt the space between them and spiked it to the ground, her knife through its shoulder. It gave a single scream before she broke its neck. Its blood was warm on her tongue when she felt herself observed from the trees behind her.

"You are the wolves," she said aloud without turning.

A wolf slipped from the trees; another rose from a depression in the ground. There were four in all, long-muzzled and gray. All animals know and fear the great killing creatures: the eagle, the bear, Korea's tiger, the wolf. The smaller killing creatures avoid them: they do not care to know how it feels to be prey. Kagaya-hime straightened and turned, the rabbit still in her hand.

"What are you?" the largest of the wolves asked—for there were no cats so far from the capital, and nothing it could compare her to. Her woman's shape meant nothing to the wolf, for it did not understand what a cat should look like.

"The people call me Kagaya-hime," she said. This appeared to be sufficient answer.

The largest of the wolves shook itself. "You are a killing animal, but a small one. We could kill you if we chose. Are you not afraid?"

"No," she said. "It does not matter. I have no *fudoki*."

Wolves have no *fudoki*—the pack is defined by blood and smell and voice; their ground can change; their tales define nothing. Nevertheless, they understood her. "Why are you here?" another wolf, a female, asked. She smelled of milk and cubs.

"The people come to kill you," Kagaya-hime said.

"The people always seek to kill us," the female said, "but they do not succeed."

Kagaya-hime lifted the knife. "I have lived among them. If they have not killed you, it's because they have not wanted to do so. Yet. But you have taken their foals—"

"Ah yes, the foals," the female said. "They tasted sweet and their bones were soft."

Kagaya-hime's mouth watered despite herself. "—and now you must leave. They will hunt you down, find your cubs, and kill you. Your tale—your pack—will end there."

"And you?" the lead wolf asked. "Will you try to kill us, too, little killer?"

She raised her chin, a cat before an emperor. "I will kill you if I can. But I would rather you leave."

"We stand together," the wolf said. "We decide together."

"Together." Kagaya-hime's face was very cold. "You are never alone."

"We stand together," the wolf said again. Its eyes flickered and it vanished, it and its priests, into the darkness of the overhanging trees.

"Girl!"—Takase's voice across the clearing. He loped to her side, sword bare and gleaming in his hand; slowed when he saw she was unharmed. "Where did they go?"

"Away. I told them we would kill them."

"Huh," Takase said. "So you talked with them, did you?"

She wiped the back of her hand against her face, smearing blood into her tears. "I don't know if they'll stay. They lose nothing by going; they carry their tale with them."

"I—" Takase said, and then shut his mouth abruptly. He gestured to the rabbit on the snow. "You will want to clean that. And wash your face before you return."

In the morning they tracked the wolves back to their den, a mere slit in a rocky slope. Kagaya-hime was the smallest of them, and she crawled in to find nothing, only the torn fur of a nest, the chewed thighbone of a foal. She backed out and brushed herself clean. "They decided to leave," she said, and no one asked how she knew this.

I have never seen a wolf, never even seen a picture of one. "They are like dogs," said Dōmei, when I asked him once about them: "Like the gods of dogs."

"Bigger, you mean?" I asked. We were sitting on the veranda, eating pickled eggs and watching one of the household's cats prowling at the edge of a clump of reeds under a bright moon.

"They have gold eyes," Dōmei said. "Flat and fierce. Think of a dog that could kill you, that would not even care whether it did so: that's a wolf."

Mutsu province, where there are wolves, and gold-eyed men like Dōmei. I shall never see it now.

8. THE FAN-FOLD NOTEBOOK

Strange. All these pages, all these brush strokes, and I have said little about my half-brother, the emperor everyone now calls Shirakawa. This is perhaps intentional: thinking of him is like scratching at a scab to see if the cut beneath is still fresh. What will I accomplish by doing this? I already know that it has not healed, and I am not brave enough to face the fresh pain.

It is not many months since the forty-ninth night rituals after his death. Some nights, when I feel the thing inside my chest pressing against my lungs, I talk to him. Some nights, I think he answers me.

He was not so many years older than me, and, when he was young, very handsome (as everyone told me, again and again — even my nurse sometimes looked at me and sighed, "Why could you not have a bit of your brother's elegance?"). For a time, when his father was still emperor, he lived with my foster father. The house was full of flurry and attendants because of him, but my women kept us far apart ("Trust me, your highness, he has no interest in having his thoughts disturbed by a flyaway girl with dirty hands and no manners").

Then my foster father said that I could no longer keep mice. Worse, he forced my nurse to take away the mice I did have. There were two or perhaps three: tiny buckwheat-colored creatures with glittering black eyes bright as prayer beads. She would not tell me what she did with them. My tears devolved into an enormous tantrum, for which she locked me into a little raised-floor storehouse, avowedly until I learned to control myself.

I did not learn control there, but I did learn that there were two planks in the floor that had not been properly secured, so that a resourceful girl could lift them and let herself down into the crawl space. I crept through the dust and emerged cautiously, on the far side from the house, then ran for the copse of white pine and *ɔawara* cypress at the garden's opposite end, as far from the main buildings as I could get without crossing the residence walls.

We called him Sadahito then, for he was not yet emperor. He must have been sixteen; certainly, he was much taller than I. He spent much of his time with his father, so I did not expect to find him in the grove—and certainly not alone; an heir is *never* alone, any more than a princess. I do not know what he was doing there—did not think to ask, caught up as I was in my own miseries.

I knew bursting in on him was a terrible solecism, but I couldn't think of what to do next: Apologize? Back away as if I hadn't seen him? Throw myself on the ground? Faint? Grace in awkward situations does not come at the age of ten, so I stood rooted to the ground, as if a tree myself. He did not seem offended; said only: "You've been crying," and pulled a soft paper from his sleeve. "Here, use this."

I took it from his hand and scrubbed at my cheeks, but I could not stop staring at him. Unless I did something stupid (now, for instance), I would probably serve Sadahito at court someday; he (and my foster father) would select the man I would marry. He controlled my destiny—he and the other gods.

"You're my half-sister," he said. We had met before, but always through curtains, as befit a princess and the heir. "I forget: what do they call you?"

"Harueme. What should I do with this?" I held up the now-grimy wad of sleeve-paper.

"Give it to me and I'll get rid of it for you," he said. "You don't want them to guess you got out, do you?"

"No," I said, amazed at his insight. He knew I'd been crying, and he knew I'd escaped. No wonder he got to be emperor. "Why are you here?"

He made a gesture, implying everything and nothing. "I am tired of studying, and I cannot visit Kenshi right now—she is in her courses." I knew who Kenshi was: she was his consort, and said to be very beautiful, though I did not meet her and learn the truth of this for several more years. He sighed heavily, though he smiled at himself as he did so. "So, little sister, why have *you* been crying?"

He had distracted me for a time; now his question brought it all back, and I started crying again. Between sobs, I sniffled out the story of my mice. He put his arm around me (though I was covered with dirt and snot and tears) and told me that they would be fine in the garden, if that's where they had been abandoned. "There's a lot for a mouse to eat out here."

"But the cats—foxes—" I said, crying in earnest now.

"If they die, they will just come back as something better. Maybe cats themselves, hmm? And who can say? Even mice may eventually attain enlightenment."

I was comforted by this, not because I believed the mice were safe (or that their enlightenment was possible; already I'd had enough mice to suspect otherwise), but because he had tried to comfort me at all. By the time he helped me sneak back to the storehouse undetected, I loved him with all my heart.

Later that night, after I had been freed from my storehouse, bathed and given a good supper, my brother's chief man came to my rooms, and left a pierced silver box, a treasure from beyond even India. Inside was a single gray-furred mouse, young enough that its eyes were still too large for its face. I named it Little Sister, and pretended that I was my brother, and the mouse me. No one could take the mouse from me—it was a gift from the heir, after all—and so I carried it inside my sleeve and fed it rice from my bowl. I wept for a half a month when it died, because he had given it to me.

Several years later (I was fifteen) I came to court to attend my half-brother. Everything happened very quickly—my father the emperor Go-Sanjō died, and Sadahito gave up his name and became emperor that very day. He asked for my company, and my foster father sent me there.

I had visited the palace before, when my father the emperor Go-Sanjō requested it, and even once when he was gone to stay with a consort's father, and I was allowed to explore a little. Still, the notion of living there made everything different. The painted floor the color of turquoises, the crimson pillars, the painted screens—these were all mine now, in some small way. Every day I would wear robes prettier than my finest as a child. I would be surrounded by witty, beautiful, cultured people, and I would (I fantasized) become immensely popular, famed for my wit and scholarship, and as elegant as Sei Shōnagon had been, eighty years before. All my lovers would be handsome as Genji; all my attendants would be famous for beauty and charm, their glory reflecting on me.

And my half-brother and I—we would spend all our time together, reading and writing, perhaps even traveling, to Ise or even the Shirakawa Barrier or beyond! I would show him my moths' wings, and my notebooks of observations; he would show me whatever it was he cared for most in the world. He would call me Little Sister; I would call him Brother.

It was not like that; I have to laugh at my naïveté at thinking such a thing was possible. His responsibilities were great; he was always with his regent or the other high nobles, discussing this or that. When his duties did not occupy him, he spent time with the other high-ranked young men at court; or his consort, Kenshi; or others of his women. He even had other sisters and half-sisters, at court or nearby shrines. A thousand thousand people wanted his time or attention. I was just one of the horde, if higher-ranked than most.

And I was no Sei Shōnagon. Granted, I was the daughter of an emperor and (I am told) exceptionally beautiful; but the people at court were all more interested in music and poetry than in water-clocks and philosophy. No one but I cared how learned I was. And the public halls and emperor's chambers were lovely, but the private rooms, even the rooms of a princess, were worn-looking, sometimes dilapidated, and always flea-haunted.

A month after I came to court, I asked the emperor if he would let me leave, to return to my uncle's residence, or enter a nunnery. He denied the request. "I need you," was all he said. It was not for many years that I understood what he meant by this, until the day we sat together and tasted the rain on our lips. In the meantime, I learned to accept my life here.

Shirakawa and Kenshi. I was jealous of her, of course. She was only a little older than I but she was beautiful and graceful, and more important, charming. In my heart I claimed to despise these things (it would never do for me to announce such a sentiment), but now I can admit that I despised them because I felt I could never attain them. I was beautiful (I say with all candor), but that meant nothing. A round face and white skin are an accident of birth; being well dressed and groomed was a reflection on Shigeko and my other women.

As a child I judged myself by the adults that surrounded me — my mother and her women; my foster father and my uncle — and they all seemed infinitely elegant, masters of mysteries I could barely perceive. I was the daughter of an emperor; if I could not be as elegant as they, well then, I would be clever.

Becoming beautiful was a process that surprised me as much as it did my uncle. He had despaired that I would ever be valued for anything besides my birth, but my woman Shigeko came to attend me (just before my half-brother became emperor, this was), and I was suddenly clean, and my robes matched, and any dead animals I might be examining were discreetly hidden away. I think my half-brother Shirakawa would have summoned me to court in any case; but it was a comfort, my uncle said, to know I was not going to disgrace everyone associated with me when I got there.

Shigeko made me polite as well as elegant. It was she who insisted I write to my half-brother's favored consort, Fujiwara sammi no Kenshi, who lived elsewhere at court. I did so, growling all the way through the required poem, something about the reeds of the east wing greeting the grasses of the north—I'm sure it's here somewhere; I'll ask Shigeko when she returns from overseeing a gift to one of the temples south of town. I still recall Kenshi's response: "The clouds visit both east and north. Grass-blades blown between us show only fragments of the wind."

And so we wrote letters, and visited one another when we could. We were never friends, both being too highly ranked to be close to anyone not assigned to us; but I found her pleasant and quietly witty. It was easy to see why Shirakawa loved her.

Even more than her apparent perfections, I envied her his attention. A half-sister and a consort fill two different places in a man's life; this is no different for an emperor. He spent many of his nights with her, and certain days when no work could be performed, due to tabus or festivals or snow so heavy no one chose to leave the shelter of their own eaves. He visited me sporadically; "Whenever I want someone to question everything," he said once to me when I asked, "whenever I want to think hard to keep up." I took this as a compliment, reluctant to look at myself closely enough to determine whether he meant it as such.

"And your consort?" I said, half-laughing to conceal my embarrassment. "When do you visit her?"

He did not laugh. "When I can."

And so my brother had Kenshi. She bore him a son that they lost, and then another who lived—my nephew Taruhito, who became emperor—Horikawa, now he is dead. These experiences brought them together; even when I saw him without her (or her without him), I felt as if I were watching a running dog who was missing a paw: the dog may not mind nor even know; but what is not there leaves an awkward bump in his gait.

After Mononobe no Dōmei and I became lovers, I was not so jealous. I had my own companion, my own fourth paw; and I spent every possible moment with him. If I did not get pregnant, it was not (as I overheard one of my women say to Shigeko at the time) for lack of trying.

And then Dōmei left the capital, to return to his family home. I claimed an indisposition and retreated for a few months from the court. I did not want to deal with the eyes of the others on me. Either they knew of our affair and would be feeling—ridicule? pity?—or they would not, and their jokes and petty concerns would grate on my sensibilities like ground nutshells on skin. My rooms at my uncle's residence were always available to me, so I retreated there, and did not come out for a time.

My memory is that I cried steadily for a month or more, that every overcast day and every ink stroke that I blotted set me off again. But I have just asked Shigeko what she remembers of that time, and she tells me I did not cry once. And yet I am sure—well, memory is strange, after all. Perhaps both of these are true, and she and I live in worlds that almost—but do not totally—overlap.

And whether I showed this grief or not, we both remember that after a time I stopped jumping to my feet every time a messenger arrived with what might be a letter from the provinces. War started in Mutsu province, and I started to read again, about war and the making of it; when the first reports of Minamoto no Yoshiee's war started trickling into court I read those as well, and pretended I was not searching for his name among the dead and distinguished.

I returned to court and even invited other men behind my curtains, usually old lovers who had become more friend than sexual partner. *I move forward with my life,* I said to myself, and felt smug about it. We can contrive victories of the most unpromising material.

A year after that, Shirakawa's consort Kenshi died.

Kenshi did not die at a good time. There is never a good time, of course; there is always something left undone, a last trunk left unemptied. But this was especially inconvenient: early in Yoshiee's war, when the situation was little understood, complicated, and not very encouraging. Kenshi and Shirakawa's son, who was—five? six? very young, in any case—was sickly, and not expected to live to adulthood. The monks from the mountains nearby were behaving badly, marching armed in the streets of the capital and burning one another's temples; and there had been a drought that was taking a year and more to recover from; and the chancellors were for some reason or other being more than usually tiresome in their requests. Shirakawa managed all such things with the grace of an expert *kemari* player, but he coped poorly with her death.

I wrote Shirakawa the letters one might expect of a sister worried for her brother, or a noblewoman for her sovereign. The answers were polite but short, and not in his handwriting. He did not visit, nor invite me to attend him, when I could have determined for myself how he was doing. I did see him, at the seventh-night rituals and at a reading of the sutras for the well-being of Kenshi's soul. He wept—tears shining like rain on his face—and yet he seemed somehow remote, withdrawn, as if his grief were something held close. It seemed, as always, that Shirakawa without Kenshi was lacking some part of himself, but now it was more serious, more acute; as if it were not a limb but some vital organ gone.

I launched Shigeko and others of my women at their friends and admirers in his train, to learn what they could of my brother's state—for no one ever *tells* anyone anything at court; we spy out what we can, and guess the rest. They returned with nothing more specific than the rumors. He did not meet with his chancellors or his high nobles. He did not read. He did not have lovers. He did not sleep.

I wrote more letters to Shirakawa; but what I really wanted to do was talk to him, face to face. I had lost Dōmei, but I had survived; there was no reason why my clever, handsome, older brother—incidentally emperor of the Eight Islands—should not recover, as well; which is why, perhaps half a year after her death, I very improperly went to visit him without a summons.

This was easier than I would have expected. The court is a thousand buildings and courtyards connected by ten thousand walkways and gates; but it covers only a small area, and (if one is familiar with or can find one's way) it is possible to walk the length of the enclosure without needing to put on clogs, or get one's head wet on a rainy day. Shigeko was reluctant to invade the emperor's presence, but she accompanied me nevertheless (in many ways, she is far braver than I). I dealt with the guards and courtiers we encountered by brushing past them without explanation. By the time they recovered from their surprise, Shigeko and I were well past, and another of my attendants was murmuring explanations, excuses—anything that might keep them from stopping us.

His rooms were nearly unpeopled: two bodyguards who started forward, and then stepped back when Shigeko spoke to them, and a woman server with a covered lacquered box in her hands. "Where is he?" I asked, and followed her silent gesture.

He was in an enclosed place that might have been where they slept, though there was nothing here now but a carving of Kannon and its offerings. He was not praying, but there was a tabu tag hung from his *eboshi* hat, meaning he was not to be interrupted. *Ha*, I thought, and knelt beside him. I pulled my prayer beads from my sleeve and began a just-audible prayer.

He sighed and put down his own beads. "Not you, too."

"Brother—" I began and trailed off. This had seemed like such a good idea; now that I was here, I found I had no idea what to say. He had been crying; his face was still wet. All the exhortations I had planned in my mind on the walk over here vanished, steam from a kettle. "I am so sorry," I whispered, and to my horror started sobbing.

He tipped his head back, and fresh tears slipped from the corners of his eyes, shining trails to his ears, his neck. "I keep—missing her," he said. "There are so many things that need to be done, I just—"

"You miss her so much," I said. "But—" *But she is dead; she's not coming back; she left you anyway, for the commonest lover of them all, death*, I did not say.

He glanced at me. "I am sorry about your guardsman."

He knew; he had cared enough to know. "I'm worried for you."

"Little Sister," he said, and his smile was so sweet that I began sobbing in earnest. He reached across the space between us, and held me close. We wept together. I cannot claim it was my doing, but after this, he again involved himself with the world.

Enough of this. I know my own story—have lived it, each day a new section added to a scroll that grows near its end now. I know this story too well to be surprised by it. My little cat-warrior—her tale has the capacity to delight me and distract me from my half-brother's loss, which just at this moment (it is very late, and the pressure in my chest prohibits sleep) is as immediate and painful as it was the day he died, when I cried until my eyes wept blood.

So:

Spring comes later to Hitachi province than it does to the capital; still, by the third month the snow was gone from the Osa Hitachi estate, and the world was buffeted by floodwater and spring winds and storms that thundered like dragons through the clouds. Takase had established a camp just outside of the estate for his war band, but camp and household had blurred until everything was a single filthy, noisome mess. The ground had been mashed to mud, ankle-deep in the places where the horses collected. The air was filled with smells: wood and charcoal smoke, wet manes and manure, the oily smell of cooking meat, the bitterness of hot metal pounded out by the smiths. Not all cats are fastidious (I have been familiar with a cat who rolled in the midden heap behind our kitchen house, and entered my chambers with wilted radish-greens trailing from her ears), but most are. Kagaya-hime was like many of her kin in this, that she did not care to have dirty feet and disliked sharp smells.

Takase and Kitsune had gathered perhaps a hundred horsemen, each with attendants and a horse or two. This was not many, but to fight the Abe without a warrant or potential amnesty was risky business. The central council might eventually offer an exemption to the usual penalties, not everyone dared take the chance. Though his had been the initial letter asking for the warrant, the vice-governor, Nakara's brother, could not involve himself directly at the risk of his position. But when certain of his retainers asked for leave he did not ask too many questions. A handful of warriors brought their men and their horses from the provincial capital—along with sixty *hoko* spears, sent by the vice-governor under the convenient if implausible fiction that they might serve as "protection for the hazardous journeys home."

This brought the total number gathered to about three hundred men—horsemen, retainers, and servants—and one hundred twenty horses. It was not a large band (though large enough withal, especially when the horses are all male) but there was an immense amount of material required even for this sort of conflict, where they expected to seize food as they traveled.

I remember reading something once, when I was at my uncle's house, waiting through my monthly courses. Alert to my interests, Shigeko chanced to bring me an overview of the codes and practices that concerned war-making. (War-things were much on my uncle's mind at this time, for this was in the months after Minamoto no Yoshiee's war in Mutsu province began: a year after Dōmei left me and returned to the east.)

I had no idea how much was required for war-making! I suppose I might have guessed, familiar with what must be assembled for even a short journey by, let us say, a princess to the shrine of Inari no Jinja, scant miles from home and a place where one might be expected to need little. There was a list in my uncle's papers of what warriors require for military duty. I have found it folded into a diary of mine from that time. What my uncle thought of such a document going missing, I can only imagine.

> —rice and *sake* and salt (*enormous* amounts of salt—why, I cannot say);
> —weapons of every sort and size—longswords, short swords, and knives; a bow and fifty arrows; additional steel arrowheads ready for mounting—as well as whetstones and quivers and bowcases and all the bits and bobs that are required to tend and store one's weapons;

—saddles and saddlebags and silk-cord bridles and steel
  bits;
—wood shields as tall as a man, to be propped on the
  ground in battle where they might serve as cover, for
  the men on foot or dismounted riders;
—axes and hatchets and chisels and saws, tents and cooking pots and copper trays;
—flints, tinder, long-handled tongs to grip coals;
—sickles (for what, I wonder? —and then think, ah, yes,
  the grass pillows mentioned in all those poems written
  by men at the frontier);
—moxas and bandages for healing;

—as if that were all. Then there are the attendants (and each
horseman has one or two of these, to work as groom and servant
and combatant as need arises), along with all of *their* food and
supplies and weapons—*hoko* and *naginata* spears and swords and
bows; and the priest who comes to give guidance, along with his
or her followers, and food and supplies; and the clerks and warrant officers; and any hangers-on that the leader believes might
be useful or cannot be naysaid. And so many supplies must have
required carts and oxen or horses, and still more men to drive
and tend them. And all of this is organized into companies of fifty
men each, and subdivided into campfires of ten and then squads
of five. It sounds as complex as court life, if not so pretty.

In the months after Yoshiee's war was declared, I read much
on the subject. I longed to understand, not what I later learned to
call logistics, nor the *why*s of it, but the *what*. What was it like to
fight, to actually shoot at someone else, to want them dead and
have the means to make them so?

There were certain Chinese classics that all the military nobles
thought essential: Sun Tzu, Ssu-ma, and the *Kōsekikō sanryaku*.
These were full of strategy and tactics and oblique metaphors,
but they seemed somewhat cold, bloodless. In addition, sheaves
of poetry floated about court, purportedly written by soldiers

156

Kij Johnson

(though this was often a literary conceit); but they said nothing about war itself, instead harping endlessly on how much the men missed their wives, and the loneliness of sleeping on those ubiquitous grass-stuffed pillows.

Some years ago a collection of stories started filtering through court—the *Konjaku*. We joked then that the *Konjaku* had one of everything, but in fact it has many more than one story about warriors, and these reports vary. In some, war seems more glamorous than horrible, as complex and formal as the presentation of the blue horses in the first month or the Gosechi dances in the eleventh: the exchange of arrows, the name-announcing; men in beautifully laced armor whirling in graceful combat on spirited horses. Others are perhaps more realistic, though in them war seems mostly to be exhortations and beheadings, usually over small (not to say absurdly petty) matters.

There was the *Mutsuwaki*, as well, all about the first war that had been going on in the north, back when I was very small. I was no longer at my uncle's house, so I borrowed a copy of this from the scrolls of my half-brother the emperor; he looked at me strangely but had it sent without comment. This was much longer. For the first time I realized that war was as filled with politics as court, but still there was the painstakingly described armor, the elegant little platitudes about this or that one's skill at archery or riding. When the author stepped down from these aesthetic heights to describe battle itself or its results, his images were improbably grisly. I still remember one: "The ground was slick with viscera, the moors wet with fat."

All these wars, these battles, in the *Konjaku* and the *Mutsuwaki* and elsewhere, are true. Names are named; Shigeko (who knows everything about everyone who has ever been to court) could probably recite the genealogies of half the men mentioned in them. They are true, but they are lies—like all tales.

Some years ago there was a night in the fifth month when the full moon was hidden behind the clouds, and I overheard three older guardsmen talking in the darkness. They had fought in

Yoshiee's war. Tongues loosened by plum wine and *sake*, they compared the lessons they had learned. These had nothing to do with eloquent speeches, and everything to do with avoiding diarrhea and keeping one's bowstrings from rotting. Their stories were hardly fit for gentle ears: an attack where foot soldiers swept blades along the ground to fell the horses by slashing their legs; a long season when everyone had dysentery and the men wore no *hakama*-trousers or loincloths, for it was pointless to do so and then clean them a thousand times a day; a man driven as mad as if he had been fox-possessed, all from an arrow-cut on his thigh that turned black and began to rot; a man hacked to pieces alive before his wife's weeping eyes; a wife raped before her husband's staring, severed head.

I listened to these things, and thought: *This is Dōmei's life. This is who he is.* But I could not reconcile this with the man who had laughed so often with me, the gold eyes that were so warm when we made love. I had nightmares for some time after listening to the men; and for years afterward their words would return to me suddenly, like a ghost story one heard as a child and can never forget.

The Osa Hitachi were a military clan, and everyone, from Kitsune and Nakara down to the oxkeepers' children, was caught up in the preparations. The buildings within the estate were crammed with the supplies that could not be left in the rain—for it still rained, naturally. Outside, fields were being prepared for the summer's crops ("I'm sure you want the space," Nakara said tartly to her brother one wet day when everyone's tempers ran high, "but come the tenth month, I'm guessing that you will want to eat, yes?"). Nakara had to send every mare within a ten-mile range twenty miles south and west to a smaller farm claimed by the Osa Hitachi, but even so the stallions sometimes fought. Kagaya-hime grew tired of trying to find solitude, and instead stayed out of the way and watched it all, rather as a cat sits on a wall watching the servants prepare to move a household to Biwa lake for the summer.

Nakara apologized one day. She clattered under the eaves of
an outbuilding and saw Kagaya-hime there, tucked into the space
between a pillar of shields and an untidy heap of new-made sickles, trimming Biter's hooves with her knife. "Be patient, Hime.
Things will settle down as soon as the men leave."

Kagaya-hime finished the hoof and stood. "I imagine you will
be grateful when we are all gone."

Nakara was holding a cedar-wood box filled with chopsticks
for moving the coals in braziers; she dropped this, and the little
iron rods rolled everywhere. Woman and cat-woman knelt and
gathered them. "*You* can't leave," said Nakara. "*You're* staying.
Aren't you?"

"No." Kagaya-hime laid her handful of sticks in the box and
stood. "I go to Mutsu province, as well."

"Mutsu," Nakara said. "They are all fools or barbarians there.
Or insane."

Kagaya-hime said, "Your brother was one of them."

"That's why I would know." Nakara hesitated, unaccustomed
to asking for favors. "We're not like city people here, my dear.
My household is whomever I say it is. A sister would be a great
comfort to me."

Kagaya-hime closed her eyes and leaned against Biter's flank,
feeling his rough winter coat against her cheek. "Why would you
wish this?"

"I know what it is to not know who—what—you are," Nakara
said. "This way you would have sister and brothers and home.
You would know that much at least."

This was what she had lost so long ago: ground to live and
mate and hunt on, a family, a tale into which she would fit.
Nakara's brother was half-fox; there was clearly room for a
woman who had once been a cat, for her to become Osa Hitachi
no Neko. And she would no longer be alone. It would not be her
fudoki, but humans' tales did not grate as other cats' had. She
would remain what she was—changed, perhaps, but still recognizable to herself. The road-kami had abandoned her; might she

not stop? *Road?* she whispered to the backs of her eyelids. It did not answer; but for an instant she saw the dark thing with a thousand eyes, and it spoke her name.

"I cannot," she said finally, and opened her eyes. "I must go."

Nakara said in a tight voice: "I do not want to lose anyone else."

"You found this place, this — family. Or made it. It is not mine."

"Where will you go? Why?" A tear slid down Nakara's cheek; she brushed it aside impatiently.

Kagaya-hime said slowly, "I thought it was the road that carried me, but we left the road behind when we crossed the water at that town. Enoura. And I still have to go."

"Where will it end? Will you fight with the men? Will you walk until you die, till you walk into the ocean and drown? And I am to let you do this thing?"

"I cannot help it." Kagaya-hime began twisting a lock of Biter's mane into a tight little rope.

"Do not pretend that you have no control over your life, girl," Nakara snapped. "You go because you wish to, because you don't choose to stay." She turned on her heel and walked away, leaving the box lying in the mud. Her hurt and anger lasted for days.

No one controls their own life. Well, perhaps some of the Fujiwara men do. Perhaps they attain manhood, and suddenly know exactly what they want from life — I will marry in two years, and have a son in five, retire at thirty, die at sixty. And my half-brother knew his life — was born knowing it. But the rest of us? I look back on my life and I see a series of decisions, each of which made perfect sense at the time, most of which led to nothing in particular.

It is true that I am powerless, that I am controlled by my family, by the Fujiwaras, by the gods and Buddhas; but I am also free: to think my thoughts, and dream of blue-green streams under foreign trees.

I thank the merciful Kannon for this tale I tell, where I can at last control a life, even if it is not my own.

❀   ❀   ❀

The days of preparation collected themselves into untidy fort-nights, and then a month and more. Takase spent much of his time in the main house, surrounded by low tables heaped with slips of paper listing the details of war. These he arranged into various piles and then rearranged the piles, his clerk scribbling completed lists onto other, larger pieces of paper. Discarded scraps drifted across the floor.

A courtier might have compared him to an aging poet writing among fallen cherry blossoms or snow. He reminds me more of my half-brother the emperor, who spent many days in precisely this manner—though it annoyed my uncle (indeed, most of his branch of the Fujiwaras), who thought he concerned himself overmuch with the running of the empire, which (in their opinions) might better be left in their hands.

Kagaya-hime saw Takase and the clerk and the countless, strangely attractive, fluttering papers, and saw a kitten's game, or a mystery. She often watched him, but Takase did not seem to mind, or perhaps even notice that she was near—it is easy to ignore a cat when she is not of a mind to remind you of her exis-tence, though otherwise it is impossible. It may also be that he sensed she was not, strictly speaking, human; or perhaps he saw that she was one of those who are born to killing, without dis-cerning the details.

On this day—it was toward the middle of the second month, when the irises by the spider-leg stream were first showing their leaves, straight as knives—Kitsune came into Takase's presence. He spent most of his time outside with the men and horses, where his voice was necessarily loud and his stride long; papers skit-tered away from his feet as he stopped and bowed. "My lord—" he began, and the eaves rang.

"Wait." Takase raised his hand. The clerk finished the charac-ter he was writing and laid down his brush, then fussed around, placing river stones on the heaps to hold them in place. Kagaya-hime knelt half-hidden by a latticed screen leading to the veranda, binding a steel arrowhead to a shaft; she lifted her head to watch. "Now," Takase said, when the piles were secure, and only the scraps on the floor fluttered. "What is it?"

"It" was many things, of course. I have learned that no one (not even Shigeko, whom I see a thousand times each day) has only one thing to say. Ask, "And what else?" and there is always another, and sometimes it is the most important of all. Lacquered stirrups from Musashi province had come in; one of the Osa Hitachi retainers had received news that his wife was ill, and left for home with his men; mice had gotten into some of the rice, though it was still salvageable. Takase was old (and wise, though these are not always paired) and asked, "And what else?" a number of times.

If there are no secrets at court, there are fewer within a household, fewer still within a war band. "The men have learned that my sister's guest means to travel with us," Kitsune said.

"And they object," Takase said.

Kitsune nodded. "A few. Monthly courses, sightseeing, endless delays for travel tabus and heating water and looking for protection from the dew."

"Do you feel this way?"

"Ha. She is tough enough."

"But you do not care for her," Takase said.

Kitsune stiffened. "I never —"

"Boy, I am old. I have no interest in listening to excuses."

Kitsune frowned and rubbed his neck. "I — do not understand her. Who she is."

Takase snorted. "Say that about any woman, not just her. Will you be able to travel with her?"

"If she slows us down, no."

"Well, girl?" Takase said. "Will you keep us waiting while you cut your nails on auspicious days?"

Kagaya-hime hadn't known that he saw her: he had not turned his head her way once in the long hours of work. Caught, she stood and entered the room, arrow and thread still in her hands. She did not meet Kitsune's eyes, but looked sidelong at him, gauging mood, threat, posture. He was flushed red with embarrassment, defiant. "No," she said. "Why would I cut my nails?"

Takase barked a laugh that became a cough. And later, when (perhaps) he thought she had left them, he said to Kitsune: "She is driven by fate, as are we all. It's a waste of energy to stand in the way."

As I write here, my cat Myōbū watches me, suddenly intent, as though a fire flickered over my head. There have been many cats over the years, and I have spoken to them all in the high tones reserved for children, drunken men, and pets. They have never spoken back, but I have never thought they would. They are not badgers or foxes, after all. They are from distant godless places, beyond my most ambitious dreams.

A month later, Kagaya-hime left with the war band. It was a bright spring day, still winter-cold, except that the trees showed a haze of pale green, and the air seemed furred with moisture and the possibility of life. Nakara and Kagaya-hime had avoided one another, but now the woman joined the cat, and in silence they watched the band form an unruly line of snappish horses and hoarse-voiced men.

"Must you do this?" Nakara said again.

Kagaya-hime said, "Yes."

Nakara sighed. "I cannot stop the wind from blowing, and I cannot stop you. I'm sorry that I was angry with you."

Certain cats hold grudges. Shisutāko, the little nun, was like this; she refused your embrace if she thought she had been slighted, or if you were to toss her from a veranda into the garden after a particularly wearisome morning of her face in everything; and she waited days if necessary to take a revenge as indelicate as it was surprising. I think it is possible that our cats learn how to bear grudges from people, for we can hold one for a lifetime.

Kagaya-hime was not of a resentful nature. This requires a sense of perogatives infringed, and she had no expectations to be dashed.

She saw Nakara's sorrow and did something she remembered from the aunts and cousins when they sought comfort from one another; she stepped forward and pressed her cheek into the curve of Nakara's neck. Nakara reached out and pulled her close, held her tightly. Kagaya-hime stood taut-muscled for an instant, then relaxed and embraced Nakara: the first time she had embraced another, felt the comfort of one's arms filled with a person one loves.

"I am—sorry," she whispered into Nakara's hair, "though I do not know what that means."

They stood joined for a time, but no matter how tender the moment, a cat grows restive. Kagaya-hime moved away, still close but no longer touching.

Nakara looked at her and sighed. "There are people who cannot settle, as if they were birds born without legs. They go on and on, to the world's end—the lands of the hairy northerners, or India; farther, even."

"What happens to them, the ones who go?"

"I don't know. They never return to tell us. Perhaps they never find a place to stop."

"I am not one of those," Kagaya-hime said. "I long for home and *fudoki*. I would stop if I could."

"Would you?" Nakara said.

"I have a gift for you," Kagaya-hime said suddenly. Tucked in her sash was a slim, shallow box carved of tortoiseshell, hardly larger than a fan-case. She laid it in Nakara's hands. Inside was a knife no longer than Kagaya-hime's hand, its blade the color of claws.

Nakara looked up. "I cannot take your knife."

"I have others," Kagaya-hime said, and held up her hands, though she showed only her palms to Nakara, so that the woman might not see the raw place where one of her fingernails had been until that morning.

"I have a gift for you, as well," Nakara said. Junshi stood a few paces away; Nakara gestured, and the woman handed to Kagaya-hime a lacquered woven box, long and narrow. Inside were gold and ivory feathers as long as Kagaya-hime's forearm: eagle feathers,

feathers worthy of an emperor's arrows. The sunlight caught them and the feathers gleamed with flecks of muted light.

Nakara continued, her voice distant, as though she chose not to feel too strongly. "My father was a warrior; my mother was the daughter of a warrior. I have learned these things. Make sure that your neckguard is low. When charging, don't get shot in the face. Trust the men beside you."

Cats have no way to share their sorrow. It is not in their nature that two cats sharing a *fudoki* can truly feel sadness—cats come and go, it is the tale that matters. And a cat without a *fudoki* has no one with whom she can share sorrow, and so she learns no habits of expression. But a woman understands loss, and can express it. And this, Kagaya-hime learned, was both advantage and disadvantage to being human.

Mutsu province. This is the end of the (civilized) world, the farthest reaches of the empire. My favorite Michinoku paper comes from there, though I have a difficult time reconciling my image of the place with the notion that there are workshops, perhaps even manufactories, whole families or villages devoting their lives to producing luxuries for the capital, so many hundreds of miles away. Mutsu is meant to be a land of savages (that drinking of blood! those arrows in the hair!), of peaks taller than the great mountain Fuji and snow a thousand feet deep, of springs of scalding water that rise from the very depths of Hell, of monkeys that speak and *tengu*-demons and monsters—it is meant to be the fringe of the world. The Mutsu province of my mind is filled with wonders.

My lover Dōmei told me that it is not really like this, that Mutsu province is like everywhere else. There are roads and estates, towns with government offices, posting stations; hills, mountains, and hot springs; peasants and nobles; nothing extraordinary, nothing I could not find nearer to home and better designed or regulated. I have to wonder whether the entire world is like this. I have learned a bit about Korea and China, and we of course share much culture with them; but if I went to India or even beyond, would I find maintained roads and public wells, town gossips and officious village leaders, peasants happy or unhappy with their lot, rice fields in varying states of cultivation, cats asleep in patches of sun?

And perhaps death will be like this, whether Hell or the Pure Land or some incomprehensible place I have not imagined. Will there be roads and sunlit verandas and sleeping cats? Would this be a comfort or a disappointment? Is there anyplace that is filled with wonder, anywhere but my imagination, and the tales?

Yesterday my great-grandnephew the emperor sent me a poem, which I correctly interpreted as a summons. It is more fitting that I attend him than the reverse; but I am an old woman, and I remember when he was born, the pup. I remember when his father was born: even his *grandfather's* birth, for I waited with Shirakawa's consort Kenshi when she was in labor. I bit back my mild annoyance at the poem. We have not visited for many months, and I may not see him again before I leave the palace altogether. And he is ten, after all. I can hardly expect more elegance of mind than I myself showed at that age.

It always takes time to prepare for an imperial visit, but it takes even more for an old woman who has been recently ill. One would think that Shigeko was accustomed to emperors by now, but for some reason this visit set her all a-flutter, and she fretted over my robes as much as she ever did when I was younger.

"Akihito's ten," I said. "He's not going to care, as long as I'm respectable."

She frowned at me. "He's not Akihito anymore. He's the *emperor*, my lady. Even if you seem to forget it; even if he doesn't care. You have a responsibility to look respectable." *Not to disgrace us all,* she meant.

"To him?" I said. "He didn't seem to care much for such things, back when he spent all his time vomiting on his clothes."

"Nevertheless," she said, refusing the bait. So many years together make all sports familiar.

My younger women were all flutters and excitement, resetting the sleeves for a green-gray robe combination that had been disassembled for cleaning. Shigeko and two others washed my face and throat and hands, and eased me into my garments, stuffing one sleeve full of soft papers to use if I coughed. They propped me up between them, and we walked down walkways and verandas and galleries at a pace I hoped looked more deliberate than feeble. (I find I have *some* vanities, after all.)

The emperor my great-grandnephew has immense rooms, but as most emperors seem to, he lives most of his time in a small area set off from the immense echoing spaces. Curtains and eye-blinds and a canopy create the illusion of walls and intimacy; the lovely floor is padded with reed mats and a phoenix-bright carpet from some unimaginably distant land. He is never alone, so he had with him his regent, a calligraphy instructor, and a number of men and women. Everyone still wore mourning for Shirakawa's death, so the room felt muted.

They all looked very young to me (as, in truth, everyone does, when one is seventy). I recognized only a few of them, but amused myself searching for resemblances to court people I had once known, all now retired or dead: *with that nose, he must be one of the Sugara boys; the girl must be the daughter, all right, granddaughter of Fujiwara no Kimiko.* One of the women (she had the square face and unconscious grace the Kuroku-clan girls all seemed to have) slipped across to me, and led me to a curtain-stand very near the emperor, placing a mat and helping me to settle.

She wafted to the emperor and murmured in his ear. The boy put down his brush with a certain air of relief and dismissed the calligrapher. "Aunt, I trust I find you well? I heard you were ill, so I burned incense for your health." His voice was clear, sweet as the high notes on a set of *shō*-pipes.

"Thank you, Nephew. Highness," I added as an afterthought.

He stared critically at me, head tilted like a bird's. It is true that he is a ten-year-old boy; still, I was glad that Kignu had goaded the women into finishing these robes. "Are you feeling better?"

"Child, I am seventy years old. Remaining alive is as 'better' as I can hope for." A ripple of stifled laughter ran through the attendants. The emperor—most of these children—were too young to understand what I meant by this; even the boy's father was born forty years after I. I must seem unimaginably old to them all, like the clay figures we find sometimes at ancient gravesites.

My nephew frowned a little. "You must take care of yourself, Aunt," he said sternly.

Why? I did not ask. "Your concern touches me," I said, and found I meant it. An attendant entered and claimed his attention: a relief, for my eyes were burning, and I had to blow my nose, which I did as quietly as possible. Shigeko took the damp sleeve-paper from me and slid it into her own sleeve with the bland look of a woman for whom such unappealing actions are duty. I watched my nephew and his court for a time, content to let the activity, the clever puns and poems, drift around my ankles.

"Aunt?" the emperor asked, later, when not so many people were paying attention to us. "Are you dying?"

"Yes."

"Huh." He thought for a time, a single tiny line between his eyes. "Well, don't."

"I have no choice, child. None of us do." I wondered if he was thinking of Shirakawa, his great-grandfather, my half-brother. "I am sorry I won't see you grow up." I realized suddenly that this was true. I have seen so many of my family grow up and then grow old and die, or die young and untimely. It would have been nice to watch this one, as well. And to see next spring, and the winter after that, and the robins returning from the south, and the dragonflies after a rain, and anything and everything.

His voice was very small. "You used to sing to me. When I was a child."

"You remember this?" I had a vague recollection of having done so when he had flu and was too ill to do more than cry and sleep.

He nodded vigorously. "All about moths and, um, butterflies."

"Really," I said. I had not offered poetry, not *ki*-chronicles nor Chinese exhortations to proper behavior: I had sung a peasant's love-song from the north. Dōmei had taught it to me, singing the woman's lines in a squeaky voice that never failed to dissolve me in laughter. "You remember this."

"I still know the words," he added. "They were pretty."

"Yes, they were," I said softly. Dōmei and I sang the song often, even sometimes when we made love, tossing lines back and forth like poetry.

He spoke the first line, hesitantly, and then sang it. And I found I could not help but join him. My nephew's voice was much higher than Dōmei's had been; mine was much lower than it had been when I was young.

A ten-year-old emperor and a dying woman sang a peasant's song taught her by a long-lost lover from the north. Life is full of wonders. Dōmei lives still, in my heart, and in words a child does not yet understand.

9. THE *SHOBU* NOTEBOOK

*K*agaya-hime traveled with eighty horsemen, two hundred miscellaneous attendants, and a hundred twenty horses. This is a good-sized village's worth of people, though *this* village sent a vanguard to scout its way; slept somewhere different each night; and was almost entirely male and entirely childless.

Kagaya-hime knew even less of villages than she did of estates. The road had taken her through a number of them, but she did not usually stay in them longer than it took to find food; she was uncomfortable in the presence of so many people and the undetectable boundaries between their territories. The war band's constant motion eased the discomfort she might have felt in such a large gathering. She knew about motion and travel; she knew what it was to sleep under unfamiliar trees.

Any gathering of men—but particularly of warriors—is like a troop of monkeys. There are continual jostlings and posturings, males circling one another looking for weaknesses. (I learned this from my lover Dōmei's stories, though I do not think this is the lesson he expected me to learn.) Even if the group's leadership is incontestable, even if the hierarchies of commander and captain are established, there is another level of dominance, based not on lineage or military rank, but on personal strength and skill, and the indefinable element that makes this man attractive and that man merely ordinary. My half-brother had this charm, if you can use so slight a word for a power that won him lifelong loyalties and affection. Takase had it, as well.

Though the war band traveled quickly, there was plenty of time for monkey-games, for most of the men were experienced at campaigning. Yoshiee's war was not so many years in the past, and these were northerners; even the youngest were accustomed to the constant scuffles to protect their lands from robber gangs. Some of the games involved the horses pushing past one another at a trot or even a gallop—on unfamiliar terrain; Kagaya-hime watched and could not see what they accomplished by risking their horses' legs in this way.

Other games involved archery—shoot at that fencepost, shoot at this twig, see if you can slice the fuzz from a rabbit's tail without hurting the rabbit. They also involved talk and bursts of laughter, and mock arguments: "You first, and then I'll put my arrow through yours." — "That rabbit there? Let's see his hat marker. He's not high enough ranked for me, but he'll do for you." — For in battle everyone wore a wood tag attached to his *eboshi* cap, to make severed heads easier to identify, one assumes.

The day was beautiful. The sun was warm on Kagaya-hime's back, but when she crossed into shade she shivered, for the air was still cold. They crossed into Mutsu province in the morning, leaving Hitachi road for a new road: another stage between her and the Tōkaidō's irascible kami. Mutsu road was as unimpressive and variable as its predecessors had been, widening to a broad lane of drying mud when it passed through villages, deteriorating to a single dirty band where it crossed the hills.

The road was littered with signs of other travelers: worn straw sandals and hoof-covers, ox and horse droppings; torn paper that once protected something; a discarded lantern, its wood frame irreparable. Occasionally the band met others, who always stepped aside or wheeled their carts into the new growth along the road and stared up at the men and their horses as they loped past. "Look!" a child said as Kagaya-hime passed: "A girl! Why is she—" but she did not hear the end of his question, already far behind.

Everywhere smelled of sun on earth and new growing things.

Biter seemed content to amble forward in the straggling line of horses and men. Kagaya-hime sat him easily, the heavy weight of her armor (though she did not yet wear her helmet or shoulder guards) eased where it rested against the saddle. She watched the land pass, and the attendants running over fields or hills to retrieve the arrows of their masters' monkey-games; and she was close to content.

When they stopped for the night, Kagaya-hime saw other monkey-games in how the men chose the places they would tie their horses and lie down to sleep. They all knew what it was to sleep on the ground and they were frankly uninterested in doing so whenever they could avoid it; but the farms and temples and shrines here were loyal to the Osa Hitachi and Seiwa Minamoto, and Takase did not choose to inconvenience (and possibly antagonize: loyalties in the north might as well be written on water) anyone by appropriating foods and roofs for his own people. Instead, dry patches and tree-sheltered knolls were claimed; campfires sprang up, and the smell of food filled the air.

Kagaya-hime threaded her way through them all, unwilling to play the games (which are as pointless to a cat as they are to a woman), but fascinated with the men's loud voices, their jokes and profanities and boasts. Takase and Kitsune and their attendants shared a fire, a little away from the others, and when she passed them, Takase gestured her over: "Have your people set up here." He returned to his conversation with Kitsune.

"I don't—" Kagaya-hime began, and then she realized she *did* have people. Two attendants had been walking beside her horse for some time; she had not noticed this, for she had been full of her own thoughts. Their presence had seemed as natural as Biter's had on that day she'd first found him.

One of these attendants brushed past her with a quick, per-functory bow, and setting down his pack started to unload rice and dried fish, striking up a conversation with the other servants as if he had known them for some time: a man of average size, neither handsome nor homely, dressed in sensible travel clothes, a peasant's straw rain cape thrown over one shoulder.

The other attendant was, amazingly, a woman: again, of average size and attractiveness, dressed in men's garb, but with a servant-girl's thick, short hair and a ready laugh in her eyes. Bowing, she eased Biter's reins from Kagaya-hime's slackened grasp, and led him toward the river, alternately cooing in his ear and exchanging greetings and insults with the other servants: the first person (if one did not count Kagaya-hime) that Biter had ever allowed to touch him.

Over the months, Kagaya-hime had learned that other people did not find that useful items (such as servants) magically appeared when needed. — Indeed, it is not common save for princesses.

I have had this experience myself, especially lately. I awaken, and there is a new woman waiting beside my bed. Without a word spoken, she helps me upright and to my chamber box, as if she has done this all her life, and mine. Dazed with sleep, I am not sure whether she is truly new, or I just do not remember her. My age is the standard excuse for my uncertainty; but as an excuse it is more convenient than true. I do not remember them all, because there have been so many of them, scores or hundreds of interchangeable women who have attended me over the decades. A few remain vivid to me because their intelligence or charm or opinions made them intriguing companions.

It is more than servants and attendants, of course. If I need a new writing brush, it appears. Leaf-shaped paper, ink sticks, sesame-seed tea, coals for the braziers, clean under robes: these things materialize as if I had prayed to some god and found him in an accommodating mood. Often I do not realize the need is there until it is met.

I know that the world is not like this for other people—if they run out of rice they must somehow acquire more—though I have no idea how this might be done. I put down my brush and ask my companion, "If you ran out of rice, what would you do?"

"My lady?" Shikujo is the girl whose marriage is so unsatisfying (though she is nearly thirty now: no girl), my visitor from the provinces. We are the only two awake: even Shigeko has returned to her bed where she can sleep off the remnants of her *kaze*-cold.

"Rice," I say again. "If you were to run out—in your household, I mean—what would you do?"

"Have more brought in," she says.

"How?" I ask.

"Send the servants for it, I suppose. I'm not sure what you're asking me, my lady."

I sigh. Of course she doesn't understand: Shikujo is nearly as artificial a creature as I am. Neither of us could feed or clothe ourselves if others did not supply the food and silk—and this goes on, layers and layers, for our attendants need attendants, and so on, all the way down to the person who actually knows how to husk rice or peel the cocoons of silkworms. But that person is as distant from my experience as she would be from a cat wandering in the northlands.

Kagaya-hime has no idea how to make fabric and cannot grow sweet potatoes. Her clothing, food, horse—and now servants— all come from the gods (or me, actually, for I am the kami of this tale). I had not thought of it before this, but it is not an accident she is called *hime*, princess.

My woman Shigeko came to me as suddenly as a sneeze. This was some months before my father died and my half-brother the emperor summoned me to court, so I must have been fourteen. I was officially a woman, but I was still awkward as a boy, all long strides and loud laughs, apt to hang around the gardeners and carry dead vermin into my rooms in my (usually filthy) sleeves.

I despised my foster father's and uncle's wives and even my own women. They had no intellect, no wit to follow my reasoning about the relations between butterflies and moths, or robins and sparrows. They did not read Chinese, or at least were careful never to be caught doing so. They cared about stupid things: *monogatari* tales; the endless stream of poetry that flowed, drab and steady as river water, from their brushes; the shapes of their eyebrows; the low quality of the silks from Mikawa province in recent years; who was having a baby, by whom, and when and why.

I would never pluck *my* eyebrows; they would never get me to care whether my robes were the correct shades of peach, and not unseasonable rose. Any husband I might get (and I did not care whether I ever had one, not knowing yet the tricky exchanges of power that demand marriage of a princess) would have to accept all this. I am sure that I was as thoroughly a burden to my family as ever they were to me.

It was early in the year, when water left in a cup overnight skins over with ice. I had escaped the woman who was nominally in charge of my behavior by the simple expedient of lying to her face. "Off to the outhouse," I said and bowed, unwilling to let her see my face. Really, I thought, she was as stupid as hens—they all were. And I spent the morning in the pine-and-cypress grove where I had once found my half-brother longing for his consort. There were beetles there, even in the cold.

I only came back when I was hungry, and my feet were so cold that I stumbled in my clogs. There was the usual flurry of activity and complaints. I ignored these as I always did, though I was grateful for the padded robes the women wrapped around me, and the brazier I knelt beside.

There was a new girl, tall and not much older than I was. Even I could see that her robes were simpler than those of the other attendants, the silks less valuable; but somehow, her manner made this look perfectly correct, and the others slightly fussy and overdressed. Her face was hardly pretty—perhaps the reason she was being sent off to attend me, and not married to someone who might improve her family's situation—but I thought it interesting. Most new girls were shy about meeting a daughter of the emperor, watching me with anxious eyes until forced forward by someone more experienced; but she knelt apart reading—some romance, no doubt, I thought with contempt.

And then I noticed my notebook was missing—I was interested in wing-shapes back then; I expect it was the gray dogshead-silk

one, filled with drawings of birds' wings—and knew somehow
that this was what she was reading.

"You, girl," I snapped out. She approached and bowed correctly, but I saw her finger still keeping her page. "Give me that."

She bowed again as she laid it before me, but she did not
retreat as another might have. "You must still be cold. Let me stir
up the fire, my lady."

I watched her use iron sticks to mound the coals. She was
right: I was still cold. I tapped the notebook's cover with one finger. "What were you doing with this?"

She tipped her head to one side, still intent on the sparking
heap. "I wanted to see what sort of mistress I was getting."

"And what have you decided?" I said, my voice arrogant to
conceal my sudden embarrassment.

She leaned forward and opened the notebook, finding a page.
I am right: it *was* the gray notebook, because I remember an outstretched wing drawn with a fine brush. Conscious of a stranger's
eyes on it, I squinted at the drawing. It looked wrong now. I had
made the largest feathers too long, I knew suddenly.

"I learned," she said, "that you need someone else's eyes on you."

Startled, I looked up. She added, "—to keep you honest. You
are too accustomed to things being easy for you."

I felt as though the floor had collapsed under me, as if she and I
were alone, sprawled in the dirt. How dare she see me so clearly?
"I could send you home in disgrace," I said, thinking about it.

"Yes," she said, and for the first time, I saw the shyness behind
the bravado. "But I would like to stay, my lady."

"Why?" I asked baldly.

"I—would like to serve you."

"Why, if I am so flawed?" I asked again, but she only blushed
and shook her head, and did not answer, even after I pressed her.

A conversation with Shigeko never really begins nor ends;
more accurately, it began the day we met, and will end the day I
die. One of us says something, and we are distracted, by a letter
or the moon's rising or a bat that has found its way under the

eaves. Later, or the next day, or the next month, we return to that thought. Perhaps years go by. Some questions are never answered: we have learned to leave silent places in this forty-year wandering conversation, and in what we know of one another.

On the other hand, I can't sleep. "Shigeko," I bark.

I am curled in my sleeping robes, trying not to drip ink anywhere while I use this not-very-practical portable writing desk. Shigeko lies burrowed into her duck's-down padded robes beside me. She has always been a messy sleeper, making a nest like a mouse. I can tell from her breathing that she is not sleeping tonight, either.

"My lady?" She rolls to her side and leans on an elbow looking up at me. Her hair is neatly tied, but strands have strayed free and catch moonlight and lamplight, silver and copper. She looks as translucent and fragile as a jade Kannon.

"Why did you stay with me?" I do not say: *when you first came*. So many years in a single conversation: we no longer find it necessary to complete our thoughts.

She wraps her arms around her knees like a girl. I can't remember the last time I could do that, even though she is older than I. "Because I knew I could not bear not to be with you."

"Ah." I had expected any of a thousand answers, but not so deep an honesty.

She continues: "You were kind, I could see; and always thinking. Your women all loved you—love you still—there had to be a reason, I knew. I remember thinking how brave you were."

"I?" I say, startled. "Brave?"

She looks sidelong at me, smiling a little. "You're thinking you've never done anything brave. But, my lady, I saw you that first day, trapped in these rooms, pacing like a fox trapped in a storehouse, born under a thousand thousand rules; and I knew that it took bravery to be happy, with all that."

"You have lived exactly the same life," I say.

Her smile grows wider. "I did not say you were the only brave one."

I have to laugh.

*   *   *

All my life I have longed to see the Shirakawa barrier, at the border to Mutsu province. As a child I imagined it would be a fabulous place, with towers as tall as cedars, built of jade and turquoise and guarded by strong-armed men and horses that breathed fire. As I grew older and moderated my daydreams somewhat, I altered this vision to walls of thousand-year oak, and slender fierce guards with eyes like Mononobe no Dōmei.

I have never been, and now will never go, to the Shirakawa barrier and beyond, into Mutsu province. And now I cannot visit it even here, in Kagaya-hime's story. I had thought I controlled this tale, but if that were the case I would demand, "Everyone must now travel Mutsu road, along the banks of Abukama river," and it would be so. But Seiwa Minamoto no Takase, old and wily, gives other orders and I find I cannot naysay him. He must bring his band to the estate where Kitsune's brother was killed, which is three hundred miles north, in the heart of the Abe clan's lands, and he must do this without drawing undue attention. Mutsu road is much too frequented, so instead he slips through the less-visited Nakoso barrier to the east and travels the sea road, with mountains to his left and the great ocean to his right.

Kagaya-hime will not see Shinobu rock, where white silk left overnight flushes rose-red and amber. She will miss the fields of *susuki* grass at Kasashima, subject of so many really rather uninteresting poems. She will never see the two-trunked pine of Takekuma; she will not cross the bridge over Natorigawa river, built of wood from a previous incarnation of the sacred pine.

The war band paces off its miles, always within hearing of the ocean: sometimes hushed like the wind in firs, at others a crashing din, louder than a peasant couple hurling pots at one another. There are estates and villages, of course, but those who live by the sea have their own concerns and alliances. They do not care about the disagreements of those whose hair is not whitened with salt-rime. The war band travels quickly and comparatively silently, and no one rides ahead to warn the Abe clan.

The men of the war band will pass the provincial capital of Taga in fives and tens, secretly and at night, so as not to draw the attention of the governor and military there. They will travel nearly a hundred miles in a fortnight — and none of it will be the Mutsu province of my dreams.

Kagaya-hime called the servants Uona and Otoko. No one seemed to find it worthy of comment that they had appeared like dew, without warning, and that Uona was a woman.

Kagaya-hime had no difficulty keeping up with the war band. She belonged to no squad and shared allegiance with no one, so she left the group often and roved far ahead and down side-paths, bringing back deer and wild calves and birds.

Even her skills did not prevent many of the men from viewing Kagaya-hime's presence with distaste, though most could not have said why they did not care for her. I have noticed this before, that there are people who simply do not care for cats, and many of these people are men. There are also men who do not care for women (except in the most rudimentary ways); and still more men who dislike women who like men-things, water-clocks and war among them. She did not talk of her family, of course, so perhaps she had been disgraced or even exiled. And (the men said), she was probably not even from one of the bow-and-arrow clans, the only excuse anyone (let alone a woman) could have to mess around with weapons and such. Kagaya-hime was cat and warrior and woman, and she was also strange; the members of the war band could sense this, even if they could not identify it.

Days passed, and miles, and landmarks. The war band made camp under stars and rain clouds and the roofs of abandoned farmhouses. Because life is full of such minor catastrophes, sad-dle-frames cracked and bags of rice burst: evenings were spent repairing things and sharpening arrows. The men determined their hierarchy, and the monkey-games settled into jokes and posturing, repeated until they became little rituals. The joke about rabbits' hat markers became dogma: every insect met along the road was asked for its marker.

Kagaya-hime continued to share Kitsune's and Takase's fire. It was a busy place. When the evenings were dry enough, the captains assembled and debriefed the day. Most of the rest of the time Kitsune and Takase were deep in plans. Kagaya-hime said little; but she listened, and watched Takase, and smelled the ever-present infection in the old arrow-wound in his side. Takase in his turn watched her, as he watched all his troops.

Kagaya-hime grew used to Uona and Otoko. They were good servants, quiet, efficient, and very loyal. Otoko got into fights with the other attendants, defending Kagaya-hime. Uona was a storyteller, perhaps the best of the war band. On fine nights, the other servants gathered around to listen to her tell the story of the daughter of the moon, or the fox-wife and the Kannon; but she refused to tell tales in the presence of people who had criticized her mistress.

Most of the men distrusted or feared Kagaya-hime, or tried not to think of her at all. (Nearly everyone hides from the thing we do not understand—death, for example.) But one or two wondered to themselves who—or what—she was. She could shoot a swift from the sky, and she never lost an arrow. She said little, yet the commander and his war leader kept her close, shared their fire with her. She appeared tireless. Even by the eastern provinces' high standards for horses Biter was exceptionally fine (if fractious)—a dragon of a horse. Her servants were exemplary.

I have said that the war band was men, but there was another woman attached, the priestess Onobe no Kesuko. A war band needs priests as much as it needs weapons, and Kesuko served a shrine to Hachiman in Omi province, which owed a certain loyalty to Takase and had sent her when he requested their benison. She was a severe woman, younger than I (but not by so very much), slim and rough-edged as sword-grass. She wore women's robes and a travel cloak and basket-hat that concealed her face

from the raff and scaff of the war band. She and her party kept
much to themselves, for they could not afford to compromise
their ritual purity; but she often came to Takase's fire to offer
advice. Kagaya-hime did not like Kesuko, but she understood her
better than she did any of the others with whom she traveled, for
Kesuko's cold manners reminded her of the cousins and aunts she
had lost.

Kesuko and Kagaya-hime circled one another warily. But on
the fourth night of travel (roofless under a cloud-stained sky, on
the mashed young stems of a trampled buckwheat field), Kesuko
stopped by Kagaya-hime, who remained by the fire as the captains left the nightly council, playing idly with a thick silk tassel
from Biter's bridle. "Come," Kesuko said.

Even the daughter of an emperor does not comfortably say no
to a priest of the myriad gods; and Kagaya-hime was not experienced with generating quickly the excuses that might have been
palatable to Kesuko or her kind (as a princess is; over the many
years I have grown proficient with such lies). Kagaya-hime only
nodded and stood, handing the tassel to Uona.

Typically Kagaya-hime navigated the encampment's chaos as a
cat passes through unfamiliar ground: remaining at its fringes,
moving from safety to safety. Kesuko moved as a tiger might, walking a straight line across the ground, men and animals scattering
before her, sidestepping only for the fires themselves. Kesuko led
Kagaya-hime directly to the stream: once clear, now churned the
frothy brown of certain teas. "Sit," she ordered, and Kagaya-hime,
who disliked orders (in truth, barely understood what they might
be), found herself sitting on a rough cold rock beside the water.

Kesuko nodded. "Now. What are you?"

Kagaya-hime turned her face away but watched the priestess
sidelong from the corner of one eye. "I am nothing and no one.
They call me Kagaya-hime. I will fight."

"No doubt these are all true," Kesuko said. "But you do not
answer my question."

Kagaya-hime looked her directly in the face. "Why should I

tell you anything? Seiwa Minamoto no Takase is commander here. I do what I wish."

The priestess thought for a moment, seemed to make a decision, and sat down on a different rock, some feet away. "No, I think you do what you must. Your wishes have nothing to do with it."

If Kagaya-hime had still been a cat, she would have hissed and shown her claws, for Kesuko saw too much: a threat, if not a physical one. "My *fudoki*—my ground, my tale—is gone. And now I have lost my body, my claws, and teeth." She gestured at herself, a short angry sweep of her clenched fist. "Ask your gods what I am; they know better than I."

Perhaps Kesuko understood Kagaya-hime's defensive flare, for she changed the subject, tipped her head from side to side as if listening to the cracking behind her ears. "I am never going to get my neck stretched out. I slept wrong the first night out, and now—this." She rubbed the cords of her neck. "There are eight million gods. Eight million million gods. They do not all speak to one another, or with me. I ask because I must know: are you a risk to Seiwa Minamoto no Takase, or this campaign, or the men of this band?"

"I am dangerous," Kagaya-hime said, "but not to these men, unless they threaten me."

Kesuko nodded her head. "That is fair. A question that follows is: are *they* a danger to *you*? It is hard to be a woman and travel with so many men."

"Because they will mate with me?" Kagaya-hime asked. "Men have tried."

"Unsuccessfully, I expect." Kesuko's eyes glimmered with what might have been a smile. "Rape is the least of the dangers. No: we are all killers here. Even I ask the gods to let us kill, and I carry this"—she touched her sword's hilt—"on the chance that I will do so, as well. Remain with us, and you lose the chance to be otherwise."

"I will cope," Kagaya-hime said.

Kesuko stood. "Will you? These men all think they will cope, as well. I have seen much fighting, girl, and I know this: most will stay to fight, because they do not wish their friends to die if they can be there to stop it. Some will find they have no taste for killing, or even fighting. Others will like it too well and will flee from this mirror to their souls, or remain to drown themselves in the killing rage. Which will you be?"

"I have killed before," Kagaya-hime said. "I will do so again."

"I still have not made myself clear. If you stay, if you fight and wound and kill—why will you have done this? Loyalty to Seiwa Minamoto no Takase or the Osa Hitachi? You had not met them a season ago. Loyalty to the men of your campfire? To protect your family, your friends?"

"I kill because it is what I have left," Kagaya-hime said.

"A dangerous path, girl," Kesuko said. "There is always more." Before Kagaya-hime could ask anything, she strode away.

I have had a bellyful of priests in recent days. I have made no secret of my plans to retreat to Kasugano and become a nun; for some reason this has brought priests and monks and nuns out in force to reassure me that I do a virtuous thing; that rebirth awaits me; that my story does not end, but only moves into a new notebook. —Rebirth or the True Land: whenever followers of different sects gather here, they start bickering over doctrine. I am not sure whether the new notebook they mention is my move to Kasugano, or death.

I have been telling everyone that I look forward to serving Buddha for the rest of my life. It is the proper thing to say, like: *I will love you forever,* and: *I care about poetry.* But I think that I am more honest if I say that what I look forward to are negatives. I look forward to not waking up each morning within these infinitely familiar screens. I look forward to having my hair cut, so that it does not take a day and a night to dry, to wearing robes that do not bow my shoulders with their weight. No intrigue. No late nights spent trying to show interest in something other than my bed. I do not long to move *toward* Buddha, only away from everything else. I have a feeling this decreases my virtue in becoming one of the Kasugano nuns.

I am not tired of life—I do not want to die; there are days when I shut myself in my sleeping enclosure and cry in sheer rage, aware that my body will betray me in the end—but oh, I am so tired of *this* life. These walls, this sky. How can I die when I have seen so little?

I think of the priests and monks and nuns because a priestess sent by Ise shrine has been with me today. She can't be more than twenty years of age; too young, I would have thought, to speak for the kami. She is some sort of grandniece or cousin's child, though I cannot remember exactly how we are related.

All my other women were gone—even Shigeko, off bidding farewell to my visitor from the provinces, who is leaving court for her monthly courses (one of the advantages to growing old has been that I no longer must relocate so frequently). The priestess knelt with me and drank tea and ate little cakes made of sweet rice and liana syrup. She is extraordinarily graceful. I wonder why her parents permitted her to be sent to the shrine, for she could have married with great success, I think.

I found the visit comforting, for it comes with no promises, no exhortations, no differences of dogma. Unlike all the Buddhas, the kami have no great lessons for me or, I think, for anyone. They simply are.

There was a day when my husband (well, husband-to-be) was considered old enough to wed. This was the year my half-brother retired from the throne, and handed it to his son, though the child (I should call him Horikawa, for he is dead now) was still quite young. I'm not sure why my half-brother did this, for he loved the work of ruling; did he really think he could be as happy retiring to one of his estates and concentrating on the sutras? In any case, he did not do so, for Horikawa was always frail and interested more in poetry than in matters of the court: if an emperor was to rule us, it would have to be a retired emperor.

Shirakawa retired to his residence south of the capital's walls, though he visited the capital often (it is only a mile, after all). I accompanied him when I could. It was a year or two after this, when we were at the southern residence, that my uncle told me that the boy he had selected for me was old enough to be wed.

I had been examining a dead crow Shigeko brought to me, and attempting to record the delicate feathering of its leg, the glossy scales that covered its clawed foot. It was of course highly improper that I bring any dead thing into the house of an emperor, retired or otherwise, but I salved my conscience by thinking of the fleas we all killed without compunction, even in his presence. If a flea (or a mosquito, or a louse) was acceptable, surely a crow, which everyone knew was a mere scavenger, could be only a little worse.

Mercifully, my uncle would not be allowed behind my curtain, so the dead bird and the mysterious stains I had somehow accumulated from its body would not be visible to him. "How old is he?" I asked absently.

I could see out, for the curtain was just transparent enough to allow this. I watched him shift his weight a little. He cleared his throat. "He is thirteen—but well built for his age. He had his manhood ceremony this spring."

I stifled a laugh, for I was then nearly thirty. Well, perhaps he would be interested in dead birds: children often were. It was arranged that I would go to my uncle's house for a time, and the boy—"man"—would come to me there.

It was the sixth month when he first visited. The convention is that visits between men and women are serendipitous; he and she are admiring the moon in the same courtyard; or he passes her house on a rainy night and seeks shelter; or he idly accompanies a friend visiting another woman in the same rooms. Of course my uncle and I—and everyone in the house, I expect—knew the day and time he was expected to arrive; but none of us were allowed to admit it.

Even as she pretended there was nothing special to the night,

Shigeko dressed me with special care that evening. I remember my robes were yellow and sea-green gauze, the outermost woven with a pattern of waves (I'm sure we'll find them in one of the trunks we haven't yet emptied)—and she refused to let me do anything that might possibly dirty the pale silk. Forced inactivity is never comfortable; I fidgeted from place to place, and tried to interest myself in a collection of poems that was popular in court just then.

He arrived at the dog's hour, along with a little army of male friends and attendants, my uncle's son among them. It was understood (if not mentioned) that my cousin had invited him to drink wine in one of the garden's pavilions—my uncle being conveniently away, busy with something or other at court. My suitor would somehow end up, not there, but on the verandas of my rooms, and it would all be very charming and poetic, and he would eventually end up in my bed.

Everything happened as predicted. The men had been drinking together, so they were somewhat more ribald than I had expected; but by the rat's hour, most of the men wilted off to other assignations; and my husband-to-be was behind my curtains. Dim light conceals much—age and youth, flaws and tics—but he looked a mere infant to me, too young to have had his trouser ceremony. Thirteen was far younger than I had remembered. His face had the perfect roundness of beauty—or baby-fat. He was elegantly dressed—no doubt some attendant had fussed over him as obsessively as Shigeko had over me. We exchanged a few conventional poems. He was as uninspired as I in creating them, which made me hope his attention was focused on some other, more interesting topic—moths, perhaps, or Chinese medicine: something we might share after marriage. I had never heard that he was an intellectual, but I knew almost nothing about him.

The lovemaking was as inept—and incomplete—as might be expected. The sky was already growing pale and he would need to leave before daylight, so we did not have much time. He smirked at me (thirteen! a horrible age) as he fumbled at my sash, trying to untie what was a very simple knot and succeeding only in tangling it past remedy.

I realized suddenly that, had I wed the first husband my uncle found for me (the one who died of smallpox), I might well have a son his age. With this came a certain sympathy. Here the poor child was, trying to impress a woman more than twice his age, his future wife, the daughter and sister and aunt of emperors. He was probably intimidated by my sexual experience (which was not inconsiderable) and simply overdoing it in an attempt to seem worldly. I tried not to sigh out loud, but I allowed him to paw me through my robes until he left at dawn.

After he left I surprised everyone, including myself, by vomiting until my throat burned and my muscles ached. Shigeko attributed this to nerves.

For the wedding to be finalized, he would visit me for the next two nights and stay late the third, and we would share wine. And then it would all be over, "and we can go back to what we were," Shigeko said, comfortingly.

Pah. I cannot bear to think of him just now. My cat and her journey are a welcome distraction from unpleasantness.

Mutsu province is a patchwork of estates that offer loyalty to any of a dozen or more great men or monasteries or temples, most of them a very long way away. Some of these estates are nothing at all, only uncut forest and fields that have been allowed to grow over and vanish back into the countryside. The farther from Hitachi province the war band came, the fewer Osa Hitachi estates and farms there were and the less certain their loyalty; and once they had passed the provincial capital Taga, there were barely a handful. This was why Nakara's brother had come here in the first place, to solidify influence in the region.

At the same time, the Abe estates grew more common, and more directly linked—for alliances and allegiances are not as simple as I am pretending. There are layers of loyalties, overt or hidden, and nuances of promise and oath, and the *only-if*s and *what-if*s

of conditional alliance. It is hard to say, "This household is loyal to
the Abe," because the household may simultaneously be loyal to
the Onobe, who are enemies of the Abe; and to the Tendai temple
at Taga, which hates both Onobe and Abe. In the end a household's loyalty is to itself—and to the emperor, of course.

Still, at some point beyond Taga the war band's journey
crossed an invisible barrier. Beyond it, the estates they passed (or
passed through) became what might now be considered enemies,
with loyalties to the Abe, and not to Osa Hitachi or Takase or to
any of the men who traveled with the war band. The men knew
now that whoever they met was an enemy, or might as well be,
and the lack of ambiguity was a relief of sorts.

Takase, Kitsune, and Kagaya-hime spent more of their time
listening to reports from scouts. From time to time Kagaya-hime
and Biter went exploring and brought back information of their
own. She knew little and cared less about the spiderweb of politics, so she brought back news of useful wells and flooded river-
fords—phenomena of interest to a traveling cat.

10. THE CHANG-AN NOTEBOOK

I have been ill for several weeks—so tired, so very tired. The thing that fills my chest and leaves no room for breath evidently left room for a *kaze*-cold of sorts, for I found myself coughing out gobbets of dull green matter, and even blood. Shigeko moved me from the palace, of course—dying here would have been bad for the palace's purity—taking me to her family's residence on Konoe avenue, since her family is one of the few exalted enough to host a princess. The coughing (and the gobbets) eased, though they have not abandoned me; but they left in their place a terrible pain, as if I inadvertently coughed out some vital organ. Still, I am accustomed to pain of many sorts, and this is not what will kill me.

Perhaps I should have gone to Kasugano rather than return to the palace. Shigeko was surprised—I suspect she is looking forward to the simplicity of life there, of a life after I am gone—but I found I could not. The emptying of my trunks is only half-finished. I recently found a little teakwood cabinet filled with letters exchanged with one of my half-sisters when she was in retreat at Ise. She was prolific (as was I, it seems), and for some days I amused myself by hearing the echoes of her voice as Shigeko read the letters to me, one after the other. What other letters, memories, remain in those trunks?

And another reason: I did not want to leave this unfinished, these notebooks of my life. Writing is a habit into which I have fallen. It is hard to break.

And so five days ago (was it? I am not sure, for I have been sleeping such odd hours lately, tucked deep in my rooms away from daylight and stars) I returned here. Since then I have slept, and stared into the coals of my brazier (will I ever be warm again?). Today is the first day I have tried to write, and even these few lines have required that I rest three times.

Shigeko has watched me write and write and write—over the years, yes, but also here, in all these once-blank notebooks. She has seen how hard writing is for me, just now, and she has finally asked me what I write.

"Memories," I tell her. "Dreams."

"Why?" she asks. "You have all your old diaries"—though this is no longer true; many have already been picked apart and fed to the flames of braziers like this one.

"It is something to do," I say. I do not tell her that I write because I must, because the price of my life is telling this story, if only to myself. If I die without telling it, I die in debt, and I will never be able to move into the Pure Land.

She does not ask more, not tonight, but no conversation between us truly ends.

There was a day when they were at last very close to their goal, and Kitsune took a handful of men and rode ahead to survey the situation at the Osa Hitachi estate. It had rained for three days, and the band had camped on steep pine-covered slopes that offered cover from the interminable tap-tap-tap of the rain—but only in exchange for irregular gouts of water that gathered and then dropped from the branches—the difficult choice between a steady small evil and a sporadic great one. Takase was not allowing patrols, so Kagaya-hime remained close to camp, and vented her irritation at being cold and wet by throwing knives into the soft bark of a yew, again and again at the place where she had seen a beetle, though nothing remained of the beetle and very little of the wood where it had walked. Biter stood under the thick rice-straw rain blanket Otoko had made for him, snapping idly at anyone who came within reach. The morning and the afternoon dripped on; and then dusk, made drab by the heavy skies. Takase sat back on his heels in silence beside the fire, absently rubbing his ancient arrow-wound. He said little, and Kagaya-hime said less. Cats and commanders know how to wait.

Kitsune did not return until shortly after full dark had fallen. Kagaya-hime woke from a doze when she heard horses walking and soft voices. Kitsune dismounted slowly, and handed his reins to a servant, then stumbled to the fire and sank back onto his heels. He was soaked through: gold and orange firelight glistened on his wet face. The horses and other riders moved away. There was a stranger with the group, a peasant by his looks, who remained near Kitsune just at the edge of the light, squatting under an immense rain hat. Peasants also know how to wait.

Takase had been sleeping beside the fire, but with the arrival he eased himself upright, and coughed and spat on the ground. "Well, boy. I didn't expect you'd find your way back through the trees until morning."

Takase's attendants always had water heated at camp (an old man — or woman — is offered such courtesies); now they poured it onto tea leaves and handed cups to their master and Kitsune. He smelled of horses and wet silks and sweat and exhaustion — and tears, Kagaya-hime realized. He was crying: that was the water on his face.

Takase watched him for a moment. "Well, and — ?" he said, and his voice was more gentle than Kagaya-hime had heard before.

Kitsune did not look up from the cup he cuddled in his hands. His voice was almost too low to hear, even in the quiet camp. "I knew they burned it," he said, "that they killed him; my nephews, my baby niece — everyone. I knew it. — And it was nearly a year ago." A tear slipped from his face, a gold flash in the light before it fell into his cup. "We got there at midday, maybe the horse's hour. Some of the buildings are just gone, just charcoal. Farmers have been breaking up some of the structural timbers, burning

what's left in their ovens. The main house is about half-ruined. —
They're keeping mares in it nights, to protect them from wolves.
My brother's house." He looked up suddenly. "It's almost a year,
now. It still smells like smoke."

"Like kitchen fires and sulfur," Kagaya-hime said. She remembered the burned grounds on Nijō avenue, the cats with burning
eyes that might have been real or might have been ghosts. "And
death." Her nails were biting into her palms. She flexed her
hands, trying to relax, and saw Takase and Kitsune looking at
her. "I have seen it," she said. "My *fudoki*. My aunts and cousins —
that is how we died."

"Well," Takase said again. "What's the situation there, boy?
Where are the Abe?"

Kitsune rubbed his eyes. "The main force went back north in
the autumn, but there's still one of the family here, the fourth son
and his family; and a cousin. They're not rebuilding; they ride
over from an estate a few miles away to check on things." He gestured at the peasant, still crouched out of the fire's circle of
warmth. "Mori here knows more. He served my brother before —"
His voice trailed off.

"You," Takase barked at the man. "Come here." The farmer
crept forward, forehead nearly to the ground. "Where is this
other place?"

"That way," the peasant said and pointed into the darkness
without looking up. "Two miles east and north of my master's old
estate. Ten miles from here."

"You have been there?"

The man nodded.

"Who is there?"

"Abe no Juro—that is the fourth son, my lord; his cousin—
families and servants—thirty horsemen—" The peasant looked
up doubtfully. "And the servants, and all the locals."

Takase looked up at the sky, as if he could see stars and moon
through the dripping clouds. "It's still early," he said, "the rat's
hour or thereabout—"

The peasant pressed his face to the wet dirt again. "The boar's hour, my lord." Peasants can often tell such things.

Takase said, "Early, at any rate. We can be there long before dawn and attack while they sleep, before they've heard we're here."

Kitsune stood, his eyes flat in the firelight. "Attack them. Yes."

"Lords—" The peasant's voice sounded as though it had been wrung from him. "Please. My sister and her husband serve there. They have children."

"So did my brother have children," Kitsune said.

"My sister did not burn your brother's family," the peasant said, as sharply as he dared. "Please, let me send her word. She will leave and never say a thing, I swear it."

"No," Takase said. "She would have friends, and she would tell them. It must be this way."

"Then they are dead," the peasant said and turned his face away, toward the darkness and the rain.

There were few guards on the estate, the inhabitants evidently trusting to the wet night as their best protection. Forerunners found only three men standing under trees. Their senses numbed by the steady rain and the late hour, they died silently, perhaps without even realizing they died.

The war books I read so long ago were full of elaborate strategies with names that sound like sexual positions from a Chinese handbook; but on the night I listened to the old warriors from Yoshiee's war, I learned that the commonest strategies are the simplest. Ambush: night attacks: destroying a bridge so the enemy cannot approach: out-and-out flight.

Burning an enemy's household while he sleeps is popular, as well. The guards gone, Takase found it simple to arrange his war band around the main buildings of the estate. The horses he left out of earshot, for they had picked up their riders' excitement and could not be trusted to stay silent.

Not everyone was asleep, of course. There is always some old woman with aching bones, or a mother soothing her colicky baby, or a man full of wine shifting restlessly, his bladder full. But they were unlucky this night, or cursed. Everyone stayed inside and no one heard the Osa Hitachi men take their positions. The dogs must have heard, and the geese with which farms are always infested, but they said nothing—or perhaps did not hear, after all, over the rain.

Kagaya-hime's eyes were better than the men's, but there was little to see: the buildings and the men brought for this attack were just variations in the darkness, more felt than seen. Takase was a black bulk a few steps from her. When he spoke, his voice was low: "Bring the torches." The order was passed until she lost it in the rain. A moment later, lights dull as fox-fire bobbed toward the heavy mass of the main house: torches guttering in the rain. The torchbearer nearest her was Osa Hitachi no Kitsune. Watching to ensure his fire did not die, he walked carefully, feeling his way over the puddled ground. Tiny red lights flicked across his face. Kagaya-hime thought about the dream-thing of eyes and flames, the killing rage, and recognized it in Kitsune. She did not recognize the other torchbearers, but guessed that they, too, had lost family.

The main house was a typical rural building, thatched rather than tiled for warmth in the winters. The structure was raised on pillars, the roof far out of reach; but in one place the thatch had loosened over the winter and not yet been repaired. It hung down in a sloppy garland, like the frayed straw rope at a neglected shrine. Kitsune held his torch high beneath the overhang until the rice straw hissed as it dried, barely audible over the rain and the dripping trees. Dull red light licked certain stems, too weak to spread.

"Did it catch?" one man murmured to another, both nameless in the gloom. "Maybe he should—"

"Wait," the other said, and there was a noise, the soft sudden movement of air as new-dried straw burst into flames.

The men around Kagaya-hime took a simultaneous step as if pushed back by the light. Kitsune ducked backward, away from the sudden fire, and tossed the torch onto the roof. The clearing brightened as pillars of fire shot up elsewhere. "Now *that's* a light you can read by," one of the men said and laughed without humor. Kagaya-hime could see his intent face. They all had this look: the expression of a cat before she jumps.

They heard the first shout inside the main building: "Fire," and then, "Fire! The roof—look!" screams and disorder. People tumbled through the doorway, a woman and two children, one an infant. One of Takase's men shouted, "She's mine," and shot her in the belly, below the baby in her arms. She fell without a cry, dropping to her knees and then side. The child beside her stared stunned at the men outside until an arrow took him in the chest. He collapsed backward into a man and old woman stumbling out. The baby of the fallen woman started wailing as the man screamed. The old woman was silent for a single white-eyed moment before she turned to shout inside. "It's an attack. We're—"

She fell to the ground clutching the flesh around an arrow set fletching-deep into her thigh. "Well, shit," she said before the next arrow slashed into her face.

The flames were young, bright and enormous as funeral pyres, though black smoke and glowing steam obscured them in places. Sparks showered the clearing; it was only when one landed on her face that Kagaya-hime realized that some were drops of rain catching the light.

The men of the war band howled, fierce as wolves, eyes shining flat and pale. They shot everything that came through the door, and after a time no one tried to escape that way except fowl and a terrified dog with a great dirty burn along its flank.

This was how it had been for her home, for the cats of Kagaya-hime's tale—not the arrows but the fire, the thatch collapsing, the agonizing death, the impossibility of escape. She had lost everything in fire; but this did not make her merciful. She killed people as they ran out, and when they stopped coming she shot arrow after arrow into the flaming door, as if to kill those still inside. Perhaps this was mercy of a kind; no one had offered the cats of her *fudoki* so quick a death.

This is the way of war—of this war, anyway. Perhaps somewhere in the world, among the barbarians beyond India or across the great ocean, there are civilized wars with rules of engagement and judges to determine proper behavior. Perhaps strategies are clever and complicated and minimize unnecessary deaths. Perhaps the only people who die are warriors sent to the scene of battle for no other purpose than to kill or be killed. Perhaps there is somewhere that chroniclers can tell the plain truth about a battle without shocking even the most delicate of sensibilities.

But I rather doubt this. We are a civilized people, in our way (dare I say it?) more sophisticated even than China; and yet I cannot forget the stories of the men from Yoshiee's war. Even for us war is unpleasant; surely it must be more so elsewhere.

Kagaya-hime understands war, accepts it as I do not. Why would she not? She is a cat, a killer by nature. She has seen children killed before this: the males of her race have been known to kill the kittens of a *fudoki* when they claim its territory. Perhaps this is the way of all males, to kill. They have no *fudoki* and so all that is left to them is life and death and their children. But I am forgetting; this is Kagaya-hime I am speaking of. Human males, men—Dōmei—surely they are more than this.

The cries ceased after a time, or were drowned by the fire. The screaming infant that had been crying fell silent; the heap of bodies before the door smoked, smelled of cooking meat. The war band's shouts stopped, and as it became certain that there would be no last-ditch escape—no one was left alive in the buildings to attempt one—men left the fire. Some wept or vomited as they walked, or collapsed as if they had fought for their lives, or shivered as if ill or injured. Some stayed: Kagaya-hime, Kitsune, Takase, others.

"Why are they sick?" she asked Takase. A man—the one who had laughed at the fire—had fallen to his knees, body wrenched with dry retching.

Takase turned to look at her, his expression harsh. "It takes some people this way. We've killed a lot of people."

"Wasn't that why you did this?"

He barked a humorless laugh. "Clever girl. We chose to kill them, but that doesn't mean we don't suffer for it."

"Why? You're alive, they're dead. This is what you wanted, and this is the way of things for you, is it not?" she asked: reasonably, she thought, but he eyed her as if she were a stranger found suddenly standing beside him.

"Yah," he said, and spat on the ground; smoke leaves a bitter taste in the mouth. "We watch death and imagine it as if it were ours, our comrades'. Because it could have been. Will be, someday."

"Is that why he vomits?"

"Maybe. Yes. No. Ask him, why don't you."

"Why don't they *all* turn away?" She gestured.

"Some lost family," Takase said. "They want to see these others die."

"It doesn't bring them back."

"You lost your family, girl. Didn't you want to kill someone, anyone, after that?" Takase rubbed his eyes. "Gah, I'll go blind from this smoke. There are people who love death, who kill because it fills them with joy."

"Oh, yes," Kagaya-hime said softly. "Because the killing reminds them that they, at least, are alive." A timber broke and collapsed inward, and a flame as tall as the trees shot up from the building's interior. They stood in silence for a while. "Why do you watch this?"

Takase said. "I watch because—" He gave a short laugh. "I'm dying; I might as well tell you the truth. I'm here because I'm better at war than at anything else."

"I also," Kagaya-hime said. Cat and commander understood one another.

Fire in the night: the priest from the nunnery has been with me, and tells me to contemplate the sutras when I cannot sleep, as happens increasingly. It is my salvation, he tells me: my hope for rebirth into enlightenment.

But tonight I cannot. It is the tenth month now (can I have written for two whole months? I recall beginning these notebooks in the eighth month). I have been cold for so long, but for some reason tonight, when winter's first frost glitters under the nearly full moon, I am sweltering as much as I did when my courses stopped, all those years ago. I do not hurt so much tonight, but earlier this evening the flush of heat drove me out walking a little, leaning on Shigeko until her back creaked. Now Shigeko sleeps, and I shift restlessly, pulling my sweat-sticky robes away from my skin.

Dōmei. His skin felt good, tasted better. Like any civilized man, he wore scent, and I remember he smelled of Chinese oranges and sandalwood; but beneath that was something rich as pheasant-meat, musky but sweet. I can remember it so vividly; if I close my eyes, it is so strong that I can imagine him in my room, and see him untying his *hakama*-trousers behind my eyelids. He looks across the room at me, his eyes glinting with humor and passion. My heart pounds; I am choked with longing, sweet and hot and tart, like biting into sun-warmed fruit. He always loved to touch my throat, even lay his cheek and lips against it as we made love. My hand (the memory of his hand) reaches up to touch my neck and I feel—this. Skin as fragile and furred and folded as much-used mulberry paper. This is an old woman's throat. My throat. Dōmei is gone, and I am dying, and I will never never never be young again and feel his touch.

In my secret heart, I curse all the gods and Buddhas who permitted me to become old, who let Dōmei go.

Dōmei could not sleep nights, or did not sleep well, at any rate. Dreams haunted him, dreams he could never (or chose never to) tell me when I awakened him, unsettled by the inarticulate sounds he made, the sweaty thrashing as he fought the bed robes.

It is not a bad thing to have a lover who does not sleep well, when he may only visit you in the hours between dusk and dawn. Nights, we made love frequently and slept seldom, and I dozed my days away. I wonder (now, with the wisdom that has nothing to do with contemplation and everything to do with age) whether we had sex so often and so enthusiastically because he wished to batter himself against my body until he was too exhausted to dream.

But there was a night I had forgotten until this moment. It was winter, and snow was falling. This numbed the air, muffled it as thoroughly as summer humidity ever did. I had a bet with Dōmei about making snow mountains, so two of my women and Dōmei's two attendants chased around the peony courtyard throwing up plumes as they pawed the snow into heaps. Dōmei and I and the rest of my attendants watched, feet close to the braziers we had brought onto the veranda. The men were faster and more efficient, of course, so I sent Shigeko out to assist my team. Dōmei protested the cheat, and when I only laughed and tossed my head, he waded into the snow himself, tossing snow between his legs, dog-style, onto his mountain.

So, improper as it was, I went out myself to regain the advantage for my side. Others of my women tumbled after me. Protesting through his laughter, Dōmei tossed a handful of snow my way, a slow bright cascade in the torches. And I tossed snow at him, and my women at the men and at one another, and soon the courtyard was filled with squeals and screeching, for all the world as if we were none of us old enough to be trusted with using ink. As with the mountain-building, at first the men had the advantage of us, but I learn quickly, and it was no time at all before I had realized that the snow threw farther and more accurately when compressed into firm balls the size of a fist. —Which is not to say I was any better at this than I had been at shooting arrows at a target: I missed far more often than I hit, and even then it was not usually what I aimed at.

Dōmei encouraged me to fling these balls at him, his laughter muffled, granted intimacy by the snow-filled air. He tossed his own carefully, close enough to incite me, distant enough not to strike me.

I tossed my balls of snow and learned: harder next time, and a little more to the right. I threw one so well that he was forced to duck. And the next time, when he was distracted by a snowball from Shigeko, I struck him solidly on the side of the face.

A face full of snow cannot be pleasant—snow crunched tight until it is hard as wood must hurt like being struck with a club. The snowball exploded into dust and smoke. Dōmei dropped into a crouch of sorts, then leapt toward me, hands out to strike, eyes unrecognizing. I dropped to my knees, preparing to die. He would not mean it. I knew this would be no more than the unconscious slap of a man at a mosquito, a dog snapping at a flea that had bitten it. But I would be dead anyway.

I closed my eyes but I did not die, instead heard him fall to his knees before me, heard horror in his voice as he whispered my name.

This was the end of the snow-games that night. I coaxed him to stay with me, behind my curtains for a while, because the look in his eyes had frightened me, and I needed to replace it in my memory with other, tenderer expressions. He stayed because—I don't know why he stayed. I loved him, lived in his sleeve (and he in mine) for a year and a season; and I think I never knew who he was. He was Dōmei, the man from the hinterlands. He was a wild animal come to stay in my garden for a time. I watched him and wondered, but I never understood.

Dōmei slept that night, though he did not often do so in my presence—slept and dreamt. I woke in the darkness, to the sound of a man crying, and it was him, sobbing as he slept. I cannot say what had happened to the lamp, the braziers, for we lay in a darkness like the inside of mourning sleeves. I called his name; when this did not awaken him, I touched his hand and then his cheek.

"What?" He thrashed awake.

"It's just I." When I stroked his face, I found it wet, and his body shaking. "What is it?"

"I was at the Moki estate, with my father—" The Moki estate: I knew this place from a casual allusion he made once to one of his attendants. The Mononobe clan and the Moki had fought; the Mononobe had won. "—and they were crying, all the women, inside the house. I heard them screaming."

"Hush, hush. It's all right. You're here now. You're awake."

"I was awake then, too, Harueme."

I barely breathed, for I had never heard this tone in his voice before.

Lamplight and even daylight change what we say. We see someone's face and adjust our conversations accordingly: catch her interest, make him laugh. Certain things can be said only in darkness, true darkness, where one cannot see fear or horror or disgust in one's auditor. In the light (and there is always light, it seems: moon and stars, embers if nothing else; but not this night, not as it lives in my memory) Dōmei spoke of a thousand pleasant or amusing things: stories of his brothers, his horses, pranks and games and delights—it is no wonder I longed to see his home! He said nothing of battles, though I knew there had been several.

But the snow-fight and now the darkness—he spoke, in a voice I scarcely recognized. He had seen just such a night-attack as this I have written, years before. The fire that Kagaya-hime watches is his story—or the story I imagined behind his disjointed fragments of image and sentence that night; for he did not say, this happened and then that happened. He gave only details: how the screams ended in gurgles, sobs, an old man's voice that said, "I'm tired, mama"; the mixed smells of wet thatch and the burning dead; a lone baby crying in the growing heap of bodies by the door until it fell silent.

I thought at first this was a nightmare he recounted. It could not be possible for someone I knew, loved—for *Dōmei*—to have experienced this. I asked no questions, for I could think of none I might want answered. I held him until he stopped shaking and squeezing out the bitter words. He fell silent and turned to me, and we had sex again: wordless this time, and fierce as cats mating. He left shortly after this, still in the strange total darkness, and never slept in my rooms again, though he visited as often as he ever had.

In the morning I was not at all sure that *I* had not been dreaming. I asked Shigeko as she picked up scattered robes and sleeve-papers from my sleeping enclosure, but fatigued from the snow-fight, she had fallen asleep and heard nothing. This has always seemed strange to me, that the one night that Dōmei spoke of war was the only night she failed to stay awake with me. —He forgot his sash, I remember now; Shigeko and I found it when we first started to empty these trunks.

"Shigeko?" I ask now. It is morning and bitterly cold. I have all my screens closed, but when one of my women came for my chamber box, I had a glimpse of the garden thick with fog, peony-colored in the rising sun. It is truly autumn now. I will leave soon, as soon as these words stop pouring from me, like a flux that cannot be cured.

Shigeko has been sleeping beside me as I fill this notebook. My favorite sandalwood-handle brush grew heavy, so I took up this brush, so much lighter in my tired hand. She awakened a short time ago; now she picks up the scraps of sleeve-paper I used to test this brush, for I tossed them on the floor. This could almost be that morning, forty years ago, when she gathered the papers left by sex with Dōmei—though her hair is frosted silver, and her movements are careful, as if her fingers were unfired clay and too fragile to use heedlessly. If the moments of my life might be sorted, not by hours and years, but by all the times I have held a brush, perhaps Shigeko's life might best be measured by the papers she has picked up.

"Do you remember Mononobe no Dōmei?" I ask her. This is the first time we have spoken of him in—twenty? thirty?—years.

She smiles slightly. "Of course, my lady."

"Do you recall the night we had the snow-fight, he and his men and you and I and—"

She thinks for a moment. "Murasaki and Tamiko and Hashi were there, as well."

"No doubt," I say to her: I cannot keep track of all the women who have attended me over the years. "That night, after we retired — were you there?"

"Oh, yes," she says. "He — had bad dreams, as I recall."

"You heard him, then? He said things?" I did not dream them? And you recall such a small thing, so many years later?

"I could not sleep, my lady. It was very dark. I was thinking about the snow, remembering the fight —" She smiles again. "That was fun, yes?"

"Yes," I say. "I only remembered it when I began —" I gesture at the notebook with my brush, which I see is drying, the ink caking into the bristles.

"Truly, my lady?" She looks surprised. "I have never forgotten."

"It was not a dream, then? What he said that night?"

"About the — fire, when those people died." She shivers and goes without my asking her to stir up the coals in the brazier. "Yes," she says absently.

"It was not a dream, then," I say, and I mean, not just that night, the words he said, but everything about Mononobe no Dōmei, and how I loved him.

"No," she says. "It was all real."

What is it like, to die by fire? I have wished this fate on my cat-warrior's family, and then on Osa Hitachi no Kitsune's brother and his people; and now on the Abe, and all the hapless others that lived at this estate. There are fires in the capital nearly every year, and each time some tens or thousands die. Whenever there was a fire, I (through my women) followed its progress through the responses the guardsmen and passersby shouted to us as they hustled past. We clung to one another and imagined the fire might veer, and that somehow we might not be saved. It would creep closer and closer, pillars of smoke and flame; choking fumes; some touching final poems exchanged —

Well, really, what were we thinking? We played with the fire, thrilling ourselves with the notion of deaths so unlikely and exciting, just as a child pokes a stick at a sleeping mastiff, confident that the rope that holds it will not break. We already knew that we would die by childbirth and disease and old age. Fire, or drowning, or freezing to death would all be *exciting* deaths, so much more glamorous than the circumscribed borders of our lives.

We were fools—or I was, anyway. No matter its form, death is not exciting. Or it is always exciting. I do not yet know which. Frankly, I have no desire to know.

In the morning, most of the fires were out at the destroyed estate. What remained burned on, sullenly stubborn but easy enough to avoid.

Kagaya-hime had never lost her cat's skill at walking over uneven surfaces, so she climbed farther into the collapsed main house than the others dared. She stooped under a beam and found herself in a strange gap where the wall had not completely collapsed, holding the ceiling beams clear. The space was slick with ash and water, and filled with the scents of burning and rain. —And ghosts: a man screaming and clawing at the remains of the wall; another bent over and weeping tears of blood that vanished when they fell; a woman lying beside a charred body, as if asleep beside a lover.

Kneeling at Kagaya-hime's feet, a ghost woman pawed at a collapsed timber.

"You can go now," Kagaya-hime said. It seemed futile work, even to a cat. "Most of the others have."

The ghost woman looked up. "My husband—I think he's here, but I can't seem to—help me. Please."

"You're dead." A drop of water landed on the back of Kagaya-hime's hand and left a black circle; she rubbed it away. "Everyone is."

"If we're both dead, why can't I find him?" the ghost said reasonably. "He should be right here, yes?"

Kagaya-hime looked around the dark reeking space. "There are others here, but I can't tell if they are your husband."

"Where?" The ghost leapt up, and Kagaya-hime could see a corpse, black as the wood that pinned it; though there was no telling whether it was the ghost's corpse, or that of the husband it sought. "Where is he?"

"There are people there" — Kagaya-hime pointed at the ghost men — "and there. But — "

The ghost whirled to look. "There's no one!" It sagged to its knees, tears red on its face. "I'm alone. Why would you lie?"

"*I* see them," Kagaya-hime said. She stepped across to the weeping ghost man, who looked up, confused. She held her hand just above its head. "Here is one."

The ghost man looked up at her hand. "What are you? Why are you alive?"

The ghost woman's face crumpled. "There is nothing there, nothing but darkness. Don't *mock* me."

"Never mind," Kagaya-hime said. After a moment, the ghost man covered its face with its hands; the ghost woman knelt again, to scrabble uselessly at the timber that trapped the corpse.

Kagaya-hime picked her way forward, through the darkness. Impatient with their stupidity, she did not speak to the other ghosts; but she heard something living, a high fast panting, and following it she found a dog with blood on its muzzle, hind legs crushed by a fallen chest. The dog did not lift its head at her approach, so she crouched and brought her face to its muzzle.

"It hurts," the dog said.

"I can make it stop," she said, "but then you'll be dead."

The dog panted for a time, then: "Yes."

Kagaya-hime slit the dog's throat. The breathing ended with a soft, wet noise. The body twitched once, and again. And then the dog shook itself free of its body, stood, and stretched. "Much better," it said. "This is dead?"

Kagaya-hime nodded. The markings on the living dog had been concealed by ash and blood, but the dog's ghost was clean:

gold-brown coat, black muzzle and paws. "I did not know that dogs had ghosts."

The ghost nosed at its corpse. "Neither did I. Now what?"

"I don't know," she said. "You're dead. Everyone is."

"I guess. Hey, there's my lady." The ghost dog pricked its ears forward.

"You can see her?"

"I see everyone," it said. "Dead, like you said. She looks upset. I better check."

"I don't think—" Kagaya-hime began, but it was already gone across the short distance to the ghost woman trying to lift the timber.

"My lady?" the dog said.

The ghost woman did not look up. "Not now, Goldie, I'm busy." The woman stopped suddenly and looked at the dog, realizations tumbling one after the other. *A dog spoke: no, it is dead: no, we are both dead, and yet we see one another. I am not alone.* Trembling, the ghost woman reached for the dog's shoulder. Ghost touched ghost; she cried aloud, and pressed her face against the glossy immaterial fur.

Dogs, even ghost dogs, are only patient with tears for a time. It wriggled a little in her arms and said, "Now what?"

She wiped her eyes and looked around. "My husband—"

"Don't see him," the dog said. "He's gone."

"Oh," she said, believing the dog as she had not Kagaya-hime. Kagaya-hime said, "You, dog—you see all the ghosts, yes?"

"I suppose," the dog's ghost said. "My lady, let's get out of here."

"Wait," Kagaya-hime said. "Are there mouse ghosts?"

The dog seemed to shrug. "See for yourself. My lady, can we go now?"

"Yes," the woman's ghost said, and at her voice a beam overhead shifted, ash and water cascading down. Shouts outside the building: "Girl! Are you in there?" When Kagaya-hime lifted her head from her protecting arms, the air was white with drifting ash. The ghost woman and dog were gone.

The other ghosts wept and screamed and slept on, unheeding. Kagaya retraced her steps carefully, but saw no mouse ghosts.

In all, Takase's party found forty corpses and another score of things that might once have been bodies. I wish I could say that the peasant man Mori's sister and her family survived, but it seems unlikely.

War and passion are caused by disturbances of the humors, an imbalance of yin and yang, too much fire or air, not enough water or wood. And yet the monks tell me that there is karma, and cause and effect; that war and passion (and sickness, and death) happen because they have been earned in some way. But this is nonsense. The peasant man whose sister died at the burned estate, and Kagaya-hime, who has lost her tale, and I, who die of this pressure in my lungs—what precisely earns these specific punishments?

Only in stories do things make sense.

11. THE TEN-OX NOTEBOOK

I have been so tired lately. We have emptied many of the trunks, but there are still what seem a thousand more. It is not the pain that keeps me awake. I am curious about this *monogatari* tale I tell: curious about the cat, and even curious about myself. My story ends, as all tales do, in death — or, more truthfully, my story ends just before that, when I put down this brush and retreat to Kasugano at last.

And that will be when the last of these empty notebooks is filled, and the last of the filled trunks is emptied. I replace *things* with *words*, I see. And after that? The notebooks are *things*, as well. As such, I suppose that even they will be put on the fire, when all is finished.

When I am done with the notebooks (and my life), there will be left the word: *remember* . . . Shigeko will think of me until she is dead, I hope with kindness. My great-grandnephew the emperor may have occasion to think of me when he is grown old; may even teach some child the song I taught him. Finally there will be no one who remembers me. I will be a name on a list, like the consorts of emperors five hundred years dead.

I should not be holding a brush when I feel like this.

I remember this from the Chinese guides to war-making that I borrowed from my half-brother the emperor: a small force in the territory of an enemy of superior numbers must utilize speed and surprise if it is to prevail. The war band of Seiwa Minamoto no Takase was still a hundred miles from the primary estate of the enemy. They (no doubt sensibly) did not choose to follow the main road north. This followed the course of Kitakawi river for many tens of miles, and led through villages and past forts and estates. There were many possibilities of losing surprise, and the almost certainty that soldiers assigned here would resent an unauthorized assault.

There was another way, a route that crawled over the flanks of mountains, and crept beside streams of icy water so fast that a horse more than knee-deep might be swept away and die. There were villages and farms along this way as well, but fewer of them, and no forts. The route followed ox-wide roads in the valleys, and hunters' trails over the mountains. Here, two hundred fifty men and their horses (for others had left the war band, summoned or lured home) had more chance of traveling north without unwanted attention.

The Chinese guides do not mention this, but there is another thing required for a conflict of this sort, something so fundamental that I think that they overlook it. *Strike fast,* yes; and *strike with surprise;* but more importantly, *strike hard,* hard enough that the enemy reels and does not regain his balance. The books were full of strategy and tactics, a million details; but at its heart, war is about a single thing: violence. The war band understood this, as all the Chinese sages did not.

The band moved quickly. Estates were far apart, sometimes no more than a handful of buildings and a series of fields carved from the otherwise unending forest. The fields were often better tended than the structures, filled with horses ("not so good as ours," Kitsune said to Kagaya-hime one day) or grain, still no more than slim green shoots in the wet dirt.

Strategy was simple: the war band approached an estate and burned it to the ground. Anyone they found—peasant, child, country noble—they killed. If it was dusk when they found a place, they made camp in outbuildings, and burned the main house and fields: lighting a fire for the night, the men called it, and laughed.

The assumption was that anyone found between the estate where Abe no Juro was killed and the main estate of the Abe would be an ally of the Abe—if you could call people this when they had no options, and were in any case more interested in whether their poultry stayed healthy. This assumption was probably true, though "ally" is a flexible term in a world where a loyal follower can leave a marching war band with no dishonor because he is summoned home by the birth of a son, the sickness of a parent, a possible blight in the buckwheat, or an ill-omened dream.

The local inhabitants did not send north for assistance; by the time they realized assistance might be required, they were dead, or too busy fighting fires and mourning the lost. Perhaps they did not think to send north. Takase's men did not explain their goals as they advanced, even to the few survivors. There was no reason to be sure that this force was directed at the Abe and not another of the powerful families that bickered across Mutsu province. The locals may even have believed the war band was no more than robbers, if better equipped and in greater numbers than usual.

There was warning for the people north of the war band, of course: smoke from a fire makes a towering signpost, the more so when it is night and the southern horizon shimmers angry orange. And messengers did get out: desperate youths on horses stolen from the fields, mothers cuddling infants in slings fashioned of charred cottons; but their messages were locally directed, to a daughter married in a neighboring village, a cousin working on one of the estates.

Men and women are full of contradiction. Even as they believe every runny nose is harbinger to the *kaze*-cold that will kill them, they convince themselves that the man idling alongside the road fingering his sword is no threat, and when they are too close to escape they are shocked to find his intentions are hostile. The residents saw the fires and they heard those few who fled; but they hoped that the band would pass somewhere else or ignore them, that the weather would change and hide them, that the gods would somehow save them.

The gods save no one. The fires continued. While there were men who loved the killing, for most men the willingness ebbed and flowed. There were moments when it was simple, others when a man could not bring himself to draw his bow. Many men grow sick of killing just after a battle: they shiver as if cold, and vomit and cry easily. This is why there were always survivors: stay quiet and hidden, pretend you are not there, and the men of the war band, grateful that the worst is over, will pretend that you are not there, either. You will not follow to avenge yourself. You will not report them, even supposing there is someone who cares, who is not grateful that the attack fell on you and not them. You will be too busy burning or burying your dead, tracking your escaped animals into the forests, saving what you can of the fields.

Some of the allies left the war band as they lost their taste for killing; others fought on out of loyalty to Takase or the Osa Hitachi, or (more often) a desire that the men of their campfire not despise them. Kagaya-hime had no bad times when she could not kill. Neither did Osa Hitachi no Kitsune, whose brother had been slaughtered and who was half-fox, which means killing-blood.

And Takase never faltered. I wonder about this, for I do not think he is a cruel man; but he is old, after all, and there are things we must finish before we die, so that we know who we are when the time comes. A military man spends his life preparing for war, and perhaps he never sees it, or sees it in an imperfect form, in unimportant squabbles and artificial conflicts. Takase had fought, and led men, but that was many years ago, and often to no real purpose. Revenge is a simple motivation: aiding loyal followers is a good one. Me, I think that he wished to be a warrior once more before he died.

❊   ❊   ❊

The boy who was to be my husband touched me that first night, a clammy, shaking hand pressed against my breast as if he were stanching a wound, and (because he could not untie the knot) incompetent gropings through the folds of my *hakama*-trousers, which grew soaked only by his nervous sweat. And then it was dawn, and he was gone.

I vomited and then slept the day away, and Shigeko made everyone—attendants, inquisitive cousin and uncle's messenger, priests and monks—leave me alone. I did not even see the morning letter he sent. Poetry is nothing but lies *(I will love you for all the years of the pine; we will share a thousand lives)*, and she guessed that I would have little pleasure in any poem he might send. She wrote the response for me, and only showed me the exchange after I awakened and washed and ate sweet foods, hoping to clear my mouth of a terrible taste I could not identify.

The second night. Again my cousin and my suitor and all their attendants, the endless idiotic conversation. I had a headache but could not allow it to interfere with this oh, so important visit, so I left the burden of conversation to others (in our years together Shigeko has suffered much for me), and watched the moon move through clouds as thin and transparent as silk gauze robes. Again came the false yawns and "appointments elsewhere," and we were alone, he and I, six feet of boxwood floor and a curtain-stand between us.

Evidently he had spent the day thinking of our night together, for he was not so shy this time. "It grows quite cold"—though in fact it was unseasonably warm, that night—"May I come sit beside you?" he asked. I could hear a hundred rehearsals in his carefully casual voice.

"Oh, no!" I said in a voice that was no doubt as artificial as his own. "That would be *quite* improper." On my side of the curtain I exchanged a glance with Shigeko (who was there, of course, with two others of my women); it had been some time since anyone had been quite so gawky in his pursuit.

The correct response to this, of course, is, "I will do nothing, just talk, I swear," a statement patently false, reassuring only in its predictability. But he was hopeless. On this, his second night, he had decided to make up for last night's clumsiness by being as debonair as possible, which at thirteen is not at all. He crawled around the edge of my curtain-stand, tangling his feet in the long legs of his *hakama*-trousers. "You're even more beautiful the second time," he smirked.

I itched to slap him, but he was my husband, after all—or would be. He would (one hoped) mature into a civilized man. In the meantime, it was my responsibility to use my skills to set him at ease, to show him desire and release. To educate him, train him into the man I wanted him to be. I was old enough to be his mother, after all: how hard could this be?

He showed an unseemly eagerness to dispense with the *hakama*-trousers and get down to cases, but it was absurdly early. "Oh! A moth!" I said. "Tell me, my dear, are you interested in such things?" I tried not to sound like an adult making polite conversation to a child.

"Not unless they eat the silk right off you," he said.

I gave it up. There would be other nights, years of them. Later, no doubt, he would display his (currently undetectable) virtues. And even if he grew no more pleasant, he would grow older and presumably less annoying; and there would be other wives and consorts and lovers. I might not even see him from one month to the next. As for tonight, at least he would not care (or perhaps even realize) that any poems I might make were uninspired.

And so I said the things I should say, and tried not to either laugh or cry. He pushed aside my robes and then loosened my *hakama*-trousers (left untied this time, the cord only looped over itself, to avoid a second disaster) and pushed them down until they clumped around my knees and ankles, an awkward and unappealing wad of fabric.

In my turn, I untied the knot that held his trousers in place, priding myself on my grace in doing so: it is strange how one focuses on tiny benisons when trapped in unpleasantness. He was erect, and not inconsiderably sized. I made the appropriate admiring noises, and touched him, gently and then firmly, feeling the heat of his skin, the texture of his flesh, soft over firm.

But it had been some time since I'd had sex with a young man and I had forgotten certain things. He spent almost immediately all over my iris-colored robes, surprising us both.

And even this might have brought us together. A shared misstep can do that, if handled with charm and humor. Instead he tried to ignore the situation, his sullen embarrassment a poor way to handle it. Since he was hard again almost immediately (ah, youth), he laid me down into the cooling stickiness of my ruined robes, not even pausing to slide the *hakama*-trousers off my legs.

Some things he knew. He entered me easily enough, with minimal fumbling, though his thrusting was feverish and clumsy. By this time I was too annoyed with him to do more than the minimum to encourage him. In his inexperience, he did not recognize the signs of my disinterest, and I resented him for that, as well. When he spent for the second time, I cried out and closed my eyes—in gratitude.

Poor boy. It is so many years since then, and now I realize it was not entirely his fault that things did not work. True, he was a smirking, self-absorbed monkey as gauche as he was stupid. But I was resentful and ungenerous, and did not conceal that I despised him. I could not stop thinking of Dōmei, and how different things would have been with him.

That was the second night of the three nights required for our wedding to be final. He stayed until dawn, as was required for the marriage to be formalized, but we said almost nothing after that. He drank plum wine as quickly as Shigeko brought it to him, and looked out at the garden, spurning my every attempt at conversation—for I knew I was behaving badly, and I tried to smooth things over with courtesy. As the sky paled, he took me again, one final time, quickly and angrily, and was gone.

❀   ❀   ❀

I was not present for the third night of my marriage.

After our second night, my husband-to-be left at dawn. He did not stalk out, as I suppose he thought he was doing, instead flouncing with all the maturity of a child in a tantrum. He gathered his closest attendants (who had spent their night on the veranda, near the screens of some of my women), and they swung off, down a long walkway that led to the residence's east gate. The sky had lightened enough that I saw them clearly, but all the curtains and eye-blinds and lattices and screens cut my view into tiny random shapes: here, half of an angry face; there, a hand caught in a gesture without meaning.

Even after they were gone, and Shigeko and the other women started to bathe and dress me, I watched the world in fragments. The lattices that hung from the eaves broke everything into tiny squares, and even these were hidden in places by the eye-blinds, which left only slivers of light and motion. In one place, a half-opened screen revealed a narrow stripe of the world: silver-blue sky, and a part of a cloud, and a tree's crown, a tiled roof, other lattices and verandas, and ivy and white stones, all no wider than my hand at arm's length. And everything was hazed by the silk gauze of the curtains of state that surrounded me.

The squares and slices and slivers hinted at the world, but did not offer it. I had grown used to this, had learned to see a splintered world and conclude the rest. Even when I stood outside, as sometimes happened, my world was a shred of the whole world, the real world, bounded by walls and roofs and carefully planted trees. And even the hill Fudaoka and the mountains to the east and west, all as familiar as the rips in the screens around my bed.

My uncle and cousin called. I could not deny them a visit, but I had little enough to say to their plans for the marriage. The boy sent his morning poem, surprisingly shy and so late that he must have spent some hours sweating to get the words right. I replied with something meaningless about plovers at dusk, crying for loneliness. *I have never seen a plover,* I thought, but I sent the letter anyway, grateful for the emptiness of poetry.

When we have been awake all night, we commonly sleep the day away; the more so when the next night promises no rest. By midday most of my women had retired, though several stayed with me, concealing their yawns so poorly that I sent them away. And then there were only myself and Shigeko, who might as well be my skin, so closely joined are we. The air was warm, and hummed with insects I could not see. The shreds of the world shifted as breezes arose and then collapsed, as the sun moved inexorably across a sky I saw only in shards. Shigeko drowsed beside me, head on a porcelain pillow padded with worn China-silk. I did not read, nor list such observations as I had been lately making, about the feathered legs of crows. I carefully, carefully, thought of nothing at all.

I said aloud: "I will leave now." I made no decision. It was as if my words decided for me.

My voice awoke Shigeko, who sat up, blinking.

"My lady?" she said. "Did you speak?" Her hair had been tied back with many little paper tapes, but strands had pulled free to make her outline hazy, indistinct.

"Nothing," I said. "I said nothing."

It does not take many days to travel from the burned-out estate to the main estate of the Abe. Despite the trail of fires and deaths left in the war band's wake, it took fewer still for the news to reach the head of the clan. After tragedy most people are distracted by their situation or their grief; but there are others who flee, salvaging nothing from their ruined lives; still others who burn, hot and fast as paper, for revenge. The Abe main estate swarmed with those few who had seen the burnings, and more who had heard the tales and run northward, away from the danger. To the south, there was always smoke in pillars or veils, and a greasy look to the air. Sunsets were astonishing reds and golds.

The leader of the clan was a man fifty years of age, Abe no Noritō. No one had lived through the burning of the first estate; but Noritō must have known or guessed that this trail of fire led straight from where his fourth son had lived and died. Grief and the desire for revenge often share the surface of a single stone. Where does one end and the other begin? No one can tell, not even the stone.

Noritō's resources for a war (even a small one) were not great. It was the middle of the fourth month: food is short, for the winter's stores have been used up and the foods of the new year — sweet potatoes and *taro* and *ðaikon* and *azuki* beans — are not yet grown. People are scarce, as well, for there are so many up in the pastures with the horses, or busy in the fields, or with the silkworms. Everyone is tired; the harder they work now, the better they will eat come winter, and the more easily they will pay their taxes to the provincial governor. Of Noritō's three remaining sons, only one remained at the estate; another was in the capital, at court as a guardsman; the third was far to the west, settling a dispute. Potential allies were mostly wrapped up in the affairs of their own estates and households; they had their own storehouses to fill and taxes to pay.

Still, Noritō could gather one hundred fifty horsemen: with attendants, nearly four hundred men. He could not know the size of the advancing war band (survivors thought there were a thousand, or a thousand thousand), but he fought on his own ground. If he himself did not know every stick and stone of the territory, he knew or could find someone who did.

Ambush would be possible but difficult. Though the advancing war band mostly traveled along the narrow stretch of flatland between mountains following a river course, there would be scouts and outriders expecting ambush, and a wary target is the hardest to hit. There were several places where the flatland widened out into a plain of sorts, which would make face-to-face battle possible. Combine what looked like a straightforward battle with sharp-eyed bowmen on the mountains; this might prevail over slightly greater numbers, and if the advancing force was smaller, it might end in the valley. If nothing else, there would be time for Noritō's household to retreat to an ancient *ki*-stockade a

few miles to the west. Noritō sent a messenger south with a challenge: battle, on the twentieth day of the sixth month, on the
plain beside the village of Ōgen.

A scout came to Takase one evening, carrying the challenge,
still wedged into its cleft stick. Takase, Kitsune, and Kagaya-
hime were in an open-walled pavilion a little way up a mountain
slope, upwind, where the smell of the smoke from the burning
farmhouse below was faint. It was too early for mosquitoes, but
the first gnats hovered in the air, annoying as dust.

"I killed someone, who was coming up from the north and the
west, moving fast," the scout said. "I found this afterward."

"You killed the messenger?" said Kitsune. "Was he attacking
you?"

"I hit him from cover." The scout gave something very close to
a shrug. "He's the enemy. He didn't exactly have a banner saying
'envoy.'"

"Unfortunate," Takase snapped. "If we respond, now we must
send one of our own. There's no reason to think they will be any
gentler with our man than we have been with theirs. Well. Let's
see what the Abe have to say."

Kagaya-hime was a little apart from the others, only there at
all because she did not care for the smoke down in the valley; it
was easier to bind arrowheads to new shafts where the air was
clear. "Girl, come here," Takase called. "They'll meet us. Find
someone who can bring us to Ōgen, and we'll finish this."

As it happened, the scout was sent with the message to
Noritō's estate. Only his family care whether he survived or not.

Ōgen was not hard to find: follow the river upstream, and it will
be one of the villages alongside: if not this one, then the next or
the next. The twentieth day of the sixth month was three days
away, which gave the war band ample time to scout the ground
and find defensible shelter—for a promise to fight on a given day
is no guarantee that one side or the other will not try to win the
night before.

They settled into a large but rustic farm less than a mile south of Ōgen. The farm was halfway up the mountain's flank, snugged against an outcropping of rock that kept even archers too far away to attack from above. There were ten or so buildings, and (once the reluctant inhabitants had been removed) these were comfortable for the men and their horses. Still: many scouts, many guards, many sentries.

This was a wet year. It is as well they found good roofs and hard walls, because it rained for two days in a row, and even the newly thatched main house developed leaks and that pervasive smell one gets in steady rain.

There were things to be done before the battle but not many, for the war band had been fighting for some days. The men slept as much as they could, and saw to the horses and their gear, swapping stories as they braided cord for new reins, or reflected arrows.

Kagaya-hime was restless. This might be expected, for she had traveled long, driven by kami and her own losses. No: it was something more immediate than that, a fever that flushed her cheeks and breasts and left her too agitated to stay long in one place. She could not be comfortable. She snapped at her woman Uona, more at her man Otoko; most of all at the men of the war band. Their presence was like sand caught in a graze, or a flea's bite: pain and an excruciating itch that she could not scratch. She scouted as much as possible, far from everyone, but even the mountains held men, bear hunters and hermits and such. She killed several; after the first day, when she returned with three quivers and five swords that were not her own, Takase forbade her to leave camp unless she could control herself. "They needed it," she snarled.

Takase was meeting with certain of his captains and the priest- ess Onobe no Kesuko beside the fire. Kagaya-hime paced the room, hands crooked into claws. The captains were always a little afraid of Kagaya-hime, who was strange in a way they could not quite define, so they avoided her eyes; but Takase and the priestess watched her with more-or-less well-concealed amusement, each for his or her own reason. "Why did they need to be killed?" Takase said.

Kagaya-hime stopped, taken aback. "I needed to get past them. And they might take reports to the Abe."

"It is a temptation to kill everyone who gets in your way, but people try not to do this too often. It leads to this." Takase gestured. "Wars."

She started pacing again. "Their smell—they irritated me."

Kesuko snorted. "I am sure it did. Listen: I recognize this fever. It will pass."

"No one feels this," Kagaya-hime snapped.

"On the contrary," Kesuko said. "Most of us do, sooner or later." She smiled slightly.

A messenger interrupted them all, and the topic was dropped. Neither Kagaya-hime nor Takase thought to ask what Kesuko meant by this, and in any case priestesses are famed for statements that make little sense, except in retrospect.

At Kesuko's recommendation, Kagaya-hime was allowed scouting again ("Better to have her far away, when she feels like this," she said), though the cat woman stayed high in the mountains where she saw few people, and none up close. Well, almost no one: Kitsune also scouted, and they encountered one another on the second afternoon.

Kagaya-hime walked along a ridge that had a good view of the valley, just inside the trees. Ahead was a small covered shrine, one side open to the overlook. The vermilion paint was nearly gone, leaving only bare wood dark with rain, and the roof tiles had gathered moss and pine needles until the shrine seemed to fade into the woods around it. Kagaya-hime knew someone was there, though there was little to hear over the steady hissing of the rain through foliage, and less to smell. Well, then: if this one spied on the war band, she would kill him. She approached silently from the shrine's blind side, short sword loose in her hand. She came around and saw sandaled feet stretched out, and leggings; and a bow tipped against one leg, ready for use. A basket-quiver stood on its block base holding a dozen arrowheads of every shape. Kagaya-hime sheathed her sword as she stepped around to see Kitsune. "Keep better watch," she snarled.

Kitsune had grabbed his bow and settled the arrow she had not seen until she saw him pick it up, a single quick motion. A leaf-headed arrow, long-shafted and designed for killing. He lowered bow and arrow to his lap, and spat on the ground. "Are you trying to get killed?" he asked.

"I think *I* would not be the dead one," she said.

"Huh. Fish?" he said. He had been eating, rice balls and pickled fish.

"Yes." She squatted on her heels, back to a post that held up the roof. The fish tasted of vinegar and salt and smoky earth. His smell, his closeness, his presence, still bothered her, but she was hungry. "You should have heard me," she said. "Or smelled me."

"Through *this?*" He pointed at the rain sifting down.

"A fox is supposed to have sharp senses. It was part of the *fudoki*, the—tale."

He picked up the leaf-headed arrow and stabbed it point-down into the ground. "I am no fox."

"You are half one," she said. "I see it and smell it on you."

"I have not been one, not since I was a boy."

"You've been a man so long? You've never wished to taste a fox's world?"

Kitsune laughed. "My brothers thought I cheated at all our games, anyway. If I had been changing back and forth—? It was easier to stay human. Human is good."

She looked away. "No. I would kill everyone I know to become a cat again."

"Ah," Kitsune said. "So *that* is what you are."

"It is what I was. The kami—someone—took everything away."

"You are Kagaya-hime now," Kitsune said. "Isn't that enough?"

"It is nothing at all." She leaned forward and her hair swept across her cheek, hiding him from her gaze. "I have no sisters and fellow-wives, no kittens, no ground to belong to us all, no tale."

She heard in his voice that he smiled. "And yet I would have said you fit very well with us. You have sisters—my sister Nakara loves you; she wanted you to stay, or at least return with me. You have comrades in arms. You have a horse and servants, and can make a new home anytime you decide to."

"And kittens?" she said, lifting her face to watch him. "Someone to pass the tale to?"

"Even those," he said.

"Where are the toms?" she said bitterly. Her gesture included the trees, the camp, all of Mutsu province. "It is my season, and none are here."

"Have you ever thought this body of yours might serve a purpose besides offering you clever paws? There are no toms here? *I* see no cats at all. *I* see a woman. You are surrounded by men. This is no problem at all, that I can see."

"Do you think their smells—all your smells—don't drive me mad?" she whispered. "But I will not have a human child."

"You're a cat, all cat. This"—he touched her shoulder—"is nothing. It's like robes; you put them on, you take them off. This"—he touched her belly, where her soul lived—"is what *you* are. Which are you? Human or cat?"

"Cat." Her eyes filled with tears. "Oh, cat."

"Then why would you have a human child?"

"Oh," she said, like a child understanding a lesson she has struggled with.

Sex. I was fourteen or so, new-come to court, and in love with every sweet-voiced guardsman I encountered. The first man who shared my robes was older than I by a few years and, I thought, handsome. Our conversations and letters would have incited a nun to sex, I think; while the experience itself was painful, I was so maddened by desire that I did not mind, even looked forward to this, since it meant that good as this was, subsequent caresses would be even better. —Though I cannot call his name to mind, my first lover. Or my second or third, for that matter — while I did not think of myself at the time as one who untied her sash for many, I loved the feel of flesh against flesh, and I suppose provincials might have called me wanton. I had no children, which certainly was easier than bearing one and finding a proper home for it.

What has made me think of sex? —Ah, yes: Kagaya-hime. I remember that burning she feels. She stalks through her days longing to ease an itch she does not know how to put her hands on. She aches; she shivers; she snarls and purrs in the same breath.

Kitsune was half-fox, and she a cat, both killing animals; but both human now. They have been speaking, words trotting back and forth. Her momentary peace is gone, and she paces the tiny width of the shrine. He stands and reaches toward her. Her hand comes up, fingers half-curled in what might be a memory of claws, or might be fingertips, curious about the texture of his skin. She touches his jawline, and his throat. He steps closer and slides his hand into her short, thick hair, soft and fine as cat's fur.

For me, releasing in sex used to be sweet and hot, like heated syrup suddenly spilled. I would shudder, throat to thighs, and then my body would float, as if in blood-warm water. I have seen cats mate; I do not think they release like this, and even Kagaya-hime, in a woman's shape, may not feel it as I do (or *did*: it has been so many years).

Kagaya-hime and Kitsune joined at the entrance to the shrine, in the rain-shadow of the eaves. This was her first time, as woman or cat, and she knew little of what it should be like. Her instincts and the lessons of the cousins and aunts made it seem a savage thing, rage and pain and desire dancing together. But Kitsune was a merry lover, with the enthusiasm of youth and the experience of an attractive man who has spent some time in the capital. Kagaya-hime mewed under his touch, panted and writhed and cried out at the end. He released, and her body relaxed somewhat; but the itch was not gone. It burned on, and she left him quickly, to pace the slopes above the village of Ōgen, trying not to howl.

12. THE *MASHI*-HEMP NOTEBOOK

Did I decide to run away, or was it fated from my birth and before? Was this boldness unique to me, or have other princesses tried? Do all women run from their fates? Do all men? I am old now; I am dying. I still do not know.

To get rid of Shigeko, I faked an indisposition of the bowels — not such an unlikely thing, after my vomiting of the day before. I ordered her to leave me alone with a chamber box, and to remove any of my women who might be within hearing distance.

Certainly it was strange for a noblewoman to refuse assistance at such a time, but I have always been self-conscious about such things. I suppose to my women this might be considered the least of my eccentricities. —And even this is gone in these my dying days: I need help more than I need my pride, it seems.

In any case, Shigeko withdrew to a distance that, if not quite out of earshot, was still distant enough to offer the illusion of privacy, which is as much as a princess can expect.

What would I need to run away? I looked down at my robes of rose and pale blue-green—eleven layers of stiff silk, not to mention the sashes and cords and the amber gauze Chinese-style jacket—and my *hakama*-trousers, so long that I stepped on them when I walked. I would need clothing, obviously, something not so obviously regal. Clogs for walking. Food, I supposed: fruits, perhaps, or rice balls.

"I am running away," I whispered to myself. I felt cunning as a monkey, full of possibility. I opened a trunk (the bound-cedar trunk with the bronze chrysanthemum lock; we emptied that one and sent it away more than a month ago) looking for clothing, and found rolls of unsewn silk in autumn colors. Useless. The next trunk held old *monogatari* tales, left over from my childhood.

I opened a dozen trunks, I think. I'm not sure what Shigeko thought of the noise from my rooms—for she must have been near enough to hear the thumps and scraping. I thought, *really, I must clean these out sometime,* and then laughed aloud, converting the sound to a realistic groan. *Let Shigeko empty them.*

It was the monkey's hour—midafternoon. Soon my women would come to me, find me robes for the last night of my wedding, feed me anise-water and ginger hoping to ease my indisposition. *Come on, come on,* I breathed, panicky now, not sure whether I was more afraid they would stop me, or catch me looking like a fool.

A small trunk held summer robes. It was daunting to think of changing all my robes without assistance, so I stripped off all but two of my rose-colored under robes. None of the robes in the trunk matched properly, but I selected three in shades of pale gold, in a rough gauze that I thought looked rather countrified. This made me laugh, even through my nervousness: I did not often care about my robe combinations, but now people—strangers—might see me.

The men tied their *hakama*-trousers up and out of the way of their feet when they played at archery games or *kemari;* but I had never seen just how this was done. I eventually contrived something with cords I pulled from two scrolls. The silk clumped in unruly bunches at my knees and ankles, but at least my feet were bare. I tied my hair into a heavy club that hung over one shoulder and down to my waist. I would have to steal a hat and some clogs at the gate—and food, wherever I could find it, for there was nothing to eat here, and I did not feel much like calling an attendant.

I had a notion that people traveling carried things with them, in little bundles on their backs. Clothes, I supposed, and—writing

materials, perhaps. Books? The room was a tangle of fabric and
carved wood and paper, heaped knee-deep in places. I should
bring a sutra, I knew; then, if I stumbled into a monastery, I
could at least become a nun. But didn't they demand that a novi-
tiate bring presents? I knew noblewomen always did so.

My bare foot was hot. I looked down and saw that the sun had
moved while I was fretting, and a tiny square of light had crawled
onto my toes. I clumped up a second set of summer robes with my
notes on mantises and an unused ink stone and brush. I needed an
ink stick still, and more paper, and—*No time,* I thought, and ran.

Poor child. I was thirty, but that seems so young to me now.
Run away, and you leave the tiger behind you, where you can no
longer see it—and it is still faster than you. Unpleasant truths are
there whether you look at them or not. I did not realize this yet.
Death is like this, and I find I face it better than I ever did my
marriage.

Shigeko must have seen me slip from my rooms. Perhaps she
thought I threw on these mismatched robes to creep to an outhouse, where I could be ill in true privacy. This is a question I
have never asked her: *Did you know?* —For if she knew, and let me
go, anyway—well, this is a Shigeko I have not imagined.

It is late and she is asleep on the other side of the crab-painted
screen, the snore she has developed over the years as familiar as
my pulse. I could awaken her and ask, this and a thousand other
questions I suddenly realize I have never been arrogant or coura-
geous enough to ask. But sleep is as precious as silver to old
women—and perhaps my courage (or arrogance) is not what it
once was. I will leave her to sleep.

I had no plans that day, except *away.* The boy would come for
the third night, and there would be more of those hopelessly
inane poems, but I would not be there. I would be free—free of
him, of the poems, of a world that had more interest in robe combinations than moths' wings. Away.

Panic and excitement feel the same; I could not tell which was stronger in me. I padded down the walkway to the west gate—the path the boy had taken at dawn. What was *he* feeling just now, in whatever rooms he laid claim to? Was he lonely, even as he fended off the well-meant advice of older, more experienced attendants? Did *he* long to flee? For a moment I entertained myself with the idea that neither of us might show up for the third night, that many years later we might meet again. We would laugh over our disastrous wedding, a wise old nun and a clever monk. But I could not reconcile this with the gawky boy who had taken me so angrily at dawn.

As a child I had many times tried to escape my residence to join the boys at their games. I was not often successful, though the gardener-boys had shared with me their secret paths: a break in the east wall, a conveniently bent plum tree that overhung the north wall. But that was years before; surely the gaps had been plugged, the tree pruned. The boys would have found new escapes by now. In any case, I was grown: larger, harder to conceal, not so quick to crawl under walkways or up trees.

But I had an advantage. Children are expected to run away. See a child somewhere she does not belong, and you know she is escaping from something unpleasant, and should be sent back to it, whatever it is. But an adult found somewhere unexpected—and, in my case it was the kitchen garden: really, I had no idea how many different plants we eat!—is assumed to be lost.

I was picking my way along a walkway cluttered with baskets of dirty greens when a voice snapped, "What are you doing here?"

I jumped and whirled. A young woman knelt among something leafy and dark green; her indigo-and-white cottons and her dirty feet and hands had concealed her somehow, made her a part of the lengthening shadows that stretched across the vegetable beds. "Oh, you're from the north wing," she said, and flushed. "I'm sorry, my lady, I shouldn't have been so—You're looking for the way out, aren't you?"

I nodded, afraid to trust my voice. Did she recognize me? I had nothing to do with my uncle's servants; she would never have seen my face. She could hardly imagine I was the princess Harueme, barefaced and alone along the radishes. She said nothing more, only led me to the servants' eastern gate, which I had never seen before, even as a child.

The little gatehouse was crammed to the eaves with straw hats and rain capes, and bits of wood that to my inexperienced eye might have been anything. She offered me a basket-shaped hat that covered my head on all sides, nearly to my jawline. The weave was coarse enough that I could see through it: *yet another screen between me and the world*, I thought. She eyed the clogs I'd found next to a storeroom entrance, for so long that I was afraid she recognized them, but she said nothing.

"Watch out for rain," she said, and waved me past the bored-looking guardsman. I could have embraced her, this excellent woman who had no interest in me. Instead we exchanged smiles, and I stepped past the guard and into Nijō avenue. *Away.*

Did she know who I was? Later, when the story could not be concealed, did she realize? Did she care? Perhaps I am not the only one who has run away from my life. Perhaps she had tried, or dreamt of it. Perhaps everyone does.

"Shigeko?" I ask, "Did you ever wish you were somewhere else?"

"Where?" she asks. She is awake now, and feeding an old scroll of bad poetry into a brazier. She amuses herself by trying to burn it as a single long roll without setting fire to her sleeves.

"Anywhere. Away."

"Ah." She nods wisely. I have not shown her this tale I write, but I think she can guess at least some of what I write from the questions I ask her, or whichever notebooks we've recently unearthed. "Oh!" Distracted, the flames have licked at her fingers, and she drops the entire roll onto the coals. They flare up, and we watch nervously, two small girls afraid that they will set fire to the eaves. The flames die down. We sigh in unison.

"Never," she says.

"Really?" I say a little enviously. "Why not?"

She blushes. "I was well content here, with you."

It is my turn to blush. Perhaps I will show her these notebooks I write.

The night before the battle at the village of Ōgen.

"We're outnumbered," Takase said. He sat with Kitsune and his captains at a fire laid in the center of the farmhouse's kitchen yard, a place high enough that the ground had drained. The fire was large, not for warmth but to keep off mosquitoes, and the bitter smoke eddied into their eyes as they spoke. Takase had ordered Kagaya-hime to stay close to camp that night, and she fidgeted restlessly outside their circle, pulling an eagle-fletched arrow through her fingers, again and again. "Ideas? I have no desire to die without getting something accomplished first."

"Night attack is useless," a captain said. Abe no Noritō's warriors camped at a temple just north of the village. The temple grounds were surrounded with a high wall of tree trunks set upright in berms of mountain rocks. The monks inside, hardened by robber gangs and the almost constant fighting that Mutsu province seems to breed, were at least as warlike as those near the capital. So: it was unwise to launch a surprise attack on the sleeping camp.

Other ideas were tossed back and forth. Sharp-eyed archers in the mountains could cut down the enemy during the battle, but Takase did not have so many men that he could spare even a few from combat. This was also the problem with sending a small force to assault the Abe from behind; in either case it was unlikely that the Abe would be caught unawares. The rice fields above the valley were still filled with water; if the war band's attendants broke down the terraces the field would be flooded, but there was not enough water to do more than swamp the fighting ground fetlock-deep with mud—and it was already close to that, after two days of heavy rains.

"What else?" Takase said.

From behind the circle Kagaya-hime spoke. "Sheathe our claws." Few men from the north had seen a cat, and none knew of this ability they have. But Takase knew cats, and had seen this. "Go on," he said.

She stepped through the circle, and stood beside the fire at its center. "You are smaller than they, yes?"

Takase nodded, eyes tight—though there was no saying whether this was because of the smoke, or annoyance, or the pain of his unhealing wound.

"Then there will be no bite to the back of the neck. You must trick them." She curled her back a little, remembering the feel of defiance. "Look larger than you are. Look fierce, and you may not be worth it."

The captains muttered among themselves, but Takase held up a hand. "We cannot look larger: by now they know how many we are. We can look fierce, but that won't stop them. Not this time. What else?"

She stared out over the heads of the council. "The hind legs are what kill," she said absently. "Your front claws pull them close, and then you gut them with your hind legs."

"What good is this?" one of the captains snapped. "If I want to listen to babbling, I will return to my wife and children."

Another said, "She shoots well, but—"

"She thinks in ways we do not," Takase said. "Four legs instead of two; hidden knives until they're needed. Run away; turn to fight. I see a way. Summon your chief attendants."

"The *servants?*" a captain said.

"The standard bearers, the grooms—yes, the servants. They have claws and teeth, just as we do," Takase said. "And I have orders for them."

So often we forget the servants. I say, "I was alone," as if I walked or read or slept out of sound of voices, isolated. I may say, "I have spent my life alone," but this is a lie—more of a lie than it would be for the baby in a family of six. I am never alone. Except for a handful of times in my life, the closest I have been is in the outhouses, and even then (unless I give orders otherwise) there is someone within earshot, just in case. There were always other women, and there is always Shigeko. Even when we were younger and she or I left court because of our monthly courses, I knew she was there, like the roof over my head at night, like the wind I breathed.

We share much, Shigeko and I. We have shared books, and laughed at the *monogatari* tales' excesses, or the egregious lies in certain court diaries that have fallen into our hands. She has corrected my paintings of insects and moths and mice with her own delicate brush. She drew the line at millipedes, but she held dead birds for me, even though touching them was impure, so that I could better observe an outstretched wing or the tiny feathers that ringed their eyes.

She knows my face better than I do: has plucked my eyebrows and painted the new ones on since I was barely a woman. It was she who knew my monthly courses, and told me when I would be well advised to retire from court, or to avoid pale fabrics. She has held me more times in the night than any lover, than even my nurse.

Do *we* share, or does *she* share? She has aided me in all these things, but what would she read if left to herself? Soon enough she need read nothing (save sutras) she does not care to. What books and scrolls will she beg to have sent from the capital? More: what will she think about? What favorite foods of mine will she gladly stop eating? Which women (and men) of the court will she drop acquaintance with?

—When I wrote those words, she was kneeling across from me, staring absently into space, one long hand holding her place in a scroll that (I realized) I didn't recognize. "What are you reading?" I asked her. Had I ever asked this before? I must have— five and forty years is a long time: most questions are asked in such a time—but I cannot remember ever hearing her response. It is true that most of us are more interested in our asking a question than in the answer: this must be even worse for a princess.

"It is nothing, my lady," she said. "Do you need something?"

"No; except to know your answer."

"Well, then," she said, a little defiantly. "Poetry."

Poetry? I hate poetry, I managed not to say. She had heard me say it a thousand times, in any case. I was curious, yes? I wanted to discover what was inside Shigeko's mind, not my own. "Tell me what you see in it," I said.

"But you *hate* poetry," she said.

"You have listened to me for the reigns of five emperors," I said. "I can listen to you this once."

So she spent the afternoon explaining what she sees in it. Her observations were not the clever interpretations of image and meaning I expected. She told me, *This one reminds me of when I was ten,* and: *My first lover used to recite this in bed.* I won't write everything she told me. They are her stories to tell if she chooses, not mine.

After a time, I said, "Do you keep notebooks?"

"Yes," she said, and laughed a little, as if embarrassed. "I started when I was a child. I suppose there must be a hundred of them by now."

"Really," I said. *Amazing.*

"Or were," she added. "I've been destroying them. I won't need them in Kasugano, my lady."

And, old woman that I am, I cried. I haven't cared about the burning of my own notebooks, but I had a thousand objections to her burning hers. What parts of herself has she hidden away or destroyed, only for my convenience? And now I may never know them.—Unless I ask, of course.

How could I have forgotten? Shigeko is more than an accessory in my life, a trunk I put things in, a notebook to record my thoughts. She is, and has always been, herself.

The war band's men set watch and sharpened their weapons and drank cold *sake,* and talked.

Armies have a *fudoki* of sorts. There are tales stretched so far as to become lies, familiar jokes a thousand times repeated, a list of the names of those now gone and how they died. There are child-ish pranks played (a hat marker replaced with a nonsense name, Prince Rabbit-toes or My Lady Blue-loins; an arrow's fletching changed from hawk feathers to rows of white down), and these, too, become part of the army's tale.

Dōmei once told me that he missed war.

"How can you?" I asked, shocked.

He was drunk and more candid than usual: he slurred as he spoke. "I have never had such good friends."

"You are surrounded by people who love you," I said, "and no one is dying here." How could war be better than this? Than me?

"We are all dying," he said. "We just forget that when nothing is trying to kill us."

I said nothing (indeed, could think of nothing to say), and he lay back, arm thrown across his eyes. And he started to talk. I held myself silent, clinging to his words.

The stories were not all interesting. Even the stories about bat-tle focused on little, often banal things: a man who lost his helmet and part of the skin beneath it, slick as skinning a rabbit; some-one-or-other's armor lacings that had rotted due to the dye used on them, replaced at the last minute with hemp cord—though I cannot even picture this, so barbarous it sounds; a man with dysentery so foul that the men who shared his campfire the night after a fight called him The Yellow River. There were a lot of sto-ries, and after a time, I saw that tears leaked past Dōmei's arm. He wept for these stupid stories.

No: he wept for something else behind the stories: the men he shared them with, and the sharing that comes only when you think you die tomorrow.

I have always thought I know what it is like when women are together: what we talk about and fret over, what matters to us—though lately I have begun to wonder whether I understand even Shigeko. But men with men? They are as foreign to me as the Chinese traders who came to court when I was nineteen. More: they are as foreign as listening to wolves talk, or tigers.

❀   ❀   ❀

I am so easily distracted these days. I tell Kagaya-hime's story, but my own is as insistent. So: I said that men set watch and drank and talked.

Takase and Kitsune sat at a sunken coal-pit in the middle of the building they slept in. Once he had brought tea and wine, Takase's main attendant, as weathered and old as his master, settled back beside him, and talked with the ease that comes from decades of service to someone. There was a fire to discourage the insects: the men were too hot, but it was preferable to being bitten.

The stories were not all about making war. Takase and his attendant (who was called Suwa, for the town he was born in) knew one another's stories intimately; but they did not know Kitsune's, nor he theirs; in any case it is no bad thing to hear such stories one last time, just before (possible) death. The men talked about their homes, their horses. As is typical, they talked about sex, swapping amusing or impressive encounters first, and, much later, the partners that mattered too much to discard thus casually, the women (and men) they loved: Takase's first lover, Suwa's wife, Kitsune's favorite mistress. Kagaya-hime's restlessness eased (or perhaps the mosquitoes grew worse than the restlessness), and she joined them in the bitter smoky air. They looked sidelong at her, but the tales went on. Such stories are not easily shared with strangers or women, but woman or no, she might die with them tomorrow: that made her no stranger.

Takase had a single wife, a woman from a branch of the Hata clan. There had been a night when he had crept into her father's residence and watched the moon with her. Just before dawn he gathered his courage ("You were afraid?" Kitsune said. "There are things more frightening than death," Takase said. "If you haven't figured that out, you're even younger than you look") and slipped behind her curtains, and they shared hurried, breathless, giggling sex, trying to be done before the household awoke.

"It isn't sex, is it?" Kagaya-hime interrupted him. "It's not being alone."

Takase wheezed a laugh. "Clever you. Some people say it's

about love, but you're right. I loved her, yes. But one of the things I loved about her is that when we were together I wasn't alone. I had other lovers. None of them were like that for me."

"What about you?" Kitsune said to Kagaya-hime. "Have you loved anyone?"

"My horse," she said, and after a pause: "Your sister Nakara. Uona and Otoko perhaps."

"Ha," Takase said. "That's not what I meant."

"Then I don't know the answer."

"Well, you will wed none of them, I hope," said Takase, and the topic changed.

Much later, when the fire was guttering, and Suwa and Kitsune slept, their heads on their bundled armor, Takase and Kagaya-hime spoke.

"A cat," Takase said, for he had been told by Kitsune. "You're new to the islands. Well, I've heard no harm of your kind; you injure no man, unless you claw him—and then I expect he deserves it. But I hadn't heard that cats are so fond of travel."

"I have no home," she said.

Takase leaned back carefully, cradling his belly as he did so. "I've governed three provinces, lived in four residences at the capital. There were things I missed about all these places, but wherever I was, was home."

I have read the war tales that float around court. Everything in a battle seems very orderly: the armies meet; there are envoys and arrows back and forth; one side or both decide to attack, and there is a scramble to be first in battle; men shout out their names and ranks, looking for suitably ranked foes; horsemen with their bows; the lower-ranked foot soldiers with their *hoko* spears and their *naginata* and their freestanding heavy shields to dodge behind.

But I am also familiar with the sorts of lies that are told for the sake of a story or to save face. I can imagine details the war tales do not bother (or choose) to mention. I can imagine a very different way of fighting.

Ōgen stands at the edge of a small plain, no more than a mile long, half that across. They grow rye and buckwheat there, rice on the nearer slopes of the mountains all around. Outside the village (which is not large—twenty houses, no more), there are wells, storehouses, farmhouses of those who do not choose to live as close to their neighbors as a village demands. With all this, there is not much space for a war band of seventy horses and their riders, and one hundred fifty grooms and attendants taking up arms as foot soldiers; even less for a defending force of nearly two hundred horsemen, and two hundred fifty more foot soldiers. Still, they manage. The two armies (for what else can I call them? The war tales are full of armies of ten thousand and more, but it seems more reasonable that armies are small. Where would one collect ten thousand horsemen willing to fight for the same thing, and where could they do so?) stand on opposite ends, north and south, of the valley. Battle is set for the dragon's hour, midmorning.

The members of Takase's war band were awake before dawn. Fighting men claim they can sleep through anything, but some part of them remains alert, and will startle awake at certain sounds. Dōmei did not sleep often in my company, but when he did he was oblivious to nearly everything—the laughter of my women and the men who visited them as they exchanged rude poetry on the verandas; shrill *shō*-pipes from a nearby garden; thunder and lightning. But he came wide awake at the tiny metallic scrape of my picking up a knife to cut my nails, or the chink of pottery cups against one another.

Few people sleep well before a battle. Many gave up with the sky's first brightening, and called softly for their attendants to build up the fires and bring them food and drink. These muted noises woke more men, and most of the camp was awake by the time the sun lifted itself above the mountains. It had been a cool night, and mist hung above the fields, dissolving only when daylight struck it. Across the plain, members of the Abe forces came down in twos and tens, early to the field.

"Looks like a calm day," Kitsune said to Takase. "The shields shouldn't blow over." Takase nodded absently, and tucked an arrow into his topknot, as northerners do.

An army's shields are man-tall and very heavy, layers of hard wood pegged together to make what must look like a door to nowhere. On the back of each shield are legs that hold it upright at a slight slant. The foot soldiers of an army erect these shields and use them as cover, jumping out to jab or slash at the riders and their horses with the *hoko* spears and the *naginata,* then retreating to protect themselves from the horses—and the riders' arrows, provided the horsemen bother to pay attention to groundlings.

It is traditional that the opposing armies plant their shields a hundred paces apart. I suppose shields might be portable in combat; but on a muddy, rain-soaked field like Ōgen, once positioned they will not move easily or far.

In any case, Takase had given other orders. Close to the southern entrance to the plain of Ōgen, the foot soldiers arranged the shields into three ranks, close but staggered. Noritō's forces would see a wall of sorts, far behind the milling horsemen and foot soldiers: a waste of the shields, no doubt part of some feeble plot on the part of the meager band (or so the Abe might think). Or perhaps they meant to use them as a fortress of sorts, to protect the spare horses; though it kept the mounts too far from the action to be useful. Or perhaps there was a mutiny of sorts, and the foot soldiers refused to fight for some reason, and instead huddled away from the battle, trying to stay safe until they could slip home.

The Abe could not have seen the part of this that did matter: hidden behind each shield was a *hoko* spear, heel sunk as deep into the mud as the attendants could make it, set at an angle toward the Abe. Forty shields; forty *hoko* spears. It was not so much, but the plain was not wide here, and this wall separated it into two halves, north and south. *Sheathed claws,* Takase had said the night before. Lure them in and then gut them.

The horsemen of Takase's war band did not much like their part in this; but the point of war is not to behave nobly or even well, or in such a way as to make it into the war tales of a future day. It is to win. You will seem noble enough once the chroniclers are done with you — but only providing you win.

I have read the war tales and manuals but despite this I know so little about what war is like. Battles on scrolls offer surprisingly little useful knowledge. Could Takase's plan work? How close do horses like to be? Will the foot soldiers and horsemen perform their parts? Will the enemy perform *theirs*? I can only guess, as I might guess what it is like to die in fire or bear a child.

So: Takase and Kitsune, and many of their horsemen stood a quarter-mile in advance of the shields. Kagaya-hime rode beside Takase. ("How can I give her orders?" Takase said to Kitsune, when he asked where she was to be. "They will just be counter-manded by the gods. Who will win that discussion?")

Some (but not many) foot soldiers and standard-bearers accompanied them. I think that, without cover, this took more courage than anything else that day. Most of the servants and foot soldiers milled about their shield-wall south of the line; prowled the slopes just above the barrier — anything to conceal the spears.

Envoys passed back and forth — though, really, what would they have to say? I have never heard that they sought to stop the battle, and why would they? Both sides long to fight. Occasional arrows crossed the space between the groups, like insults or boasts. There was shouting, of course, though it was hard to hear the words over the noises of the river and the restless horses.

And then battle.

Everything fights to survive. A worm in a bird's beak writhes. A rabbit struggles, even tries to kick and bite the cat that catches it. A fox in a snare gnaws her paw to the bone trying to get free. Battle may start with great goals, but I think it must always end up being a fight to survive, each man doing whatever he must to stay alive.

The arrows and shouts that flew between the Abe and the Osa

Hitachi men came faster; the horses approached one another at a walk, then a trot and a canter; and at some point, the abstract *we ride to battle* changed to *I must survive this*. Horses everywhere, the enemy all around. A man lifts his bow and awaits his chance, circling his horse to get to the right angle to shoot while staying out of his enemy's line of fire. And of course there are many foes, all circling, all looking for their chances: and one's helmet makes it hard to see to the sides and impossible to turn one's head. Arrows have a harsh sound in the air, harsher when they strike one's armor: sick thuds when they sink into flesh. And there are shouts and the frightened horses' neighing, and hooves and feet scrabbling in mud. Even the shouting is cacophony, men's and gods' names and wordless screams, jumbled into a sound like the million voices of the kami.

I must survive this alternates with *How can I?* even in the bravest fighters. The killing rage can change to white-lipped panic and back within a breath. No one who is not mad wants to be the bravest man, not if this means all the enemies' attentions are focused on one; but no one at all wishes to be the most cowardly. Terror and courage shift places as deftly as the horsemen struggle for clear (but safe) shots.

Fighting with arrows means that nearness is defined not by distance, but by lines of sight—the clearer, the closer. An arrow can come from anywhere, even (if one has been so unfortunate as to select an armor-lacing pattern that matches one of the enemy's) from one's own people.

But arrows run out, and the battle becomes too close. One draws one's sword, strikes at anything, horse or man, near enough to hit, trying in turn not to be struck. The blade often fails to cut through armor, but it can knock a man from his horse, to be dealt with on the ground.

And there are the foot soldiers, as well. They mostly do not waste their time aiming for riders, but horses are easy game, their fragile legs within easy reach of a nine-foot *naginata*. The Abe's foot soldiers and their shields are everywhere. An Osa Hitachi rider fights to keep his horse safe as well as himself: if your horse stumbles — or if, injured or unbalanced or hit, you fail to keep your seat — you fall among the foot soldiers. You may live awhile, but their pole-arms are longer than your sword. They will kill you.

It is no surprise to the Abe that the Osa Hitachi horsemen, outnumbered and unsupported by foot soldiers, retreat. The Osa Hitachi horses sidle back toward the shields. At some point a signal runs through the Osa Hitachi men. They appear to panic, spin their horses, and bolt to the south end of the plain, back to the shields.

The Abe men had thought that the shields, the apparently reluctant foot men, were perhaps a trap; but their blood howls in their ears. They ride and shoot, hunters now, prey scattering before them.

Takase's horses dance through the zigzag paths between the shields. And at a shout from Takase, the foot soldiers behind the shields heave them up and sideways. The Abe horses see barriers where the paths used to be, and jig to the new-made gaps. Some stumble onto the deep-set *hoko* spears. They scream and fall, dumping their riders to the ground. The men just behind the leaders don't see what's happening and their horses do not have the time or room to react; they crash into the spears and the fallen shields and the struggling clots of horse and man. The Osa Hitachi foot soldiers stay out of range of desperate hooves, and slash anything they can reach with their spears and *naginata*. The lacings of everyone's armor have loosened in battle, and there are a hundred gaps at neck and arm and breast and groin. It is easy work.

The muddy ground is too wet to absorb the blood, which runs along its surface in glossy dark streams. Takase and Kitsune and Kagaya-hime watch; but many of the Osa Hitachi horsemen do not and turn their heads away; or focus instead on shooting at the Abe horsemen who have managed to stop their horses before they become part of the tangle.

There is little the remaining Abe horsemen can do. They shoot at any Osa Hitachi they can see, but the foot soldiers are half-hidden behind the chaos, and the horsemen are well armed and shoot back. There is no headcount, not yet, but the Abe have lost a surprising number. Shocked and demoralized, they retreat. A few, trapped, wave their hat markers to show they surrender.

There is a lot of death this way. Noritō loses sixteen horsemen outright; twenty are caught or injured in the broken heap of men and horses, and beheaded by the Osa Hitachi men. This is a slaughter by the standards of war, for a thousand horsemen can fight all day and suffer only twenty deaths, despite hundreds of injuries.

As Noritō retreats, another twenty of his men flee like clouds, scatter like divining sticks, returning to their own homes. By the time he makes it to the *ki*-stockade to which he has evacuated his family, he has fewer than a hundred horsemen and their attendants—less than two-thirds of what he began with—by the village of Ōgen.

The battle changed nothing. Tomorrow it would begin again: the riding and the burning, and it would not end until there was more fighting, more injuries, more death. And even *then*, supposing the Osa Hitachi destroyed the Abe, there were many hundreds of weary miles riding or walking home again, and more fighting, injuries, death along the way. Tomorrow it would all start again. This would be cause enough for despair.

—Although this is what life is. In our most painful times—a brother dies, a lover leaves, the world is not what it was—we claw through our days and weep as we fall asleep, grateful to be done with the day. And then morning comes and we have it all to do again, breath by weary breath. There is a difference, in that my battles have always been within myself.

How can men do this? It is horrible enough to imagine, let alone to be there. We are willing to suffer unbearable things for those we love, or because we must; but how can a man (anyone, of course, though it is only men who do so) walk into a battle for no great reason beyond this, that someone he respects wishes him to do so?

Perhaps this respect is love, a man's sort of love. Dōmei spoke more warmly of the men he fought with than anyone else—than even, I suppose, me. After he was gone, I brooded long on this, trying to understand, and concluded that only men could understand this, or practice it. Now that I am old, I realize this is too simple an answer. I would walk into all the Buddha's hells for Shigeko, not from courage but because I would not willingly leave her alone in such a circumstance. I love her more than I fear Hell.

—I find that insights grow more frequent as I have less time to take advantage of them.

After the attack, Kagaya-hime and Kitsune walked together, pulling arrows from the bodies. It was not easy work. Arrows often wound, seldom kill. An armed man with an arrow buried deep in one thigh does not give up the arrow unless his life goes first. *Hoko* spear in hand, Uona followed, collecting the arrows they retrieved.

The village of Ōgen wanted no part of the battle but suffered nevertheless, as a mouse does caught under the feet of a panicking horse. The same concerns that drove the war band to destroy the farms they passed burned Ōgen, as well. Some of Noritō's men had thought to hide here, as well; to prevent retribution, Takase had ordered them ferreted out and killed. If village men died as well, it was regrettable but unavoidable.

"Gah," Kitsune said. "This is making me sick." They walked through a kitchen yard, blinking against the smoke that stung their eyes.

"Why?" Kagaya-hime asked. She had lost an arrow, one of the three she had fletched with the golden eagle feathers given to her by Kitsune's sister Nakara: her first friend. She did not often miss; it must be *in* someone.

"It's one thing when you're caught up in the fight. But now—"

She said, "We are killing animals, even in this form. Perhaps it is our nature." A dead man lay facedown, his blood a gelled puddle. He had been running. The arrow (not her eagle-feathered one) stood straight up from his back.

"No," Kitsune said. He turned his face away when she pulled the arrow free with a wet grinding noise.

"Man *or* fox, it's your nature," she said absently. An injured man had crawled behind a tumbled cart, but she heard him cursing, and came around to where he lay on the ground, arms wrapped tight around the arrow sunk deep in his belly.

"Hush . . ." Kagaya-hime knelt beside him.

His eyes focused for a moment on her—a woman in armor, naked sword in her hand. "Jingū?" he whispered. "Goddess?"

"No," she said, and stabbed him in the throat: a clean death. When his body uncoiled, she pulled the arrow free and inspected the feathers. "Not mine," she said.

Running footsteps behind them: Kagaya-hime leapt to her feet and spun, cat-quick. A village woman had been hiding behind a tree; seeing them ready, she paused, still some steps away. Her single coarse robe was kilted high enough to leave her legs clear. She held a long knife.

"Go away, woman." Kitsune had raised his bow with her approach; he spoke past his bowstring, the arrow beside his face. "Unless you want to die."

"You killed him." The woman wept, her face twisted in rage and grief. "You killed them all."

"Be grateful we did not kill *you*," Kitsune said.

"For what? You've taken everything." Her anger seemed to dissolve, and she fell to her knees, knife loose in her hand. "They're gone, they're all gone."

"I know this feeling," Kagaya-hime said.

Kitsune turned to say something, but she ignored him and crouched beside the woman, taking the knife. It was a cheap one; someone had died to preserve his possessions, when he had owned nothing nicer than this.

"You're a woman," the woman said in weary surprise.

Kagaya-hime said, "I have lost everything, too. Family, tale, place. Gone. But I am alive. Do you have a name?"

"I am Otomi no Seishi. This was my family." She pointed to corpses in the yard. "Brother. Uncle. Cousin."

"Do you know how to do anything?" Kagaya-hime asked the woman.

"I can farm," she said.

Kagaya-hime stood. The village woman remained kneeling, face wet. "Uona, give this woman my stores, the food from my packs, the rice: everything. Keep your things, Biter's gear." Uona bowed and left them.

"*What?*" Kitsune lowered his bow. "And have her hunt us down for revenge?"

The woman opened her mouth to reply, but Kagaya-hime spoke first. "Why would she? It won't bring them back." The woman shut her mouth abruptly.

Kagaya-hime leaned forward until her face was close to the village woman's. Cat-woman: farm woman; voices too soft to be heard by any but one another. "I have been alone," Kagaya-hime said. "I have longed for death. Life is better, even life alone."

"Alone—" The woman cried in earnest. "I can't—"

"There may be others," Kagaya-hime said, "but only if you live."

Later, when Kagaya-hime and Uona had given the village woman rice and dried fish and salted birds and a short sword and robes, and returned to her one of the village's horses, they spoke again.

"Do what you must," Kagaya-hime said, "but stay alive."

"I still hate you all," the woman said. "This changes nothing. But—thank you."

Kagaya-hime nodded. "And do not follow us, or I will kill you."

Members of the war band had different opinions of Kagaya-hime's kindness. Some assumed it was feminine softness on her part. Others: "Soft? She's soft like oak is soft," said with a wise look—for her skill and savagery had not gone unnoticed, and there were those who whispered she might be a kami in human form; and no one knows why the kami do anything. The priestess, Onobe no Kesuko, said only, "She is no god. She has her own reasons." Takase just shrugged.

But Uona said later, "It was a kind thing you did, my lady."

"I wouldn't have her starve. I can hunt for *my* food."

"Still," Uona said, and bowed deeply. "I am proud to serve you."

Kagaya-hime, who had never done so before, blushed.

After this, they were together more than they had been. Kagaya-hime had not the human gift of light conversation, but Uona did, and Kagaya-hime found she liked the quick rippling of her woman's voice, even when she did not listen to the words.

—Another thing changed, as well. After this, the magic no longer produced whatever Kagaya-hime needed. Food ran short until the next estate they burned down, and after this, she and her attendants ate and drank and wore and used what they found and carried, just as everyone else did.

The night after the battle, Takase and his men camped at the same Buddhist monastery the Abe had used. The monks had made it clear that they did not care which side had won, provided no one threatened the monastery's considerable riches; and Takase's gift of horses and armor (everything left behind when Noritō's fighters retreated) soothed any concerns they might have had.

Takase had forty-two heads lined up on the ground before his quarters: the thirty-six Abe horsemen and six of their foot soldiers, too injured in the early stages of the battle to escape. The foot soldiers' heads were of no account, but might as well be removed as left on the corpses, now a mile behind the Osa Hitachi forces. The whole made an impressive display—if already foul-smelling: the day was ending warm.

(I have seen such a display of heads, back when I was very

small. They had been sent all the way from Mutsu province pickled in kegs of wine. I had nightmares for weeks afterward about
their distorted faces and the smell—I cannot think what my
nurse thought she was doing allowing me to see them.)

The Osa Hitachi casualties were much what might be expected:
six deaths. One man broke his back when he fell from his horse
trying to navigate the barrier of shields. Another fell, uninjured
until he was trampled: a strangely crumpled, concave form. Two
men had been killed outright by arrows, one struck through the
eye, the other barely touched, though the blood pulsed from a nick
in his neck until he turned pale and died. Two were skewered on
hoko spears and died before the battle ended.

There were many injuries. An arrow often does not kill immediately. It is possible for the broad-headed killing arrows—the
forked, the leaf, the four-sided—to slice a great hole in a man; but
more often they do not even pierce his armor, if shot from too far
away or striking at an angle. If the arrow does pierce, the wound
will be painful and bloody, perhaps even incapacitating an arm or
leg; but the man who suffers it may still be able to fight that day,
the next, ten days hence. Or half a lifetime later: Takase's arrow
wound was taking twenty years and more to kill him.

But many of the wounds fester. They ooze clear and then colored fluids. Dark lines crawl across a man's skin, reaching from
the injury toward his heart. When the dark line reaches his chest,
he dies. I have seen this once, a guardsman nicked in a fight with
the monks who were harassing the capital some years back. We
had been lovers a few years before, and he still visited from time
to time. I saw the festering and the dark lines, and I smelled him,
like rotting pheasant in the sun; but he denied all this: "Just a
scratch," he said, and laughed a little, though his face was twisted
with pain, and he could not stop touching the flesh beside the
stripes. In the end he wept for death, and his superior gave it to
him. I had bad dreams after this, thinking of Dōmei in Yoshiee's
war.

And more. There is a sickness of the soul that settles once the war-madness drains away, a weary nausea in the belly. Men remember what they have done and cringe or weep or relive it endlessly, remembering certain sounds, screams, voices: searching for something, though they could not say what. Everyone who has fought is injured in this way. There is little they can do but wait for their flayed spirits to scab over. Some will. Some will not and their hearts will fester across a lifetime.

Men have their various ways of coping with this. There was a group who celebrated their victory with bragging shouts and overly loud laughter, as if noise itself might heal. Others made themselves busy cleaning their armor and repairing their arrows; their voices were hard and practical: work to do, things to make ready. Many men sank (or retreated) into sleep, half-eaten food forgotten in their hands; or they wept openly or in secret. Everyone drank too much. Everyone's hands shook a little.

Kitsune was one of those who threw activity into the empty place left after the fever is gone. The battle had been directed by Takase, but the men of the war band were his men, Osa Hitachi men. He walked through the groups, talking to each warrior: loud with the shouters, brisk with the practical ones; quiet, even tender, with the broken ones. He stayed long with the injured men, keeping them from thrashing when their squad-mates laid burning moxas on their skin or pressed crushed leaves into the wounds.

Takase and Kagaya-hime sat together. There was a veranda framed by pillars painted with flying Buddhas, faded with sun and weather: a welcoming place, but it was inhabited by the forty-two heads, so Takase and the cat woman sat upwind in the garden. He still wore the red brocade commander's robe he had fought in, but it had been loosened by his attendant, who had checked the unhealing arrow wound in his side, found it open and weeping, cleaned it, and bandaged him. Now he drank *sake*, which he downed little bottle by little bottle, as if it were iced water on a hot day.

Kagaya-hime was perhaps the only one not haunted by the things she might have done differently or should not have done at all. She herself had taken three of the heads: an odd way to kill, for an odd reason, but people did stranger things than this, so she had shrugged and accepted it. The restless heat of her mating season still ran through her, but her exhaustion was strong and it was pleasant to slump against her bundled armor, and watch the fire Otoko was building.

"You don't seem upset," Takase said after a time.

"Should I be?" Kagaya-hime said.

He laughed, and stopped in midbreath. Sweat broke on his brow, shiny in the light. At last he let out his breath. "I keep thinking, this is the time it will kill me, and I keep being wrong. Hah."

The fire gave a flat brilliant yellow light: pinewood, still fresh enough to sizzle and pop. It erased the lines drawn by pain and fatigue and age on Takase's face, leaving him what he had been; a strong-boned man with fierce eyes. Even the *sake* did not dim the intelligence, the strength, there. A strong man with a hawk's expression: wise; a leader.

Kagaya-hime stood suddenly, and reached a hand down to him. "Come," she said. Wordlessly he allowed himself to be heaved upright; wordlessly he followed her into their rooms; wordlessly they mated there.

As men so often do, Takase slept afterward. But a cat's heat leaves her little peace, so Kagaya-hime dressed and walked out to pace beside the fire. Otoko and Uona drank wine with some of the other attendants: occasionally one would come back and stir her fire up or add new wood. The severed heads looked at her with glittering half-closed eyes. The flames gave a foreign life to the heads; as she paced their mouths moved as if trying to frame words with stiff lips.

She paused for a moment at a cry from the other side of the temple enclosure, one of the injured men. When she turned back to her fire, a shower of sparks flared upward, and the heads became the thing of eyes and flames that had haunted her dreams. "What?" she said aloud. "Why are you here?"

Because, they seemed to say in voices that were like and unlike the chittering of the million kami: *grief and anger, you, joining.* It did not seem to her to be an answer.

"I have no patience with gods," she said. "There was a kami, and it left me."

Ask yourself why it/they/you are gone. The flames settled and the heads grew silent, and nothing she said earned more response than the light in their eyes.

I have given the early parts of Kagaya-hime's tale to Shigeko. I watch her as she reads, all the while pretending that my mind is engaged in recording great thoughts here.

I am as nervous as a child writing her first poems to send to her father. I wonder and fear what she thinks as she reads. Why should I care so? She has read everything I have written before this. —Ah, but this is different. Those were just my life. This is *real.*

The fire had burned to embers before Kitsune returned, the grief and tension that drove him all night eased at last. Kagaya-hime offered wine and he gulped it down, and then more, as fast as Takase had. He dropped to the ground beside her, resting his head on her bundled armor.

"So many of them are going to die," he said without looking at her. "The healers will work, and the monks will chant, and the priestess will pray, and none of it will make any difference. They'll die anyway. Some of them, I know their families."

"But you wanted this fight. Yes?"

He rubbed his eyes. "So I shouldn't feel sick about it? Don't *you* feel anything?"

"Sorry for the horses. Some of the attendants," she said. "They didn't want to be here. Everyone else?" She shrugged. "They're here by choice. People die in their beds, people die as infants. Where's the difference?"

"I'd cry for those, too," he said, a little tartly. "How can you not?"

"Should I weep for every kitten who dies without becoming part of the *fudoki,* every mouse I catch and kill?" She touched her cheeks, her eyelids. "We do not cry for this, we cats."

"What do you cry for, then?" he said. When she said nothing, he added, "Why did you leave the capital? Your—what do you call it?—tale was gone, maybe. But I've been in the capital. There are a million places you could have lived. And toms everywhere; I heard them. You could have built a new home, a tale. And you didn't. Why not?"

"I—" she stammered to a halt. "I ran and then kept running, and then there was the voice, the road-kami. So I went. And then this happened." She touched her human thigh.

"Huh," said Kitsune. "Maybe cats are too stubborn to learn anything unless you throw it at them."

"What was I supposed to learn? I knew every cat, every inch of ground, in my *fudoki.* I didn't *need* more."

"And when they were gone? A brave cat would have stayed and built a life."

Noises from inside the rooms: Takase rolling in his sleep, mumbling the names of the men who had died that day—and other names; a lifetime of fighting leaves a long list. Kitsune and Kagaya-hime exchanged glances.

"I can't," Kitsune said. "I am so tired," so Kagaya-hime went to kneel beside Takase, and soothe him in his sleep, and wipe the tears from his face.

13. THE BLUE-GREEN NOTEBOOK

Kagaya-hime mated six times in four days:

—Kitsune in the shrine.

—An Abe scout she found the day before the battle; she did not learn his name, only coupled with him, and then (because she fought for the Osa Hitachi) she killed him as he slept.

—Takase, the night after the battle.

—A captain of the Osa Hitachi, a married man from Shimosa province.

—A strong-backed man from the village of Ōgen, when she remained behind the war band to look for her arrow.

—And Kitsune again, the second night after the battle, in the charred remains of a storehouse the Abe had burned to make the war band's pursuit as irritating as possible. Six in four days: really, a cat in season makes even a woman at court look chaste.

And after this her season was done. She was no more restless than she ever had been, a cat without a *fudoki* in a woman's body; and no more interested in men. Kitsune watched her a little wistfully sometimes, but he was not importunate. It was a momentary thing; he could not have hoped for it to last, except that between men and women it sometimes does.

Not so many trunks left to empty. I had not thought I lived in clutter, but my rooms seem twice as large as they used to, and there is a hollow sound to the space. Shigeko empties a pawlonia-wood box, making neat stacks: gifts for the women, gifts for the temples. She pulls free a rumpled mass of hemp fabric and shakes it out. A blizzard: a hundred paper cards settle to the ground. The pieces from a poem-matching game were unaccountably bundled into a child's robe that none of us recognize and hidden here. Whose game? Whose robe? Why is it here?

There have been other surprises: the desiccated mouse, a teak-wood box filled with unknown hard white seeds that smell like anise, a baby duck's beak threaded on a black cord, a river rock with the word *twelve* painted in vermilion. I still have the rock beside my ink stone, cool and smooth when I lift it. Who painted it? I do not recognize the calligraphy. Why, and where, and how did it end up wrapped in a error-riddled page copied from a *monogatari* tale and stuffed into a box designed for combs?

I have been full of questions for Shigeko lately. It is as if I wish to see another life, one that will extend beyond my own. Or perhaps it is just love.

We have spoken much of her lovers lately. Her stories make me laugh, since we shared certain lovers, and can speak of their virtues and (far more often) their flaws with what we at least consider wit. But there were others we did not share. She has always had an incomprehensible taste for *shō*-pipe players ("Their hands;" she smirks, "their fingers are always so agile"), and the sorts of men who cry easily ("Self-absorbed," she says, "they never demanded much of my heart"). Me, my taste ran more to tall men with dry humor, such as the Fujiwara boy, Munesuke, who grew up so interested in bees. And Dōmei. Dōmei did not play flute, and he was no cryer. Still:

"Do you recall Mononobe no Dōmei?" I say, as casually as I can manage.

Shigeko is a little tipsy. We have been drinking too much hot wine; since the latest healers have demanded that I take divers noxious herbs in wine, I have chosen that I at least have the comfort of warm wine, which seems to make the medicines go less vilely. Shigeko takes hers without herbs, of course, but she has been matching me cup for cup, even though wine no longer seems to affect me. She slurs only a little, but her hair has become slightly disarrayed, a black-and-white wisp trailing over one eye. Her face is relaxed, seeming younger. "Dōmei? Oh, yes, my lady," she says.

"Were you lovers?" I say.

She pushes the strand to one side, but it slips back immediately. "Once. You were in seclusion. We talked for a while, and then he came behind my curtains."

"What did you talk about?" I ask.

"Horses, mostly." She frowns slightly, trying to remember. "Oh, spotted horses, and how much trouble they can be. And horse breaking. My brother used to be interested in horses. Dōmei quite made me want to see his family pastures."

Horses? In all our time together, Dōmei and I had never spoken of horses, except as tools to a purpose. I am surprised by the stab of jealousy that shoots through me. Shigeko seems not to notice. She is turning her cup over in her hands, a single line between her brows.

"He was all right," she says. "And charming, I suppose. But I was just never interested after that." She shrugs. "In truth I liked a lot of your other men better. The Genji man, Akifusa, for one. And what was his name? his brother—Toshifusa, something like that."

"But Dōmei was—" *Wonderful.* Charming and warm, and— Perhaps the wine *has* affected me; I cannot think why I am even discussing this.

She shrugs. "Some horses eat soybeans. There's no accounting for tastes."

I realize to my shock that she means that is it *my* tastes that are strange, for loving Dōmei. How odd.

And I do not even know whether she has ever felt for anyone as I did about Dōmei.

Away was all I had wanted from my escape, and *away* brought me through the servant's gate into Nijō avenue. Fine: I was out, an emperor's aunt standing under the incurious eyes of a low-level guard, wearing stolen clogs and unmatched robes and watching the sky to the east blur the purple of wisteria or rain. At any moment, Shigeko or my cousin or someone—*anyone*—would enter my rooms and find the wreckage I'd left behind, and the alarm would go out, and they'd catch me, ten feet from the residence walls. Something I learned immediately: the fear of embarrassment is a sharper goad than a chopstick in a child's hands. I briskly walked off, as if I knew where I was going.

A second thing I learned: walking is hard. It had been twenty? twenty-five? years since I had walked with vigor; and then I'd been a girl. The rutted dirt of eastern Nijō avenue was awkward, not to mention cluttered with carts and vendors and overgrown weed-patches. The dog-path alongside was little better, with an added risk: the clusters of noblemen in informal robes, drifting off to this or that assignation. Anyone might recognize me—or, more accurately, these robes, since my face was hidden. But I had forgotten that people see what they expect to see; I was just another attendant scrambling to complete an errand before the rain.

A third: rain is only pleasant if you are tucked under deep eaves, watching it mist across your pretty little garden. Standing under a dying oak in one of those icy, soaking autumn rains is hardly the stuff of poetry, unless there is a poetry of howls. The street and dog-path remained rutted, but over time transmuted, dirt to mud. The oak's few leaves were such inadequate cover that I gave up and walked on. I held my robes up to my knees and then my thighs, and even so mud splashed my hems as I clomped through the deepening puddles. The hat was of mixed advantage: while it did conceal my face and even protect my hair and neck, the brim dumped most of the water down my back.

At least the rain would discourage pursuit, I thought: cold comfort, when warm robes and brazier sounded better all the time.

I was lost, of course. I knew little of the capital outside the court and a handful of houses in the east quarter. The city was a collection of scattered places I had visited or heard of, separated not by a navigable grid of streets and avenues but by allotments of time spent in the rush-scented shade of a carriage; blurred shapes seen through woven palm-frond walls; the sounds of bells or street-vendor's cries or horse hooves on dirt.

I was learning that *away* is not really a plan. The only temples allowed within the capital walls are at the city's southernmost edge, and I knew that they would be too far to walk (whichever way south was; I had turned myself around in the rain), and I was sure that my uncle and cousin would look for me there. I might have retreated to the house of a relative or an attendant if I had any idea where any of them lived—and if this were not the third night of my own wedding I evaded.

There was a gate to the east, the fastest way out of the eastern quarter—where at any moment I might run into my husband-to-be—and, incidentally, the city. It led to the Tōkaidō, and which led eventually to the Shirakawa barrier and Mutsu province. It was not much of a plan, but it was something: I would find the gate, and then something would turn up.

Poor little princess, poor me that was. I thought myself so clever, my mind stuffed with mouse-pelts and military theory. I despised poetry because it was useless (as it is; that is its charm, I am learning from Shigeko). But life is much more than utility, even supposing that familiarity with the patterns of moths' wings can be considered practical. All that cleverness, and I did not realize how lonely I was.

The rain did not stop, the day I ran away. Perhaps the kami were warning me to return to my uncle's home, or marriage with the boy, or my life, but I do not think so. The kami are not convenient; they do not teach lessons. They are what they are, and they are everywhere; but they are as unfamiliar with our way of thinking as a cat might be.

I might have asked which way was east, but those few people

outdoors moved quickly, running to avoid the rain. And I couldn't think of how to ask them a question. How did ordinary people call to one another? Did one say "please"? Did one bow when one's question was answered? I did not know any ordinary people.

I guessed which way might be east, and walked and walked, eyes on my path more than my surroundings, which already faded into the early dusk of autumn rain. The walls that surrounded the blocks grew older and showed breaks where the stones or wood had collapsed; there were even places with no fence at all. This surprised me: everyone (even princesses) knew that the east quarter was where everyone of rank and influence lived, so how could there be so many ruined residences? Well, I supposed, the blocks nearer the wall and therefore farther from the court might be less attractive. I'd always heard that there were a thousand of us, men and women above the fifth rank; but there was no list I'd ever seen; perhaps there just weren't enough families to fill the eastern quarter.

My feet hurt, a general thudding pain in my soles and heels, and sharp wet pains where the clogs rubbed. I saw a little gate-house, isolated, its fence fallen. It looked dry under the remains of the ragged thatch. I stepped gingerly through the knee-high grass that buried the walkway, and into shelter.

The rain did not seem so bad now that I was at least somewhat protected. The space was filthy with dust and spiderwebs. I balanced myself with one hand on the doorpost and stepped from a clog to inspect my foot. The flesh was angry red in places, and slick with the remnants of a burst blister, my first since childhood.

When I was seven I studied the six-string *koto* as ordered by my foster father. I cannot remember the name of my instructor, a gaunt woman who looked as though she might have been carved of bamboo. I was a reluctant student, eager for any excuse to get out of lessons, which raised blisters on the tips of my fingers.

There was a day I cried, and my instructor said, "A woman of culture gladly suffers for art; she does not whine." "I don't want to be a woman of culture," I sobbed. She said coldly: "An emperor's daughter may never whine; her *life* is art." And she ordered me to continue. The blisters broke, ruining a set of sumac-colored silks, but I did not complain in my lessons again.

The rain eased a bit, so I returned to the dog-path and limped on, trying to walk in such a way that the clogs would not hurt, a futile attempt. There was no traffic: a dog and a man far down a side street; a gaunt ox, grazing the weeds in the ditch across the street. I smelled a fire, the fatty scent of cooking meat. I was hungry, I realized, but there didn't seem to be anywhere one might find food, and the cooking smell was not distinct enough to follow.

Night was falling, changing my world into indeterminate shapes of varying darkness. I could see almost nothing, but a dark mass across the street a block or so ahead would be the wall that ringed the city. I could not see the eastern gate, but once I got to the wall, I could look for torches, fires—something that would lead me there. I had no idea what would happen when I found the gate. I trotted forward, ignoring the pain and the burst-blister stickiness in my clogs.

I was wrong, of course. The *eastern* quarter does not decay into disuse as one approaches the wall (which is not really a wall, in any case, with stones and a roof cap and all, except in the south). It is the north and western section of the city that does this. Unfamiliar with the world outside my walls, I had turned around in the rain and walked west instead of east.

Even in the darkness, I saw that the "wall" here was a ridge barely waist-high, worn flat by the many tens of years since the west had been an important neighborhood. The western gate did not exist at all, except as a pile of rotted timbers. I reached through the weeds and touched the wood, which crumbled in my hand, soft as mulberry paper. This was not the *away* I had expected.

Masako. That was the name of the woman who taught me six-string *koto*.

There was a crooked storehouse across from the gate's remains: all ghost-shapes, dark and darker. I felt my way to the open doorway and up a step to the raised floor. From inside, the doorway showed as a blue-black shape but did nothing to relieve the darkness. I inched forward feeling for holes. There was at least one, for I reached out with my foot, felt nothing, and stumbling backward lost my clog. I kicked the other off: one clog is worse than none. The floor felt cold but soothing on my blisters. I knelt and felt around carefully—no other holes within reach, no stones or boxes or unclaimed bones—and laid my bundle down.

I shivered in my robes, which were too few and too light for the deepening chill of an autumn night spent, for all practical purposes, outside. I had not brought a lantern or a candle to warm myself (and had no way to light one, even had I been so clever); I had no food; and I was (more or less) lost. Leaving the capital was not going at all the way I had imagined. I could return to my uncle's house or to court, but I thought I could better bear dying here than that embarrassment. I curled tight as a new moth's wings, trying not to shiver. I felt queasy from so many hours of excitement and fear and no food.

I was sure I would die. Every horror my women had ever gossiped about came back to me: rape and robbers and wild beasts, death by fire, death by cold, death. I had not thought of myself as imaginative, but they came vividly to mind. The air smelled musky, as if some animal lived here; but I could not tell whether the scent was fresh or might be only my own fear. I was dizzy and my chest hurt from my heart pounding. I strained to identify every noise—and in a ruined outbuilding after rain, there are many noises. In my fear, each drip was a voice, so that the night was filled with their chittering.

This is how my mice were, I recall: shaking and startling at anything unexpected. Poor mice. I had not realized that to them I was every evil.

I still don't understand how I could fall asleep. When the moon came up, I could at least see things through the doorway, dark shaggy trees and stars, and a haze of moonlight. My panic eased. I burst into tears, and cried as I had not since I was a child.

I recall my dream that night. Even now, so many tens of years later, it returns: something about watching a fish at the bottom of a river of blue-green water. Sometimes in the dream I jump in after the fish; other times, I reach down and it leaps into my hand. Sometimes the fish speaks to me, though the words never remain when I awaken. Perhaps I will finally hear them when I am dead.

I did not fall asleep so much as fall unconscious, and I was not aware of either until I startled awake, disoriented and cold and oh, so very stiff. Somehow I'd slept through first light, and the sky was already the color of pearls. Through the storehouse door I saw a streak of rose-colored sunlight touching a single tree. The storehouse was worse than I'd thought in the dark. The tile roof sagged down nearly to my eye's height, the timber that should have held up the roof rotted through and hanging loose. It looked as though any jar might collapse it. The dirt on the floor was patterned with so many paw prints that I could not identify them: fox? *tanuki*-badger? something else? Whatever it was had not visited in the night. I hoped.

I retrieved my clogs and crawled cautiously through the door, stretched and relieved myself, and assessed my situation.

—which was not good. I had no food, and while water stood all around me in puddles, I had nothing I trusted to drink. On a rainy day, when everyone keeps their eyes on the ground in front of them, my robes might pass as ordinary, but on a sunny day they stood out, both for their glorious shimmering amber color and for the mud and dirt ground into the weave. My hair and

face could be no better. The first man to see me would recognize
that I did not belong—anywhere.

I was ill-equipped for tending myself. I longed for Shigeko,
who always knew (or could at least find someone who knew)
how to do anything. Shigeko made food and hot drinks appear
(and despite the sun's growing warmth, I was still chilled from
my night on bare boards), filled quiet comfortable sleeping enclo-
sures with soft bed robes and padded pillows. Undoubtedly
Shigeko could make something pleasant out of even this
unpromising situation. No: Shigeko would never have allowed
this in the first place. She would have wept and clung to me, or—
harder to resist—reasoned with me; and I would have endured
another night of my husband-to-be's awkward gropings. And I
would be married. Even starvation seemed preferable to that;
though I learned soon enough that starvation only seems an
acceptable alternative to something else until you get really
hungry.

I was in the northwestern quarter of the city; now that it was
daylight, I could see that—there was the hill Funaoka to the
north, the mountains like walls to the east and west, all so familiar that I could have aligned myself from anywhere in the city. I
walked south along what would have been the capital's western
wall, had there been anything but rubble and a fading mound;
sometimes I came to clear places where I could see a glimpse of
the Red Sparrow gate to the court.

I was hungry, but afraid to address anyone directly. It was
unlikely anyone I met down here would have heard of my flight,
wrapped up in their own survival as they must be; but I knew I
looked a perfect fiend, and I wanted no one to run screaming for
an exorcist. More immediately, I wanted no rape or robbery: no
one to steal my clothes and leave me naked.

Many of the city blocks were untamed as countryside, with for-
est-thick copses of trees and weed-choked pools; but I learned
that enterprising folks planted gardens of grain or vegetables on
some blocks, hidden behind artfully placed windfalls. As a child

playing (improperly) in the kitchen yards of my foster father's residence, I had learned a little about what plants (and which parts) were edible. Looking for a private place to relieve myself at midmorning, I stumbled into one of these gardens, and ate carrots and radishes raw. The dirt I could not scrape off was gritty on my teeth. Still, I was comforted: I would not starve, not immediately.

I did not walk fast, for I had nowhere I planned on going. *Away* had been my only thought, but I did not have the courage to go far. I could not bring myself to cross the western wall, though there was not much difference between the city's blocks and the countryside, squared-off dirt streets on this side of the wall and apparently random dirt roads on that. If anything, the countryside seemed better mannered, for it had not been allowed to grow shaggy with disuse. I was not used to walking far, and had nowhere to go, so I stopped often, hiding whenever I saw someone.

It was midafternoon when I next stopped, perhaps the sheep's hour. No, it was the monkey's hour; I remember hearing the gongs of the guardsmen announcing the time. I was smug with the notion that I could scavenge for my own food, but I had been lucky earlier: it was not so simple. I had learned to see the paths that people left when they snuck into ruined residences or secret fields. The first path led to a pool of relatively clear water, left over from a fine garden—but no food. The second took me to a set of collapsed buildings full of nothing. The third took me to a little field where buckwheat or something similar had been harvested. Perhaps I could pick through the field looking for fallen grains: that would be something at least. It was backbreaking work, but I grew absorbed in my gleaning, intent on each tiny, crunchy, unsatisfying bite.

A shout took me by surprise. I did not see who spoke, or where they were. I leapt to my feet and fled the way I had come: the panic of prey. Whoever it was did not follow me, no doubt was interested only in protecting his fields. When I stopped,

I waited until my heart stopped hurting in my chest, and then I
turned north and east, toward court and my uncle's residence.

Three days north and east, following the path of the defeated Abe
forces. Takase drove the Osa Hitachi war band hard, hoping to
intercept their enemies. In any case there was little to slow them
down—no food or horses to claim—for the Abe were as destruc-
tive in their flight as the war band ever had been.

But a band in retreat will always travel faster than those pursuing, and there were tricks the Abe played to slow them down.
Takase's men found a path seeded with jagged iron caltrops half-
hidden by dirt and underbrush; three horses and an attendant on
foot were injured before they realized what was happening, and
it took nearly half a day for the band to work its way past.

The pursuit crossed a mountain river at the bottom of a small
gorge. Rocks and wooded slopes overlooked the gorge: a perfect
place for an ambush. Takase sent scouts out to search for Abe
archers, but Kagaya-hime and the others found none, and no sign
that any had been left behind. The war band broke its loose ranks
and threaded across the water one at a time, the men leading
their horses up the steep slope opposite. No attack.

This was repeated at the second river they came to, and the
third. By the fourth the scouts were careless (and the archer well
hidden); and four men and two horses were struck before
Kagaya-hime's sharp senses showed her the movement in a tree
upstream, and she killed the sniper.

The wind was from the north and east and blew the smoke
from the fires set by the Abe straight into the war band, making
the horses choke. Men wrapped scarves over their mouths, and
the lucky ones, the horsemen, closed their streaming eyes, relying
on their mounts to get them through. The smoke was nearly
unbearable the first night, when they trampled a field of hemp to
the ground to make camp; the village nearby was still alight, the
surviving peasants so crazed with grief and rage that they shook

their hoes and bear-claw rakes at Takase's men. When horses panic, mice are trampled; to the mouse, it does not much matter which horse did the trampling.

By morning the wind had changed, and they were able to make better time, despite the second batch of caltrops.

Takase had (in his word) "borrowed" a man from Ōgen to tell him the lie of the land. The man, Yui, was tall, strong-armed, and young: enough used to having things his way that he argued with Takase instead of begging. "I have a wife, children. And my fields—haven't you done enough, without taking away our only chance to survive? I'll have to replant—"

"Serve well, or your family will be fatherless as well as field-less," Takase had said at his dryest; and took the man.

Now Takase brought Yui forward. "They're off the path for their estate," Takase said. "Where are they going?"

Yui had become somewhat more accommodating after Takase left five horses for the people of Ōgen, an exchange for the food he took and the trouble. "I've been wondering this myself, my lord. There's not much this way: a hot spring, this crazy old hermit who's been living under a rock. There used to be a *ki*-stockade out here; my mother's sister married a man from a family that kept their mares in what was left of it during foaling. There, maybe."

Takase nodded. The *ki*-stockades had been bases for the men who conquered the northern barbarians a century and more ago. So long ago; but the dirt walls and earthworks might still be in place. There would have been great logs set upright to make a spiked wall; even if it had collapsed, most would not have rotted away. A good place to fight from—a place where the battle would not destroy your crops, nor frighten your animals into flight. "How far to the stockade?" Takase asked.

Yui pursed his lips. "Ten, twelve miles. In land like this, a group like yours—a day's travel. A little more for the injured to catch up."

It was the monkey's hour, midafternoon. Arriving after dark was not a good idea. "Have you seen it?" Takase said.

"When I was a boy, once," Yui said.

Takase said, "We will stop here, and move tomorrow."

I went back, of course. Kagaya-hime may be strong enough and resourceful enough to find her own way, but I was the daughter and sister of emperors, and in the final reckoning, this turned out to be less useful than being able to find your own food, and knowing how to sleep safe and warm.

I was lost, but I found the Red Sparrow gate and then recognized Seisenden park across Nijō avenue. I had been there a number of times, though always at night; by daylight it looked tawdry, full of rubbish people had dumped there. I stumbled around the northeast quarter until I recognized a thunder-struck magnolia that I had passed many times on my trips between my uncle's residence and court. I'd never seen the entire tree. I rode in palm-leaf carriages for the (I saw now) short journey; the magnolia had never been more than slivers and squares, glimpsed through the woven walls or the grille at the carriage's front. It was larger than I had imagined, the patterns of its burning more complex. Hidden in my cloud of carefully mixed scents, I had not smelled its earthiness: charcoal and bark. I laid my hand on it, and then my cheek. *There*, I thought. *I will go back, but I will always have this with me.*

Another block. Another. My uncle's residence and grounds filled a city block. I walked around it—four identical walls—and I saw seven gates. This was a problem I hadn't even considered. I didn't remember what the servants' gate looked like, so I could not slip back in unnoticed—even supposing it were possible. Had that guardsman been disgraced?—that woman, the one who had wished me good luck, turned away from her work? How could I not recognize my own gate, the gate my carriage had entered and exited a thousand times? All those years, and

I had never actually looked at it, always thinking of something else. I knew I might slip into any gate, but the last thing I wanted was to enter the one my uncle and cousin used most often and possibly meet them. It would be hard enough to deal with their anger without stumbling into it unprepared, unwashed, and unfed.

And whichever door I entered, there would be guards. They would see me looking like this. I would have to tell them who I was, since they'd never seen my face; and then I would have to wait there, ragged and barefaced, until one of my women came and got me. I would be a mockery.

I had run away from my marriage; humiliated my future husband, my family, and even, perhaps, my half-brother Shirakawa; disgraced myself by behaving like a peasant, a child, a badly trained dog. By now, the entire court would be aswarm with this scandal. All this, and what I was really worried about just then was a servant laughing at me. I straightened my shoulders and limped to the nearest gate.

There are not many mercies in this world, and they all seem to be small ones — hot wine on a cold day, fresh-washed hair, a *kaze*-cold that finally lets go. It was a little-used gate, and there was only one guard, and he too young for me to take seriously. I stepped onto the covered walkway, kicking off the hated ill-fitting clogs. Young maybe; but I still could not quite bring myself to meet his eyes. "Please find Shigeko for me," I said, my face averted to inspect the blisters on my feet. He hesitated a moment, probably worried about leaving his post unattended, then he was gone, feet drumming across the gardens toward the north wing, my wing.

I tipped my head back, looking into the small eaves of the gate. In the eaves' light I saw movement: a spider, one of the brown-and-silver ones I had called in my notes (when I was still interested in spiders) Lady Teishi, for a woman at court who favored those colors and displayed certain familiar characteristics. And there was a fly the iridescent purple-green of crow feathers, caught in the spiderweb: trapped. The web was too high to reach, and there was nothing to stand on. "I am sorry," I whispered to the fly. "I cannot help you."

More feet drumming: lighter sounds this time, women's bare feet running on walkways. Then the gateway was crowded with women laughing and crying and talking: "We thought we'd lost you, my lady, that you were drowned, murdered, assaulted." One of the women had snatched up a robe, and she threw it over my filthy clothing—a gesture that would have been even more thoughtful, had the robe not been one they were stitching together, and had both sleeves been in place. Another threw a scarf over my head; another fell to her knees and touched my blistered feet with soothing cool hands, exclaiming.

Shigeko said nothing and helped the other women not at all. She stood a little aside watching all this, her hands tucked in her sleeves. I thought perhaps she was angry until I saw tears slip from her jaw, and leave widening circles on the collars of her robes.

Another mercy: my uncle and cousin were away from the house just then, no doubt at court or my husband-to-be's house, trying to find me or (more likely) to contain the scandal. I returned to my rooms. My women bathed me and combed the dirt from my hair and clothed me in clean silk. They fed me *ayu*-trout and little salted birds, and rubbed herbs onto my blisters, and then they left me to sleep in my familiar little enclosure. I fell asleep immediately, and awoke once, when I felt Shigeko's tears on my hand, and heard her voice whispering, "Never leave me again. Please."

I was let off lightly. I had caught a *kaze*-cold while I was running away—convenient since my uncle had told the boy (and, the next day, his insulted and infuriated family) that I had been taken suddenly, frighteningly ill, and that all anyone could do was pray that I lived. Within a day, I was sent out of town, to recover somewhere no one could report on my true state of health.

"We will attempt to patch things up with his family," my uncle said before I left. "My lady," he snapped as an afterthought; for I was still a princess, after all.

"I will not marry him," I said, and coughed.

"If you do *not* marry him," he said, "or he does not want you, you will become a nun, and there won't be any more of this childishness. My lady."

"*Out*," Shigeko said. "My lord. The healers have said she must not be disturbed." She had no authority over this man—quite the contrary—but she has a certain way of speaking that I think would bring all the demons of Hell into an eager, servile line.

And out he went. And by sunset, off I went, to the temple at Uji.

Uji, while distant enough from the capital to be considered exile (and for most of us, this means anywhere outside the walls, with the possible exception of our summer homes on Biwa lake), was close enough for frequent visits from anyone with a carriage and half a day free, so I had a number of visitors from court. Since I was in disgrace (or might be, anyway; there had been no formal statements, of course, but I *had* fled the city, a sure sign that *someone* thought I was in disgrace) their visits were purportedly to leave offerings at the temple; but their perfunctory prayers were followed by long visits in my rooms.

My uncle and cousin were frequent visitors, though it was clear they could barely speak to me, so angry were they at the failure of their plan—for my erstwhile husband's family expressed no desire to overlook the slight. Visits with them varied between icy silence meant to express displeasure; bitter animadversions on the ruin I had wreaked on their family, my good name, my half-brother's and nephew's patience, and the court's sympathy; and furious shouting: what had I been thinking? Was I mad?

I knew they could not see me well through the screens, so I learned to slip a small notebook into my sleeve, to have something to read during these visits: if they had nothing useful to say, I saw little reason to attend carefully. I actually read all the way through the Diamond Sutra in this fashion, which I am sure did more for my soul than any remorse they might have hoped to engender.

My nephew Horikawa was emperor by now, but I heard nothing from him beyond a short note expressing regret that "illness" had taken me from the city. It meant nothing, though it was well expressed; my nephew was always very elegant in his phrasing. My half-brother and I exchanged many short letters. I ached to be the little girl who could tell him all and then cry on his shoulder, but we were adults now. Nothing was stated clearly anymore. Our obliquities depressed me, and I stopped reading his letters, leaving them to Shigeko.

Shigeko behaved with kindness and restraint throughout all this. I was grateful, for I think a harsh word from her would have broken down my careful strength, and left me crying for a hundred days.

In many ways, my life changed little. One set of walls looks very like another; a set of chrysanthemum-colored robes do not lose their intensity when one is disgraced. My women were still with me, if somewhat prone to weeping as they served. Shigeko still oversaw them all, and harassed the temple's cooks into providing meals not appreciably different from those at court. The temple was a prosperous one, and its courtyards were as elegant as anything at home—and better maintained, for there were a vast number of young, otherwise useless acolytes set to such things as removing fallen leaves from the graveled areas.

I developed quite a liking for the abbot of this place. He was a cousin of some sort, but had gone into the temple so young that I had met him only a few times, when we were both young. He had grown into a witty, articulate man, and he visited often. We discussed doctrine whenever he felt compelled to do so by his position; but mostly we played *sugoroku*-backgammon and gossiped about mutual acquaintances.

There was a day when we spoke of life at court: my nephew the emperor's flute-playing; the rain in the galleries; the mice that seemed to be everywhere; the snow-mountains my half-brother and his consort oversaw a winter ago, before he had retired. When we were done, the abbot said, "I am told you are to stay, and we would gladly offer you shelter from the annoyances of court if you wish it. But you don't belong here, do you?"

"No," I said, in that moment wishing I did. "Not yet."

"I will see what I can do." He left me; eight days later, my half-brother wrote requesting my company at the Ōi residence, one of his homes. The emperor my nephew could not have done this: he was too young, and not strong in resisting the desires of my uncle—who was still infuriated, and even went so far as to argue with Shirakawa. But Shirakawa had disregarded my uncle's advice back when he was emperor and my uncle his regent; he had no difficulty in doing so now.

Shirakawa was everything kind to me, but we did not speak of the failed marriage, nor of why he had rescued me (nor indeed how). After a year, my nephew the emperor summoned me to court, and except for a private coldness on my uncle's and cousin's part, life returned to what it was.

Some years later, I saw the boy I was supposed to marry, when he was grown and wed to a niece of mine. We did not speak directly, but I overheard enough of his conversation to learn that he grew up well mannered, polite, and kind—everything I had tried to comfort myself with when I still thought I must marry him. In spite of this, I went back to my rooms that night, and wept with gratitude that I had not married.

I asked my half-brother once why he had brought me back without urging that I reconcile with the boy. "Why should you marry him?" he said. "It seemed foolish to punish you for not wishing to do something you hadn't chosen in the first place." I thought then that, himself a retired emperor and constrained by ritual and the demands of others as I was, he sympathized with me for the restrictions of my life, and offered this one small freedom, the right not to marry someone I did not choose for myself.

But now I think that he also understood about Dōmei.

14. THE BAMBOO–PAPER NOTEBOOK

The ki-stockade was near the Abe's main estate, but sturdier and better-placed for launching or defending against an attack. The stockade was small, just large enough for six buildings and a courtyard with a square well. It has been a long time since the northern barbarians have been a nuisance to anyone but themselves, so the place had been abandoned, and the thatched roofs and even some of the original walls were gone. The walls around the stockade were a rank of tree trunks upended into earthworks; it was obvious that many of these had tipped and been repositioned, for there were signs of hasty construction everywhere. Several of the upright logs were new, so fresh that green leaves still hung from the scars left by lopped-off branches.

The Abe had nearly a day in the *ki*-stockade before the war band arrived: enough time to throw up hasty entrenchments and create sturdy platforms behind the upended logs, high enough for archers to fire over the walls. When the war band approached the stockade, arrows whistled down, and curses; and when they got closer, large stones and boiling water, though Takase's men were not near enough for these to have any effect.

The only injury was someone who had not tightened the laces on his armor since the battle at Ōgen; an arrow slipped through a gap and lodged itself in his shoulder. —And the men's pride, of course. No one likes having things thrown at them, especially if one cannot retaliate.

The war band withdrew out of arrow-range. "Fine," said Takase, and set the men to establishing two camps on the little plain around the stockade, one on each side, both just out of range.

Takase sent Kitsune and a squad to explore Abe no Noritō's estate; Kagaya-hime rode along. They found it abandoned by anyone of rank, none but peasants and servants left to defend the tumble-down walls—for what country estate does not have collapsed walls? There is always something better to do with one's time: mares to foal, crops to oversee, stories to share; sleep. Walls keep some (but not all) animals out, and they offer a certain sense of protection from robbers and undefined enemies, but they do little more. A single enemy within the walls makes them frail as grass.

Kagaya-hime and the others shot everyone who showed his face and burned everything flammable. The pillar of thick smoke was just becoming visible when they returned. Howls of anger rose from behind the walls: a flurry of arrows shot at extreme range. One arrow ticked against Kitsune's shoulder armor, and dropped like a fallen scroll. He picked it up and fired it back at the stockade. It skinned over the logs and vanished: "Should have written your name on it, my lord," one of the men said, "then they'd know who to look out for."

Takase looked tired and irritable. He'd sent envoys to the *ki*-stockade with letters to Abe no Noritō; the responses had been short, sharp, and defiant. They had fired on the returning envoys, and the closeness of the misses indicated not sloppiness in their aim, but great skill. "Well?" he snapped at Kitsune when they met with the captains at dusk.

"They evacuated everyone to here," Kitsune said. "And they brought the contents of one storehouse. Rice and buckwheat, it looked like from the dust everywhere. I can't say how full it was." Takase looked at Kagaya-hime, who added nothing, only nodded.

"I see these options," Takase said. "They mean to come out and attack us tomorrow or the next day, when they are rested. Or

they mean to sneak away from the stockade the next moonless
night, or during a distraction of some sort. Or they mean to stay
inside the stockade until we grow tired of waiting and leave."

"Siege?" a captain said. "Are they *mad*? It's the wrong season;
they won't have enough food this early in the year"—for last
year's crops would be nearly eaten up, and this year's were still
no more than new greenery.

Takase held up his hand for silence. "The place isn't well
designed for sneaking away. We'll remove the underbrush, just to
be sure. I think that we will wait for them."

This startled everyone but Kagaya-hime. Common as siege
may be in the Chinese manuals of war, it is not a usual thing here
in the Eight Islands. We are too impatient to wait for a mouse at
its hole; if our enemy goes to ground, we are more likely to give up
and return another day. Only Kagaya-hime knew that sooner or
later the mouse comes out. —Unless he has another hole, anyway.

Siege. I think it must be hard for everyone involved, this mix of
tedium and gnawing fear. Is there enough to eat, to drink? Does
the enemy plan some trick that we are too weary or bored to see?
Have the gods changed the rules in the night, so that we are now
somehow within range of their arrows? And how do my distant
family fare as I wait here for something to happen? Have the
crops been planted, the silkworms harvested? Both sides in a
siege fret; neither can do anything to ease their concerns.

The small river that ran through the valley was clean water,
safe to drink, but food was short at the camp. The war band had
carried some food and stolen more; but it is astonishing how much
food even two hundred men (they were sixty horsemen now, and
one hundred thirty grooms and attendants) can eat. Takase sent
out people to take what they needed from nearby farms, but the
longer a war band stays in one place, the more time there is for the
neighbors to grow nervous and relocate what little they have to a
secure location; and he was forced to rely increasingly on his
hunters. The monkeys came down from the mountains to steal

their food and mock at them, but after the first day the men did
not waste arrows on them, for they had a tendency to grab any
arrow that missed them and swing hooting into the trees. It was
only half a joke when the men talked about going into the woods
to find the monkeys' secret armory.

The horses were accustomed to fending for themselves; but the
valley was not large, and they had grazed parts of it down to bare
dirt within days.

The days of siege were perfect weather: the seventh month,
brilliantly clear and as warm as it gets so far north. The members
of the war band wore their *kote* over their torsos instead of the
full armor as they moved about the camps. It rained twice, summer showers as pretty and translucent as gauze, good only for
damping down the dust the camps kicked up.

As the siege continued, many of the men injured by arrows
at Ōgen died, their deaths variously tranquil or violent. Some
death-blows are obvious, as when bright blood froths on a man's
lips, or a wound turns color and begins to smell of carrion. Others are subtler: a man loses his appetite as dull bruising spreads
across his abdomen; a man's breathing bubbles in his chest until
he turns blue and dies; night by night a man's fever grows until
his skin burns like iron in sunlight.

There was little news from inside the stockade. They saw the
thin smoke of cooking fires; gold light from lamps and fires on
cool, foggy evenings. A breeze brought the scents of cooking
onions, boiling *taro* root, hot metal. They heard smiths' sounds, for
the ringing of hammers can carry for a mile: new arrowheads and
hoko spearheads, no doubt. Sometimes men shouted, or a horse
whinnied. On certain nights when the air was still, they heard the
faint rumble of men talking behind the stockade walls, or sudden
unexpected noises: a baby crying, a woman shushing it.

As the moon thinned and the nights became darker, men
slipped from the *ki*-stockade, one or two at a time. Some vanished
unnoticed; others were caught and questioned. This was no
organized plot on Noritō's part, though one of the captured men

admitted that his goal had been to return with reinforcements from his own lands. Most wanted only to return to their families, their crops. Takase and the war band learned from these men that there were three hundred in the stockade; that there were a thousand, or one hundred; that Noritō had sent for allies who were coming, who were not; that he had six months' food, or half a month's; that Noritō's wives and children were there; that they were all at a monastery far to the south, to the north, anywhere but here. People are not by their nature honest; they say what they must to survive—though in this case, they did not survive; Takase killed those he captured if he thought they would bring help for Noritō. The rotting heads had been dropped into kegs of brine; the row of barrels downwind of the camp grew longer.

This trickling loss of men was not one-sided. Siege has no glamour, no excitement to keep men distracted from their own concerns, and the men of the war band started to think of their own crops and wives and horses. Every so often someone gathered his attendants and his spare horses (if he still had any) and rode away to the south. The remaining men mocked him, but when he had ridden out of sight, they spoke wistfully of their own homes.

"Let them go," Takase said to Kitsune, when he complained. "They are drawn away by their homes, not driven by cowardice."

"*I* would not leave," Kitsune exclaimed. "I will stay 'til this is finished."

Takase smiled slightly. "It's different for you, and me, and the girl, here." (Kagaya-hime, who was with him often now, and cleaned the hole in his side when his attendants were not near.) "She has no home to call to her, and my family is dead these fifteen years. I want to finish this before I die. And you—your brother was killed. Your way home is through this. In any case," he said, "a reluctant warrior is no warrior at all."

Better than any, Kagaya-hime understood siege, the waiting at a mouse-hole; but this did not mean she liked it. A cat waits for an hour, perhaps, and she either catches the mouse or she doesn't. This siege—day after day with nothing edible at the end of it—did not appeal to her. Cats love the warmth of sunlight and brazier, and she spent long hours lying along a broken wall, blinking in the sun. The men of the war band greeted her, on their way to this or that task, and in the evenings invited her to their fires lit for the smoke that shooed off the insects. Sometimes she did stop for a time with one or another of the groups, listening to their stories.

Men like to hear their own voices; but every so often, one of them would think to ask her about her own family. She would say: "They are gone now; there is nothing to tell." But she would remain at the fire, and when most men had fallen asleep or left for duty she would speak in a near-whisper about the cats of what had once been her *fudoki:* The Cat Who Ate Watercress, The Blue-Ink Cat, The Cat Who Would Only Sleep on Silk. The tales clung to her like the barbed seeds of certain grasses, but she gently plucked them loose and told them, and they fell from her, one after the other—no more than stories now. She felt herself grow lighter, felt the festering bitterness ease, replaced by a cleaner pain.

The men listened with surprising patience and gentleness, and no one seemed surprised that the sisters and aunts she spoke of were all cats. Without anyone actually saying something, the men had learned already that she was a cat—there are no secrets in a war band, after all. Not everyone had seen a cat, but they had heard of them, from their comrades who had been to the capital.

In some strange way, they found it easier to accept her being a cat than any of the alternatives. A woman fighting was bad enough. It would be worse if she were a kami or a demon, each equally untrustworthy, their motives equally unknowable. In any case, what excuse had *anyone,* male or female, god or demon, to fight if they did not come from a bow-and-arrow family, from *gunki?*

But a cat—well, if a cat was not from *gunki,* what was?

Often she returned to Takase's fire. There were fewer of the captains' meetings; there is little strategy to a siege once begun, *don't let them out* and *don't let them surprise you* is about the sum of it, so many nights there were only the two of them. Kagaya-hime had taken to cleaning Takase's unhealed arrow-wound, like a mother-cat cleaning a kitten's cut. The flesh around it was hot under her fingers, but there was little she could do for it, except bathe the area with warm water, and wipe away the liquids that oozed out.

Takase liked the softness of her touch. "Softer than your bony old paw," he said to his man Suwa; "you're gentle like an ox."

"You're dying, aren't you?" she said one night. Kitsune was with them: a sharp breath expelled, as if in shock; but there are no secrets in war bands. Everyone knew Takase was dying, though Kagaya-hime was the first to say it outright.

Takase sighed heavily. "We're all dying, girl: you know that as well as any of us. But, yes. It's always hurt, but it's worse now. I'm tired, weak."

"How soon?" Kitsune asked, and then gave an embarrassed laugh. "I'm sorry. Of course you don't know."

"Don't I?" Takase said. "There are days I think I could tell you the number of breaths between now and then. Soon, boy."

Kitsune bowed. "I'll have a sutra read for your soul, my lord."

"Don't waste your money," Takase said. "I've seen my wife die, and I've been in a thousand fights, cut off a man's head when his mouth was still moving. And here's what I think happens: we live, we die, we rot. Save your money, spend it on pretty silks for your mistresses."

"Something lives on," Kagaya-hime said. "There are ghosts. I've seen them."

"Then where are they all?" Takase said. "My wife's ghost? The men who died?" He pointed to the row of barrels, their brine-pickled heads inside. "Where are *their* ghosts?"

Kagaya-hime squinted at the barrels, but saw nothing. "Gone. They don't stay long, most of them."

"Where do they go then?" Takase had little artifice; the mockery in his voice was forced and brittle as ice over a pond.

"I never asked," she said.

"Weren't you curious?" Kitsune asked.

"Not really," she said. "Now, a little. Perhaps I will ask the next time I see one."

Takase said, "If you are there when I die, *I* will tell you."

There are good days and bad days. Lately I have had a whole series of bad days, bad enough that I found myself crying when I thought no one (but Shigeko) would see me. The thing that fills my chest has always been inappropriate, shall we say, but now it grows more *wrong*, somehow: *evil*, like cursing the gods or mocking one's mother's ghost. I can tell it does not belong in me, does not belong *anywhere*. Everything I try to eat makes me ill, so I have learned to take a little bite and then wait, and then another. It may take half a day to eat the segments of a Chinese orange. Shigeko is infinitely patient, getting me to eat.

I think if I had finished telling Kagaya-hime's story—if I knew how it ended—I might already have summoned the priests, taken my oaths, left the court, and died these last days. —Though there are still trunks to finish. Ten now; I can count them on my fingers.

Today is the first day I have done more than sleep, and eat my single bites. I asked Shigeko to open my screens, take me onto the verandas to see the sun. It is full autumn, the leaves the colors of saffron and dandelion-dyed silk. The air is so cold that it seems almost a liquid; it leaves my fingers chilled and my nose running, but scorches my lungs.

The sky. Strange how no one ever seems to write poems about the varied clouds. Today they are stretched thin and transparent, a great sweeping arc over watery blue. This is not the thick clotted sky of summertime, the hammered gray silk of winter. Why did I never think to study the clouds?

I was unwilling to die when there was still much to say and do. But there is always something left undone, and if I were to die today, I would do so with the memory of the cold lambent sky; and that might be enough.

* * *

Kagaya-hime took to hunting again, looking for meat she could bring back to Uona and Otoko. The other hunters strayed far, looking for large creatures that might feed several men at a time, but she had learned a trick.

Early on, the monkeys had learned to use even the slight amounts of cover on the plain to approach the camps and steal a box here, a sack there. They had learned that the containers made for a very interesting game: while some held things useless to a monkey (clothes, for instance, or replacement reins), others were crammed with enough rice to gorge the troop; or salted fish, which was not a usual food for monkeys but was at least amusing, well worth the game of seizing it, fighting over it, chewing it, and spitting it out.

Now the monkeys stole everything that was light enough to carry on the off-chance that they would find something edible; and they tasted everything they stole, edible or no. The men of the war band could do little, so they watched their possessions closely, and cursed the monkeys with great dark oaths whenever they saw them.

Kagaya-hime learned to wait near something sure to be attractive to monkeys, which meant anything otherwise unobserved, conveniently near the trees. The monkeys saw her, of course; but after a while, their curiosity would overwhelm their caution and they crept forward. As they came into range, she would shoot one with a slim leaf-shaped arrow that would not shred the meat much. Whichever monkey she struck screamed and fell; the rest of the monkeys leapt for the trees and swore at her from their shelter. Sometimes she saw the ghost of the monkey she killed, plucking at its side or chest or face with immaterial fingers; but having no interest in the souls of monkeys, she did not listen to its chattering or ask where it went. The survivors were wary for a time, but monkeys are just clever enough for their curiosity to kill them. They returned eventually.

She killed many this way—though there were always more:

the woods seemed to grow as many monkeys as pinecones. None of the men of the war band tried to imitate her, for she was the best shot and more patient than any of the men, willing to wait for a morning, or a day.

There was a day when she was hunting in this fashion, staking out a handful of barrels stacked on top of a shield to keep them out of the dirt. Spilled rice made a mound near the barrels: irresistible to the monkeys, she figured. The monkeys were proving slow to arrive (she could not know this, but they had found a stack of boxes at the other camp. They were busy running their hands and mouths over wood stirrups and saddle-frames, and growing more irritable by the moment), but she was content to wait. The air was warm, gold with pollens. It tasted sweet and grassy.

Uona had taken Biter for a ride, to use up some of the energy that tended to show as irritability. Otoko was playing a gambling game with some of the other attendants. Takase slept; Kitsune watched the walls of the stockade, and amused himself by shooting arrows with his name written on them over its walls, hoping to hit something. There was nothing better to do.

Because she was watching for monkey-sized things, she didn't notice the smaller movements in the trampled grass near the barrels. Tiny actions, a rustling so faint she could hear it only when everything else in camp fell silent for an instant, as happens in even the busiest camp. She squinted, trying to separate the movement she'd caught into its elements: grass growing, the tiny breeze, the whatever-it-was.

Mice. Once she recognized the movement, she saw them easily: here eyes, small as seeds; there a tail, waving too slowly to be a grass stalk. They were using the trampled grass to get a short (human) pace from their goal, and then dashing, pausing, dashing across to the mound of rice. With her attention on the trees, she had not noticed them as they passed her foot, so close that she might have shifted her foot and stepped on one.

Mice had been her favorite thing, so many miles ago, when she still had a cat's form and lived in the abandoned residence at the capital. They had been sweet and salty at the same time, full of the sharp shards of crunchable bones, with none of the feathers that made sparrows so difficult, or the gaminess of voles. How long had it been since she had eaten one? Months, miles. Her hands were full of arrow and bow. She had no hand free to throw a knife, and they would all be gone if she moved quickly.

She had never watched them without hunting them. One of the mice stuffed rice into its mouth, grain after grain until its cheek bulged, as absurd as a squirrel storing nuts. Another crept around one of the barrels, sniffing at the iron binding that protected the wood. When it started to chew a splintering stave-edge, another joined it. A fourth mouse, fawn-colored, stood on its hind legs beside her foot, as if watching.

"Mouse," she said. A flicker, a rustle, and the mouse by her foot had whisked itself to a broken tree stump three paces away.

"What?" it said, a little impatiently.

"You *do* speak," she said. She lowered her bow and arrow carefully, rolling her shoulders as she did so. Within their limitations, monkeys are clever; hunting them required that she keep her arrow nocked and bow drawn, and this made her stiff. "I've always wondered."

The mouse said, "You are a killing animal?"

Kagaya-hime was silent, already knowing the answer.

"There is no record of your type," the mouse added. "What are you?"

"A cat," she said. "We're small and quick and silent, and designed for killing little things." Kagaya-hime bared her teeth: a small smile. "Mice, mostly."

"Ah," the mouse said, as if storing the information for later. "Yet humans are not killing animals."

"I'm not human."

The mouse said nothing, its bright eyes fixed on her. Kagaya-hime laid her bow down slowly, and leaned back against a sapling's trunk. The mouse-path to the barrels had moved out of reach, she saw. "You steal our grain," she remarked.

"It is necessary to appropriate resources. There are many of us to feed," the mouse said.

"We don't stay forever," she said. "You'll have to find other resources."

"We will find others when you are gone," the mouse said. "Other districts report resources for utilization, as well."

She chewed on a stalk of grass for a time. " 'We'?"

"Oh, yes," the mouse said absently, its attention on the mice by the barrels. There were more mice now; several had joined the one that had found the weak place in the barrel, all gnawing steadily. "We are a large empire."

"Why are *you* here?" she said. "You gather nothing."

The mouse flicked her a sideways glance from one tiny brilliant eye. "I am here to report on this appropriation to my superiors. I will mention you, and 'cat' as well."

"I see." Kagaya-hime had spent much time with people; something in the fawn-colored mouse's pose, its steady focus on the others' labors, reminded her of men she had met: quartermasters, with their constant cataloguing, their brushes and portable ink and ever-present notebooks and scrolls. "You are a recorder."

"I am third assistant comptroller of grains for my district's secondary storehouses," the mouse corrected. "But I hope for a promotion soon. We do not always live so long, you see."

"Why report at all?" she asked. "The grain is there or it isn't. Why not eat it yourself, or take it home to your family?"

"A family is small, of no account," the mouse said. "We are a large kingdom. It is necessary to catalog things: potential resources, storehouses, census rolls, properties."

"But you would have these things, even if you didn't keep track. There would still be food and young and holes."

The mouse crumpled its whiskers, as if in distaste. "It would mean nothing. The records define the kingdom of mice." She said nothing, and the mouse seemed to sigh, like a tutor with a dull student. "Perhaps you are faster in this form than you look; or a fox will eat me as I return to report; I will be trampled by one of those immense clodhopper horses; I will drown in my hole in a storm. Or my superior will die, and I will be promoted, but there will be another third assistant comptroller for grains, and one after that, and another. I am not so important, so long as the role remains filled. It is necessary to keep track of things, you see. Do you—'cats'—not do this?"

"We have the *fudoki,* our tales. That is what we save."

"Hmm," the mouse said. "Perhaps that is why there are not so many of you. No organization."

There are many mice in this world—many more than cats, more even than people. We—the men and women of the court— have always thought of ourselves as the center of an immense empire, a thousand miles from Mutsu province to Ōsumi province, ten thousand villages and temples and shrines; but we know in our hearts that China is a thousand times more vast than we.

But an empire of mice—what might a million mice create? Kagaya-hime had a sudden image of such a land, its families and clans, villages and districts, provinces and regions, overseers and governors, courtiers. And the cities of the mice, underground plats squared and vast as Chang-an on a mouse's scale. A mouse would never be alone, always part of the strange *fudoki* of the mice, a tale without individuals.

"I'd like to see your land," Kagaya-hime said.

"That is not a good idea," the mouse said. "I do not think my superiors would approve."

Kagaya-hime snorted. "Perhaps not."

Where the mice had chewed the barrel, rice trickled from a new hole and formed a little mound. The third assistant comptroller straightened and tipped its head as a weary man might, hunched for too long over some list. "I must report, and send laborers."

"Wait," Kagaya-hime said. "I've killed so many of you; I'll do so again"—the mouse gave an impression of shrugging—"I'm curious. Do you have souls?"

"Why do you care?"

Kagaya-hime blinked. "I want to know what tales I end."

"Would it change anything?"

She thought of the taste of mice, hot and squirming on the tongue. "No. Oh, no."

"I thought not," the mouse said, dryly. "You might as well ask, do rice balls have souls? I have as much of a soul as a rice ball. Or a cat," and the mouse slipped from the tree stump and vanished from her sight.

She waited there until dusk, but the fawn-colored mouse did not return. She did not disturb the visits of the mice who slipped into the barrel and left, cheeks fat.

Well? she asked the endless chittering of the kami; but they said nothing.

My rooms echo. They seem much larger, and harder-edged, the corners all rediscovered, bare to the eyes. And the hollowness: soft as it often is, my voice rings now. Shigeko's footsteps are no longer muffled, and I hear her approach from rooms away. As my possessions have gone, so have my women, sent back to their homes, the younger ones first, more recently the older, the women who have been with me for years or decades. A few begged to accompany me to Kasugano, but I remain sure that I want no one but Shigeko. It's not as though I will be there long before my death, and I will have no visitors (or trunks) to need the attentions of attendants.

I offered to send Shigeko home. She has a brother still, and she's always gotten along well with his wives, who express (in a series of fatuous poems) the honor they would feel in welcoming so valued a courtier into their midst. There would be nieces and nephews, and even grandnieces and grandnephews; a wing in the house that she could fill with trunks of her own; the chance to be pampered by others, to be the unreasonable one. She is older than I, but her health is very good. She might well live another decade; the women in her family are notorious for living well past any realistic age.

To my no-doubt poorly concealed relief, she has refused. She will attend me to Kasugano, and after I am dead, she will remain there. The assumption is that she will spend the rest of her life praying for a better next life for me; but I rather hope she does not waste her time brooding about this dead woman she once served. Even at seventy there are better things to think about. I hope she does some traveling, for she has always enjoyed that; and pilgrimages are a perfect excuse to see the sky ringed by new mountains. She might even see the great sea. She has her share of friends and old lovers who might welcome a visit.

What would it have been like if *she* had been the princess and *I* the attendant? Would I have been as good as she? Would I have loved her as selflessly? She is not here just now (out relieving herself, I think: an old woman's bladder is like an autumn grape, small and always close to bursting), so I cannot ask her what she thinks.

—She has returned, and I have asked her, and she has said, "Swap clothes with a monkey, and you end up with two monkeys, my lady." I laugh until my belly hurts, and now I think oh, yes, I would have loved her. I am "my lady," and she is my woman, but we are more than this. Swap clothes and we are still friends.

It was the mice that ended the siege. Kagaya-hime in her woman's shape had not much need to kill mice, but she was curious (and provident: if she ever returned to her cat's form, anything she learned now would have immediate and useful applications), so she spoke with them. She never saw the fawn-colored mouse again; she did not ask where it might have gone, knowing as well as it had that an individual mouse's life is short and hardly worth the recounting. Clearly it filed its report, for the mice seemed to recognize that she was a threat without teeth, a killing animal in useless human form. From one of these mice, she heard that the siege accomplished nothing: the Abe and their mice ate well, if boringly, on rice and salted fish; their well was deep and showed no signs of drying up, even as the summer stretched out into a series of bright hot days. The Abe had taken apart a ruined building and used its timbers to strengthen the other buildings. They hacked one of the logs into shakes, which they used to shingle the empty spaces in the roofs, to keep out the rain that fell sometimes from indigo clouds in the afternoons.

Back when I was so interested in warfare, siege seemed simple enough to me, something every woman understands. Someone undesirable starts to haunt your rooms, hoping for an invitation to join you behind your curtains. His constant presence makes it impossible for you to entertain anyone else, or even perhaps to leave your chambers. He looks for any contact: bribes your women, steals the food you send away after meals.

The solution is simple, if dull: you outwait him. You do not respond to his ten thousand poems either with direct excoriation or indirect sarcasm, since these might be (indeed, will be) taken as encouragement. You wait patiently behind your screens and curtains. Sooner or later he will be summoned away by duties at court, or another woman's elegance, or even boredom. You wait; eventually he leaves.

Men, it seems, do not think this way. Not only do they avoid siege, preferring instead to feed one another's rages until face-to-face battle is inevitable; even when they do have a siege, they seem pantingly eager to break it at the first opportunity. While I might expect this of the besieger, since he has everything to gain by facing his opponent, I would not have thought the besieged have any incentive to leave their safe den, provided they have food and water enough.

Takase's war band tried to coax the Abe out with daily insults sent by envoy. The Osa Hitachi horsemen played their monkey-games, bragging and jostling one another until someone donned armor, raced his horse to the wall, and hurled a torch, hoping to set something, anything, on fire. Archers wrote their names and rude comments on the shafts of their arrows and then shot them over the walls. It was unlikely that they would hit anything, but the insults might incite someone to open the gate and charge out. But the Abe stayed cozy within their walls, disdaining all efforts.

The captains debated attack options for days, but there were no secret caves, no forbidding but passable cliffs. No one had a sister inside the stockade who might consider betraying her master. No one imagined that a prayer to the kami or the Buddhas would cause one of the walls to collapse.

If Abe no Noritō had been a woman, I think the Abe might have stayed until winter, when the lack of firewood would at last drive them out; but by then, the war band would have left, returned to their own fields and estates. The winter after a summer without crops would be hard; but surely easier, less dangerous, than war. But Noritō was male, and so this conflict could only end with battle: this month, next month, the tenth month.

The Osa Hitachi did not lift the siege; they merely lost interest in it. Kagaya-hime told Takase and the captains what the mice had told her. Faced by the possibility of no clear end to this waiting, Takase ordered the men to be ready that night at the rat's hour, midnight. The men of the war band would ride against the stockade's wall and shoot anyone who showed his head, while the foot soldiers pulled down the timbers. The Abe (it was as certain as if there had been an agreement between them) would open their gates and attack; there would be a lot of killing, and injuries that would lead to death, and it would all be over by dawn.

Men.

The night the siege ended was very dark: the new moon, the fifteenth day of the seventh month, when the air is so thick that the stars seem small and blurred. It is hard to conceal the preparations of two hundred men, the restless noises of warhorses who sense battle, so the Abe were not precisely unprepared.

Kagaya-hime and Biter stood beside Takase at the center of the ragged line of the war band. Many of the horsemen held torches, but the light was murky, as if the air absorbed half the illumination. No wind: smoke went straight up until it vanished into the darkness. The air was filled with waiting. A foot soldier murmured the Amida Buddha's name three times; in the momentary silence it was as audible as if she shared a room with him. A horse stamped and puffed; the metal of its bridle jangled gently. The priestess Onobe no Kesuko and her acolytes were far behind the line of horsemen, but Kagaya-hime smelled incense, and heard soft bells and chanting: prayers.

"Well," Takase said, his tone measured, as if he were about to comment on an arrangement of irises. "We will kill them. They will kill us. But it will be done. Go on, then."

Sound can make a wall as thick as wood and plaster. The men shouted, and the air was solid with noise, a barrier to push through. Kagaya-hime had never shouted in battle—why scare the prey?— but the sound pounded through her heart and bones, so loudly that she could not feel her own pulse, or tell whether she joined them.

There was no strategy and little tactics to this battle. Everyone bolted for the base of the walls, riders hunched over their horses' necks, foot soldiers racing behind. The Abe behind the walls shot, and shot and shot more, but many of the arrows missed, and most of the hits were an annoyance only.

The Osa Hitachi skimmed arrows over the wall or threw torches against its base. The hot days had dried the grass, and flames caught in the underbrush, licked the dry timber. Elsewhere, foot soldiers dug at the berm holding the logs upright, and horsemen used their horses' shoulders or flanks as bludgeons against the timbers. Two logs loosened, like teeth in old gums, and crashed down, leaving gaps that filled with arrows and *naginata*. A third post came down, a fourth.

Despite this, the stockade was still defensible. The Abe had to use their kettles of boiling water to put out the fires instead of pouring them over the attackers, but they still had stones to throw down, and an almost infinite supply of arrows, since they could pick up the Osa Hitachi arrows and return them a thousand times. They could have stayed, protected themselves. Waited.

But the Abe opened their gates, and their horsemen crashed into the Osa Hitachi men with a shock like an earthquake.

Horses slammed into one another, trampled foot soldiers. The wall of sound made of arrows and whinnies and war cries turned to screams, shouts of rage.

Everything is dark, remember, like a rape on a moonless night, noise and buffets and terror. Everything is motion and uncertainty. A horse backs into Biter, and Kagaya-hime whirls, sword already flying. At the last instant, a flicker of torchlight shows her the colors of the armor's lacing: *kon*, fox-call blue. This is Kitsune she has nearly killed. She jerks the sword back and up and nearly clips Biter's ear. He leaps sideways, away from the hiss of moving steel. His hooves sink into something soft that screams in the shadows; when he jumps away he lands on another man. There is no telling whether these are soldiers or grooms, or for whom they fight. She feels a sharp shock on her thigh and a blazing pain, hot as touching a brazier; but when she reaches down, she feels no wound. She cannot tell what struck her or what damage it has done.

Kagaya-hime sees a little better than the men: she stands on her stirrups to get her head above the immediate fray, and sees helmets, *eboshi* caps, manes, and ears. A horse's eye catches the firelight, rolling white in pain or rage. Otoko and Uona are utterly hidden to her, lost in the roiling darkness; but for an instant she sees Takase, standing on his stirrups as well, arm slashing down at something she can't see. Her own arm hurts; when she glances down, she sees an arrow jammed there, slipped through a loose place in the lacing of her shoulder guards. The feathers dance in the corner of her vision, distracting her, so she breaks it off. A wave of white pain blinds her for a moment, but no one attacks until she has time to blink it away. The arm doesn't seem to work well, but a cat uses the claws on either side equally: she shifts her longsword to her left hand.

Strange, these little gaps in the middle of battle. She looks for someone to kill, but everyone is just beyond her reach. She picks someone she doesn't think she recognizes as one of her war band, and moves Biter toward him. Movement from the side catches her eye; her longsword comes up, just as someone else's swings down. It strikes heavy as a timber falling. She loses a stirrup and drops from Biter's back to her knees on the ground. None of the foot soldiers are close enough to kill her, but the man who struck her jumps down, ready to stab her with his short sword. She lurches upright, steps inside his swing and grapples him, tips him backward to the churned dirt. His armor makes him fall heavy, knocking the wind out of him. She takes his short sword from his loosened grasp and stabs him with it, in the throat just above his *kote* armor. The blood looks black in the bad light. His quiver has fallen to one side: in all the chaos, she sees a slip of wood attached to it and with her cat-sharp eyes reads a poem he has written there, about rain and fish.

"My lady!" Uona is by her, *naginata* dripping. Otoko is nowhere near, but somehow Uona stayed close, and even managed to catch Biter's leading rein before he fled. Kagaya-hime shares a bare-toothed smile with her woman, and swings back astride Biter, feels her armor settle onto the saddle, lightening the load. She whirls Biter in a tight circle, but the field is growing strangely empty. She cannot find any Abe, so she gallops forward. It is surprisingly dark. She notices that light no longer pours from the opened gate, because the gate is closed again.

The Abe have retreated. Stupid as it is to leave the safety of shelter, it is stupider still to do so, and then return, nothing accomplished but death and more injuries.

Men.

I thought I understood war, but truly it is this: brutish and tedious and terrifying. This tale, the tale of the cat Kagaya-hime, is lies. But so were the historical chronicles I saw, of Yoshiee's war and others; the Chinese manuals; even the guardsmen's stories, Dōmei's nightmares. All lies.

Why do I tell her story, then? For that matter, why do I try to make sense of my own life, when I cannot say which things have happened exactly as I have written them, and which have been revised by wishes or regrets?

Tales and memories, however inaccurate, are all we have. The things I have owned, the people I have loved—these are all just ink in notebooks that my mind stores in trunks and takes out when it is bored or lonely. It is necessary to keep track of things, the third assistant comptroller of grains said. It is the recording of things, in our memories if nowhere else, that makes them real.

My *fudoki* is precisely as long as my life has been. Without my *fudoki* I am nothing, because it and I are the same.

15. THE SILVER-FOIL NOTEBOOK

It is time: there are only a handful of trunks left, a neat little line of them down the center of my rooms. So I have written the emperor my great-grandnephew and asked his permission to leave court eight days from now. It is an auspicious time: no kami objects; the goddess Kannon does not mind; Kasugano temple has offered to send escorts. The emperor has written back, a kind little letter. He says he will miss me.

Now we are two: I and Shigeko. Well, there are three other women: a woman of sufficient rank to drive off visitors politely; another of a rank low enough to carry my chamber box away whenever required; and a third, of intermediate rank, to do everything else.

It is hard to believe that these are my (or anyone's) rooms. They have the empty look of a space between owners — which is close to the truth, for I know that one of my grandnieces, the princess Kasiko, has already claimed the rooms for her own, and waits, not very patiently, for us to leave. Well, and she may have them: I have been sick these forty years of that irritating sag in the roofline of the building across the peony courtyard.

It was six months ago? eight? that my half-brother Shirakawa died. He was living in the Ōi residence outside of the capital's walls. I had not been summoned, but I went to him. Months passed, even years when we did not see one another much; but then, whole winters passed when I never saw the sun, always hidden behind gray skies or high eaves. And yet it was there. I knew I would see it again, in spring if not sooner.

Now is perhaps the first time I cannot safely say this. Strange.

He was my brother: strong and clever and sensible and kind. He gave me a mouse when I was a child; he rejoiced with me, barefaced and laughing in the rain; he gained forgiveness for me when I refused the husband my uncle chose. He chuckled when I said something amusing, and listened patiently when I droned on (as I am sure I did) about the structure of claws or wings. He sent me poems when we were apart for one reason or another; he didn't seem to care whether I responded in kind. He played *sugoroku*-backgammon with me, and even (one sleepless night after his consort Kenshi had died) told me a dream he had had.

His hair grew gray and his waistline spread a little. A few years ago, when I was reading (some dreadful *monogatari* tale, all about a bat and some sparrows), I noticed that he had wrinkles around his eyes, and frown lines set deep on his brow. He laughed at my surprise then: "We race toward the Pure Land, Sister; but it's a race everyone wants to lose."

Half a year since his death. The heaviness was already in my chest when I last saw him, though I still thought it was indigestion—an indigestion that had lasted for what seemed forever—or simple weariness.

The dead seem so close to me sometimes. My mother, my father, half-brother and -sisters, my nephew, attendants and cousins and relatives of every sort—mine will be the last in a series, like the twelfth picture-scroll in a set showing the months. Really, I have seen a battlefield's worth of death; gather the bodies of all those I knew, and they would carpet the ground.

Now it is my turn to fight, in this war that no one ever wins.

The last time I saw him. How could I have forgotten this, the things he said? —Or did I dream it all?

Shirakawa never liked lying down unless he was actually

asleep. Weak as he was, he was elegant in informal hunting robes, leaning against a stack of cylindrical bolsters. He was pale and had lost some of the flesh on his bones, so that his face had the thinness I have always associated with certain Buddhist hermits and wise men. I mentioned this to him, and from his half-reclining position, he gave me a mock bow. "Neither hermit nor wise," he said, and laughed.

It was spring, but still cold, so we huddled around the brazier, putting our feet up on its edge like peasants. We both knew he was dying, so we talked of everything but that—the weather (what conversation, in all the ages of the world, does not include the weather?); Shigeko (they had been lovers several times, many years before, and they retained their fondness for one another; indeed, they exchanged occasional letters independent of my own correspondence with him); the mouse he had sent me, and the set of drawings of it that I had sent him; our father the emperor Go-Sanjō and his consorts our mothers and an argument they had when we were small; old lovers and lost friends.

"I saw him once," my half-brother said. "That provincial Mononobe man you favored. Thirty years ago? Back at the end of the Kahō era. Where was he from? Some backwater."

"Mutsu province," I said faintly. Dōmei had returned home just before Yoshiee's war, fifteen years before the end of the Kahō. How could Shirakawa have seen him since then?

"That's right," Shirakawa said, pursuing some memory of his own. "He had those strange eyes, I remember: almost foreign. Mononobe. Mononobe no—Dorei?"

"Dōmei," I managed to say without actually stammering. "Why—?"

"He brought news from up north. Fujiwara no Kiyohira is building some sort of fake capital up there. Hiraizumi, I think it is. He was warning us. Very sensible: he has a lot of land up there, and it could be a problem. Not mine, though."

"He didn't fight for the Mutsu forces in Yoshiee's war?"

He wasn't an enemy? I had been so sure of his betrayal.

Shirakawa waved off the notion. "I think he mostly kept his head down, offered support to our forces when they came through. Sensible," he said again.

"But he was a warrior!" I said. "He'd fought many times."

My half-brother raised an eyebrow. "Then he'd know better, don't you think?"

Truly, I could not tell. Dōmei told me once that he missed the kinship that comes with sleeping in the shadow of shared death. But was it worth it? The nightmares, the dark days, the night he nearly killed me only because I had startled him? "Why didn't he speak to your regent?" I said at last. "I can't believe they let you meet him."

He smiled at me, his warm eyes almost lost in the wrinkles. "I was curious, Little Sister. About what sort of man you would like."

"You knew about him." What I meant was: *you cared.*

"'A strong emperor knows how well his people sleep, and whether their bowels are healthy,'" he intoned, his rough voice a clever imitation of a tutor we had both known fifty and more years ago. "An interesting man, I thought," he said in more normal tones. "Content with his life."

"Was he well?" *Why didn't you tell me?* I did not say, but Shirakawa understood.

"He was—older," Shirakawa said at last. "Married. Three sons and a daughter."

"Ah," I said. Dōmei would have been forty at the end of the Kahō. *Married.* I wasn't sure what I was feeling. Sorrow? Loss? Jealousy? None of these, I decided. Relief. See: he had been a good man. He was no traitor. My instincts had not been bad.

What if it had been possible to wed Mononobe no Dōmei instead of the irritating pup my uncle had chosen? What if I had accompanied him to Mutsu province, given up my rank to sleep on his shoulder every night of my life?

The Dōmei of my memory was not the real Dōmei—but then, the Harueme I recalled was not the Harueme who lived through those days and nights. And neither Harueme was the woman who would have gone to Mutsu province.

I looked up to catch my half-brother watching me, frowning slightly: worried. He said softly, carefully: "I think it wasn't him you loved, but the places his eyes had seen."

So. The attack against the stockade ended in nothing. The men of the war band dragged their wounded and dead out of arrows' range and lit more torches, built the fires higher. Ten deaths: three men trampled or crushed between the horses, five slashed deep, one pierced through the throat with a turnip-headed arrow, and one who started howling and then died, though no one could find a mark on his body. There were many wounds, of course, arrows and broken bones and cuts; a severed hand, a crushed leg. Five horses were injured. Their screaming made everything seem worse; when they had been killed, the camp grew calmer.

Kagaya-hime examined her thigh where she'd felt the blow and found a bruise, thumb-sized and already hard as callus, where she was hit with a spear butt, or perhaps a spear tip deflected by her sword's sheath. Otoko bandaged the arrow-wound on Kagaya-hime's arm, but when he went off to help Uona with Biter, she removed the wrappings, and licked the deep little hole until it hurt a bit less.

Exhausted but sleepless, she limped through camp. There were no celebrations, not even the false ones born of bravado and weariness.

Kitsune was easy to find. He moved through the war band, spoke to everyone who was conscious to hear it, and touched the others, as if skin on skin might somehow ease their dreams. His head had been cut in the fight—shallow but bloody, as head wounds are—and his face was still masked in drying blood, twin tracks cleaned by the tears he didn't notice.

She didn't find Takase until the tiger's hour, for he had been pulled out of range on the opposite side of the stockade, where the trees clustered closer to its walls. Suwa, the old attendant who had brought them wine so many times, had settled him half-leaning against the trunk of a pine and cut the lacings on his armor, to bare his chest and belly.

Takase was not dead: not yet. He looked ash-white in the light just before dawn, his chest hollow, skin waxy with a sheen like sweat. She knew the shape and texture of the ancient wound in his belly, had cleaned the fluids that wept from it. Everything was changed now. Ragged lips of flesh peeled back at a new angle. Fresh blood, surprising red in the gray light, slipped down his leg and dripped onto the pine needles beside him. "You were hit," she said as she knelt beside him. "Again."

"Same place," he said. "A relief, really. It doesn't hurt so much now. I think we've lanced it, hey." He wheezed out a laugh. There was blood on his lips; it shivered with each breath. He opened his eyes. "Ha, girl. Didn't think I'd see you again." His voice was thin and dry as spiderweb.

Suwa laid a hand on his shoulder. "Quiet, my lord. Please —"

"It's all right, Suwa," Takase said. "Find the boy. Kitsune."

"But —"

"She'll stay with me. Yes?" He rolled his head to look at her. She nodded.

"Keep him quiet." Suwa stood slowly. "I'll bring a litter."

"They left," Takase said, when Suwa had limped away. "In the dark."

"The Abe?" she said. She reached up to brush something from her face. Tears.

He nodded, then drowsed for a time. She settled herself more comfortably, her back against a neighboring tree. On the opposite side of the stockade, she heard the camp's muted sounds, then the sudden shouts and bustle that must have meant Suwa had come.

"They're gone," Takase said, waking suddenly. "Did I tell you? They passed me, so close I could have shot every one of them. If I wanted to, hey." He stopped to catch his breath. "Is there wine?"

"Just water." She helped him drink the last swallows from the water-skin she'd carried all night. "But you didn't."

"No," he said. "Too dark. No strength. Anyway, it's over. They're done. *We're* done."

"Will they try to avenge this? Attack the Osa Hitachi?"

After a while she realized he'd fallen asleep again. Not dead: his chest still moved, slow tired breaths. Blood still slid from the wound, darker, thicker. A fly rested on his upturned hand: waiting.

When she heard running footsteps, she turned her head to watch Kitsune approach with Suwa; behind them walked the priestess, Onobe no Kesuko, a sword still bare in her hand.

Kitsune dropped to his knees as Kagaya-hime held up her hand. "He's sleeping," she said, just as Takase spoke again.

"They're not going to come after you," Takase said in a conversational voice, as if he had not nodded off at all, as if they were discussing capital politics in a courtyard a million miles away.

The priestess arrived as Takase nodded off again. She bent to inspect the wound, and straightened. "That's that." She sheathed her sword, announced to the men beginning to cluster around Takase: "He will die."

"Please, can you do anything?" Suwa asked.

"You mean, ask the gods to heal him?" She snorted. "They know as clearly as he does that he will die."

Takase roused himself suddenly. "I heard them whispering, as they slipped past. It's over. A war where everyone retreats, hah."

"We should go after them to make sure," Kitsune said.

"No," Takase said. "Let them have whatever lives they can. Same as all of you. Go home."

Kitsune clenched his fists. "Then all this was for nothing?"

The priestess said, "They killed some people, you killed some people. And now it's done."

Kitsune opened his mouth and then closed it.

"Go home," Takase said again. "My last order, hey." He slipped into unconsciousness and did not wake again.

Last night we found the strangest thing in the bottom of one of the last trunks: a letter.

There have been a thousand letters in the trunks, a thousand thousand—and I have not always been able to recollect who sent which and when. It became a game between Shigeko and myself: which lover wrote *these* deathless words? These two poems, of identical image and nearly identical language: were they written years apart, their similarities merely serendipitous; or do men crib their love-poems from one another when their creativity fails? And these—an entire packet of letters, clearly from one of my half-sisters—but which? Shigeko and I have played the game of unraveling my past, and burned the letters when the game palled.

But there is one that we have not been able to identify, written on a rich tricolored paper flecked with gold. The calligraphy is very fine, delicate and precise as whiskers. We are not even sure it is a letter:

"I have been fishing in a river a thousand miles from you, eyeing the trout beneath its surface. For some reason this brought you to my mind."

Who wrote this? we exclaim to one another, but I already know. I fought so hard to keep Kagaya-hime and her story in line, but it kept breaking out of my expectations. Once you have opened the gate to alternatives, it can be hard to get it closed again.

All those places I have never been, and now, never will see. Wait—

All those months of preparation and travel, all those injuries and deaths, and this war ended with all the drama of a fan falling. The men of the war band broke camp quickly and were gone by midday. Most would travel together until they were far enough south not to fear retribution, and then the band would dissolve into groups that grew smaller and smaller, each man traveling as fast as he could toward home. It was three hundred miles to the Osa Hitachi estate, farther for those who had come from Shimosa or Kozuke provinces. Some traveled with injured men (which generally means dying men); it might take them a month or more to return home.

Most of the dead were buried in the forest, wooden hat markers and paper prayer slips hanging from the branches above their heads. There were other tributes, as well: a pair of torn reins hung like straw rope over a shrine; an arrow driven into the ground over a grave, a poem written on its shaft.

Before she left, the priestess Onobe no Kesuko took Kagaya-hime aside. "It will not be long," she said, nodding at Takase. "Half a day: less."

"Yes," Kagaya-hime said, and then: "May I ask something?"

"Ha," Kesuko said. "Finally. Yes."

"The kami—I hear them," Kagaya-hime said, feeling her way, "but they never make sense."

"Why should they make sense to you? You don't even make sense to yourself, cat," Kesuko said. "Where's your ground, your tale, your, what was it, *fudoki?*"

"Gone," Kagaya-hime said, and felt the familiar grief, the wrench of loss.

"No," Kesuko said. "You're the first cat I've met, but I thought they were supposed to be smarter than this. *This*"—she gestured around them, at the striking camp, the empty stockade, the mountains and everything beyond them, the hot cloudless summer sky over all—"is your *fudoki*, girl. It lasts a lifetime, but you never noticed that.

"Why should they make sense to you? They have their own tales, their own shared grounds. They don't have to make sense to anyone but themselves. No one does."

Kagaya-hime and Kitsune and Takase's man Suwa knelt with Takase as he slept out the last hours of his life. "There's no point to taking him from this place, my lady," Suwa said, and Kagaya-hime nodded. The smell of death was strong on him. Even the crows had picked it up; though many pecked for the blood that had soaked into the ground, some lined themselves neatly along a branch over Takase's head, waiting. Servant and half-fox and cat-woman took turns digging a grave and gathering stones to place over it.

Farmers, peasants, and poor people came even before the war band was gone, to glean the battlefield, the war band's campsite, the stockade's grounds. They left with whatever they could carry, and there was much of it after a month of siege, ranging from a longsword dropped in the woods in the darkness to half-filled barrels of rice.

Takase died in the heat of the afternoon, his last breaths fainter and fainter, until only Kagaya-hime could tell he still lived. "That's it," she finally said, and stood. "He is gone." She did not see his ghost: not then.

She and Kitsune left their attendants to bury him, and walked a little way up a slope, into the forest. The sun did not reach all the way to the ground, so they walked in a false dusk that hummed with insects. They had removed their armor, but had not changed clothes (and after a month of siege, there is little worth changing into), and sweat and bloodstains made patterns on their trousers and vests.

A flash of vermilion caught Kitsune's eye, and they made their way to a small shrine to Inari, newly painted and still bright. The stone foxes stood on either side of a red-painted arch scarcely taller than a fox itself. She nodded to the little arch.

"What is that called?" she said.

"A *torii*," he said. "A gateway."

"It's not very impressive," she said, remembering the great Rajō gate in the capital. "What does it go through? There's no wall."

He laughed a little. "It's a passageway between *here* and *there*." He pointed. "A sort of road for gods and spirits."

"Oh," she said. They listened for a time to the humming air and a stick cracking in the heat somewhere, the almost inaudible whistle of the pine needles crushed under their feet. Kagaya-hime ran her finger along the head of one of the foxes: a porous stone, rougher than it looked.

"Once in a while," Kitsune said into the silence, "I wonder what it is like, being a fox. Being human is supposed to be better. But. Do you see things differently? Does time move faster, slower? Do you get hungry for different things?"

"Better?" Kagaya-hime said. "Different."

"I remember when I was little," Kitsune said into the humming silence. "Mostly I was a boy. I had this pony, and there was a dog, and then Nakara; she was my nurse. You knew that, right? I think my mother didn't like me being a fox much. So I wasn't. And then there was a fire and my family died, and Nakara brought me to her family. I have not been a fox since then."

"You were, though. Are," Kagaya-hime said. "You mean you have not had a fox's shape; but it is there in you. I smell it. It's in your blood."

"Hmmm," Kitsune said. And sometime later, "But how?"

"I don't know," Kagaya-hime said. "You're half of each. How hard can it be to move from the one to the other?"

And just like that, as if her words had caused it, he was a fox. He looked up at her for a moment: gold eyes to gold. She smiled at him, and he was gone, slipping through the trees, ears and head high.

Kagaya-hime walked back to Takase's grave and watched the men lay his already stiffening body into it, and push the frozen earth back in place. After a while, she noticed Takase's ghost stood beside her watching the burial: a young man now, taller than the living man had been: slim. "Well?" Kagaya-hime asked.

"What a lot of trouble *that* was," the ghost said, nodding at the body. "Why did I wait so long?"

"The others all cried," Kagaya-hime said. "The ghosts."

"Did they?" the ghost said. "I suppose they left things behind that they missed."

"And you?"

The ghost turned to her. "I will miss you a little, cat-girl."

"And I you," she said. "A little."

The ghost smiled. "I think you will have plenty to keep you

FUDOKI

busy." It reached out a hand as if to touch her belly, but she felt nothing, only the sun and a breeze against her clothes. "I have given you something; now give me something. If a male deserves it, give him a place in your *fudoki.*"

"There is no *fudoki,*" she said, but without bitterness.

"Hah," the ghost that had been Takase said. "You are a one-cat *fudoki.* Don't you realize that yet? Promise."

"If a male stays, if he earns a place in the tale, he will be allowed into it."

"Already has, I'd say," Takase said. "Remember the fathers of your children, cat-girl."

"Tell me —" she said; but he was already gone.

The half-fox Kitsune returned, a rusty shimmer of movement, at the bird's hour. It was nearly dusk, the sky through the trees strange shades of peach and amber and blue. A fox loped from the trees, and then he stood there, breathless, a man again. "Oh," he said, but nothing else.

"I know," she said. "I would do anything to go back to that."

He shook his head slightly, settling into his man's shape again. "Then do so. Who do you think keeps you in that body?"

Uona came shouting in the woods trying to find Kagaya-hime, and disturbed them. Kitsune gathered Takase's and his attendants together. "They won't be too many miles ahead," he said. "We'll ride until dark and then catch up with them tomorrow. But you're not returning with me, are you?"

"No," Kagaya-hime said. "I am not finished, not yet. Tell Nakara that I love her."

"I will," Kitsune promised, and they were gone.

Me, I'm waiting. It is four more days until I leave the capital.

Northward again. Kagaya-hime and Biter and Uona and Otoko traveled slowly through the summer days, accompanied by a packhorse, a pretty roan that Otoko loaded with most of the armor and what little food they had. They found a rough little road that led north and west through the forest. After half a day, it faded into a path and then, a day later, a track over the shoulder of a mountain—though their route would have been easy enough even without the path, for the weather was beautiful, and the ground soft from fallen leaves and needles.

Their path met Noshira river and turned west, to accompany it to the sea. They followed its shores for several days until they found a boat large enough for Biter. The woman who ferried them across had a barbarous accent but a ready laugh; they paid her with the last of Kagaya-hime's ancient coins and turned north again.

There was plenty to eat. Kagaya-hime hunted, and her attendants were clever at gathering food, or even stealing it when there was someone to steal from, though in those cases it was often easier to trade meat for rice. Biter ate whatever green things came his way and grew a little thinner, evidently missing grass. He allowed Uona to ride him, but still snapped at Otoko whenever he was close.

The journey had no urgency. There was no Osa Hitachi, no Nakara longing for her home, no Seiwa Minamoto no Takase pursuing his war to drive them forward, and so they traveled slowly, at a walking pace. They did not often find farms or even cultivated fields, though sometimes they passed an abandoned house built in half-buried, in the old style. Uona was pregnant with Otoko's child, in her early months, so she did not often feel well enough to travel immediately in the morning, and there were days they went nowhere, everyone content to drowse cat-like through the afternoon. The few people they encountered did not ask where they were going, or how they would fare through the winter.

In the north, mountains are common as geese, and there always seems to be another just beyond this one. But as one travels north they get smaller, just as horses and dogs seem to grow smaller. When the party left Noshira river, they aimed for a smooth-sloped mountain, a perfect little sister to the great mountain Fuji.

"Softer country," Kagaya-hime said.

"Not easy, though," Otoko said. "Look." He pointed to a nearby ridge, its firs and pines bent nearly double. "They'll have snow here, and winds. Bad years, it'll be higher than my head."

Otoko had somehow become their guide. It did not occur to Kagaya-hime to wonder how he had learned any of the ten thousand things he seemed to know, or even why they still traveled. She nodded and said no more.

Their path angled across the mountain's flank. It didn't seem steep until they started walking it, an endless steady climb that was more tiring than crags would have been. They stopped often for the sakes of Uona and the packhorse ("Both of us"—Uona laughed breathlessly—"we're carrying extra baggage"), so that by midafternoon they had only ascended part of the way. Kagaya-hime stopped them beside a *torii*-gate in a little clearing, having no wish to leave everyone huddling on a ridge when the sun set and the wind grew bitter.

Building camp was quick, for there was little to do. Kagaya-hime unloaded the horses as Otoko settled Uona in a nest of cloaks, with Biter's saddle as a pillow. She fell asleep almost immediately as Kagaya-hime and Otoko gathered wood for a fire. They still had the better part of a deer's haunch wrapped in its own hide left over from the day before, but: "Mushrooms, my lady," Otoko said softly, and pointed downslope. He took a cloth for gathering and vanished among the trees.

There was little for Kagaya-hime to do. The packhorse nosed over the weeds in the clearing; as he did every evening Biter chewed on his hobbles trying to find a flaw that hadn't been there the night before. Uona stirred a little and said, "Don't forget . . ." before sinking back into sleep. Kagaya-hime walked across the clearing to examine the *torii*-gate.

It was taller than Kagaya-hime could reach, painted a red now faded to dust, and hung with a braided straw rope and slips of white paper, soft-edged with weather. Offerings had been heaped by the posts, but the foods were long gone, only trays and leaves left to mark them. Other, more permanent gifts remained, but they meant little to Kagaya-hime: a padded amulet necklace shredded by sun and rain to show glimmers of something inside; the ghost of a scent of sandalwood; and, amazingly, a full set of court robes in spring colors, now faded nearly to white.

Every gateway implies a road that passes through it, but this was a gate that led nowhere: there was no shrine beyond the *torii*-gate, not even another *torii*-gate that would also lead nowhere. She walked around pillars, but saw nothing. Looking up she glanced through the gate in the other direction, and gasped.

Spread out before her was a thousand miles of mountains and river-plains and marshes. The path they'd followed was a thread across the land, leading—she knew where it led. She could not see the great mountain Fuji, which was many hundreds of miles to the south, but it felt as though she ought to be able to; perhaps, if she knew just where to look, she might even see the Tōkaidō, the shrine where she became human, the Rajō gate to the capital, the path of her panicked running through the streets: her vanished home on Nijō avenue.

It was a gateway, and there was a road; but she'd been looking in the wrong direction.

She still wore the torso of her armor, though she'd removed the skirts and shoulder pieces long ago. Now she ran back to the camp and gathered the rest of the armor: leggings, arm protectors, shoulder-guards—everything. She carried the awkward weight to the foot of the *torii*-gate and laid it there. She bent over and shook the *kote* over her head, catching it with her hands as it dropped, before it could fall and awaken Uona. The tortoiseshell colors of the lacings flared with the afternoon's gold light. She hopped a little dance, like a cat chasing a dust mote, feeling light, almost insubstantial with the removal of her armor.

The kami voices that were always in the back of her mind rustled like tree leaves in a breeze. She had grown used to them, and scarcely ever listened to their words anymore; but she listened now, wondering if they said different things so far from her old home.

"*Ah*," something said suddenly, very loud and close in her mind: the road-kami.

"Where have you been?" she said. "I left you behind, I thought."

"I am the kami of the road, but *I* never said which road. People occasionally misinterpret things."

Kagaya-hime looked down the slope to the path. "This is a different road. Can you be both?"

"Who says you are on a different road than you were?" the kami said. "There are a lot of roads, and they go everywhere. Some of them can't be seen. You are coming to the end of this one."

"But then what?" she said, her eyes filling with tears.

"You will settle down. Make a new *fudoki.*"

"Alone?"

She had the impression of snorting. "When's the last time you were alone? Your tale is a thousand long already—men, women, horses. Not to mention you have a belly full of kittens."

Her hand came to rest on her belly. "I have wondered—they'll be kittens?"

"Cats are clearly as dense as humans. Yes, kittens."

"I have been locked in this body for a thousand miles," she said, a little bitterly. "It's no surprise if I wonder."

"Who locked you there, hey?"

She opened her mouth to speak, but a thought came to her and she said nothing, her mouth gaping open, forgotten. "I never tried," she finally said. "I wept and complained and mourned, but I never thought to change myself. And it's that simple. Oh, I *see*. But why?"

"You needed a home. Could a cat come a thousand miles? It's cold up here; I expect your children will get sort of shaggy. But you'll come in handy."

"Which road did you say you were?" she asked suspiciously. "Did I come here, or was I summoned?"

"You need a home; they need cats. Seems straightforward to me."

And the kami's voice was gone, as simple as that.

*   *   *

Today is my last here. I have been sitting out on the veranda, writing the last of the oh, so necessary good-bye letters and poems, and warming my hands beside the brazier when my fingers start to stiffen. All day I've received letters from relatives and friends and former attendants wishing me well. I write back to them all: *Kasugano will be lovely; I will pray for you; I look forward to spending my final days in quiet contemplation.* I say this, secure in the knowledge that they will have no opportunities to discover the truth of my statements.

It is blustery, and the wind carves clear but concrete shapes from the air, limning them with gold and red fallen leaves. When I look into the sky, I feel as though I am staring down into a stream, at a shifting blue-green fish—though I cannot say whether it is the fish that moves, or the water that makes it appear to do so.

Perhaps it is not the wind, and not the fish (fish? There is no fish here. What am I thinking of? It is the trees I see, tossing in the wind). Perhaps it is my eyes, which weep continually now, from exhaustion, I think. Or my mind, wavering.

There was a day, beautiful and surprisingly cold: autumn, though winter was a clear omen in the air. The forest shivered gold and red and pine-green in the wind. There were ducks overhead, shouting directions at one another as they arrowed south in great untidy flocks.

The mountain where Kagaya-hime heard the kami's voice was the last between her and the sea. She came around a curve in the path and there, miles ahead, across thinning forest and a broadening plain where a river wandered, was the distant glitter of a bay cupped in the land's arms. "Well, that's the end of journeying, then," she said aloud; cats do not like water.

Otoko walked beside her leading the horses. "Down there." He pointed. A stream joined the river on the plain; there was a small village at the conflux, too far away to see clearly—perhaps ten shaggy-eaved buildings nearly the color of the fields that surrounded them. The pale lines of stone fences made ragged

calligraphy against the ripe gold of grain, the heavy green of *taro*
fields. Otoko crouched, turned over the dirt with a knife's edge.
"Good soil." He straightened. "It's even better down there."

Uona astride Biter nodded toward the plains, the village. "Will
they welcome us, husband?"

"Why wouldn't they?" Otoko said. "We have horses, we're
strong. And"—he grinned suddenly, a look Kagaya-hime had
never seen on him—"my family is from here."

"You have *family?*" Kagaya-hime said; even a cat can be surprised. "Are there mice there?"

"They're terrible," he said. "They get into everything and—"

"Then I will stay," she said.

Otoko said, "You'd be welcome, but it's no place for a cultured
woman."

"But I'm not a woman, am I?" Kagaya-hime said. She kicked
off her sandals, grateful to feel even cold earth underfoot.

"What are you doing?" Uona said.

"Starting a new tale," Kagaya-hime said, and started to untie
her short over robe.

"No men, then," Uona said. "It wouldn't be proper."

Otoko said, "We—would not have thought of this," and Kagaya-
hime knew he meant: *becoming real.* He bowed. "Thank you, my
lady." He turned and led the packhorse down the slope toward
the far-distant village.

Uona slipped from Biter's back and busied herself loosing ties
and lacings. "You're sure?" she said, kneeling to remove Kagaya-
hime's *hakama*-trousers. "You will give up all this? Hands and the
skills to make things; arrows, knives?"

"Oh, yes," Kagaya-hime whispered, a voice soft as a purr. She
dropped her vest and under robe on the ground: a shapeless
untidy heap, like a snake's skin when the snake has discarded it.
Naked in the sun she stretched, a small fine-boned woman with
thick black hair to her shoulders, gold eyes under straight brows.
"You will let me sleep by your hearth-pit, yes?"

And there was no woman there, but a small cat, fur black

flecked with gold and cinnamon and ivory, like the tortoiseshell of a hair ornament. She blinked up at Uona through eyes slitted to threads in the brilliant light. Biter reached down to touch noses with the tortoiseshell, and the cat leapt in a single fluid movement to Biter's shoulders, balancing there until Uona pulled herself into the saddle. Cat and horse and woman started down, toward the village.

Another piece of this story: a small tortoiseshell cat stands on the banks of a stream. The sun is out, but it is very cold; snow has mounded into strange shapes on the ground. Her breath puffs from her nostrils, like smoke from an inner fire, but she does not feel the cold through her winter-thick fur.

The stream's water is brilliantly clear, and there is a fish there, a trout as long as her tail. She can see it hover, every blue-green scale as brilliant as Mikawa silk, or a butterfly's wing. The fish's shadow hangs against the warm gray stones of the streambed. The tortoiseshell is reluctant to risk falling into the water, which she knows would be horrid. Still: a fish, and *such* a fish, fat and beautiful, and so close to the water's surface. And she is always hungry, keeping the kittens in her womb fed until they are born. She creeps down to a stone that touches the water, and crouches low, one paw raised over the water, patient.

The fish seems to examine the paw, as if it were an insect hovering above the water. Its eye is bright and shallow as a blade. It flicks a fin and raises higher in the water, closer to her claws.

"Cat!" Otoko's voice, behind her. "*There* you are." The tortoiseshell blinks and the fish is gone, as quickly as that. She stretches and sighs, and saunters closer to the man.

"Look what I have, girl." He cracks open his basket to show her the contents, all blue-green scales and blade-bright eyes; half a dozen trout. "Let's go home and have Uona cook these up, hey?" The tortoiseshell lets him stroke her head for a moment and then follows him home.

This notebook is nearly filled, but I have enough room to tell this much more. Kagaya-hime will have six kittens, from five fathers. This new land will belong to her, a part of a new *fudoki* that begins with her.

16. THE LAST NOTEBOOK

There is nothing left in these rooms: only two small trunks, and several bundles of indeterminate shape—and, I am afraid, contents; there are always a thousand last-minute requirements for anyone traveling, and they never fit into the storage space allotted to them.

I have burned all the notebooks but this one. I wrote them for my own reasons. When their job was done, I burned them, converting ink on paper to the loose calligraphy of smoke. Before I leave these rooms, I will burn this one as well.

The priests have been with me all morning, preparing me for my entrance into Kasugano—and, eventually, the Pure Land, though I'm afraid I daydreamed through their interminable prayers—regrettable, since I expect I will have need of their good wishes. I kneel behind a curtain (for not even now am I expected to be barefaced before these men; really, this makes me nearly laugh), so when I receive my nun's robes, they are handed past the curtain, and it is Shigeko who drapes them over my own blue-green robes and then kneels again beside me. She and I share a smile, but we say nothing.

The priests have offered to clip a mere hand's length of my long hair: a polite symbol of my separation from this world with none of the embarrassment (not to say shame) of having hair short as a servant-girl's. The priests sound impressed, if a little

shocked when I demand that they cut it to my shoulders; even
Buddha's servants are not impervious to social proprieties.
Shigeko gathers the lengths of my hair in her hands, tugging at
my head a little as she passes them through an opening in the curtain. The shears make a grating noise, and then a cascade of black
and white pours back through the gap: the new ends of my hair.
They aren't willing to go so far as shoulder-length hair, but it only
hangs to my waist now, and my head feels weightless, light on my
neck. If I decide it is still too long, I can always have Shigeko cut
it shorter.

They give Shigeko her robes, and cut her hair, as well. There is
a little more praying, and they bow themselves out. They do not
stay to accompany us: we have told them that the emperor very
kindly offered men and carriages to carry us the short miles to
Kasugano. I nearly laugh out loud.

For I am lying to everyone except Shigeko. I am running
away — or rather, we are running away together, two old women
sneaking away to see what sights they can before they die.

Shigeko has found a useful man of no rank whatsoever, but
immense virtue in that he understands animals and traveling.
And the Tōkaidō. His mother accompanies us to empty chamber
boxes and makes sure we are fed; she used to wash for us, so we
know she is patient with the foibles of old women. He has found
others to assist us, guards and grooms and carters; and some
quiet horses and two pairs of (I am assured) extremely well-mannered oxen. If we need further help, we will find some useful
peasant-girl and exchange hair ornaments for her exertions.

I can't say how far I will be able to travel before the weight in my
chest kills me. It may be no farther than Otsu, just past the walls of
the city, or the first ferry (I might cross water in a boat! Think of
it!). I think it's too much to hope that I will see the great mountain
Fuji before I die, but at least I will see the sky unfringed by walls.

And I have this letter, in whisker-fine calligraphy, about fish
that "mention my name." It was unsigned, of course — she never

did have a name, only what she was called—but there is a single line after the poem. If it is a poem: I still cannot decide:

I look forward to meeting you.

Of course it is she, now mother and grandmother to a thousand cats, The Cat Who Walked a Thousand Miles. She returned to her cat's shape, but she is no longer just a cat. Why might she not have questions for me, just as I have questions for her? And why might we not meet?

Shigeko and I have talked much about her these last days. I know that she is as real as I am. I thought that I invented her, that she had no more existence than any other set of words on paper; but I know now that this is not true. She saw things I did not expect, and felt things I did not mean her to. She is as real as flesh, as ghosts.

I am not sure if she means I will make it all the way to Mutsu province; or that we travel toward one another and will meet in some monastery or temple between here and there, when I grow at last too ill to travel; or even that she will meet me in the Pure Land when we are both dead. I am not sure whether she will be a woman or a cat—or, for that matter, what I will be. But then, I will still be Harueme, and she will still be the cat Kagaya-hime.

I would like Shigeko to meet her.

AUTHOR'S NOTE

Fudoki, which may be translated as "records of wind and earth," were eighth-century documents collecting information about individual provinces for the imperial court. They included descriptions of natural features and population centers, local resources and products, bits of folklore and history—anything that the compilers thought might be of interest back in the capital. I adopted the word as the closest parallel to my cats' shared reality.

Harueme writes her notebooks in the year 1129, during the reign of her great-grandnephew, Sutoku. While she is fictional, she shares some characteristics with Shirakawa's real sisters, Atsuko and Reishi. She has somewhat more in common with the noblewoman in the tale-fragment, "The Woman Who Loved Vermin."

Favorite primary sources for this book were: *The Emperor Horikawa Diary* (tr. Jennifer Brewster), and the war-tales *Mutsuwaki* (tr. Helen Craig McCullough), and *Hōgen monogatari* (tr. William R. Wilson). Secondary sources I found useful were *Insei* by G. Cameron Hurst III, and the second volume of the Cambridge History of Japan, edited by Donald H. Shiveley and William H. McCullough. Favorite material on feral cats included Paul Leyhausen's *Cat Behavior,* Claire Necker's *The Natural History of Cats,* and especially Jack Couffer's *The Cats of Lamu.*

Karl F. Friday proved a generous and invaluable resource. His book, *Hired Swords,* was a fascinating and useful exploration of

Heian-era military power. In addition, he very kindly answered even my stupidest questions with patience and clarity, and allowed me to see unpublished material on Heian combat technique. I can never fully express my gratitude for all his help.

I wish to thank the following for their assistance: Irene Michon for her insights into the writing process; writers Walter S. Williamson, Melissa Shaw, Louise Marley, and the Kilomonkeys (Wolf Baur, Ted Chiang, Jeff Grubb, Bridget McKenna, Marti McKenna, Chris McKitterick, and Lorelei Shannon); formerly feral cats Baby, Bro, Meerkat, Helen, Tatsuko, and Sanjū; and especially Peg Kerr and Chris McKitterick. Mistakes in this book are entirely my own.

Since it all happened a long distance away, I am sensible of having made a great many blunders, which anyone acquainted with the truth is at liberty to correct.

—*Mutsuwaki*
translated by Helen Craig McCullough